Also by Kelly Braffet

Josie and Jack

Last Seen Leaving

SAVE YOURSELF

a novel

KELLY BRAFFET

B\D\W\Y

BROADWAY BOOKS • NEW YORK

Published in the United States by Broadway Books,
an imprint of the Crown Publishing Group, a division of Random
House LLC, a Penguin Random House Company, New York.
www.crownpublishing.com

BROADWAY BOOKS and its logo, B \ D \ W \ Y, are registered trademarks
of Random House LLC.

EXTRA LIBRIS and colophon are trademarks of Random House LLC.

Originally published in hardcover in the United States by
Crown Publishers, an imprint of the Crown Publishing Group,
a division of Random House LLC,
a Penguin Random House Company, New York, in 2013.
www.crownpublishing.com

Library of Congress Cataloging-in-Publication Data

Braffet, Kelly
Save yourself : a novel / Kelly Braffet. — First edition.
pages cm
1. Teenagers—Pennsylvania—Fiction. 2. Parent and child—Fiction.
3. Stalkers—Fiction. 4. Families—Pennsylvania—Fiction.
5. Suspense fiction. I. Title.
PS3602.R3444S28 2013
813'.6—dc23

2012048148

ISBN 978-0-385-34736-5
eBook ISBN 978-0-385-34735-8

Printed in the United States of America

Book design by Maria Elias
Cover design and photograph by Oliver Munday

10 9 8 7 6 5 4 3 2 1

First Paperback Edition

For my mother, and for Linda

Men talk of heaven,—there is no heaven but here;
Men talk of hell,—there is no hell but here . . .

Rubáiyát of Omar Khayyám

I think I might be sinking.

Led Zeppelin, "Going to California"

SAVE

YOURSELF

ONE

Patrick worked the day shift at Zoney's GoMart one Wednesday a month: sealed into the vacuum-packed chill behind the convenience store's dirty plate-glass windows, watching cars zoom by on the highway while he stood still. When he worked nights, the way he usually did, the world was dark and quiet and calm outside and it made him feel dark and quiet and calm inside. When he worked days, all he felt was trapped.

So by the time he made it out of the store that evening, he was just glad to be free. His eyes were hot with exhaustion and the odor of the place lingered on his clothes—stale potato chips, old candy, the thick syrupy smell of the soda fountain—but the warm September air felt good. As he rounded the corner of the building and headed toward the Dumpsters where he'd parked, back where the asphalt had almost crumbled into gravel and the weeds grew tall right up to the edge of the lot, the car keys in his hand were still cold from the air conditioner. That was all he was thinking about.

Then he saw the goth girl leaning against his car.

He'd seen her before. She'd been in the store earlier that day, when Bill came by to pick up his paycheck. Patrick had kept an eye on her because he didn't have anything else to do and because she'd been there too long, fucking with her coffee and staring into the beverage cases. Not that Patrick, personally, gave a shit what or how much she stole, but as long as she was there he'd felt at least a nominal responsibility to look concerned for the security cameras. Then Bill had called her Bride of Dracula and made an obscene suggestion, and she'd called him a degenerate and stormed out in what Patrick assumed was a huff. He and Bill had laughed about it, and he hadn't thought any more about her.

But now here she was, leaning on his car like she belonged there and staring at him with eyes as huge and merciless as camera lenses. In the dimming light, her dyed-black hair and her almost-black lipstick made her pale skin look nearly blue. She held a brown cigarette even though she looked all of sixteen, her expression a well-rehearsed mixture of indifference and faint amusement. When she saw him her lips curled in something like a smile.

"Hello," she said.

Patrick stopped. Her earrings were tiny, fully articulated human skeletons. He tried to figure out if he knew her, if underneath all that crap she was somebody from the neighborhood or somebody's kid sister that he hadn't seen since she was ten. He didn't think so. "If you're looking for weed," he told her, "you got the wrong night. That guy works Mondays."

"You mean your degenerate friend from this morning?" She laughed. It was a Hollywood laugh, as stale as the air inside the store he'd just left. "Hardly."

"Whatever." Patrick was too tired for this shit. He pointed to his car door and she moved back, but not enough. It was hard to avoid touching her as he got in. He slipped his keys into the ignition, buckled his seat belt, and rolled down the window, all the while acutely aware of the girl's big spidery eyes staring at him through the dirty glass. He turned on the engine.

She waited, watching him.

He hesitated.

"Do I know you?" he finally asked.

"No." She leaned down into the open window. "But I know you." There was a ring shaped like a coffin on one of her fingers. Patrick wondered if the skeleton earrings fit inside it. She smelled sweet and slightly burned, like incense. To Patrick's dismay her black tank top fell in such a way that he could see her lacy purple bra, whether he wanted to or not. Jesus. He looked back up at her face.

Staring at him through thickly painted eyelashes, she said, "You're Patrick Cusimano. Your dad was the one who killed Ryan Czerpak."

Patrick froze.

"Ryan's family comes to my dad's worship group," the goth girl said, peering curiously past him into the backseat. "I used to babysit for them sometimes." Then she saw Patrick's face, and her blood-colored lips opened.

"Hey," she said, but before she could say anything else, Patrick heard himself growl, "Get your tits out of my car," and then his wheels spun in the gravel and she was gone. His heart was beating so fast that his ears ached.

The year before, on a warm day in June, Patrick's father had come home from work two hours late, crying and smelling like Southern Comfort. His hands were shaking and there was vomit down the front of his shirt and pants. Sitting on the couch, white-faced and bleary-eyed, he wouldn't look at either of his sons. *Holy god,* he'd said, over and over again. *I did it now. Jesus Christ. I sure did it now.* Patrick tried to get him to say what was wrong, but his father wouldn't or couldn't answer. Patrick's brother, Mike, brought a glass of water and a clean shirt (throwing the dirty one in the wash and starting the load without even thinking about it) but the old man wouldn't touch either, just rocked back and forth and clutched his head in his callused hands, chanting the same refrain: *Holy god. Holy fucking shit.*

It had been Patrick, after too much of this, who went to the garage and saw the dented bumper; Patrick who smelled the hot gasoline-and-copper tang in the air; Patrick who stared for a long time at the wetness that looked like blood before reaching out to touch it and determine that, yes, it was blood. Patrick who realized that the tiny white thing lodged in the grille wasn't gravel but a tooth, too small to have come from an adult mouth. It had been Patrick who had realized that somebody somewhere was dead.

Up until that point, there were two things that Patrick could count on to be true: the old man was a drunk, and the old man screwed up. And as far as Patrick was concerned, the first priority was fixing it. When he worked the morning shift at the warehouse you woke up before he did so you could make the coffee and get him out the door. When he passed out on the couch you took the cigarette from his limp fingers. When he ranted—about the government that wanted to take his money, about the Chinese who wanted to take his job, about the birth control pills that had given Patrick's mother cancer and killed her—you kept your cool and had a beer yourself, and you tried to sneak away all the throwable objects so that in the morning there'd be glasses to drink from and a TV that didn't have a boot thrown through the screen. You took evasive action. You headed disaster off at the pass. You made it better. You fixed it.

Staring at the bloody car, Patrick thought, wearily, I can't fix this.

Inside, Mike, his eyes wide with panic, said, *No, little brother, hang tight, we can figure this out. Just wait.* Even though there was nothing to figure out. All through that night into the gray light of dawn and on until the shadows disappeared in the midday sun, the three of them hunkered down in the living room, the old man sniveling and stuttering and saying things like *Jesus, I wish I still had my gun, I ought to just go ahead and kill myself,* and Mike—who would not even go into the garage, who point-blank refused—trying to force the reality of the situation into some less horrible shape. The longer they sat, the more it felt like debating the best way to throw themselves under a train. Patrick, it seemed, was the only one who realized that there was no best way. You just jumped. That was all. You jumped.

So, at one o'clock in the afternoon, Patrick called the police. Nineteen hours had elapsed between his father's return home and Patrick's phone call. He'd thought it through: they couldn't afford a private lawyer, and the old man couldn't get a public defender until he'd been charged. When the police arrived, the detective came back from the garage with a steely, satisfied expression on his face. *We've been looking for you,* he said to the old man, and all the old man did was nod.

Patrick remembered very little about what happened after that. Except that Mike said, *Jesus, Pat*—nobody had called Patrick Pat since he was ten years old—*he's our dad.*

Well, it's almost over now, Patrick said.

He had been wrong. It was just starting. None of Patrick's friends had explicitly told him they didn't want to hang out anymore; the cop who came into Zoney's every night had never said, *I'm keeping my eye on you, Cusimano; like father like son.* The supervisor at the warehouse where all three Cusimanos had worked had never suggested the remaining two find other jobs (and in fact, Mike still worked there). But always, from the very beginning, Patrick had read a sudden wariness in people, as if bad luck was catching and he was a carrier. The sidelong glances and pauses in conversation that stretched just a beat too long; the police cruisers that seemed to drive past their house on Division Street more often than they once had, or linger in the rearview a block longer than was reasonable; the weird sense of disengagement, of nonexistence, when cashiers and waitresses and bank clerks who saw his name on his credit card or paycheck couldn't quite seem to focus their eyes on him. Like he was nonstick, made of Teflon, and their gazes couldn't get purchase.

Nothing overt. Nothing you could point to. Just a feeling. If he'd never bought the newspaper at the SuperSpeedy, it wouldn't have come to anything more than that. He could just have bulldozed through, like Mike, waiting for people to get over it. He'd avoided coverage of the accident as much as he could. He didn't want to see the roadside shrine, with its creepy collection of plastic flowers and cellophane-shrouded teddy bears that wouldn't ever be played with, and he didn't want to see the kid's stricken mother holding a photo of her dead kid in the bedroom where he'd never sleep again. He'd bought the paper that day because his job at the warehouse had already started to feel impossible, but he hadn't taken anything from the rack but the classifieds. It hadn't occurred to him that the obituaries would be in the same section. Even if it had, it wouldn't have occurred to him that the kid's obit would still be running a month after the accident.

But he'd turned a page and there it was, oversized in the middle of all that sad muted eight-point death. Until then he hadn't actually seen the dead kid's photograph. Looking at it, at the kid's gap-toothed first grader grin, he'd felt—not bad, bad was his new normal. He'd felt worse. He wouldn't have thought that was possible.

The obit listed a memorial website, where you could make donations for the family. It took a few days for him to work up to it but eventually Patrick had suggested to Mike that they give some money. Anonymously, of course. Not out of guilt, although that was certainly part of it; more out of a sense that here was a thing, albeit a small thing, that could be done. But Mike, who had been drinking beer and watching Comedy Central in near silence ever since the accident, had only glared. For a moment, Patrick had thought his brother might hit him.

Instead, Mike had asked why the hell they would do that, since it wasn't like the old man had killed the kid on purpose. And it wasn't like they had any money to spare—only the old man had made full-time union wages, and losing his paycheck had hurt them badly—and it also wasn't like anybody was offering them free money, were they? "Fuck the kid, fuck his fucking family, and fuck you," Mike had said. "Dad's going to be in jail for fifteen years. They don't get anything else."

Determined to send the money anyway, Patrick had used one of the computer terminals in the public library so Mike wouldn't catch him, typing in the web address with his almost-maxed credit card ready to go. He'd scrolled down the page past the kid's picture, trying not to feel cynical about the sappy graphics and badly rhymed poetry *(My broken heart can only cry, I pray to God and ask Him why)* and looking for the donation link. He'd found the other one first.

Click here for more information about John Cusimano and his sons.

Gravity had done something weird just then. Patrick had felt like his limbs might float away from his body, but he clicked, anyway.

No flickering candles on this page. No sweet angels with electronic wings gently flapping. No poetry, no flowers, and most of all, no grinning first grader. The page he'd landed on was stark white, with red and black lettering: double underscore, bold, italic, and very, very angry. And it wasn't about the old man. It was about him and Mike.

John Cusimano's two ADULT sons, Michael and Patrick, were alone with him for NINETEEN HOURS after their father KILLED RYAN!! The car that took our Precious Baby away SAT IN THEIR GARAGE COVERED IN RYAN'S BLOOD and they DIDN'T BOTHER TO CALL THE POLICE!! THEY WASHED THEIR FATHER'S CLOTHES TO DESTROY THE EVIDENCE!! Call the Janesville County District Attorney's office and demand that they be charged as ACCOMPLICES AFTER THE FACT!!! DO NOT LET THESE MONSTERS GET AWAY WITH MURDER!!!

There was a photo, which Patrick had already seen when it ran in the local paper, of the brothers leaving the courthouse after the arraignment. There was also a message board. Patrick had known he shouldn't read it.

Michael and Patrick Cusimano you will burn in hell forever.

Those boys better hope they never meet me in a dark alley. Once upon a time somebody would have GOT A ROPE already.

In twenty years monsters like this will be ruling the country. This is what happens when you take prayer out of the schools.

Only one (anonymous) poster had said anything even remotely positive—*I knew Mike and Patrick in high school and I thought they were nice, I am so sorry to Ryan's family but Mike and Patrick are suffering too*—and the responses had not been generous.

It is obvious you do not have children and I hope you never do!

If you think their nice your probably just as evil as they are. I notice your not using your real name.

The messages made it sound like the old man had pulled up in the bloody car, said, *Hey, boys, look what I did,* and the three of them had traded a round of high fives, tapped a keg, and popped some popcorn. The dislocation was dizzying. Patrick had spent almost an hour reading those messages, all about what a monster he was. He never made the donation. He knew it was unfair, punishing the kid's family for being angry that they'd lost their son in such an ugly way. Their kid was dead, and other people's kids were alive. Patrick's dad was a

drunk and a murderer, and other people's dads were insurance sales-
men and orthodontists and air conditioner repairmen. *Fair* didn't
seem to have anything to do with it.

He'd been thinking of the accident as a tragedy that had happened to all of them, Czerpak and Cusimano alike. He'd been hoping that the guys at the warehouse were just being awkward-weird,
the way his teachers were when he was eleven and his mother was
dying. But after seeing the website, his eyes were open. He felt every
chill, noticed every look and nonlook and casually turned shoulder
and half-heard whisper. At that point he'd still had a few friends,
people he knew from high school and work, but within three months
of the accident they'd all fallen away in a litter of voice mail messages
saying *We totally gotta hang out, like, soon,* but not tonight and not
this weekend and probably not next week but *soon.* By the time the
old man had pled guilty to all counts and been transferred to a state
facility in Wilkes-Barre, the messages had stopped. Patrick had been
relieved. There was nobody he wanted to talk to.

Then it had just been Mike and Patrick alone in the house until
Mike met Caro and the two of them took over the room where Patrick's parents had slept: cleaned it out, redecorated it, filled it with
the smells of laundry soap and sex and Caro's perfume. Patrick quit
his job at the warehouse and took the night shift at Zoney's GoMart
(except for that one day shift a month, which he hated). Mike worked
every shift he could get at the warehouse, and Caro waited tables at
a seafood place in downtown Ratchetsburg. To Patrick it felt like the
three of them were planets that came into alignment once a week
or so, shared a few beers and some hot wings, and then spun back
out into their own separate orbits. The other world, the world he'd
belonged to before that afternoon when the old man had stepped out
of the Lucky Strike and decided he was sober enough to drive—that
world, presumably, kept spinning, somewhere out there, but Patrick
didn't live there anymore. He'd fallen into a numb kind of stasis and
after a while he couldn't tell the difference between the long quiet

nights he spent alone in the store and the long quiet days he spent sleeping off the nights. They both felt the same. They both felt like nothing.

You're Patrick Cusimano. Your dad was the one who killed Ryan Czerpak.

That night, as he drove home from work, he hit a deer. He'd taken the back way home, down Foundry Road, which at that time of day was a green-black tunnel through the trees. It was hard to see anything clearly; headlights didn't do any good, and the best you could do was squint and hope. Patrick had been awake for almost twenty hours. He'd left the goth girl behind him in a cloud of dust, but her voice was still in his ears. He was distracted. The world seemed like a movie scrolling by outside his windshield. Then he saw the tawny flash in his right headlight, and: *thud.*

His knees and elbows locked. He stomped on the brakes, steeling himself for the dreadful bounce of the wheels driving over the deer. It never came. When he pulled over to the side of the road, his chest felt tight and it was hard to breathe. For a moment he could only watch his hands clench and unclench on the steering wheel. Then he made himself get out.

He could hear the rush of traffic on the highway, but Foundry Road was deserted. In the faint glow of his own headlights, he stared at the four-inch fissure that had appeared in his bumper. There was no blood, for which he was thankful. He thought that if there'd been blood he probably would have flipped a circuit breaker and somebody would have found him by the side of the road in a few hours, twitching and drooling in a patch of poison ivy.

His legs felt weak but he walked toward the back of the car, stopped, and stared down the road, listening. He didn't know what he expected to hear. The spastic scrabble of dying hooves against asphalt. Something. His nose searched among the smells of exhaust and scorched rubber for the heady tang of blood. But he heard nothing, and he smelled nothing. He'd just clipped it, he thought, and it had run off. Or limped off, somewhere into the woods around him to die of shock or fear or internal bleeding. And what could he do about it either way? It wasn't a cocker spaniel; he couldn't wrap it in his coat and race it to the nearest vet. Even if it had been lying there on the asphalt in front of him, there would have been nothing he could have done except pull it off the road so it wouldn't get hit again while it was dying. So its death would be long and painful instead of quick and violent. A questionable mercy, at best.

The tightness in his chest grew worse. It was only a deer, he told himself. Not a jogger, not a pedestrian. Not a little kid chasing a kickball.

The air was warm and dewy and smelled like growing things. The leaves on the trees around him rustled, a gentle susurration that he found almost mocking. A drop of sweat ran down his ribs from his armpit. All at once he was so tired he could barely feel his feet. He turned around and went back to his car, turned the key with numb, trembling fingers, and drove away. Leaving the deer, wherever it was, behind.

At home, Mike's truck was in the driveway and Caro's car on the street, so Patrick parked in front of the house next door. He grabbed his phone from the console and the emergency twenty from the glove box, saw a few CDs on the floor and grabbed those, too. He wasn't consciously aware that he was emptying his car of everything he cared about until he turned at the front door and looked back.

The car crouched at the curb like a piece of roadside litter, the way you sometimes saw shoes or gloves or undergarments lying forlorn in puddles of mud, growing black with exhaust as the world passed them by. He'd owned the car for ten years, since he'd turned sixteen. Even in the yellow glare from the streetlight he could see how dirty it was. Although he couldn't see them, he knew the gas tank was half-full and the washer fluid reservoir empty. He couldn't see the cracked bumper, either, but he could feel it throbbing like a bruise.

Inside the house, he dropped his keys on the little table next to the door. Dead deer or no dead deer, he had no intention of ever driving the car again.

That night was one of those planets-in-alignment times. Four hours later he was steadier, drinking beer and watching television with Mike and Caro. She was sitting on his brother's lap, still wearing the white blouse and black skirt she waited tables in; Mike hadn't even taken off his work boots yet. His hand was tucked between Caro's knees. Patrick knew without being close to them that Caro smelled like fish and hot butter and Mike smelled like the picnic table out behind the warehouse, sweat and dirt and cigarette smoke. Patrick was watching a horror movie; not a very good one. On the screen, a mutant bear tore off a hiker's arm. The blood spatter hit the camera lens. It was that kind of movie.

"Come on, man," Mike said. "Normal people don't watch this shit. This is sick."

"Change it if you want." Without much interest, Patrick tossed over the remote.

Caro caught it and put on some sitcom with a laugh track. "You're in a good mood. Tough day at the office, dear?"

Your dad was the one who killed Ryan Czerpak. "Same shit, different day," he said. "I hit a deer on the way home."

"Grab me another beer, will you, babe?" Mike said to Caro.

She reached into the cooler behind them, pulled out a can of beer, and shook away the melting ice before handing it to Mike. "Did you kill it?"

"I don't know. It ran off."

"It's a deer. What's the big deal?" Mike cracked open the can.

"The big deal is that it sucks to kill something," Caro said.

"I see a dead deer, I think jerky."

She bit Mike's ear. "That's because you're a jerk."

"I'm your jerk, though," Mike said, and kissed her. Patrick looked away. He liked Caro and she made his brother happy, but nothing said *you don't exist* quite like being in a room with two people who couldn't keep their tongues out of each other's mouths. The fake family on the television screen was now embroiled in some sort of wacky misunderstanding involving a tray of lasagna and he missed the mutant bears.

"So, Patrick, did you mess up your car?" Mike said, finally.

"My sources say yes. It's all over the road."

Mike nodded knowingly. "The alignment. You want me to take a look?"

Caro slapped his arm. "You said you were going to get me a new battery."

"I will, I will. Quit nagging."

"You're the one who has to drive my sorry ass around when my car won't start."

"I love your sorry ass," Mike said, and kissed her again.

"I could not be here for this," Patrick said. "That would be okay."

"Patrick, you need a girlfriend," Caro said sternly. "You're the loneliest bastard I've ever met."

"Right. Because all of my problems would be solved if I just had more sex."

"I didn't say sex. I said girlfriend."

"You might not believe this," Mike said to her, "but there was a time when my brother was a devil with the ladies. He used to take them to this graveyard, up in—where was it, Cranberry?"

Patrick's jaw clenched, hard. He forced it to relax. "Evans City. And I only did that once or twice."

"They shot some movie there," Mike told Caro.

"Calling *Night of the Living Dead* 'some movie' is like calling a 'sixty-eight Camaro 'some car,'" Patrick said.

"You don't know shit about cars."

"You don't know shit about zombie movies."

"Now, boys." Caro curled an arm around Mike's shoulder. "I

didn't know they made movies in Pittsburgh. Is it still there? Can we go see it?"

Mike shook his head. "I'm not driving all the way up there. You want to see a cemetery, I'll take you out to St. Benedict."

"Did they make a movie there, too?"

"No, but that's where my mom is buried."

"We can do that if you want. But I want to see the movie one."

"It's really not that exciting," Patrick said. "It's just a cemetery."

"Exciting is not the point. The point is that we never go anywhere and we never do anything and all this will cost is gas."

"Gas is expensive," Mike said. Caro's face went flat and he pulled her closer. "Cheer up, girl. We'll go out tomorrow night. Do something fun."

"Sure," she said, and gave him a limp smile.

Patrick got quite drunk that night. Drunker than he meant to; drunker than was warranted, given that it was just a Wednesday and he was just in his living room and tomorrow he had to work (although not until midnight). Mike and Caro drank, too, and eventually Patrick noticed that the hand Mike was keeping between Caro's thighs was becoming less and less appropriate, so he stumbled upstairs to bed. It wasn't long afterward that he heard the thump-and-giggle sound of Mike carrying her upstairs to their room and the double thud of their bedroom door being kicked shut. Caro said words he couldn't quite catch and Mike said, "Oh, god," but it was more of a moan.

Patrick fumbled for a CD. It turned out to be Metallica and the empty space in the room filled with noise like it was water. He was drunk, he was drowning, he was sinking into blackness. He went down gladly.

There were a few times the next morning when he was dimly aware of Mike or Caro moving around the house: a door closing, the sound of the television downstairs. Once, he dozed off to a fragmented dream of tawny hide flashing in headlights, dream-felt a thud, and woke in a startle with his heart pounding. But he fell back asleep again in a few minutes.

When he woke up for real everyone else was at work. He did some laundry and made himself an over-easy sandwich with a slice of American cheese, hungover enough that the previous night felt far, far away. He had no desire to bring it closer. After he ate his sandwich, he decided he wanted a Coke and got as far as grabbing his keys and stepping outside. Blinking in the noon sun, he saw his car parked where he'd left it, in front of the house next door. A thick layer of grime coated the windshield. Everything he'd forgotten snapped back into brutal clarity and he looked at the car and thought, no, hell no, he didn't need a Coke that badly.

He spent the day doubting that he really had the gumption to walk to work that night, but when he stepped outside at eleven thirty, one look at the car made his skin crawl and the night was warm-ish, so he set off on foot. It wasn't entirely unpleasant. The dingy strips of paint peeling off the houses on Division Street didn't show so much at night, and when he got onto the highway and away from the streetlights, the wedge of moon blurred the speed limit signs into afterimages. He was between haircuts at the moment, and the feel of the breeze moving the long strands against his neck—like gentle fingers—almost made him want to never cut his hair again. There was a dreamy quality to being out this late, when everything else was shut down: like time had stopped and the rules no longer applied.

When he walked through the door at Zoney's at midnight, the blue-white fluorescents frizzled that nice blurry dreaminess into nothing. The back of his candy-striped work shirt was damp with sweat and his hair stuck to the nape of his neck. The guy he was re-lieving signed off on his deposit and left; Patrick counted the drawer, shoved it back under the register, and wiped the counter clean. It felt like he'd only been away from the store for a few minutes, like he'd stumbled through some reality loophole to a universe that was all Zoney's, all the time.

By the time the cop who stopped in every night for a scratch ticket and a Snickers left, Patrick had downed two cartons of chocolate milk, and no longer felt perched on the edge of his own grave. If it had been a weekend, a steady stream of drunks would have trickled in through the early hours, with a surge around four when the bars closed and then nothing much until sunrise. But on Thursday nights, even people who drank their paychecks were back in bed by two so they could drag themselves through the next day to get to the real weekend. The highway outside was so deserted that he could have stretched out in the middle of it for a nap. The classic-rock station playing in the store was automated, all music and condom ads. When Patrick had first started working at Zoney's, there'd been a CD player, and he'd played Black Sabbath while he worked. The loud and angry was a nice antidote to the quiet and bright and made him feel more *him*, as if, candy-striped shirt or no candy-striped shirt, he could broadcast this little piece of his soul to every poor schmuck who came through the door for a Red Bull at three in the morning. It got people's attention, reminding them that the world was real, that it was alive. But one morning he forgot to take the CD home with him, and when he came in for his next shift, the CD player had been replaced by a note from the manager about appropriate work music. So that was that. One more fragment of his being shaved away, and all he got in return was minimum wage and a nearly perfect command of every Eagles lyric ever. You could check out anytime you liked, but you could never leave: truer words, man. Truer fucking words.

Things started to pick up around six, and by seven he'd fallen into a kind of waking coma of jingling change and beeping cash registers. When a voice in front of him said, "I brought you coffee," he woke with an unpleasant start.

On the other side of the counter, paper cup extended, stood the goth girl. Today she wore a purple dress with a half dozen belts hanging loosely from the waist. Her boots were big and cartoonish and she'd probably had to drive to Pittsburgh to buy them. The bag over her shoulder looked like it had come from a surplus store.

She smiled. "A peace offering, okay?"

Patrick didn't smile back. He looked at the impatient-looking woman in panty hose and sneakers in line behind her, and said, "Come on up." As he rang up the woman's Slim-Fast and got her a pack of Capri cigarettes, the goth girl stood and watched with an almost anthropological interest.

"What to avoid becoming, exhibit A," she said, when the woman was gone.

"Fuck off."

The girl rolled her eyes. "Relax. Do you want milk and sugar in your coffee? I left it black because I didn't know. It's the good stuff. From Starbucks." When he didn't move to take the cup she grimaced. "Look, you've got me all wrong. I'm not going to go psycho on you. It's not your fault Ryan's dead. You didn't kill him."

This wasn't happening. He was not standing here among the raspberry-coconut Zingers and jerky sticks, earning minimum wage and listening to her say these things. "Next," he said, and sold a large coffee and a chocolate cream doughnut to a fat guy who didn't need any more doughnuts.

"Let's start over," she said, smoothing her already impeccable black hair. "My name is Layla. Like the song. You know: *you got me on my knees.*"

This girl. This little high school kid with her stupid boots and her Addams Family wardrobe and her skin as white and floury-looking as unbaked bread. Pillsbury goth girl, just out of the can. He wished she'd go cut herself or snort Ritalin or do whatever the hell goth girls did when they weren't blocking his counter and saying things like *It's not your fault Ryan's dead. You didn't kill him.*

He sold five dollars' worth of gas to a kid in a Slayer shirt and then there was nobody left in the store but the two of them. The girl leaned her elbows on the counter and said, "I looked your yearbook picture up in the school library. You had a really dumb haircut back then."

Patrick cashed out the register, taking the keys to the storage cabinet from behind the bill tray. He unlocked the cabinet, pulled out a carton of low-tar menthol something-or-others, tore it open, and started stuffing the packs of smokes into the overhead racks. "Why?" he said.

"I wanted to see what you looked like in real life. I have kind of a thing for monsters. Are you going to drink your coffee?"

The paper cup with the Starbucks logo sat on the counter where she'd left it. "I don't drink coffee."

"Oh." Her face seemed to fall. "Do you want something else? Gin and tonic?"

Patrick finished the cigarettes and slammed the cabinet door closed. "I want you to leave me alone."

"People think I'm a monster, too. Zombie Girl, Freakshow, Bride of Dracula—your friend yesterday wasn't exactly the first person to come up with that one, you know." She shrugged. "I don't really care. If they didn't call me Zombie Girl they'd call me Geek Girl, or Blow Job Girl, or whatever. I used to be Jesus Girl, if you believe that." There was a display on the counter of plastic toy cell phones filled with gum. Picking one up, she pressed a button on the side, and the toy went *Brrreeeep*. "Hey, are you doing anything this afternoon?"

"Why? Do you have an open slot in your stalking schedule?"

She laughed. "Funny. No, monster, if I was stalking you, we'd be having this conversation in your living room. I just thought maybe if you weren't doing anything, and you wanted some company, we could hang out, that's all."

Patrick stared at her, incredulous. Before he had time to say anything the bell over the door jingled again and this time it was Caro. Her unwashed hair was pulled back in a messy knot. Mike's Penguins key chain dangled from the front pocket of her cutoffs. She pointed toward the back of the store, said, "Coffee," and disappeared behind the Hostess display.

The goth girl lifted one perfectly penciled eyebrow, her white-powdered face faintly amused. "Busy after all, are we?" she said, then lifted the toy phone up, hit the button—*Brrreeeep*—and dropped it into her army-navy bag.

"Hey," Patrick said, but she had already turned and walked out of the store. Caro emerged from between the aisles with a large coffee in one hand.

"Your store does not have good coffee. I ate a doughnut back there." She yawned.

Patrick bit back his annoyance. "That's cool. People have apparently given up paying for things around here, anyway."

"Don't get snippy. I didn't say I wasn't going to pay." Caro handed him a five. "Who was your shoplifter, Marilyn Mansonette? You didn't try very hard to stop her. Do you know her or something?"

Through the window, he watched the goth girl climb into her big shiny car, one of those new round retro-modern things that looked like a cartoon hearse. As the driving lights came on, a pounding bass line kicked in. Nu-metal techno shit. "Not even a little bit," he said, and made Caro's change.

"That's some car she's driving," she said. "Somebody is certainly Daddy's best girl."

He wanted to change the subject. "What are you doing out this early, anyway?"

"It's not voluntary." She folded her arms on top of the cash register and rested her chin on her wrists. The top of her head bobbed with each word. "Mike let me take his truck since my stupid battery has been so flaky lately. I just drove him to work. You can get him tonight, right?"

"Nyet."

"Fuck you, why not?"

Because driving scared him and he didn't want to do it anymore. "My car's out of commission. From hitting the deer. I told you."

She blinked her green eyes and frowned. "You didn't say it wasn't working at all. How did you get here?"

"Walked."

"You're not going to turn into that creepy long-haired guy who walks everywhere, are you?"

"My hair's not that long."

"It's getting there." She yawned again, bending her face down toward her shoulder to cover her mouth. "You should have asked for a ride."

The door bell jingled yet again. This time it was an old duffer wearing a flannel shirt that looked as ancient as he did. "Need a Match 6," the duffer said, pulling a scrap of paper with some numbers scrawled on it out of his pocket.

Caro stepped back. "I'll tell Mike to call you." Then she lifted a hand and left. The duffer started reading off his numbers and Patrick punched them in. As he waited for the ticket to print, he happened to glance out the big plate-glass window and see Caro. He watched as she put her coffee cup down on the running board of Mike's huge jacked-up truck, pulled the sleeve of her sweatshirt over her hand, and reached up to open the door. Then she freed her hand, picked up her cup, and hoisted herself nimbly into the cab. She didn't even spill the coffee. It was impressive.

The lottery machine whirred. Patrick looked back at the old duffer. His eyes were the same place Patrick's had just been. "Wouldn't mind a piece of that," the duffer said.

"You want her number?"

The duffer laughed, his mouth opening wide to show stained teeth and a yellow tongue. Patrick asked him if he needed anything else.

"That'll do me," the duffer said.

. . .

Bill had the next shift. A few minutes before he was supposed to ar-
rive, the phone rang. "Dude," he said, sounding at least as hungover
as Patrick had been the night before. "Cover for me for a few hours."
And extra money was extra money, so Patrick did. By the time he
got home, it was close to noon. Caro was at work and the house was
empty. He took off his candy-striped Zoney's shirt, dropped it on
the floor next to the armchair, and dropped himself onto the couch.
ESPN Classic was showing an old Pirates game; it was the playoffs,
and the Pirates were winning. The last time that had happened, Patrick had been nine. His mom had been alive and his dad had only
been a social drunk. He vaguely remembered this game, these play-
ers. Baseball cards at recess, or something.

He fell asleep before the fifth inning and woke up to a clattering
crash. Which turned into a fast riffing guitar, and the Zeppelin song
he used as his ringtone. He grabbed for his phone and pressed buttons until the noise stopped. "Hello?"

"I didn't know your car was that bad," Mike said.

Now the TV screen showed a man in a cowboy hat clinging to a
bull the size of a Volkswagen Beetle. Patrick groped for the remote.
The announcer's cornpone accent was the most annoying sound he'd
ever heard. "Yeah," he said, still groggy. "What's up?"

"Caro's phone is dead. Probably out of minutes. When she gets
home, tell her I picked up a double, so she doesn't need to come get
me. I'll get a ride with Frank tomorrow morning." Patrick heard a
shout and a laugh in the background. Mike was calling from the
phone in the warehouse office. "She might be pissed. We were supposed to go out tonight. Tell her something nice for me, okay?"

"Tell her yourself," Patrick said, but Mike had already hung up.

Patrick looked at the clock on the cable box. He'd been asleep for
six hours, but it wasn't enough, and his skull felt stuffed with cotton.
On TV, some poor son of a bitch from Tulsa got dragged around the

arena by his left arm and the cornpone announcers said, *Good golly he shore did get hung up there dint he* and *I tell you what that is one tough Okie.*

Patrick changed the channel.

He was watching a slasher flick—*Oh, no,* the group of attractive young people trapped in the department store were saying to each other, *however will we escape the murderous psycho who is creatively and elaborately killing us one by one?*—when he heard Caro fighting the lock on the front door, which stuck. "The minute we have some extra money," she said, as soon as she got inside, "we're fixing that door. It's impossible to open."

"Keeps out the undesirables," Patrick said, muting the television.

"That's the antisocial recluse we know and love. I brought food." Caro put two foil take-out containers on the coffee table and then flopped down next to him on the couch. She looked like hell. Her makeup was smudged and caked under her red eyes. Patrick knew it was just the long day she'd had, but she looked like she'd been crying. Picking up one of the containers and passing it to him, she said, "That was a day. That was most certainly a goddamned day. Here, eat. I have to go get Mike."

"No, you don't." Patrick peeled the cardboard lid off the container and looked inside: penne and chicken in some kind of white sauce. He picked up a few pieces with his fingers and shoved them into his mouth. "He took an extra shift. He'll be home in the morning. He said to tell you sorry he couldn't take you out tonight."

Caro stuck her tongue between her lips and blew a raspberry. "I'm dead on my feet, anyway. You could use a fork for that."

"I don't have a fork."

"So go get one." On the television screen, a pretty girl was pounding on the inside of the department store display window, trying to get out. Caro unlaced her shoes. They were the practical, solid, spend-all-day-on-your-feet variety but she still winced as she pulled the first one off. "I hate my job," she said, conversationally. "My feet feel like they've got nails through the bottoms and I spend all day watching things get boiled alive." She eyed Patrick, sitting on the other end of the couch. "I don't suppose you want to move and let me stretch out, do you?"

"I was here first." He ate another three fingers' worth of pasta. The sauce was kind of congealed.

"You're such a youngest child."

"What's that supposed to mean?"

"Constantly fighting for position."

"Bullshit."

"I'm just telling you the theory." Caro reached down, flipped her shoes upside-down on the floor, and then rubbed the ball of her foot. She had a hole in her sock. "They've done studies about this stuff. Like, Mike is solid and respectable, because he's the oldest, and had the most responsibility growing up, and you're the youngest, so you always have to prove yourself."

"Complete bullshit. What about you?"

"Doesn't apply to me. I was raised by wolves." She swung her feet up into his lap, narrowly missing his pasta. "If you don't want my gross waitress feet in your face, you'll move."

"I have an unusually high tolerance for gross." A bucket of acid fell onto the prettiest and most nubile actress in the movie, causing her face to melt with an excruciating slowness. The fake skull under her flesh looked a little plasticky. Caro made a face. "Nice special effect, huh?" he said.

"I wish those lobsters were just a special effect." Shuddering, she tucked her feet underneath her. "Scrabble scrabble. Can we watch something happier?"

"Like what, sports? Earlier I fell asleep watching a Pirates-Braves game from the 'ninety-two playoffs and woke up to some guy getting his arm torn off on the back of a bull. How is that less horrible than this?"

On-screen, the nubile actress's boyfriend was wading through the puddle of her dissolved flesh. Caro stood up. She pulled at the elastic holding her ponytail, and her hair, which was the color of sun shining through a bottle of cola, fell around her shoulders. "Watch your movie, sicko. I'm going to go take a shower and wash the dead fish smell out of my hair."

"I like the dead fish smell."

"Nobody likes the dead fish smell," she said, and went upstairs.

Caro had moved in a month or so after the old man went to prison. Mike had brought her home from a bar, and Patrick had awakened the next morning to a series of unmistakably breakfastlike smells drifting up the stairs. Coffee, bacon, French toast. He'd come down to find the two of them sitting at the table, a third place set for him. Caro had looked vaguely embarrassed and Mike had looked happier than he had since before the accident.

She followed me home, he'd said with a grin. *Let's keep her.*

And, sure enough, by the end of that first week, her toothbrush was next to the sink and her tampons were in the medicine cabinet. To his relief, Patrick liked her. She was smart and funny and not obviously crazy; also, she could cook, and she liked folding laundry, and she didn't ask questions. Or answer them, really. He knew she was from Ohio, and he knew she did strange things sometimes, like turning her shoes soles-up on the floor or pulling her sleeve down over her hand before touching a doorknob. She kept books under the couch cushions not secretively, but mindlessly, as if out of long habit. Once, when he'd asked her about the sleeve thing, she'd turned scarlet and ghost-white in rapid succession and the whole set of her body had changed, curling into itself as if she were trying to shrink. He'd never asked her anything like that again.

She came back downstairs wearing a T-shirt and an old pair of Mike's cutoff sweatpants, returned to the other end of the couch, and tucked her feet underneath her again. She'd washed off the caked, smeary makeup, and her cola-colored hair was clean and pulled back in one of those plastic clips. Now she smelled girly, like conditioner or something. Sweet but not cloying.

"Did you really used to take girls to have sex in that graveyard?" she said.

By now, the last two survivors in the department store were crawling through a heating vent. "Not all girls. It had limited appeal, although you'd be surprised how many went along with it."

"You'd be surprised how little I'd be surprised. When was the last time you were up there?"

"I guess I was—seventeen? Eighteen, maybe." He hadn't been to Evans City since high school. After that, he'd just brought his girl-friends back to the house. The old man had never cared.

"Who was the girl?"

"Debbie Mayerchek. She still lives behind us. Me and Mike used to tie her to trees when we played cops and robbers."

Caro's eyebrows went up. "Your version of cops and robbers in-volved tying girls to trees?"

"She was a hostage."

"And I thought my childhood was screwed up. You guys were into bondage. Was she your girlfriend?"

"Nah, we just went out a couple of times." And in fact, after the night he'd taken her to the graveyard, he'd never called her again. Or spoken to her in school. Or spoken to her, ever.

"Was she into horror movies?"

"Not really."

"Me neither," she said. "Life is horrible enough." The clip in her hair was slipping. She reached up and pulled it free, then twisted her hair into a rope and pinned it back again. "When I was a kid, my grade went on this field trip to SeaWorld in Geauga Lake. And you know how they have the killer whale shows, right?" He nodded. "So we're all there, every second grader in school, and we're all laughing and cheering and having a great time and then—" One of her hands shot across her body, grabbed the other wrist, and yanked it down, like a crocodile taking down a gazelle. "*Bam*. The whale grabs the trainer by the leg and pulls her right down to the bottom of the pool."

Patrick stared at her. "It killed her?"

"No. It let her go and she crawled up onto the deck. Smiling, can you believe it? She'd just been munched by a killer whale in freaking *Ohio* and she had to smile because it was her job. We just thought we'd get to see some neat animals, maybe pet a sea urchin in the tide pool, and then suddenly it's all *Wild Kingdom*."

"That's why I like horror movies," he said. "Every night I wake up and go to work and come home and go to sleep and wake up and go to work and come home and go to sleep. A couple of showers, some pizza, the occasional autoerotic incident—"

"Don't tell me that."

"We keep getting eaten by the whale, is my point. Day after day, and day after day we have to smile about it."

"Patrick, Patrick, Patrick. Sometimes I'm sad for you." Her face belied her words, though. She understood exactly what he meant. He could see it in her eyes.

"But most of the time you love me," he said.

"Some of the time," she said. "Some of the time, if you're lucky, you grim bastard."

Soon, they said good night, and went to bed. Not long afterward, Patrick, who was semi-awake and restless, heard a tap at his door. Caro didn't wait for him to answer. She came in and closed the door behind her. Her hair was down loose around her shoulders again and in the moonlight it didn't look like cola, it looked like ink.

Half-convinced that he'd fallen asleep after all, he moved over on the bed, and she lay down next to him. She brought her knees up so that her shins pressed against his side. They didn't talk. The silence was a membrane between them, thick and organic.

When he put his arm around her it felt like something they had done before. When he kissed her it felt like he was crawling inside her, down her throat and into her chest, where there was a warm quiet place that was safe and private and only his. She put a hand on his stomach, under his shirt. He tasted salt on her face but her neck was sweet and mild under his tongue and when he closed his eyes and touched her, the world slipped away and it didn't matter what he did, it didn't matter what they did. So they did it all.

He awoke to find her sitting on the edge of the bed, not looking at him. The sky was lighter than it had been and he must have been holding her because his arms felt conspicuously empty. The place on his chest where she'd been sleeping seemed to ache.

He reached for her. She stopped his arm in midair. "Don't."

Confused, not fully conscious, he sat up. Put his hands on her shoulders.

She jumped as if he'd burned her. "Jesus. Leave me alone. Can't you just leave me alone?"

Then she was gone, and if not for the inexorable *oh-fuck-what-have-I-done* ringing through his brain, he would have thought he'd dreamed it all.

TWO

Once, when Verna Elshere and her sister were children, their father took them to a place in Janesville where someone he knew was erecting a church. He showed them piles of waiting materials: huge sheets of glass, rolls of pink insulation, shining aluminum ductwork. After the church was built they attended the consecration. In the sleek lobby, redolent of paint and new carpeting, Dad reminded the girls that everything they saw had been built by man, not God. They'd seen the building half-formed, he said, so they knew what he said was true. The building was nothing but a clever assemblage of goods. It was the spirit that made the place holy, and the spirit was in the people, and that was why he held his worship meetings in their basement, and not in a church.

Ratchetsburg High School, too, was nothing but a building. The doors were only doors, and behind them were only hallways and classrooms and lockers and drinking fountains, all of it—every hinge, every rivet—built by man. There was nothing permanent, nothing that could not be thrown down. Nothing to be afraid of.

"Hey," the boy behind her whispered. "Hey, Elshere."

She didn't want to turn around, but she had to. You always had to turn around.

This was only the first day, but the two boys sitting at the table behind hers in the biology lab clearly knew each other well. They were handsome and healthy-looking, with clear skin and muscular arms. The one on the left, the one who'd tapped her shoulder, had nearly black hair and striking blue eyes. At the table with them sat a girl with the kind of face that came preinserted in picture frames, her gorgeous red hair styled like that of a movie star from a grocery store checkout magazine. Verna wondered if there was any chance that she could change seats, or schools, or selves.

The striking boy gave her a dazzling smile. "What kind of freak are you?" he whispered.

His voice was loud enough for everyone around them to hear, but quiet enough to blend into the general murmur. At the front of the room, Mr. Guarda was working his way through the class roster. Verna didn't want to answer, but she had to. You always had to answer.

"What are you talking about?" she whispered back, trying to sound contemptuous.

The boy's lovely smile broadened. "I said, what kind of freak are you? Are you a Jesus freak, like your sister used to be, or are you a vampire freak, like she is now?" His blue eyes were sparkling, his voice friendly and musical. "Or are you some new kind of Elshere freak we haven't heard of yet?"

In the open collar of the boy's shirt, Verna saw a gold saint medallion on a chain. Verna's father said Catholics prayed to saints because they didn't trust God. She wondered if there was a patron saint of torturers.

"What was your name again?" he said. "Venereal?"

The redhead giggled. Grinning, the less remarkable-looking boy said, "Venereal Elshere. She's a sex freak."

Verna's arms and legs felt very heavy. She turned around.

Mr. Guarda passed out the textbooks. The covers were new and bright, but the spines were uniformly broken. Instead of sitting stable and strong, they slumped to one side.

The redhead raised her hand. "Yes, Calleigh?" Mr. Guarda said.

"Somebody cut out a hunk of my book, Mr. Guarda." Her voice was cool as cream.

"I'm aware of that. We've decided not to teach that chapter in this school district." Did Mr. Guarda's eyes flicker toward Verna, or did she imagine it?

"Why not?"

"Would you like me to write you a pass to the principal's office so Mr. Serhienko can explain it to you?"

"Why don't we ask Verna Elshere to explain it to us?" Calleigh said.

The class made gleeful *oooooh* noises. Mr. Guarda sighed. "That's enough, Calleigh."

Verna wanted to disappear. She wanted to fold herself into her frizzy brown hair, vanish into the folds of her too-long skirt. At the end of class she stuffed her crippled textbook into her new purple backpack, the one she'd picked because the color was cheerful, almost sassy, just as Calleigh brushed by in a wave of shining red hair and sugary perfume. "Hey, Venereal, Barney called. He wants his bag back," she said, and the two boys, right behind her, laughed as if they would split in two.

At her locker, Verna emptied the bag, stuffed it inside, and carried her books for the rest of the afternoon.

Verna had not expected her first day of high school to be fun, but she was surprised by how dreadful it actually was. In homeroom, the pretty young Spanish teacher, Ms. Kiser, read Verna's name off the attendance list with a face that looked like she had a mouthful of soap. The math teacher's expression would have melted sand into glass, and the gym teacher actually rolled her eyes. The other girls in the locker room had giggled. Including Calleigh, the gorgeous red-head, who, once the teacher left them to change, had said, "So Freak-show Elshere has a little sister. You'd think their parents would have stopped fucking when they saw how the first one came out."

Freakshow Elshere. She was surprised by that, too. People here hated her sister.

Her sister: beautiful, blond, beguiling Layla, who climbed trees fastest and highest, who testified most passionately at Worship Group, whose very name had brought forth enthusiastic smiles from church camp counselors and homeschool outing organizers for as long as Verna could remember. She had trailed her sister through life like a moth after a torch; unbeautiful, unblond, and unbeguiling, shy and mousy and utterly content to bask in her sister's reflected light. Public school had been an experiment. Be in the world but not of the world, her father told them, and for a few months it had seemed that the experiment was working. Then one day, Layla had come home from school and reported that her biology teacher, one Karen Hens-ley, had taught them an unsanctioned sex-ed lesson, complete with condom demonstrations and lists of birth-control clinics. Her par-ents had complained to the school board, and the battle had quickly grown ugly. Local news crews started showing up at board meetings. The newspaper published editorials and letters to the editor. Dad had even done a twenty-second interview with a cable news network.

In the end, Karen Hensley retired. A week later, Layla came home from school with her lovely hair chopped to her chin and dyed jet-black. Her wardrobe quickly followed suit. Soon she was haunting the dinner table like a snarling, sarcastic ghost. The rapid transforma-tion left Mother and Dad hurt and angry—they called it concern, but it felt like hurt and anger to Verna—and the members of her father's home church baffled. Everyone blamed Layla's new attitude on the corruption of the secular world. But now it seemed that even the sec-ular world disapproved of her, and Verna didn't know what to think.

Her last class of the day was Art. She'd been hoping for the refuge of a solitary desk where she could sit by herself and recover from Biology, but this room was full of tables, too. Most of them had already been staked out by obvious groups, but one, off to the side, was empty except for a boy in a gray sweatshirt with the hood pulled up over his face. Sitting alone with a boy was risky, but there wasn't anywhere else. She took the stool farthest away from him. He didn't look up.

The studio smelled like the art room at camp: chalk and mud and wood shavings, not like school at all. Mr. Chionchio grinned and winked, saying, "Uh-oh, another Elshere. We'll have to keep an eye on you." But it was okay, somehow, it was friendly. Their first assignment was their own self-portraits, drawn in crayon, because—he said—this was one assignment he didn't want them to take too seriously. As they worked, the teacher wandered around the room, glancing over shoulders and making comments.

When he came to her, he said, "Are those wings?" He was the silly-tie type of teacher; today's was covered in white cartoon sheep, one black sheep among them next to an arrow and the word *me* printed in a childish chalk-scrawl.

"You said to have fun with it." Verna could barely hear herself.

"Wings are fun." He sounded amiable. "Hey, I've got your sister first period. Try to get her here on time once in a while, will you?"

Verna blushed and said she'd try. After he walked away, the boy in the sweatshirt raised his head. "Are you into fantasy?"

Verna shrunk away from him. "What?"

He pointed at the paper in front of her. His sandy bangs fell to the tip of his nose. Underneath them was a pair of glasses that couldn't possibly be clean, not with his hair hanging down against them all day. "The wings. Are they, like, elf wings, or fairy wings, or what?"

Verna opened her mouth and closed it again. If she said yes, would she be Venereal Elfshere for the rest of the year? "Just wings," she said. "Regular wings."

Then, quickly, she picked up a crayon and bent over her drawing. After a moment the boy muttered, "Whatever." They didn't talk again for the rest of the period.

After the final bell rang, Verna found Layla standing by her new car with a tall, lanky boy, a stranger. Their mouths were wide-open and pressed together, their eyes closed, and their expressions strangely solemn, as if the act were more communion than congress. (Verna's grandmother was Catholic, she knew what Communion looked like.) The boy's mouth moved on Layla's as if he was eating her. He wore a long black coat despite the pleasant weather, and his hair was the same glossy raven-black as Layla's. Layla's olive-drab army surplus bag, hanging over her shoulder, was the most vivid color between them.

Verna did not want to stand around the parking lot watching Layla kiss a strange boy. She wanted to go home. "Layla," she said.

The couple stopped kissing but didn't move apart. The face Layla turned toward her sister, far from being embarrassed, was cool and annoyed. Which didn't mean anything. Layla always looked like that. "Christ, Verna. Where's your backpack?" Then the older girl shook her head. "You know what? I don't even want to know. This is Justinian. We're giving him a ride." She hit the button on her remote and her car chirped.

Verna managed a thin smile, but this boy, this Justinian, only looked at her as though she were a music box or a snow globe, some small, curious thing with no actual use. He had blue eyes, just like the boy from Bio. She opened the back door, pushed aside an assortment of clothing and empty paper coffee cups, and climbed in. The car, with its tinted windows, was a black bubble in the sunny parking lot, and Verna felt safer the moment the door closed behind her.

Fifteen hours. Fifteen hours until she would have to come back.

"So," Justinian said, as Layla buckled her seat belt. He sat in the front seat like the car belonged to him, and he was letting Layla drive it because it pleased him to do so. With a long, thin hand—a dragon ring with red-jeweled eyes wrapped around his first finger—he tilted the rearview mirror so that his eyes met Verna's. "You're the child of God."

His nose was long and hawkish. "We're all the children of God," Verna said.

Justinian raised an eyebrow. "Then God owes my mother a lot of back child support."

His voice wasn't exactly unkind. Layla snorted a laugh, tipped the mirror back, and hit the ignition button. The car filled with droning music. It was too loud to talk, for which Verna was grateful.

Layla drove them to a shabby, undistinguished corner in downtown Ratchetsburg. Then she pulled over. "You'll come out later," Justinian said to her. It should have been a question but it wasn't, quite.

"If I can," Layla said.

He leaned across and kissed her, then got out. Verna got out, too, to move to the front seat, and found him holding the door for her. "See you, Verna," he said, and gave her a somehow-familiar smile. As Layla drove away, Verna could see him in the side mirror, walking purposefully in the opposite direction, his long coat billowing in the breeze. He'd lit a cigarette and smoke swirled around him like a halo.

"Is he your boyfriend?" Verna asked.

Layla didn't take her eyes from the road. "*Boyfriend* is a word that the sheep use to make their lives feel less pointless."

Verna didn't know what to say to that. "Oh," she finally said, and didn't ask anything more.

Later, both girls were in the garage, putting together information packets for their father's ministry. Verna was, anyway. Around and around the long table she went, picking up one piece of paper from every stack: rising incidences of venereal disease, explicit sexuality in prime-time television, pregnancy rates, AIDS-related deaths. Each packet was tucked into its own folder, and each folder was printed with a glossy photograph of a smiling teenager under a blue sky, her sun-kissed face looking as if the photographer had caught her in between tennis sets. Her corn-silk hair was pulled back in a neat ponytail and a gold cross gleamed above her collar. Layla, two years ago.

Now-Layla was stretched out on the scratchy brown carpet among the fallen staples and lost paper clips, her combat boots propped up on a chair so that her skirt fell almost to her crotch. She wasn't helping Verna collate. She was only in the garage at all because of the contract she'd signed with Dad, which was supposed to bring a little peace back to the family but which mostly resulted in moments like this, when Layla was somewhere she didn't want to be, tasked with something she refused to do. According to the contract, Layla had to spend one night a week working for the ministry, attend all family meals, not leave the house on school nights, be in bed by ten thirty on weeknights and midnight on weekends, and drive Verna to and from school each day. In exchange for all of this, Layla had received a new car.

"Don't get us wrong," Dad had warned her. "All that we're asking of you is that you fulfill your obligations to this family. The car isn't a reward for that. The car is a sign of our faith in you and our recognition of how difficult it's going to be for you to start making different life choices." Dad was very into life choices, and contracts, and God. Because Proverbs said a virtuous woman was worth more than rubies, he called his ministry Price Above Rubies. Pledge your virginity to God, he told teenagers—primarily girls—and in return you'll receive His love, and also a sterling silver ring set with a lab-created ruby. The rings were mass-produced in Mexico and came sealed in tiny plastic bags. ("Just like coke," Layla liked to say, although Verna didn't think she actually knew that firsthand.) The rings were cheap. Verna's made her finger itch. Mother said the itching was a reminder of her pledge; Layla said she was probably just allergic to the metal.

Privately, Verna wondered if it wasn't a sign that God found the whole thing vaguely ridiculous, because either He guided you or He didn't and if He did then how could you really do anything wrong? When nobody was around, she slipped the ring off and kept it in her pocket. Until she felt guilty, wondered if maybe God at least appreciated the gesture, and put it back on.

Layla, of course, never wore hers at all anymore.

Dad had made the garage into an office by installing the brown carpet and snap-together modular walls. With the huge garage doors still intact, the space heater in the corner wasn't nearly enough in the winter. "God's love will keep us warm," Mother always said, but she'd also knitted a box of scarves and fingerless gloves to wear during the winter. It was September now but Layla was wearing a pair of cherry-red gloves with yellow stripes, pulling at the stitches, trying to make a hole. As Verna dropped yet another completed folder with Layla's face on it into the box, the door opened and their father's assistant, Toby, walked in. He wore combat boots like Layla, but his jeans were clean and pressed and so was the long-sleeved shirt he wore. Verna could see the edges of his tattoos peeking around his cuffs and collar. He looked down at Layla and her skirt gathered mere millimeters away from indecency, and his face grew stern with disapproval. "Layla, you're being immodest. Sit up."

Layla smiled a slow, small smile, and Verna realized why Justinian's smile had seemed so familiar: there it was in front of her, spreading across her sister's face like a cold sore she'd caught from him. "C-c-caught you looking," she said, uncrossing and recrossing her ankles. The movement was measured and deliberate.

Toby didn't rise to the bait. He was used to Layla. "Do you need help, Verna?" The *V* sound was dogged by the faintest hint of the stutter the older girl had mocked. "I have some time."

Verna nodded. The entire office smelled like Toby's herbal cologne and spearmint nicotine gum. "So, how was your first day of school?" he said.

Verna picked up a flier. *Venereal Disease in Teenaged Girls: It's Scarier Than You Think!* She looked away from the word *Venereal*. "Good."

He asked about her teachers, then said he'd had Ms. Kiser ten years before, and she was nice. "Incorrect," Layla said from the floor. "Kiser is not nice. Kiser is a dumb bitch who kisses up to the jocks and cheerleaders and completely ignores everyone else."

"Don't call her that," he said. "Say she's got a strong personality, or that she's a challenging person."

"Wouldn't change the fact that she's a bitch."

"It might change the way you look at her, which might change the way she looks at you."

Layla made a face. "Gee, Toby. You're so wise. How did you get so wise? Was it the meth? I bet it was the meth." Toby said nothing, just dropped another folder into the box. Layla turned back to Verna. "Now, Chionchio, I like. Guarda, of course, will hate you on principle. I thought he and Pastor Jeff were going to throw down at that last board meeting. It's actually sort of ironic, because Guarda's supermega-Catholic. Goes to St. Joe's three times a week, gives shit up for Lent, everything. Sex ed was Hensley's thing. Guarda wouldn't touch it. But he's the head of the department. So."

They have the right to know how their own bodies work, one of the letters to the editor had said. *All they need to know is that God wants them to wait,* Dad had written back. His response was still pinned to the refrigerator downstairs by a papier-mâché butterfly magnet that Verna had made when she was seven.

"It's not a biology teacher's place to teach sex ed," Toby said. "When I was in school, they taught that stuff in Health."

"Were you out sick the day they covered drug abuse?"

Toby, shaking his head, said, "You can't get a rise out of me, Layla," and she grinned and said, "Oh, I think I could. If I really wanted to."

"I'm going to go tell your father we're done," he said, curtly, and left.

"What a loser," Layla said. "Doesn't he make you want to stab yourself in the eye?"

"Not really," Verna said. "Are you going to help me finish these?"

"No. Those make me want to stab myself in the eye, too." Layla stood, picked up one of the folders, and made a face at her own image, then held it up in front of her face and Verna. "Bleah!" she said, in a monster voice, waggling the folder back and forth. "I am the Jesus zombie! I will steal your soul! And your eyeliner! And any skirts less than twenty-four inches long! Bleah!"

Verna rolled her eyes. Layla laughed and tossed the folder back down.

"Oh, I kill me," she said. "Hey, Vee, by the way, speaking of death and zombies and other unpleasant things—there's this girl at school, Calleigh Brinker? Hot redhead, legs up to wherever?"

"I met her."

"Yeah, well," Layla said. Suddenly all the humor was gone from her voice. "Steer clear. She's Hensley's niece. She's also just the tiniest bit psychotic."

Verna wished the ground would open up and swallow the school building overnight, so she never had to go there again.

At dinner, Dad said, "Toby said you could have been more helpful with the information packets, Layla."

"Toby was high as a kite," Layla said. "I'm surprised he didn't say I could have been a flying giraffe."

"Toby has a lot of wisdom to share, if you'd let him."

"As well as more than one blood-borne disease, I don't doubt." If Layla's previous smile had been a perfect mirror of Justinian's, the sunny one she flashed now was a perfect mirror of their father's. "Shall I let him share those with me, too?"

The big muscles at the corners of Dad's jaw clenched and unclenched. He did that a lot when Layla was around. The shirt Dad was wearing and the way he was wearing it, open down the front with a T-shirt underneath, reminded Verna of the boy from Biology.

Mother was setting out bowls of turkey chili and salad and arranging plates of cheese and chopped onion and cilantro on the Lazy Susan. Her hair, a darker blond than Layla's used to be, was carefully pinned up, and her nails were freshly manicured. Even pulling open a bag of corn chips, Mother was lovely: well-groomed, well-exercised, well-dressed, all of it. Dad was the same way. When you ran a ministry you had to be presentable. The two of them played a lot of tennis and used a lot of personal-care products. They smelled nice, but they made Verna feel like Sasquatch.

Passing the chips—and changing the subject—Mother asked if they'd had a good first day of school. Layla said that it promised to be the best year ever, if only she could make cheer captain. Everyone ignored her.

"How did Biology go, Verna?" Dad asked.

"Fine."

"Layla, do you have salad?" Mother asked.

"I'm a vegetarian," Layla said. "All I have is salad."

"Mr. Guarda didn't give you any trouble?"

Verna shook her head.

"At least eat a little of your chili," Mother said to Layla.

"If you want me to eat it, don't put corpse meat in it."

"You're going to become anemic."

"This is good, Michelle." Dad poured chips onto his chili. "I wouldn't mind taking a look at your textbook, Verna."

"Karen Hensley never used a book," Mother said.

Verna swallowed. "They cut the reproduction part out, though, so . . . "

Her voice trailed off. Dad smiled at her. "Verna, honey, we know you don't like to make trouble."

Verna looked down at her food.

"I, of course, love to make trouble," Layla said.

"Layla," Dad said, a note of warning in his voice.

"What? You didn't mind so much when it was your trouble. Back then it was, 'When's your next protest, Layla? How many signatures did you get on your petition, Layla? Hey, Layla, maybe you should organize a walkout, I'll call Channel Seven.'"

All of which was true, Verna thought. "All trouble is not created equal," Dad said now. "I wouldn't object to you using physical force to defend yourself, but that doesn't mean you should walk around hitting people for fun."

Layla stuck her knife in her chili. "I'll cancel my weekend plans, then."

Mother sighed. "Layla, must you? Now that knife is going to have to be washed," she said, and Layla answered, "If you didn't want us to use them, you shouldn't have put them on the table."

Dad cleared his throat. "Anyway," he said to Verna, "this particular issue is bigger than whether or not Guarda teaches the same lessons Karen Hensley did. It's about our right to believe what we believe. Persecution versus freedom, truth versus lies—all of those big ideas that seem very abstract, but in the end they come down to everyday people like you, and everyday battles like this. And in the end, the world is a better place."

"Truly moving, Father," Layla said. "What a speech."

Dad's eyes narrowed. "You do know that it's because of you girls that I'm called to fight. Everything I do is for the two of you and the world you're going to grow up in—the world your *children* are going to grow up in."

"Nothing's even happened yet." Verna's voice came out much softer than she intended.

"I'm not having children. In fact, I think I'm a lesbian," Layla said.

Mother made an exasperated noise and threw her napkin down on the table, and Dad put a hand on her arm. "She's just trying to get to you, Michelle." He looked at Layla. "You know, just because you're going through a phase where you don't think big ideas are cool doesn't mean they're not important."

"Oh, I'm an enormous fan of big ideas. Free will. Intellectual curiosity."

"God gave us those things," Mother said. Her cheeks were pink but her voice was level. "It's up to us to use them wisely."

Layla laughed. "Sure. And waging Holy War Part Two to keep Verna from finding out how to use a condom is totally using God's gifts wisely." Layla pulled her knife out of the chili and put it on top of her white cloth napkin. "Maybe if you'd taken Hensley's class, you wouldn't have had to buy your prom dress in the maternity section."

"Enough," Dad said. There was a long silence. When he spoke again, his voice was deliberately gentle. "A year ago, you didn't think our fight with Karen Hensley and Tom Guarda was unimportant. You didn't think it made your life a living hell."

Which was also true; Layla had walked around for weeks like one of the old Christian martyrs, almost seeming to shine from the inside. But at that last school board meeting—which Verna had found terrible, Dad's sticky red face and the unpleasant jut of Mother's chin, kind-looking Mrs. Hensley nearly reduced to tears and everybody in the room shouting for one side or another—even Layla's brow had furrowed. She hadn't been shining then.

"Wrong," Layla said now. "I didn't tell you that it was making my life a living hell, because you told me I was doing God's work, and I was stupid and naïve enough to believe you."

Dad shook his head sadly. "Why are you so determined to shut God out of your heart, Layla?"

"Oh, fuck off," Layla said, and then things really exploded. Mother was screaming and Dad was screaming and Layla was screaming, and Dad's face grew redder and redder and at one point Layla screamed, *Fuck fuck fuck fuck MOTHERfuck,* and Verna put her hands over her ears because she didn't want to hear any more.

Later, after Layla left the house in a cacophony of slammed doors and thumping bass from her new car's stereo (bedtime came and went and still no Layla, so much for the contract), Verna lay in bed and prayed: *Lord, I love my family, but I hate them when they're together. Forgive me, Lord. Help me not to hate them. Amen.*

Verna was surprised at how bleak life became, and how quickly. Her classes all covered bland introductory stuff that she already knew. Calleigh Brinker hit her in the back twice with a tennis ball on Wednesday. In the locker room, she dumped Verna's gym bag out on the floor and said, "My aunt is teaching day care now, by the way. Thanks to your dad she's up to her arms in shit, and so are you."

Verna said nothing. What could she say?

Once upon a time, going to school had meant spending a few pleasant hours a day at the warm honey-colored wood of her mother's kitchen table: classifying leaves, reading about Laura Ingalls and Betsy and Tacy, doing math worksheets printed off the Internet. Now she ate lunch at one end of a long empty table in the lonely, deafening cafeteria, a table covered with battered gray Formica into which somebody had scratched *Ashleigh Riccoli is down to fuck.* On her way up to history, she often caught a glimpse of Layla standing by the fire exit at the end of the second-floor corridor with Justinian and another girl, whose cropped blue hair and pierced lip marked her as one of them. Lots of kids at school had dyed hair and a few even had piercings, but Layla and her friends stood out. If there was one thing that Verna's first week of high school taught her, it was *Thou shalt not stand out.* Thou shalt not stand out by wearing the wrong clothes, the way Verna did the day she wore a long flowered dress that her mother had made and Calleigh called her the Little Whore on the Prairie. Thou shalt not stand out by having a father who'd threatened to take the school board to court. Thou shalt not stand out by having a strange name. Like, for instance, Verna Elshere.

Hey, Venereal, I'd tell you to suck my dick, but I don't want to catch anything.

Layla and her friends might skulk in the hallways like disdainful crows but Verna's goal became complete anonymity. She wanted to be colorless, featureless, a perfect, bland blank. And so on Thursday afternoon, she found herself standing in the hallway outside the art studio, staring at the wings she'd so innocently drawn on her self-portrait three days earlier and wondering if she could get Mr. Chionchio to take it out of the display case. What had she been thinking? Who had she thought she was?

"I figured it out," somebody next to her said. "They're angel wings, right?"

Her tablemate, Jared. They'd been sitting together silently all week. Verna's cheeks grew hot and she wished again that she'd never drawn the stupid wings in the first place. She shrugged.

He nodded. "Like the Nephilim. That's cool." He wore the same baggy sweatshirt and the same dirty glasses, but today she could see a little of his eyes, peeking through his bangs like a rabbit's through grass. He had a nice voice.

"You know about the Nephilim?" Verna said, surprised.

"Sure. I've got a game character who's a Nephilim." He looked at her. "Is that right? A Nephilim? Or is Nephilim already plural? Is it Nephila? Anyway, he's a badass. His charisma is, like, nine billion and any sword he touches bursts into flames."

Verna had absolutely no idea what he was talking about. "Your picture is really good."

He'd drawn himself in bold, confident strokes of black crayon, sweatshirt, scraggly bangs, and all. The cartoon boy had no eyes—just hair and glasses—and only a straight line for a mouth. In one hand he held a guitar; in the other, a book. At his feet sat a huge, shaggy dog. The real Jared looked at the picture as if seeing it for the first time. "Oh. Thanks." He sounded dismissive and a little embarrassed.

"Is that your dog?"

They had walked into the classroom together. Jared dropped his bag next to his stool. "It's a wolf. Wolves are my power animal." His ears turned red. "Not that I buy into the whole power animal thing, exactly, but my mom's boyfriend does, so—you know."

Verna didn't know. "What's a power animal?"

"They help you."

She dropped her books onto the table. Her backpack was still stuffed in her locker and her arms and back were always sore. "Do they carry heavy objects?" she said, without really thinking about it. "Because that could be really useful."

The corner of his mouth twitched. "Not exactly. They represent your strength, and protect you and stuff." Jared pulled his fingers through his bangs, tugging them farther down over his nose. "It's just some New Age crap Keith is into. You're Verna, right?"

She nodded, and—because it would come up anyway—said, "Layla Elshere is my sister."

"The goth chick who hangs out with Justin Kemper?"

"You mean Justinian?"

"Huh. Yeah." Jared's face was invisible behind his hair, but Verna thought she heard a hint of contempt in his voice.

"I don't really know any of Layla's friends," she said. "You don't like him?"

"I've never really talked to him. I only moved here in April." He paused for a moment and then said, "It's sort of stupid that he calls himself Justinian, though. And the whole vampire thing. It's just— come on, you know?"

Just then, Mr. Chionchio said, "Okay, folks, listen up," and started explaining their first unit, which was drawing. Verna only half-listened. The boy in Biology had said something about vampires, too. As soon as Mr. Chionchio had set up a cut orange and a vase for them to draw, she said, "What vampire thing?"

"Oh, you know." Jared was bent over the paper in front of him. "The whole 'bright light hurts my spooky night creature eyes' thing. Look, forget it. He's your sister's friend. I'm sure he's cool. You're Christian, aren't you?"

Had somebody noticed her sitting next to him and warned him that hers was the nutso family behind the sex-ed saga? "How did you know?"

"Your cross." He pointed to Verna's necklace. "I'm not, though. Christian. And don't take this the wrong way, but I don't really want to be. I'm open-minded and all that, it's just not my thing."

She heard her father's voice saying, *We can work with open-minded.* But Verna didn't want to work with anything. Jared was nice and he didn't make fun of her for drawing angel wings on herself and she'd just spent forty-five minutes being called Gonorrhea Girl by the boys in Biology.

"You probably think I'm a jerk for saying that," he said. "I just knew this one girl at my old school and she was all, hey, let's hang out, but then it turned out she only wanted me to go to church with her. They got some prize for bringing new people."

Verna sighed. "Well, are you a jerk?"

He stared at her for a moment. Then, softly, he said, "No."

"Good," Verna said. "I'm tired of jerks."

Friday morning, Layla came to breakfast wearing a tight T-shirt with *god is dead* printed across the chest and nobody mentioned it. Before they ate, Dad read from the book of James: *Whenever you face trials of any kind, consider it nothing but joy, because you know that the testing of your faith produces endurance.*

Layla, of course, laughed. "That's nice. Am I facing the trial, or am I the trial?"

"Each of us faces trials, and each of us is somebody else's trial. So I guess you could say a little of both." Dad smiled wanly and then looked at Verna. "Do I see wheels turning up there, Verna?"

Verna was trying to think of somebody whose trial she might be. "Math pretest."

"You heard the verse," Layla said, poking at her cereal. "Be joyful."

"And bring a calculator. Calculators on math tests! Now that's something you can be joyful about." Mother smiled at Layla in her *god is dead* shirt just as if they all shared a joke together. It was always like this for a day or two after a big fight, with both parents trying hard to act relaxed and forgiving. The sweat practically stood out on their brows. Consider it nothing but joy.

In the car, Layla screwed her face into a simper and her voice into a falsetto mockery of their mother's. "'Let's all thank the Heavenly Father for blessing us with calculators! Praise Jesus! Hallelujah!'" Her voice dropped back down to normal. "You know who gave us calculators? Texas fucking Instruments, that's who."

"I don't think that's what she meant."

Layla thumbed the steering wheel, changing the music until she found a suitably aggressive song. "Yeah? And are you going to remember to feel grateful today when Kyle Dobrowski calls you Venereal Elshere? Are you going to consider it nothing but joy?"

Verna flinched. "How do you know about that?"

"Justinian told me."

"How did he know?"

"He knew because, unlike most people, he actually pays attention to the world around him." Layla sighed. "If it makes you feel any better, they screwed both of us in the name department. My sophomore year was one long, endlessly repeating chorus of 'Layla, I had you on your knees.'"

It did make Verna feel better, weirdly. "Which one is Kyle Dobrowski?"

"Pretty eyes. No soul." Layla snorted. "Mother and Dad are idiots. Satan doesn't look like Justinian. Satan looks like *him*."

Verna clung to that all through Biology, while Kyle and his minion, whose name was Brad Anastero, asked her in harsh whispers how many genital warts she had and Calleigh snickered. They were getting bolder. Mr. Guarda talked obliviously about cell structure, mitochondria, alleles; either he couldn't see what was happening in the second row or he felt no obligation to intervene, despite Verna's magenta cheeks and damp eyes. She tried to pay attention anyway, but it was hard. Because why should she care about his world if he didn't care about hers.

After Bio came Art, and Art was jumping into a lake on a hot summer day, the first pain-free step after shaking the rock out of your shoe. When the bell rang, Jared was telling her about religious themes in *The X-Files*, so they walked out together, and then Verna made her way to the parking lot alone.

Where Justinian sat on the hood of Layla's car with his arms draped over her shoulders, his fingers laced loosely together in front of her throat. Layla leaned between his legs, one languid finger tracing the faint blue veins on the back of his hand. "Verna Faith Elshere," she said, with a lift of one carefully plucked eyebrow. "Was that a boy I saw you talking to, you slut?"

Verna's cheeks grew warm. "He's just a friend." Trust Layla, she thought bitterly, to take the one decent thing in her day and turn it into something horrible. Even if she was joking.

Justinian jumped down from the hood of the car like a lanky, trench-coated cat. "I know that guy. He draws wolves." If Jared's voice had held a note of contempt, Justinian's played the entire symphony.

This time, instead of dropping Justinian downtown, Layla drove home. The driveway was empty; their parents were gone. Layla put the car in park and turned around to look at Verna. "All right. Should Pastor Jeff or the Whore of Babylon inquire, I am studying at a friend's house. I will not be home for dinner, because I was invited to eat with my new friend's family. Should they inquire further, this friend's name is—oh, let's say Brittany."

Verna glared at her. "I'm not going to lie for you. Tell them yourself."

"I could tell them water was wet and they'd assume I was lying."

"Maybe you shouldn't lie so much, then."

"Maybe you should lie more."

"Well, I'm not going to start now. You can just forget it."

"Such a sweet little lambkins," Layla said. "Such an obedient little zombie."

Justinian glanced at Verna in the rearview mirror, but said nothing. She wanted to wither up and blow away like a dead leaf. "I am not."

"Prove it," Layla said.

"Fine." Verna grabbed her books and climbed out of the car.

By the time her parents came home, she'd changed her mind a hundred times but, in the end, she lied. Not because Layla wanted her to, but because she couldn't listen to another huge screaming fight. Not tonight. She even invented a blue sweater for the imaginary Brittany to wear, thinking of the cardigan Calleigh had worn that day. Every syllable she spoke seemed to shine with untruth, but her parents accepted it.

After dinner, she wiped the table while her parents talked in the kitchen. As she listened, the arcs her rag made grew smaller and smaller and Verna grew smaller and smaller, too; because she had discovered, long ago, that if she was *very* small, people often forgot she was there. This was how she'd learned that the original manufacturer of the Price Above Rubies rings had employed eight-year-olds in his factories, and that when Toby slept on their couch for a month it was because the director of his sober living facility had found a fifth of vodka under his bed, and that there was a GPS transmitter hidden in Layla's new car.

"A friend named Brittany, huh?" Mother said now.

"Who wears blue sweaters. Maybe we're coming to the end of this thing, praise God."

Mother, sounding dubious, said, "I'll believe it when I see it."

Verna heard a cabinet door open and close. She often prayed for the strength to stop eavesdropping, but God never gave it to her. Maybe because the things she learned left her less baffled by the mysteries around her. How could a ruby ring cost less than four dollars whole-sale? Why did Toby, who was in his twenties and an official grown-up, always have to be home by ten o'clock? Why did Mother and Dad buy Layla a car when she'd been nothing but trouble for months?

"Verna doesn't lie," Dad said. "She doesn't have it in her."

"If Layla pushed her, though—"

Mother still sounded doubtful, but when Dad said, "Verna is a good girl," his voice was confident and sure.

Verna's hands gripped the rag and wrung it until it wept. Verna was a good girl. Layla was bad, Layla was fallen, but even Layla could almost be redeemed if sweet innocent Verna vouched for her. The child of God, the harmless sheep. The obedient little zombie.

Anger rose up in her, hot but good. We are not those people, she thought. The distinctions were too clear and tidy and people weren't like that, people weren't clear and tidy. *She* wasn't clear and tidy.

Answering calls from home was part of the contract. Verna called Layla from the cordless phone in her parents' room. When the older girl picked up, Verna could hear faint music in the background, a long, sibilant inhale. Layla was smoking. "What," she said, sounding bored.

"If they ask you about Brittany's sweater," Verna said, "tell them it's blue."

Later, Layla said, "The sweater was a nice touch. Added verisimili-tude."

The two girls sat on Verna's bed, Verna propped up against the headboard—she'd been reading when her sister came in—and Layla sitting at the foot. Verna was wearing her pajamas, a tie-dyed shirt from church camp and flannel pants with kittens on them. Layla was dressed to go out. Verna could smell the patchouli oil her sister used, the leather of her jacket and boots.

Verna didn't look away from her book. "I don't know why I helped you at all, after the things you called me today."

Layla looked surprised. "What did I call you? Sheep? Oh. Slut." She nodded. "Yes. That was bitchy. I apologize." Verna still didn't look at her, and Layla touched her blanket-covered foot. "Seriously, Vee. I'm sorry. You did good tonight."

"Well."

"Well what?"

"Grammar," Verna said. "I did well."

Layla smiled. Her real smile, not the Justinian one. "You're priceless. I bust out a fifty-center like *verisimilitude* and you're jumping on me about *good* versus *well*?" She patted Verna's foot again. "Get up. Change your clothes."

Verna stared at her. "Why?"

"Because Justinian wants me to bring you to the fire circle, and you can't wear flannel pants with kittens on them."

So Verna traded her pajamas for a long black dress of Layla's, and—even though she was so nervous she was shaking—managed to hold still while Layla ringed her eyes with black kohl and covered her lips with waxy, wine-colored lipstick. "It feels weird," said Verna, working her sticky new lips and blinking her stinging new eyes, and Layla said, "That's just Satan taking over your soul."

Down the hallway, close to the walls to avoid the creaking floorboards, and through the silent kitchen they crept. Then out the sliding door and across the lawn toward a car idling at the curb, old and boxy but as silver as moonlight. The passenger door opened and the blue-haired girl stepped out. "You brought her," she said, not sounding annoyed or even disappointed. She took Verna's shoulder and hustled her into the back, where Verna found herself pressed against a boy with a shaved head that she'd never seen before. He laughed, slapping his knee, and Verna heard something clink. The blue-haired girl squeezed in on Verna's other side.

"Hello, Verna," Justinian said from the front seat, where he'd just finished kissing Layla.

"Verna, Criss, Eric," Layla said, pointing in turn. "Let's go."

The blue-haired girl—Criss—giggled. "Aw, Layla, you gothed her up." When she spoke the stud in her lip glinted.

Eric laughed again. The sound was grating and slightly manic. "Still wearing her Jesus Saves chastity belt, I hope."

Verna huddled deeper inside her cocoon of borrowed black. Layla glanced over her shoulder and said, "Eric, be nice to my sister or I'll stomp you."

"Take a fucking joke," Eric said, and Layla said, "You're a fucking joke."

"Children," Justinian said. His tone was dry, ironic, but the car went silent.

He drove fast. The music was loud, and at night, all the roads looked the same. Perched on the raised middle of the seat, Verna felt off-balance and precarious. She could see Layla's boots propped up on the dashboard, wrists crossed lightly on top of her knees, the red coal of her cigarette an orange firefly hovering around her hands. The smoke made Verna dizzy. She wasn't wearing a seat belt and she couldn't stop imagining herself flying through the windshield as it shattered around her.

When the car stopped, before the headlights cut off, Verna saw trees: thin trees, broad trees, trees in layers, trees upon trees upon trees. They were parked on a single-lane dirt road. Outside, in the blissfully fresh air, Verna saw no lights and no houses, heard no highway sounds or barking dogs. Criss had a flashlight and was already disappearing into the woods. Justinian took something from the trunk of the car and handed it to Eric, and then he and Layla, arms twined together so they looked like one creature, melted into the shadows. "Come on, Vee," Layla called over her shoulder.

Verna hesitated, then followed. Twigs and branches caught at her and her feet couldn't seem to find the flat spots. She prayed she wouldn't fall, not in front of everybody. Although technically she was behind everybody. From somewhere in the darkness, Layla called, "Verna, hurry up!"

"I'm trying." Frustrated, she pulled at a grasping frond. "It's dark."

She heard Justinian say, "She doesn't have any light?" The sound carried clearly in the silence. A moment later, Verna saw a white beam gliding through the woods toward her, a black shape behind it.

"Sorry. I thought you had a flashlight." If there'd been contempt in his voice that afternoon, there was none now. His face seemed to float.

"I'm okay. Just clumsy," Verna said. He reached out a shimmering hand to help her. She couldn't imagine taking it. But then her toe caught a root and she found herself not just holding his hand but clutching it, almost desperately. His fingers were warm.

He steadied her. "I doubt that."

"You haven't known me long." She sounded bitter even to herself.

"How long you've known someone isn't important," he said. "Sometimes you can see somebody every day for years and not know them at all. Other people, it seems like you're born knowing. Come on. Eric has the fire going."

Indeed, a warm light flickered through the trees and the air was full of the fumy tang of lighter fluid. Justinian led Verna to a small clearing, where Layla was draping a blanket over a fallen log. On the other side of the fire, Eric was doing the same thing; Criss was bent over, struggling with some object she held between her knees.

"Sorry, Vee," Layla said. "I thought Eric gave you a flashlight."

"Eric didn't have a flashlight to give," Eric said, settling down on his blanket. "Eric is not made of flashlights."

Verna heard a hollow pop. "There, you son of a bitch," Criss said triumphantly, and passed the thing she'd been fighting with—a bottle of wine, now open—to Layla. She tossed a small, silver thing down onto the blanket. "That corkscrew is a piece of shit, Layla."

"Next time I steal a corkscrew from my nondrinking parents,

I'll try to make sure it's top-of-the-line." Layla took a swig from the bottle, spilling a little; a drop of wine ran down her chin. Grinning, she wiped it away and then held the bottle out to Verna. The look on her face was the same one she used to cast down from the tops of trees. "Drink, Vee?"

Verna could see Justinian over Layla's shoulder, watching. The fire popped; the heat from the flames lay against Verna's cheek like a warm hand. She didn't want the wine, she didn't want to drink. But Layla had brought her here, these were Layla's friends, and it would be a long grim night if they thought she was an idiot. "No, thank you," she finally said.

Eric snickered. "Shut up, Eric," Justinian said, and Eric did. "If she doesn't want to, she doesn't have to."

There was a bare instant of charged silence. Then Layla said, "Of course not," and Criss said, "We don't do that peer pressure shit."

What they did do was talk: about music Verna didn't know, books she hadn't read. The smell of woodsmoke and cigarettes mingled with the loamy smell of the forest and Verna wished she could say something witty and cool. She wished she could say anything at all. Eventually Justinian whispered in Layla's ear. "I'll be back in a while. Don't worry," Layla said to Verna, and she and Justinian walked off into the woods together, back toward the car. Leaving Verna alone with the two strangers. She listened for the sound of the engine and was relieved not to hear it. Across the fire, Criss was chain-smoking, throwing one cigarette butt after another into the flames.

"Give it up, Crissy," Eric said eventually. He was reading, by flashlight, a sheaf of papers that seemed to have been printed on somebody's basement photocopier. "It's a lost cause."

"Eat shit." Criss sounded cross.

Eric looked at Verna. "Criss suffers from unrequited love."

Verna thought of Justinian and Layla, of the way the tall boy had looked at her sister in the firelight, and felt sorry for Criss. "What are you reading?" she asked him, to change the subject.

"*The Anarchist Cookbook.*" He showed her the cover. She heard the metallic clink again and saw that it came from a set of handcuffs he wore doubled on his left wrist. "Tells you how to fuck shit up, make bombs and gunpowder and stuff."

Verna stared at him. "Why would you want to do that?"

"To bring power to the powerless. And to get revenge on all the assholes. There's way better stuff than this on the Internet these days, though. I'm just reading this for kicks." His mouth bent into a smirk. "Actually, it's sort of funny. The guy who wrote this is one of yours now."

"One of my what?"

"People. A Christer. Keeps trying to get the book recalled so people don't use it. Which is pretty goddamned typical, if you ask me. Just like your dad. Knowledge bad, ignorance good. Thinking everyone else is too stupid to make their own decisions. Not that people aren't stupid, generally."

"But if it's dangerous—"

"Fuck that. It's not about danger, it's about control. Keep people scared and stupid and you can make them do anything you want. Anyway, sometimes you got to set off a few bombs to get things done. Ask your friends from Operation Rescue."

"I don't have any friends from Operation Rescue," Verna said. Even her father said the Operation Rescue people were crazy. It was never right to kill somebody, not even to save another life. Not even in abortion clinics.

When Justinian and Layla came back, they brought another bottle of wine. Criss complained again and with particular vehemence about the corkscrew as she uncorked it. The bottle was passed, and Layla curled against Justinian like a sleepy kitten, reaching up occasionally to play with a lock of his long, black hair. Eric was still reading and Criss was still moping and Layla stared into the flames. Verna wondered what time it was. It felt late. She didn't want to ask Layla when they were going to go home.

"I wish everyone in the world but us would disappear," Layla said, sounding wistful. "I wish we were the only ones on the whole planet."

Justinian nodded. "Like the Rapture. Except that instead of calling all the deserving away, only the deserving get to stay." He looked across the fire at Verna. "Death will come like a thief in the night. Right, child of God?"

It wasn't death that came like a thief in the night, it was Jesus; but then Verna remembered Kyle Dobrowski saying, *Hey, Venereal, which bathroom do you shit in, because I don't want my girlfriend catching your VD from a toilet seat.* Wouldn't it be lovely if all the Kyle Dobrowskis were taken by thieves in the night? Did God really build this beautiful world, all starry skies and rustling forests, just to fill it with people like him?

"I've got a few people I'd like to visit in the night," Eric said.

Justinian nodded. "Don't we all."

Layla yawned. "Crissy, can I go to sleep on you?"

"Sure," Criss said. Layla put her head in the other girl's lap and closed her eyes. As Verna watched, Criss plucked a leaf out of Layla's hair.

"Verna," Justinian said. "Do you want to come back to the car with me? Take a walk?"

Verna hesitated.

"Go on, Vee," Layla said, sleepily, and so Verna scrambled to her feet.

They didn't need a flashlight this time. The moon had come out. The forest was filled with a soft, silvery light, and Verna had no problem stepping over the roots and branches that had tripped her before. At the car, Justinian picked up a pack of cigarettes from the floor of the backseat. Then, instead of going back to the fire, he leaned against the front fender. "Having fun?"

Verna nodded. She didn't seem to be able to speak around him.

"Good," he said. "The fire circle is important. We're young, and so nothing belongs to us. Here, we have a place of our own, even if it's only for an hour or two. Criss and Eric seem to like you."

They did? "Criss is nice. Eric seems sort of angry, though."

"Eric is extremely angry. You'd be angry, too, if you had his life. His dad barely notices that he's alive, and his mom—" Justinian shrugged. "Since he dropped out of school all he does is play video games and plot the end of the world. Don't let him get to you."

"What about Criss?"

He smiled. "Poor Crissy. Your sister has her spellbound."

"What?"

"She's in love with Layla."

What Verna knew about homosexuality was that there were people out there who had been so bombarded with sexual messages from such a young age that they became confused. Such people were to be pitied, treated with compassion, and gently led to Jesus, who would help them back onto the path that God had charted for all mankind. Verna had always thought of them like disfigured burn victims: she had never met one, but hoped she would react correctly when she did. Trying to sound nonchalant, she said, "Oh. I sort of thought she might be in love with you."

"Criss and I love each other, but not like that. What Layla and I have is different. It's like when you hear a song or see a painting that touches you. You feel like you've found some part of yourself that you've never even seen before, but you know it's yours."

Verna didn't know what to say. "That sounds nice."

"Nice." Justinian's mouth curled in that patient, disdainful smile. "Sex with Layla is like having a thousand-piece orchestra playing in my head while the concert hall burns down. *Nice* isn't the word I'd use." Her eyes must have widened, because he said, "What, did I shock you?"

"No. I guess I knew— She never said, but—" Verna heard her own words and hated them for sounding so young and so stupid.

"Human beings spend a lot of time feeling small and lonely and trapped. Sex is a way out." He flicked his ash. His face was all planes and angles, as if he'd been designed instead of born. "Layla was feeling particularly trapped tonight."

Verna stared at him. "You mean—now?"

"What did you think we were doing?"

Verna looked around, at the ancient car and the deserted road. "Here?"

"Why not here?"

Why not, indeed. "It's not exactly warm," Verna said, although her face was hot.

Justinian laughed. "Warm enough, child of God."

The laugh was friendly. Emboldened, Verna said, "Why do you call me that?"

"It's what you are. Layla is the child of sin, and you're the child of God. Layla was born when your parents were still in high school, right? And your parents used to be metalheads. I'll bet they drank, did drugs, all of it. Then they got saved, and then they had you. So Layla's named after a Clapton song, and you're named after the woman who told them about Jesus."

It was true. Her parents had been on their way home from a rock concert in Pittsburgh and their car had broken down. Hitchhiking home, they'd been picked up by a Christian woman, and instead of going back to Verna's grandmother's house, where they lived in the basement with the infant Layla, they'd ended up in the woman's living room, reading the Bible. By dawn, they'd both been saved.

"Child of sin, child of God," Justinian said. "Don't think your parents don't know it, too. Why do you think they're so hard on her all the time? She reminds them of everything they don't want to admit they used to be."

"They love Layla."

"No, they love you. They hate her. They're nicer to your dad's tweaker assistant than they are to their own kid."

Uncertainty nipped at Verna. "My parents are good people."

"Possibly, but they hate their daughter." He shrugged. "It happens. Love's not mandated by nature. Do you love them?"

"Of course!"

"Why?"

In the silver light his face was the luminescent blue of skim milk. Why did you love somebody? Why did Verna like green more than orange and fried chicken more than pork chops? Verna didn't know how to answer, but she knew that the question made her feel awful.

"Because you've been told you do, that's why. And you're a good daughter who does what she's told. Yet another reason why they love you and hate Layla." He shook his head. "You didn't ask to be born into that family, for those people to be your parents. So you're not bound by what they expect you to be. Layla understands that. She knows your parents hate her, and she knows it's not her fault. I'm more concerned about you, actually. You have a right to be happy, no matter what they tell you. And you're not happy."

All at once, Verna's eyes stung with unshed tears. She wanted to wipe them away, but he was watching. "What makes you think that?" she said, trying very hard to sound surprised.

"Everything," he said, and that did it, that was all, the tears spilled up and over her eyelids and she couldn't stop them. School and home and Bio and dinner and all of it, everything pushed down inside her all week, the crushed feeling, the flatness. She swiped at her eyes, folded her arms in front of her chest, and hoped that the night would hide her; hoped that he wouldn't laugh, or make fun of her, or tell everyone else, back at the fire circle.

But Justinian just stood, and smoked, and waited. When she'd more or less composed herself, he blew a smoke ring into the air. "Like I said. Everything." He stood up. "Come on. Let's get back."

He turned and headed back through the woods. Verna followed.

THREE

Lying in bed that morning after Caro left, Patrick considered suicide: not because he didn't want to live, but because it seemed the most leakproof way of making sure the situation went away forever, and *forever* was exactly how long he wanted to avoid having a conversation with Mike about how he and Caro had slept together. But Patrick had never been the wrist-slashing type. It had taken his mother a long time to die, and he had no illusions about death being anything other than the biological defenestration that it was. There was no poetry in death. People died because they were animals and all animals died. Sometimes they got cancer and sometimes they were hit by cars and sometimes they just stopped breathing. And sometimes they slept with their brothers' girlfriends.

Fuck.

He had, it seemed, developed a talent for seeking out the worst possible thing he could do in any given situation, and then doing it. He and Mike had fought about many things over the years but never a girl, and since the accident, they hadn't argued at all. Not once. The tenuous peace between them would have pleased and astounded their mother, who had spent a fair amount of her parenting life serving as the world's least willing referee, but to Patrick, it felt unnatural. Which didn't mean that he wanted to destroy it. And destroyed was exactly what it would be, if Mike ever found out what had happened.

He tried to think of some nondeath thing he could do to make it right, or at least less awful, but there was nothing. Avoiding Caro all day was easy because she was at work. When he saw her again that night Mike had just woken up, and the three of them ate pizza together as if everything was normal. The pizza had mushrooms on it, like always, which Patrick pulled off and left in a limp gray pile on his plate, like always. He knew the grease-stained box would sit on the table for a week, just like always. Mike said, "We got any red chili?" and Caro got up to get it. She smelled like fabric softener and hand lotion and the combination settled in Patrick's nose, coating his throat, dancing over his tongue, and that was when he realized that the situation was even worse than he'd thought. Because before she'd come into his room, he would have sworn that he'd never even considered what she smelled like, or what all of that cola-colored hair would feel like in his hands, or what her mouth tasted like, or what her breath would feel like in his ear. Now he could think of nothing else. When Caro came back with the chili, Mike pulled her down into his lap; she pushed back, said, "Get away, you smell like manual labor," and Patrick wanted to explode. Did that mean anything, that she did that, or did Mike just stink?

They finished eating and the feeling got worse. He left for work thirty minutes earlier than he had to and even then, it didn't stop. This wasn't the fun kind of could-think-of-nothing-else that he'd been through with other girls, when it felt like their naked bodies had moved into his brain and everything smelled like them and felt like them and he spent every waking moment seeing them or try-ing to see them or, if all else failed, imagining them. No, this was a miserable, seasick could-think-of-nothing-else. Caro was in his head but the reality was Caro and Mike together on the couch, in the armchair, in bed on the other side of the wall, and he had nobody to talk to about it. Nobody.

Nights were agony.

He felt flipped, inside-out. As the days passed even a beer run with Mike felt like an exercise in self-mutilation; standing in front of the refrigerator case at the six-pack store, Mike said, "What do you think, Iron City or MGD?" and Patrick was so filled with *I think I slept with Caro and I want to do it again* that he could barely open his mouth enough to say, "Iron," because he was afraid of what would come out.

He wanted to do it again, and again, and again. As many times as possible. He hated himself for it, but there it was.

It got so bad that the first time he found Caro home alone, which was Wednesday, he couldn't take his eyes off her. She was washing dishes and when she looked up, there he was, standing in the doorway and staring like some kind of psycho. Her face filled with apprehension, and that made him feel bad—but after four days of being afraid to look directly at her, he couldn't seem to do anything else. A lacy tracework of suds braceleted her wrists and the small hairs around her face were damp. She was beautiful.

"Stop it." There were wet spots on her dress where she'd splashed herself. "Stop looking at me like that."

"I'm sorry," he said, and he was.

"It was a mistake. You know it was a mistake."

"I know," he said, and he did.

"You just have to not think about it. Just put it out of your head."

That was rich. *Put it out of your head,* as if he hadn't been trying to do exactly that every second of every day. As if he wasn't trying to do it now, seeing the way her hair curled against her shoulders, the fine straight lines of her nose. But her face was wrought with tension and he knew she was right even if she was wrong, so he made himself grin and say, "Caro, it's okay. Everything's cool," and she managed a smile back but he didn't buy it.

Nothing was cool. The few conversations they managed to have felt like spun glass, fragile and carefully constructed—even stupid things. Were they out of milk yet, or had he seen her car keys. It would have been funny if it didn't hurt so much, and who would have laughed about it with him anyway, except her. On Friday, Bill asked if he wanted to go drinking with a bunch of people and even though Bill and his friends were stoner idiots Patrick was so desperate for relief that he said yes. As they drove to the bar, the windows down and the music up, Bill's truck smelled like weed and stale beer and coconut air freshener, and the smell made Patrick think of women, of the smell of a girl's hair after you'd been out at a bar with her. Find a new girl, Patrick thought. Erase what had happened, wipe out all those sense-memories that he couldn't shake and fill up the emptiness with new, unsullied ones.

Instead, he got drunk. The bartender was pretty, but not as pretty as Caro; her nose was a little snubbed and her front teeth bucked out. At one point, he found himself standing next to a girl he'd actually dated back in high school. Which wasn't a big deal. She wasn't the lost love of his life or anything. She was just a nice-looking girl that had always been a little out of his league. When she'd dumped him, right before Biology, he hadn't been very surprised. The breakup had happened on day four of a five-day preserved-rat dissection: the wonders of the rodent intestinal system. The smell of the preservatives and the rat's whitish-pink nose that would never twitch again were far clearer in his memory than anything about the girl. When he saw her at the bar, it took him more than a few seconds to realize that the reason she looked so familiar was that various parts of his body had spent time inside various parts of hers. So he said hello, and she said hello back, and he said you don't remember me do you, and she said not really should I, and he said nah, that's okay, and walked away. She wasn't as pretty as Caro, either.

As he nursed his last beer in a dark corner by the pool table, the two guys waiting for the table started talking about bars. This bar, other bars, bars they liked, bars they hated; the best drink specials and the best pool tables and where they'd gotten laid most often. He had to get out of there. He couldn't find Bill, but he was getting used to walking. The night was warm, sticky in that dying-summer September way. Like most small towns in Patrick's experience, Ratchetsburg was built around a triple nucleus of the schools, the city hall, and the shopping mall. The schools were surrounded by nice houses and a scattering of playgrounds, the city hall was surrounded by small shops that sold sandwiches and copies and office supplies, and the mall was surrounded by car dealerships and chain restaurants. Apart from those three areas, a sprinkling of churches, and a subdivision or two, what was left could all be filed under Don't-Give-A-Shit, USA: bars and beer distributors, auto body shops and dry cleaners. Places everybody wanted, but nobody wanted to live near, so the neighborhoods around them—neighborhoods like the one where Patrick lived, like the ones he walked through now—were neglected and crumbling. He moved carefully, not too fast and not too slow and in as straight a line as possible. Walking drunk wasn't nearly as illegal as driving drunk, but it would still get you busted. Out in the open air like this, he felt okay, but logic dictated that after five beers he wouldn't pass a Breathalyzer. His name being what it was and small towns being what they were, he didn't think he should take chances.

Halfway home, he saw the lights of the SuperSpeedy, a cool white beacon of civilization. Zoney's was Ratchetsburg's crappy convenience store; the SuperSpeedy was the nice one. If you wanted a meal after midnight in Ratchetsburg and didn't feel like sitting down at the twenty-four-hour diner, it was the SuperSpeedy or nothing. They had hot food and coffee, six different kinds of creamer to stir into it, and a machine that dispensed three flavors of cappuccino. They also had bathrooms you could use without worrying about your inoculation history and the most expensive gas in town, except for the times when it was inexplicably the cheapest. The SuperSpeedy kept you guessing.

The store was filled with hollow-eyed people standing in line: at the sandwich counter, at the soda fountain, at the register. All of them waiting, waiting, their hands full of candy, chips, cups of coffee, money. It was like purgatory, with snacks. Not just the customers; the employees, too. They worked the registers, squirted ketchup on hot dogs, piled limp lettuce onto flaccid lunch meat and waited for it to be over, waited until they could go home. At least when he was at work, he didn't have to make sandwiches. The SuperSpeedy might have been fancier than Zoney's, but damned if it didn't smell just the same. He took a red Gatorade from the refrigerator case and joined the line. None of the things he actually was showed here, not the job quitter, or the son of the drunk kid-killing piece of shit, or the prick who slept with his brother's girlfriend and wanted to do it again and again and again. Somewhere out there a deer with a shattered pelvis had died painfully of thirst and hunger and infection, and it was his fault, and nobody in this store knew it except him.

Then a female voice said, "Patrick Cusimano," and he turned. The goth girl stood behind him, wearing a knowing smirk and a frantically red plastic dress. Most of her black hair was up in two ponytails and she'd painted her eyelids metallic silver. If Hollywood ever made a creepy-doll movie set in outer space, she would have fit right in.

"Fuck," he said. "Not you."

She pointed to the bottle of Gatorade in his hand. "Those drinks are all sugar and sodium, you know. Plus high-fructose corn syrup. Completely artificial and completely terrible for you. Particularly for your teeth." Her own teeth were straight and white, in an expensive, magazine-ad way.

Patrick gripped the clammy plastic bottle harder. "Go away. Leave me alone."

"I'd take that personally if you weren't so drunk."

"I'm not drunk." It was mostly true.

"No, *I'm* not drunk. So which of us is more qualified to judge?"

Her pert little nose wrinkled. "You smell like cheap beer, you know. Really. You reek. You're not driving, are you? Because driving under the influence has not worked out well for your family."

"You're a bitch," he said, but didn't feel any real anger. He felt too tired and defeated to be angry. She was standing quite close to him now. The black barbed-wire bracelet on her bare upper arm was almost touching his sleeve. Anybody that didn't know better would think that she had his permission to be standing that close to him, that they were friends.

"Wait," she said, and walked away.

Patrick, his eyes fixed on the woman in front of him, didn't look after her. Maybe he could get out of there before she returned, he thought as the line shuffled forward—but then she was back, pressing a pack of gum into his hand with slim fingers. "In case you *are* planning to drive home like that. You should eat, too. We could get some nachos if you want."

"I don't want."

She smiled her snarky little smile. "Everybody wants."

The line crawled forward. The girl twisted her coffin ring around and around on her finger, a gesture that could easily have seemed nervous on somebody less—less what? Self-assured. Rehearsed. Insane. "I didn't see your car outside," she said. "Where did you park?"

"I didn't."

"Did somebody drop you off?"

"I walked."

She stared at him. "You walked?" From her tone, he might as well have told her that he'd hopped here naked on a pogo stick. It almost made Patrick smile.

Almost. "That's what I said."

"To buy Gatorade at one in the morning."

"To get home."

"From where?"

"From where I was." Then they were at the front of the line and

Patrick put his drink on the counter. The clerk, his face slack with an all-too-familiar mixture of fatigue and resentment, barely glanced at them as he punched buttons on the register.

"Six eighty," he said.

Patrick stared. The SuperSpeedy had an intense markup but this was ridiculous. "For a bottle of Gatorade and a pack of gum?"

"She ordered nachos," the clerk said, nodding at the goth girl as one of the gray-faced sandwich trolls behind the deli pushed a plastic container bulging with cheese-covered tortilla chips onto the counter. When she'd gone to get the gum. "I'm not paying for those."

But the goth girl picked up the container anyway, her coffin ring glinting in the light. "See you outside, killer," she said, and disappeared through the automatic glass door, her ponytails bouncing like the tails of two actual equines and her red plastic ass gleaming under the artificial light. The clerk watched her go, his eyes temporarily lit with ugly interest. Completely unaccountably, Patrick—never much of a fighter—found himself wanting to hit the guy. He could practically feel that greasy nose breaking under his fist.

But then she was out of sight, and the clerk looked back at Patrick, his eyes lifeless once more.

"Like I said," he said. "Six eighty."

He found her across the parking lot, sitting on the hood of her hearse and licking orange sludge from a tortilla chip held between two fingers. When she saw him, she grinned, her eyebrows darting up. "Serves you right. You are consistently not very nice to me, despite all my best efforts. The least you could do is buy my nachos. Which I shall, of course, be kind enough to share." She held out the plastic tray.

Patrick sighed. "You don't give up, do you?"

"I'm tenacious."

"You left tenacious behind a long time ago. You're more like herpes." He took a nacho. The chip was crisp and the sludge was hot and the combination was appealing, in an unwholesome way. Next to him, the girl grinned and licked away at the orange goo. It was horrible to watch, but difficult to turn away from—the salt crusted around her fingernails, the orange smears of sludge on her pink tongue—and all of the colors seemed preternaturally intense: red red dress, yellow yellow chip, black black hair, orange orange cheese. It was as if she were under a spotlight, shining more brightly than everything else.

"So why do you hate me so much?" she said, licking. "Is it because of the whole Ryan Czerpak–worship group thing? Because I have to tell you, I couldn't really give less of a shit about my dad's worship group."

Patrick took another chip. "Maybe it has something to do with the way you show up everywhere I go saying things like 'drunk driving hasn't served your family well.'"

"You don't find my candor refreshing?"

Candor. This time, he really did smile. Just a little. "I do not." Although, after almost a week of working as hard as he could to avoid saying what he meant, he kind of did. "What's a worship group?"

"Like a church, but independent. It meets in our basement." She took another chip, too. This time, instead of licking the chip itself, she ran a finger through the cheese and licked that instead. Her nails—painted black, of course—looked like she bit them.

"Speaking of your dad, do your parents know where you are?"

The girl tossed the second chip after the first. "Of course. My conservative Christian parents fully endorse me hanging out in parking lots in the wee hours of the morning."

"Wearing skintight plastic dresses." When he'd been in high school, the freaky kids had made do with concert T-shirts and thrift-store rags. Internet shopping had apparently blown the teen angst universe wide open.

"PVC, technically. You told your parents everything when you were my age, of course."

Patrick smiled again, but this time it wasn't because anything was funny. When he was her age, his mom had been dead and his dad was knocking back half a case of beer on the nights when he took it easy. "Let's not compare you at your age to me at your age."

"Why not?"

"Because I wasn't crazy, and you are. Christ." She had taken another chip and started the cheese-removal process all over again. "What do you have against tortilla chips?"

"Nothing. They're the perfect vehicle for cheese. Anyway, you're not the first person to think I'm a weirdo, Patrick Cusimano. Look who's talking. You're like Norman Bates with facial hair."

Somewhere in the parking lot, somebody leaned on their horn, an angry, discordant noise. "At least I'm not dressed like Raggedy Ann on LSD."

She laughed. "Raggedy Ann on LSD. I love that. That's great." She shook her head. "Look, you can't walk home. Only losers walk places. Let me give you a ride." His wariness must have shown on his face, because she added, "Oh, come on. What's the worst that could happen? You get home quickly and without incident?"

"Or we get pulled over halfway there, and I get arrested for contributing to the delinquency of a minor. No thanks."

She folded her arms across her shiny plastic chest. "You're only nine years older than I am, O paranoid one."

"Nine legally very important years," Patrick said, "and how the hell do you know how old I am?"

"I told you. I looked you up in the yearbook." She jumped down from the hood of her car, tugging at her skirt in a way that utterly belied all of her phony sophistication, and held out the tray of nachos. "You want the rest of these? If I eat any more of that cheese, I'm going to puke."

"If I watch you eat any more of that cheese, I'm going to puke." The inside of Patrick's mouth felt greasy and synthetic. He looked away from her, toward the road that led, more or less, to his house.

When he and Mike were kids, the SuperSpeedy had been Mick's Market—smaller, dingier, owned and staffed by an actual guy named Mick—and they used to walk here to buy Coke slushies, shoplifting candy bars by burying them in the thick, opaque goo. It was a twenty-minute walk. Twenty minutes of picturing Mike and Caro in their room, doing things he didn't want to imagine but knew he would imagine, in great detail. If he took the ride, he'd be in bed in five minutes with some loud music to drown out his thoughts. The kid was crazy and Caro would say, *Jesus, Patrick, don't encourage her,* but—

The goth girl was watching him with a faint smile. As if she could see the path his thoughts took, as if she knew she would get her way. "Coming?"

"Yeah," he said. "Whatever."

Patrick liked his music angry, but the noise that blasted out of the car speakers when the girl turned her key in the ignition felt like being slammed against a brick wall, and not in a good way. It was like her: plastic and crafted and fake. Not a real guitar string or drumhead anywhere to be found. She moved her thumbs over the buttons on her steering wheel and the sounds changed, went from aggressive and soulless to deep and cool. It still wasn't his kind of thing, but it was better than the noise. "This is my current favorite song," she said, as they pulled out of the parking lot. "Where am I going?"

"You know where Division Street is?"

She nodded. Away from the arc lights of the SuperSpeedy, the too-much makeup didn't show. Her car smelled new and spicy and expensive. He'd smelled that smell before, that first night, when she leaned in his car window behind Zoney's, and with that memory came the image of her lacy purple bra, the soft white flesh disappearing into it and an increasingly familiar *we're-here-now-we-can't-go-back* feeling. He'd spent the last three hours in a bar full of legally drunk girls and now he was alone in a car with jailbait. He pushed that thought away.

"I scare you," she said. "Why do I scare you?"

He looked out the window at the dark houses. "You're seventeen. You're a stranger, and you're strange. And my life is complicated enough right now."

"From what I can see, your life is about as complicated as a piece of Wonder bread."

"Yeah, well, you've got a pretty limited vantage point." Her dashboard lights were red and purple, very gothy. He wondered if she'd had to special-order them that way. "Anyway, you didn't exactly make the best first impression."

"So it was the worship group thing. I would have had to tell you eventually, you know. I thought it would be weirder if I waited, like we were friends under false pretenses."

"It was plenty weird the way you did it, actually. And we're not friends. Friends have something in common."

"Like a fetish?"

"I was thinking more along the lines of school or work."

"Is that where you met that girl from the store? At work?"

"Girl?" he said, like he didn't know.

She smiled. "Oh, aren't you coy. The brown-haired one. Pretty, if you like that type."

"Which type is that?"

"Ordinary."

Nothing about Caro was ordinary. He didn't dare say so. This girl didn't miss a trick.

"You didn't go to school with her. She wasn't in the yearbook." Dangling from her earlobe was a silver rectangle with a cutout center and notched corners. A razor blade, too small and polished to be real. "So how did you meet her?"

"She's my brother's girlfriend. I think they met in a bar." He tried to sound casual but failed miserably, even to his own ears. Talking about her felt like hitting his own funny bone with a hammer.

"Your brother's girlfriend?" They were stopped at an intersection. When she turned to look at him, her razor blade earring caught the red light along its edge. "Is that what you meant when you said your life was complicated?"

Her tone was a little more amused than Patrick would have liked. "Yeah, that's it all right. Nothing to do with my dad going to prison or my face being plastered all over the Internet."

"Quit changing the subject. What's her name?" He chose not to answer that, and she laughed. "Okay, then. What's *my* name? Do you even remember?"

"What if I don't?" he said, feeling belligerent.

"Nothing. It's only a word my parents liked the sound of. It doesn't mean anything." Her thumbs moved again and the song started over.

"Try saying that when your name is Cusimano. Pull over on the right."

She did. "Everybody in town thinks you come from a family of murderers. They think I come from a family of zealots. Every time I talked, it was because my dad had his hand up my ass, making my lips move. People have been putting words in my mouth for so long I don't even know which ones are mine anymore." She shook her head, making the razor blade dance, and turned to him. Her mascara-smudged eyes were serious, the lines of her face like an ink drawing. "Look, forget my name. Forget yours, too. Let's give each other new names. Be new people."

He wasn't sure what she was talking about. "It wouldn't change anything."

"It would change everything. Didn't you ever want to erase your whole life, everything you've ever done? Because I do. I want to be somebody completely new. I want to be somebody I've never even met."

Somehow, the way she said them, the words were an invitation. Division Street was deserted. The parked car was filled with the croon of her music and her eyes on him were so huge and so dark that he almost felt suffocated. Her lips were full and round and black, a perfectly outlined patch of night in the middle of her pale face. Like bitter coffee with no milk. Nobody knew her. Nobody knew he was here.

Everybody wants, she'd said, back in the SuperSpeedy.

"Is that your house?" Her voice was intimate. She nodded toward the window.

It wasn't, he'd deliberately told her to pull over too early, but he looked anyway. He could see his parked car, Mike's truck and Caro's white Civic. All at once the moment broke, like a rubber band stretched too far. When he looked back at the girl, he saw her for what she was: a weird, screwed-up kid, wearing too much makeup and saying things she couldn't possibly understand. He wanted desperately to be away from her before he did something stupid. Since stupid seemed to be his stock-in-trade these days.

"No," he said. "I'm pretty sure I don't want you knowing where I live."

"How weird and secretive of you." She gave him that same goddamned knowing smile, and even though he'd seen it on her face a dozen times he was suddenly filled with the unpleasant certainty that she knew how close he'd come, that she'd seen it in his face. The urge to be away from her quintupled and why was he still *sitting* there?

"Thanks for the ride." Sounding rude, not caring. He got out of the car and stood there on the sidewalk until she left: his fists jammed in the pockets of his jeans, so she wouldn't see how they trembled.

The next morning, he took some solace in his headache. He stayed in bed until he heard Caro in the shower and Mike tromping around in the kitchen, then went downstairs. "Jesus, little brother, you reek," Mike said. "Where'd you go last night?"

"That place out on Thirty."

"How'd you get there?"

"Bill."

"He drive you home, too?"

"Yeah." Patrick poured himself a glass of chocolate milk.

Mike laughed. "You liar. You totally picked up some chick last night. Sat in the car making out for ten minutes."

"What, were you watching from the window?"

"Don't get pissy. We were cheering you on."

We. Patrick finished his chocolate milk and put the gray-filmed glass in the sink. It made a small, sad clink on the chipped ceramic. "That explains why I kept hearing megaphones."

"Maybe if you start getting laid again you'll stop being such a miserable bastard," Mike said cheerfully. "How long has it been, anyway?"

A week, Patrick almost said. He almost said more than that. The words sat on his tongue as uneasily as the previous night's five beers sat in his stomach, and felt just as likely to leap out.

Mike snapped his fingers. "That girl Angie, with the red Kia, right?" He laughed. "Remember the time you and me pushed that damn thing all the way to the Shell station?"

"Vaguely."

"That car sucked. She was hot, though."

Had she been? She'd worn long acrylic fingernails and thong underwear, she'd been obsessed with this television show about two brothers who fought demons, and she'd liked having sex in semi-public places. At the time she'd seemed fun, but now Patrick barely remembered the sound of her voice.

"Hey," Mike said. "You want to go to the SuperSpeedy? Throw a little egg and cheese on that hangover?"

The rush of water through the pipes in the walls abruptly ceased and Patrick heard the bathroom door squeak open upstairs. "Yeah," he said. "Sure."

In direct contrast to the nastiness inside Patrick's head, the weather outside was idyllic—sunny and clear, with that wide-open weekend feeling that automatically made a person want to relax outside somewhere. When he was a kid, on a day like this, he and Mike would have wolfed down their Cheerios, hopped on their bikes, and ridden off in search of a game of kickball or street hockey or guns or whatever, and they wouldn't have come home again until hunger drove them there. Or at least, that was how he remembered it. Patrick didn't generally trust memories that glittered like that, because he'd found that if you spent too much time with them you discovered unpleasant things you'd tried to forget: a broken finger that never straightened again, a treasured ball or glove held where you couldn't reach it even if you jumped, a monster lying in wait to terrify you at home. Drunk monsters. Dying monsters. Rooms with open curtains that still felt dark.

Nonetheless, it was the kind of day that made a person want to do things. And what Patrick wanted to do right now, he quickly realized, was not be in this truck, listening to cheerful shitkicker music with Mike, who wouldn't let the previous night's parked-car incident drop. Saying, "Do I know her? Is it some girl I've been with? Is that why you won't tell me who it is?"

"Actually, yeah," Patrick said. "In fact, it's all the girls you've been with. Every single one, all the way back to Krista Porter in ninth grade. Like those circus cars with all the clowns." He rubbed his forehead. Despite the beautiful weather, he was sweating. "Last night was nothing, okay? Just some chick I'm never going to see again." And wouldn't it be nice if that were true, but somehow he doubted it.

"Why not?"

"She's not worth the trouble."

"Dude, trust me. She's worth the trouble."

"You don't know her."

"I know being alone sucks," Mike said. "Even for you."

Patrick gritted his teeth and said nothing.

The SuperSpeedy was just like Zoney's. The place never changed. The lights and the smells and the lines felt the same as the night before, distinguished only by a thin veneer of sunlight. They ordered two egg sandwiches with double cheese and double sausage, but the smell of cooking meat and burned coffee was too much for Patrick so while Mike waited for the food he went back outside. Across the lot, he could see the parking space where he and the goth girl had eaten their nachos. Soggy tortilla chips littered the strip of lawn separating the asphalt and the sidewalk like used condoms. In his mind's eye he saw her car from above, the way it would look from Mike and Caro's bedroom window: the fumes billowing from the tailpipe, the night-quiet street, the car's roof a blank slab of metal under which anything could be happening, anything at all. He turned away.

Layla. Her name was Layla.

Back at home, Mike settled down in front of the TV with a beer, his sandwich, and an exhibition race, but sitting on the couch watching a bunch of guys drive around in circles felt too goddamned metaphoric for Patrick. He put his running clothes on, grabbed his MP3 player, and left through the back door.

Where he found Caro, sitting on the step. He'd assumed she was at work because he hadn't heard her in the house, but there she was, painting her toenails and reading the kind of magazine that you could smell long before you saw it, full of perfume samples and glossy photographs of lipstick. A pen stuck out from behind one of her ears and a checkbook topped off the stack of envelopes on the concrete slab beside her.

"What are you doing?" he said.

The brush she held above her big toenail hovered for a moment but then kept going. Swift, smooth strokes, unwavering and decisive.

"Theoretically, I'm paying my bills. But since I don't have anything to pay them with, I'm doing my toes instead." She stuck the polish brush back into its bottle, pulled the pen from behind her ear, and stuck it between the two smallest toes on her right foot. Her toes were soft and nubby-looking, like a baby's; the polish on her tiny nails was the color of pistachio ice cream and Patrick found himself wanting to lick them. "So, was she cute?"

Her tone was friendly, even playful. "Yeah, Mike told me you two had a good game of I Spy last night," Patrick said. "Who won?"

"You're changing the subject." She picked up one of the envelopes and ran the corner of it around the edge of a toenail to wipe away a bit of errant polish, which oozed up and over the paper. Melted pistachio ice cream. "Was she cute?"

"Do you mean cute like a duckie or cute like a bunny?" he said, and she said, "I mean cute like a girl you want to fuck."

She emphasized the action verb in a way he couldn't ignore and the sudden hardness in her voice turned the bright sun sour, like milk on the verge of going bad. His gut grew hot. He regretted stopping to talk. He should have just kept going. "Jealousy seems like a weird reaction from you right now."

She glared at him. "Shut up. Mike's right inside."

"Watching the race." He wouldn't come up for air until it was over and they both knew it.

A long, sore moment passed.

Finally, Caro said, "That car last night—I've seen it before. It was that goth chick from Zoney's, right? From the other day?"

The soreness flared into anger. "You mean the other day that never happened? That other day?"

"Come off it, Patrick. That girl looked like she was all of sixteen. I'm just trying to keep you from getting in trouble."

She sounded as angry as he felt. The backyard smelled like grass and dirt and nail polish, the back of Patrick's neck was beginning to prickle under his hair in the hot sun, and his insides were being pulled like taffy. He could feel a vile bubble of rage pushing its way up and out of him. "Then try staying out of my goddamned room at night."

Her cheeks turned pink and she looked back down at her toes, her hair falling to hide her face. He stood up, turned his back to her, and started toward the alley: away from her, from the house, from the wreckage in his head.

"Patrick, wait," she said, sounding—even through his fury—incredibly sad. "Where are you going?"

He didn't care if she was sad. He couldn't care. It was her fault. Hers. "To find that goth chick and ask her if she wants to fuck." He tucked his earbuds into his ears, turned on his MP3 player, and cranked up the volume. If she said anything as he left the yard, he didn't hear her.

When his shift was over on Monday morning, he had to stay after for a staff meeting, which was beyond tedious. Everyone gathered out back by the Dumpsters, the only space big enough to hold them all. Patrick chose a spot by the corner of the building, as far away from the rotting-garbage stench as he could get. If he leaned back a little he could see the gas pumps and the highway and freedom. And shit, fuck, and goddamn, who should pull up but the goth girl—Layla—in her big shiny hearse of a car.

Standing there in the dust and the stink, weeds tickling his ankles and trucks rumbling past on the highway, Patrick watched her fill up her car. Her black tank top made her skin look almost reflective, as if she was made out of chrome. She used a credit card to pay and didn't even bother to watch the rising total the way most people did, staring instead at her own reflection in the car window: huge sunglasses, wind teasing at her hair. For the first time, what he could see of her face looked—normal. She looked bored, but not calculatedly so, and that irritating, knowing smirk was nowhere to be seen.

When a truck rolled by on the highway, shifting gears with a loud, grating bleat, she lifted her face toward the sound. Patrick wondered what she was thinking.

The passenger door opened. The girl who got out was short, like Layla, and she was dressed in black with huge clunky boots, like Layla. Her nose and her chin and the shape of her face were all just like Layla's. But she wore her brown hair in a sloppy ponytail and kept her arms folded tightly in front of her body, with her shoulders hunched and her head down. As she crossed the parking lot, her walk held none of Layla's insouciance, none of her swagger. Not to mention that Layla had curves in places where this girl didn't even have places.

Jesus. What was *he* thinking?

That he felt so friendless and stuck that he was almost glad to see her, that's what. He waited until the mousy girl was gone and then slipped around the corner. When he said, "You send your sister in for coffee?" she jumped. Just a little, but it was enough.

She recovered quickly. "I did. Although the coffee here is terrible."

"Nobody ever washes the pots."

"That's appealing. Where's your car? Do you not ever drive anywhere anymore?"

"I do not," he said, "ever drive anywhere anymore." Saying it aloud made him feel a little giddy. She had a mole on her chest, a few inches below her collarbone. Perfectly round, like a drop of chocolate. The wind blew a few strands of her hair into her mouth and she pulled them away with one finger. Her nail polish today was a slinky reptilian green.

The gas pump thudded. Layla pulled the nozzle out of the tank, dripping gasoline onto the car and the asphalt and everywhere, it seemed, except herself. If he'd been that careless he would have smelled like gasoline all day but Layla seemed to be one of those stain-resistant people that errant drops of effluvium broke the laws of physics to protect. She pressed a button and the pump spat out her receipt. "Let's do something tonight," she said.

Some small thing inside him twisted. "I don't think so."

"Do you have something better to do? Because I assumed you were just going to go home and spend all night sitting in your crappy house."

"My house could be amazing inside. It could be a goddamned wonderland."

"So show me sometime," she said, and the thing twisted harder. "But tonight, I want to go out. Are you coming or not?"

"Not," he said, but even he could hear the lack of conviction in his voice.

She smiled. "Great," she said. "I'll pick you up at six."

He didn't know what to say, so he said nothing and walked away, back around the corner. When he stole another look at the gas pump, the sister was standing next to the car with two cups of coffee. Layla said something to her. She made a face, and they both laughed as the sister took off first one lid and then the other, and emptied them onto the asphalt. Patrick wasn't very far away, but he was far enough for the sound of their laughter to be lost before it reached him.

He wouldn't have gone if he hadn't returned home to a neat pile of laundry sitting incongruously on the maelstrom of his sheets. Caro's work. All of the shirts were tucked into tidy squares with corners that lined up perfectly; the socks were turned right side out and balled together, and the waistbands of the boxer shorts all faced the same way. Even now, after everything that had happened, Caro still folded his underwear. He could not get her out of his life. He could not get her out of his head.

Fuck her. Fuck her and her obsessively folded, wrinkle-free laundry. When five thirty rolled around, he shaved for the first time in days, combed his hair, changed his shirt, and put on an extra layer of deodorant. Telling himself all the while that this was nothing, this was just a way to kill time. Reminding himself that Layla was clinically insane, that she was jailbait. But he hated having nothing and he hated being nothing and before he left he took the pile of laundry and dumped it on his floor.

Layla told him he smelled good. He said, "If we're going to go, let's go," and in a few minutes they were on the highway driving toward the turnpike. Her music was electronic and bass-heavy and sounded as if it were sung in German. The sun was going down and the light was that creepy, corpselike blue; Patrick saw the remnants of a dead deer by the side of the road and let it drift out of his thoughts. On the other side of the Squirrel Hill Tunnel the trees abruptly became city. Patrick had never liked the city. Pittsburgh was just a label attached to the sports teams he supported. These days not even that, very much. Getting away from the house and Caro had seemed so urgent just an hour before but now he knew he'd made a mistake. He shouldn't be here. Here, with her.

She parked on a side street. Patrick was used to being out at night but not like this, on a well-lit sidewalk full of glittering shop windows and people strolling briskly between them. With great purpose, she led him to a coffee shop where the menus on the wall were artfully lettered with colored chalk, but all the furniture looked like it had come from Vincent Price's garage sale. Somebody had tried to open a place like this in Ratchetsburg a few years before, but it hadn't made it. This one was full of people around Patrick's age who didn't seem to have just come from swing shifts at warehouses or counter jobs at convenience stores. Patrick, whose boots and haircut had both seen better days, felt first sloppy and disheveled and then defensive and confrontational. So what if his boots looked like shit. So what if his jeans were faded through actual wear. He didn't belong here. He shouldn't have come.

"I drove. You get the drinks," Layla said, dropping her army-navy bag into one overstuffed armchair and herself into another. "Double-shot Americano, and one of those marshmallow rice things if they have it."

Which they did, although due to the glories of trademark protection it was labeled a Krispy Rice Treat. It was also the size of a small shoe box, and cost nearly six dollars. When he brought the thing (on a plate, with a fork, although who ever ate those with a fork) and her coffee back to Layla, she took it from him before he could even sit down. "Most excellent," she said, and pried it into two more or less equal pieces with her fingers. Her decay-colored nails sinking mercilessly into the Treat's Krispy Rice flesh made Patrick think of lions on the Serengeti.

She held out a huge sticky chunk. "That's your half."

"Just put it on the plate." The Treat smelled like butter and vanilla and his grandmother's house. It probably smelled like everybody's grandmother's house, which was why they could get away with charging six dollars for it.

Balancing her coffee on the arm of her chair, Layla sat back and tucked her feet underneath her. She held the Krispy Rice Treat in one hand and pulled pieces of it off with the other, as if she were eating cotton candy. When she opened her mouth he could see smears of scarlet lipstick on her teeth. "So, Patrick Cusimano."

He took a drink from the bottle of water he'd bought. "So, Layla whatever-your-last-name-is." Jesus. He didn't even know her last name.

"Elshere. Layla Nicole Elshere. The Layla is for my dad's favorite Clapton song and the Nicole is for my mom's favorite soap opera character. This is what happens when teenagers breed. Your turn."

"My turn to what?"

"To reveal. In one fell swoop, I just told you that my dad likes Clapton, my mom has shit taste in television, and they had me when they were in high school."

"So now I'm supposed to reciprocate?"

"Only if you want a ride home."

He was at least partially sure she was joking. "Patrick John. The John is after my father. I don't know about the Patrick."

"Your father, who art in prison," she said, and he said, "Exactly how personal are these questions going to get?"

She didn't miss a beat. "New topic, then. Where's your mother?"

"Dead."

"I'm sorry."

"Thanks."

She blew air out of her nostrils and looked exasperated. "You're not very good at this."

"What do you want me to say?"

"Anything you want. What did she die of? How old were you? Do you remember her? Do you miss her?"

"Why do you want to know?"

"Because, dumbass, I can't know you if I don't know anything about you, and I can't know anything if you won't tell me anything."

"The flaw in your reasoning," Patrick said, "is that I don't necessarily want you to know anything about me."

"Then why come here with me?"

"To get out."

"Of your house?"

"It's actually not that much of a wonderland."

She leaned back, crossing her legs. Under the stupid French mood music on the coffee shop's sound system he could hear the creak of her boots, the hush of her tights as her legs rubbed against each other. "Your brother's a real all-American stud type, isn't he?"

"What," Patrick said, "did you look him up in the yearbook, too?"

"That, and I saw him kissing that chick outside your house one day." She sipped at her coffee. Her black eyes never left him. "There was a lot of tongue involved for seven in the morning."

The vanilla-butter smell turned cloying. When he spoke again he sounded angrier than he'd expected. "Are you staking out the house now?"

She only smiled. "Not habitually. I just drive by every now and then to see if you're there. Although I've been looking for your car, which I guess doesn't mean anything since you've given up driving."

"I guess you'll have to go creep out somebody else, then."

"Blah, blah, blah. Tell me you've never once cruised a girl's house just to be close to her, or called and hung up just to hear her voice."

And of course he had. He had to admit that he'd never given much thought to how the girls in question might feel, looking out the window and seeing his car drive by at eleven o'clock at night, and again at eleven thirty, and again at twelve.

"It's not like I'm leaving dead rodents on the doorstep or anything," Layla continued. "I just drive by occasionally on my way to other places, that's all. And, by the way, I *could* leave a dead rodent if I wanted to. One of my friends is doing a rat dissection in Bio. I could even leave *parts* of a dead rodent."

He smiled despite himself. The rat again. "You're nuts."

Layla settled deeper into her shabby Vincent Price armchair, looking satisfied. "It's not for lack of dead rodent availability, is what I'm saying. When you're curious about somebody, it's only natural to try and find out more about them."

The boots she wore today were tall and pointed and hugged her ankles, making her look as if her calves were made of smooth black leather. "What about you and your sister?" he said, trying to turn the tables.

Layla winced theatrically. "My sister is sweet and kind and gentle and the world is eating her alive. The dark side is her only chance. Besides, the good-sister-bad-sister routine is getting tedious. I'm tired of being the only one who ever gets in trouble."

"What does she want?"

"To sing with the choir of angels," she said. "My turn. This thing with your brother's girlfriend. Is it an unrequited love-that-shall-never-be thing, or did you just get really drunk one night?"

"Pick another topic."

Layla smiled. "I knew it. You've got, like, serious lust issues with her. You two totally got it on, didn't you?" She took another sip of coffee and licked at her upper lip to catch a stray drop. "Was it only once, or is it an ongoing habit? Are you utterly racked with guilt?"

"I'm not going to talk about this with you." He was blushing so fiercely that he was almost sweating. "Why do you care, anyway?"

"Because it's salacious and filthy, why do you think?"

"No," he said. "I mean, why do you care about any of it? Why do you care what I do or when my mom died?" He shook his head. "And you wonder why I'm suspicious of you. You know why? It's because you don't make any damn sense. I feel like I won some stalker lottery, like you were flipping through those goddamned yearbooks, found my picture, and said, 'Okay, *that* guy.'"

She popped the last of the Krispy Rice Treat into her mouth, chewed for a moment, and then swallowed. "Actually, it was that picture from the newspaper of you and your brother leaving the courthouse. He looked sad, but you didn't. You looked pissed off. Why did you look so pissed off?"

A hot day, overheated in a suit reeking of wet wool and sweat and worry. The photographer scuttling in front of him like a bug as he walked across the courtyard; the old man somewhere behind them, being loaded into a van and driven away. *Forget about me, I ruined your lives enough.* Mike's fists balled up so tight that his tendons looked like high-tension wires. Like Patrick's own fists, right now, on the arms of this dumb velvet armchair, a broken spring jutting into his ass and French love songs on the stereo. This girl. This fucking girl.

"Because they were taking our picture," he said, "and we didn't do anything wrong. Stupid question."

She blinked, hard, as if he'd spat at her, but recovered just as quickly. "My dad used to make us all pray for you. That God would find his way into your hearts. And that Danny and Rachel—Ryan's parents—"

He knew that, she didn't have to tell him that.

"Could let go their hatred and forgive you. Not like they're per-fect, by the way. Danny was married before. He and Rachel had an affair and everything. They're all hypocrites."

"Did they?" he said.

"Did they what?"

"Forgive me."

"No," Layla said. "I don't think that's on the immediate horizon." She shrugged: a tiny gesture, just the barest twitch of her shoulder, as if the issue didn't really matter. "I used to imagine you, sitting in that house for all those hours, knowing that car was there. My dad and all his acolytes act like they'd know exactly what to do and exactly when to do it. Like they're so infallible, like every choice they make is blessed by heaven and they're never, ever selfish." She sounded bitter. "Which is a crock of shit, of course."

It took Patrick a moment to find his voice. "And what did you do," he said, "when you imagined you were me?"

"I didn't imagine I was you. I imagined I was with you."

Across the coffee shop, two people about his age—a man and a woman, both wearing trendy glasses with heavy rims and both car-rying laptop bags—leaned in toward each other over cups of steam-ing coffee. The man reached out, touched the woman's arm, and she smiled at him. He pictured Caro carrying a basket of bread through the restaurant; or maybe she was home by now, in the house. In his house. Where his mother had been pregnant and sick and all but died, there hadn't been much left of her when she went into the hospital for the last time; where his dad had been sober and drunk and sat on the couch weeping while Ryan Czerpak's blood dried on the Buick in the garage, where he'd been arrested. Where every night now Mike and Caro went to sleep in the bedroom that had once belonged to Pat-rick's parents, the bedroom where for all Patrick knew he and Mike had been conceived, and where, every night, Patrick himself went to sleep in the same bed he'd slept in since he was a child. And the last girl he'd slept with there was the last girl in the world he should have had anything to do with, the girl who slept every night in his parents' bedroom and the girl who was sleeping with his brother, and the whole thing was so microscopically collapsed, so inescapable. A black hole.

Like the rest of his life. Across from him Layla sat in that shabby armchair, her boots tucked beneath her now; her face was calm, like a porcelain doll's. She seemed quite happy to stare out the window and sip her coffee and he knew she would wait for as long as it took him.

"Hey," he said. She looked up at him. Her eyes were bottomless. "You want to get out of here?"

"If you do," she said, and he said, "Yeah."

In her car, she flipped down the sun visor and opened the vanity mirror. Then, reaching across him, she took a makeup bag out of her glove compartment and produced a package of some kind of pre-moistened wipes. Her makeup was smudged, just the faintest black haze under her eyes, and she used one of the wipes to clean it away. The way she did it, it was obviously a habit.

"There was this thing that happened last year," she said.

Patrick hoped she wasn't going to tell him about the time her teacher touched her, or whatever.

"It was very—" She stopped, considering her own eyes in the mirror. "Very public. And very ugly. My bio teacher showed us how to use a condom in class. And I was stupid enough to tell my repressed asshole of a father about it, and he got the God squad all up in arms, and the next thing I know everybody—and I do mean everybody—hated me. That teacher was incredibly popular. Not to mention that, thanks to good old Ratchetsburgian inbreeding, she's related to half the school." She closed the mirror and tossed the wipe into the backseat. "So, on one hand, I've got my dad writing statements for me to read at school board meetings about how I didn't want anything to do with condoms because Jesus hates latex, et cetera, and on the other,

I've got the girls' varsity volleyball team setting my hair on fire in the second-floor bathroom."

She looked better without the smudges under her eyes, he thought. "They set your hair on fire?"

"It was longer then. And blond." She reached into her pocket and pulled out a long black cylinder, which turned out to be eyeliner. "Anyway, fun times. Then, one day, when I thought I was just about to go insane, this guy from school—who everyone said was a Satanist, by the way, although those people, like most of the world, were stupid and wrong—walked up to me in the middle of the hall and told me I was being used. I thought, great, yet another dimension to the lunacy. But that night, at yet another school board meeting, I'm sitting there watching my dad shout and yell and mention his ministry every third word— Let's just say the lights came on." She smiled. "My friend. I told him once how weird it was that we'd been in school together for a whole year and never met, and he said that sometimes people find each other when they need each other. What do you think?"

Patrick was restless and he didn't care. He thought that probably her friend wanted to sleep with her. "I don't know."

"They used you, too," she said. "People are messed up. You give them a chance to vent their sad little rage at their sad little lives, to feel morally superior, or powerful, or whatever, and they take it. They don't care who you are or what you've done. They just care that it's socially acceptable to hate you in public." Layla reached out and ran her fingers over his temple—they were cool and moist, probably from the wipe—and through his hair, where it curled behind his ear. "I think you need me. You wouldn't be here if you didn't."

He put a hand on her wrist, meaning to push it away—but then somehow she was sitting on his lap and the hand that was supposed to be pushing her away was under her creaking black leather jacket that smelled like clove cigarettes and new boots. The sweet chemical smell of her makeup remover was strong in his nostrils and she was kissing him and he was kissing her back. She tasted like coffee and vanilla. There was nothing tentative about her: her tongue plunged against his and her hands were strong and direct, as if they knew where they were going and knew what they wanted to do when they got there. He felt drunk, almost, like he was two seconds behind everything that was going on, and at the same time he was dimly aware of his own hands and what they were doing under that jacket of hers and did he always have to do the worst thing he possibly could, did he always have to fuck it up so absolutely supremely?

With great effort he took control of his hands again and pushed her back. He couldn't see her face; her hair hung down on either side of it, shielding her features from what little light came in through the car windows. Her breath was slightly rough but not as fast as his.

"I can't do this. You're too young." His tongue felt thick in his mouth.

"That's what they tell you," she said. "I'm telling you that you can do whatever you want." Then her mouth was back on him, her tongue licking at his, her body pressing closer, closer. She was like eating hot fudge with a spoon, bitter and sweet and almost overwhelming—he was tired of restraint, he was tired of control. He was tired of being the only person in his entire world. He gave in. He kissed her. He knew it was wrong. He didn't care.

He didn't sleep with her, at least. There was that.

FOUR

Calleigh and Kyle had friends everywhere. If it wasn't one of them in Gym or Bio, it was Brenna and Sam in English, Trevor and Matthias in Spanish. Often there was nothing more than a *Hey, Venereal,* but there was never less, and sometimes they got creative. Sharp triangles of folded paper pitched against the back of her head, a stack of venereal disease brochures left on her desk. (Her own father's brochures; she'd typed the originals. She didn't think they knew that.)

Verna liked eating lunch on the loading dock with Layla and Justinian and Criss, sitting on the rough concrete and knowing that she was safe. At the mall with Layla, she spent all of her birthday money on a pair of high black boots. The next day, seeing her own black-booted feet among the others on the loading dock pleased her. As did the wood-shaving smell of the art studio, talking to Jared, the knowledge that the day was almost over. She felt smaller every day. In Biology, Kyle Dobrowski and Brad Anastero kept up the endless whispers. *Hey, Venereal, you ever do a helicopter? You ever do it like Superman?* She didn't understand and the confusion only annoyed her more.

"Good boots," Jared said, in Art.

"Thanks," she said.

After school, at Eric's—he lived with his dad in a low-income housing development; Verna had never been there before, but it was just like any other apartment complex, with parked cars and tricycles in front of the houses—Layla told Verna that they wanted to dye her hair.

Sitting on Eric's bed, which was unmade and didn't smell clean, Verna felt cornered. When Layla had dyed her hair, Mother had cried. She wasn't a crier, their mother. "I'm not sure," she said.

"You hate your hair," Layla said. "You've told me that a thousand times."

"If you hate it, change it," Criss said.

Layla picked up a piece of Verna's hair. "Come on, Vee. It'll be beautiful."

And then Justinian, standing in the doorway, said, "Go ahead, do it," and it wasn't as if it were Verna's photo that her parents had chosen to splash all over the ministry mailers, so she let them: hunched over the side of Eric's bathtub, staring at the layer of grime that coated its floor; bleach burning her scalp, her hairline and ears thick with Vaseline to keep the dye away from her skin. Layla and Criss painted a few pieces with gray goo, wrapped them in plastic wrap, and covered the rest with grape-colored dye. They made Verna sit on the floor while it set. The bathroom wasn't clean, either. There were unidentifiable hairs in the corners and no bath mat and it smelled like urine. Eric's father spent most of his time with his girlfriend, and the town house felt like a place nobody cared about. The tables were dirty and all of the glasses were plastic and there was an old pizza box tucked behind the garbage can in the kitchen. In Eric's room, where he and Justinian played video games while the girls worked on Verna's hair, every surface except the bed was covered with a thick layer of magazines and car parts and stray pieces of wire.

Finally, Criss and Layla bent her over the bathtub again and rinsed her hair for what seemed like a very long time, then unwrapped the gray pieces and rinsed them for a very long time, too. They didn't let her look in a mirror but while Criss blasted her with a hair dryer, the strands of hair that blew in front of Verna's face were the color of raspberry jam, and she began to feel shaky inside. When Criss finished, Layla made Verna sit for a few more minutes while she circled Verna's eyes in thick rings of black, like she had before they'd gone to the woods; then they let her stand up, and look.

Her drab, mouse-brown hair was now an intense burgundy, and the wrapped bits had turned into long silver streaks on either side of her face, gleaming like starlight. Her pink-rimmed eyes and unremarkable eyelashes were hidden behind Layla's makeup. Verna reached up to touch her hair and was faintly surprised when the image in the mirror did the same, the strands feeling soft and alive under her fingers.

"Gorgeous," Layla said, looking pleased.

Justinian gave Verna a graphic novel; the cover showed a girl leaping from a stone tower, a thick mane of silver-streaked burgundy hair streaming behind her. "That's the Sorceress," he said. "Her hair turned silver when she threw herself from the top of the tower. Then she fought her way back from the land of the dead, and now she's immortal. You should read it."

His own hair was as black as anthracite coal, his eyes as blue as a Siamese cat's. Verna was fascinated and slightly awestruck by him, and she gripped the glossy book tightly as Layla drove her home. Her nostrils were still filled with the smell of hair dye and her eyes felt sticky and weird under her makeup. As she snuck peeks at herself in the side mirror, her unease grew. The closer they got to the house, the stronger it became. When Layla stopped at the corner and told her to get out, Verna blanched.

"You're not making me go in there by myself," she said, trembling at the very thought, but Layla only said, "Surely the Sorceress isn't afraid. Should I tell Justinian he picked out the wrong colors for you?"

So into the house Verna went. Her own reflection in the front hall mirror stopped her. She just had time to wonder if she shouldn't at least have taken off the makeup when she heard a gasp and looked up to see Dad staring at her, his eyes wide with shock.

"Oh, Verna," he said. "Oh, no."

Dinner was awful. Dad stared down at his plate with profound and silent disappointment while Mother sawed angrily at her pork chop, the knife grating on the stoneware with a horrible screech. They mostly seemed to be angry with Layla. As if Verna herself wasn't responsible for the decisions she made. As if she was a doll that Layla had ruined. As if she was *their* doll.

"When your sister gets home," Mother said, leaving the threat unfinished as she stabbed fiercely at a piece of spinach. "When I get hold of her."

Verna had never disappointed her parents before, not once. Her anger fluttered and burned in her chest.

Upstairs doing her homework, the vocab sentences were easy and the algebra was hard and as she factored equations and solved for variables, her indignation surged and roiled. Because when Layla had cut off her corn-silk hair and dyed it black, it had been just one link in a long chain of broken curfews and immodest hems and inappropriate eye makeup. "I hope you're happy," Mother had said through her tears. "You look just as ugly as you've been acting." But here Verna sat at her desk, ceramic praying hands on the wall above her. She'd be in bed by ten that night and awake by seven the next morning, when she'd wash the breakfast dishes before nagging Layla into her car so they wouldn't be late. After school she'd start the laundry and dust the living room and six weeks from now she'd bring home a straight-A report card and none of that counted with her parents. All they saw was their little broken doll with the wrong color hair.

In the window over her desk, the two silver streaks and the black holes of her thick-lined eyes stared back at her. That face might be unfamiliar but at least she knew it was hers. It was her own.

Somebody tapped on her closed door. Her father. "Can we talk?" he said.

Verna nodded, and he sat down on her bed. His hair was thinning on top, but what was left was the same color hers had been, four hours earlier. Behind his glasses, his eyes looked tired. "So, was the hair your sister's idea?"

"No." Verna wasn't lying. It had been Justinian's idea, Layla had said; he'd chosen the colors. "Nobody made me do it. I wanted to."

"I'm sure you did. Have you thought about why?"

"Why not? It's not like it was anything special the way it was."

He winced. "Verna, honey, everything about you is special."

She didn't say anything.

"Do you know why I think you did it?"

No, but I bet you're going to tell me, Layla's imaginary voice said.

"I think you miss your sister," he said. "I think now that you're both at the same school, you're starting to realize how far apart you've grown, and you want to make it better. So you start dressing like her, and dyeing your hair the way she does, because you think that maybe if she doesn't want to be like you, you can be like her, and then you'll be friends again, like you used to be."

When Layla had been golden and shining and Verna had been her faint, silent shadow. They had more in common now than they'd ever had then.

"Really, I think all of this is coming from your heart," Dad said. "Your good, sweet, loving heart."

Her good, sweet, loving heart, that wished daggers and poison and death on Kyle Dobrowski every day.

"But here's the problem, Verna. Layla's in a dangerous place right now. And I love you for going there to find her, but I'm not sure you can bring her back and I don't want you getting stuck there, too. I don't want to lose both of my girls."

Wrong, wrong, wrong. She wanted to tell him: what school was like, what Layla was like, what she, herself, was like. What the world was like, because she was starting to wonder if he knew. All she could say was "Neither of us is lost."

"Layla has to come back on her own, honey," he said, shaking his head. "And we can be there for her when she does, we can welcome her and make it as easy as possible for her, but we can't make her come. I know you want to help her, but you're not going to help her by letting her push you into being somebody you're not."

It was hopeless. She tried to smile. "Dad, I'm still me. I just have more interesting hair."

"I liked your hair the way God made it." He stood up. "Look, I can't tell you to stay away from your sister. I'm not sure I would if I could, but I know I can't. Will you make me a promise, though? Will you listen to God before you listen to her?"

He'd always told her that God spoke deep in her heart, and that she would know what He wanted her to do because it would feel right and everything else would feel wrong. Nodding, right now, felt wrong. She did it anyway.

"That's my good girl," Dad said. "You know I'll always love you, no matter what, right?"

"What about Layla?" Verna said.

He blinked, and then smiled. "Yes, Layla, too, although I'll admit that she doesn't always make it easy." He cleared his throat. "Speaking of Layla, do you know where she is tonight?"

"I think she's at Brittany's," she said. "I think they're doing homework."

Although it occurred to her, after the door was closed, that Dad just needed to check the GPS website to see that she was lying—but the only computer in the house was the one in the office, and she didn't hear him go in there, not for the rest of the night. As she fell asleep, she found herself thinking about what she would be like, if she were the person that Kyle Dobrowski and Brad Anastero liked to tell her she was. Her dreams were troubling and strange. When she woke up her pillowcase was stained with hair dye and Mother was furious.

. . .

The next day, Justinian gave her a bracelet, black leather with a silver ring attached to the outside of it. It was like the one the Sorceress wore in the comic. "I got it at a convention a few months ago," he said. "I was going to give it to Layla, but for some reason I never did. Then, last night, I found it. I think it was meant for you." She was surprised that he thought of her at all, so she let him fasten it around her wrist. The leather was stiff and tight, almost uncomfortable. It was like being held in somebody's fist. As the day passed she decided she liked it. It rubbed a bit, and it smelled of new leather and solvent, but it was a reminder: there were places in the world that weren't the bio lab, people in the world that weren't Kyle Dobrowski and Calleigh Brinker.

She wore the bracelet to Worship Group on Wednesday night. The group met in the Elsheres' basement and there were no pews, just folding chairs and a crucifix and an old *Twilight Zone* pinball machine that hadn't ever worked. Layla sat on top of the pinball machine, as she always did—Dad said the important thing was that she came—picking her fingernails and looking aloof, but Verna sat in one of the chairs arranged in loose concentric circles around the room. Normally she sat next to one of her parents, but this time she chose the chair closest to Layla. Around her were faces that were as much a part of her history as her own flesh. She'd gone to church camps and weekend retreats with Jenna Latshaw and the Costa twins; she'd helped babysit the little ones, the Czerpak kids—before Ryan died—and the Ferarrini kids and Debbie Mayerchek's little boy, Jayden. Last week she'd worn a pink blouse and a flowered skirt to Worship Group, and now she wore her kitty-skull T-shirt and fishnet stockings and boots and none of them would look at her. It was as if she gave off some kind of polarity that repelled direct eye contact. When they looked in her direction, their gazes just sort of slipped away.

Verna cast a stealthy glance over her shoulder, trying to catch Layla's eye, but Layla was hunched into herself, staring down at her own crossed ankles. The Black Sabbath shirt Layla wore wasn't what she'd worn to school. Verna hadn't ever seen it before, but it didn't look new. The black cotton had faded to a musty gray, and the image of four scowling men on the front was crazed and worn, their long painted hair chipped around the edges. Their faces made Verna think of Justinian. Mother and Dad had made much of the shirt at dinner. Apparently Dad had once owned one like it.

"Your father used to be the world's biggest Sabbath fan," Mother had said.

"Ironic, isn't it?" Layla said. "The first thing I wear in months that you haven't hated reminds you of your bad old days of sin and damnation."

Dad said, "It's our youth that we're remembering fondly, not Ozzy Osbourne. Where did you find that, anyway?"

"A friend gave it to me," Layla said.

What friend? Verna wondered now. She tried to imagine Justinian wearing the shirt, but it was too ragged. Justinian's clothes never looked worn. The shirt he'd worn that day had been intense black, the red lettering crisp. *And Darkness and Decay and the Red Death held illimitable dominion over all.* Thinking of it now Verna shivered.

Meanwhile, Dad finished talking about this week's Bible verse, and asked if anybody had anything they wanted to share. There was a smattering of the usual stuff: someone's friend had cancer, somebody's brother lost his job, someone's troubled niece had been packed off to a Christian wilderness camp. The group prayed for them. Verna snuck another look at Layla. She was picking at a hole in her jeans.

"I have something," Danny Czerpak said. The man who'd hit and killed Ryan with his car had been drunk; he and his sons had waited nineteen hours to report it. Those had been awful hours. Mother and Dad had spent them at the hospital with Danny and Rachel while Verna, at home, had prayed for the impossible, that the boy would live. Now Danny said that he and Rachel had decided to sue the man who'd done it. He was in prison now but he still owned the house where his sons lived. "It's not about the money," he said. "It's about making those boys understand that what they did was wrong. Other than their father being in prison, their lives haven't changed at all, and that doesn't seem right to us." He cleared his throat, looked at his wife, and said, "So, anyway, I just wanted to ask all of you to pray for us, to help us do the right thing in Christ and for God's justice to be done. Amen."

"Amen," Dad said, gently. So did everybody else.

Layla was chewing a fingernail, and—for some reason—smiling. Faintly, bitterly.

Toby frowned, and shifted, and said, "Are you sure? Romans says, do not take revenge, right? It is mine to avenge, I will repay, says the Lord. Shouldn't we be trusting Him to punish those guys? I mean, the Bible says"—his tongue stumbled a little over the *B* in *Bible*—"feed our enemies when they're hungry, do good to those that hate us. You're talking about taking away everything they have. It's a serious thing."

Verna wondered. She spent thirty-five hours a week in school and Kyle, Calleigh, and the rest made her dread almost all of it. They were a weight she could never shake off, a misery that never eased. If she had the chance to punish them, would she be able to leave it up to God? You couldn't compare a few dirty words to a dead child, you couldn't. But still. She didn't know.

Meanwhile, Danny's fists clenched. "My son is dead," he said. "Last time I saw him he was wrapped in bandages and I was signing away his organs."

"Why don't we give it to God?" Dad said. "Come on, everybody. Let's pray."

Afterward, everyone drifted upstairs, where Mother had laid out refreshments. The sticky smells of fruit punch and brown sugar cookies were, for Verna, the smells of church, and the little kids playing tag up and down the hallway were just as they had always been, but nothing else was. Rachel Czerpak stood by the punch bowl, her eyes red and damp, and watched as her two surviving children romped with the others; Verna could see the grief inside her, the way she felt Ryan among them even though he wasn't. Verna herself was here but felt like she was elsewhere.

Jenna Latshaw, with the Costa twins in tow, cornered her by the punch bowl. Verna could practically feel their excitement: finally, they had an opportunity to save a falling soul. And not just any soul, but Pastor Jeff's own daughter. "We're worried about you," Jenna said.

"There's nothing wrong with a little hair dye. I had that pink stripe last year," Amberleigh Costa said. It was disconcerting, the way she was looking at Verna's hair instead of her face.

"It's not the hair dye we're worried about. It's what's behind it."

"Or who," Spencer Costa said, sounding ominous. "We think it's your sister."

Dad said that they were supposed to do this, to watch out for each other and keep each other on the right path. Across the room, he was watching, and Verna knew that in his eyes the others were reaching out to help bring her back from the edge. Walk with the wise and become wise, and so forth. But the Costas went to a private Christian academy, and Jenna was homeschooled. They weren't in Biology with her. They weren't on the tennis courts when Calleigh Brinker practiced her forehand on Verna's back. They didn't know what it was like, and they didn't know Layla, and they didn't know Verna, either.

The room felt too hot. As soon as she could, she made her way to the sliding glass door, eased it open, and slipped out into the backyard. The sun was setting and the dwindling light brought the yard's contrasts into relief: the house on one side, all rough stucco and sharp corners, and across the grass the dense trees, overgrown with ivy. The air was cool and felt like fall. The prickly heat inside Verna dampened.

The glass door slid open and shut behind her. Layla said, "Broke away from the Jesus brigade, did you?"

"Were they always so awful?"

"Good Christians, all." Layla sniffed. "Hey, do you smell ciga-rette smoke?"

They traced the smell to the side of the house and saw Toby squatting against the wall on his haunches, cigarette held like a dart between the fingers of his right hand. There were no windows and no landscaping on that side of the house, just a thin swath of grass and the high board fence that separated their house from the one next door. Toby started when he saw them, and then looked guilty.

"B-b-b-b-busted," Layla said. "Give me a cigarette, T-t-toby."

"No."

"I'll tell my dad you've got porn in your car."

"You think he'd believe you?"

"So I'll tell Verna to tell him." Layla held out a hand. "Officially, she doesn't even know what porn is, though, so if you make me do that, you'll really go to hell."

Toby frowned, but tossed her the pack. "You shouldn't l-let her use you like that," he said to Verna.

Verna rolled her eyes, feeling very Layla-esque. "Relax, Toby. It's just a cigarette."

"Ah," Layla said, taking a cigarette and returning the pack to Toby, "but that's how the devil gets you. First cigarettes, then straw-berry wine coolers—next thing you know, you're in the park, giving blow jobs for meth. Right, Toby?"

Toby stood up. "God still loves you, Layla. You can come back to Him whenever you're ready." Then he stubbed out his cigarette on the sole of his boot, carefully palmed the butt, and walked away.

"You're mean to him," Verna said, without much conviction.

"He loves it. It gives him an opportunity to be all superior and holy. Speaking of people who love feeling superior and holy, Amber-leigh Costa and Jenna Latshaw seem to think I've cast a spell on you. And not with my charisma, either. With, like, candles, and goat's blood."

Verna half-laughed despite herself, but said, "Nobody said it was because of a spell when you dyed your hair."

"I didn't have the benefit of a scandalous older sister to blame it on. Justinian always says the way we look is an expression of how we feel. If you don't feel like them, don't look like them." Layla flicked her ash. "I can't tell you how much of a revelation it was, that I could choose not to look like Dad's virginity poster girl anymore."

"Is that why you cut your hair?"

"I cut my hair because Calleigh Brinker and her friends set it on fire." Layla smiled humorlessly. "They said they wanted me to know what burning in hell would feel like."

Verna stared at her. "You never said."

"What, so Dad could parade me and my burned hair in front of a bunch of news cameras? Pass." She paused for a moment. "It was better just to cut it off. Cut that part of my life away. Justinian's idea, of course. And he was right. He usually is." There was a note in her voice that Verna couldn't quite identify, something as small and bitter as her smile during Worship Group. "He was right about you."

"What do you mean?" Verna asked. Baffled, as always, that he'd thought about her at all. Sometimes she lifted the bracelet he'd given her to her face to smell it and think of him. Which was the sort of thing that she imagined somebody in love doing, but Verna wasn't in love. Being in love with Justinian would be unfathomable, like being in love with a star—not a famous actor or musician but an actual star, like Polaris. Layla could be in love with him; with her confidence and her cool Layla sometimes seemed nearly celestial herself.

"That you were miserable," Layla said. "He likes you, you know. Criss, too."

"Eric doesn't," Verna said. Although warmth was filling her like cocoa, utterly unlike the prickly heat that had come over her inside the house.

Layla laughed. "Eric doesn't like anybody. He and I got it on once and the whole time he was telling me what a bitch I was. And not in a fun, dirty-talking way, either. He meant it."

Layla's calm demeanor didn't match the words leaving her mouth. "That sounds kind of scary," Verna said, carefully.

"No, it was profound. Hate can be just as intimate as love. You know, Eric's family is a disaster. His mom's been in prison for assault since he was ten."

"I didn't know."

"How would you? He never talks about it and nobody ever bothers to ask. People just see the shaved head and the boots and figure he's an asshole, so that's how they treat him." She took a drag of her cigarette. "Not that he's not an asshole, ninety percent of the time."

"If you think he's—then why did you—"

"I'm sorry. I seem to have lost my ability to speak Repressed Virgin," Layla said. "Are you trying to ask me why I fucked him if I thought he was an asshole?"

Her cheeks hot, Verna nodded.

"I did it for the same reason that I made out with Criss." Layla saw Verna's face and laughed. "Didn't know about that, did you? True story. Say 'fuck' and I'll tell you why. Come on, Verna. Make an independent decision."

Verna could guess why Layla had done those things. Because their parents wouldn't want her to. "I'm making an independent decision not to say it."

Layla grinned. "Fair enough." Then she looked down at the tip of her cigarette, and the grin faded, as if she saw something in the red-orange fire and didn't entirely like it. After a moment, she said, "You know, Vee, if you want to dye your hair back, we can."

Verna imagined the clothes in her closet, as neat and orderly as parishioners on a pew: flowered dresses, cheerful sweaters, pretty pleated skirts and crisp cotton blouses. Like candy sprinkles on a strawberry sundae, sweet-colored and sunny. If she let Layla dye her hair back, tomorrow morning she could be the old Verna from a week ago. Ignore the stark black and purple exclamation point hanging in the center of the clothing rod, put on some nice flats instead of her boots—smile at Mother, because her family was not a violent mess and her mother was not in prison, and then go to school—

No. "I like my hair. Amberleigh and Jenna can jump in a lake. Everybody thinks I just do things because you tell me to. Why? Why do they think I'm this simple little thing with no brain?"

Layla blew a column of smoke into the cool evening air and said, "Because you let them."

"Okay," Jared said on Thursday. "I've been trying to figure out all week if you dyed your hair to look like the Sorceress on purpose, but that bracelet you're wearing—you did, didn't you?"

Verna smiled. "Christians can't read comic books?"

"Yeah, but the *Sorceress*." It was rare to see Jared looking as animated as he did now. He even pushed his hair out of his eyes so that he could see her better. "I mean, that's some serious stuff. She's gang-raped by soldiers in the first five pages, and then she kills herself and goes to hell and— Wait, have you read the whole thing?"

"I liked it. Although it just sort of stopped after they left the winemaker's."

"That's just the first volume. I'd loan you the second but it's the only one I'm missing."

"That's okay. I'll get it eventually."

Jared bent over his drawing for a moment. Then, without looking up, he said, "If you wanted, I could borrow my mom's car tomorrow, and we could go to the mall after school and get it, maybe."

Jared was Layla's age. He could drive. "Really?"

"We could even go tomorrow night, if that's easier." She couldn't see his face. "Maybe see a movie. No big deal."

"Why would it be?" she said, and then she understood. He was asking her out. One hand flew involuntarily to her mouth. It was the hand wearing Justinian's bracelet, the smell of which was still strong in her nose. "I—I don't know."

"That's cool." Jared sounded casual but his tone rang false.

"No," she said, helplessly. She had never even considered dating, her father didn't approve of it. "That's not what I meant. I meant—" She took a deep breath. "I meant, I think so."

He stole a glance at her, from behind his hair. "You mean, you think you want to go?"

Make an independent decision. "Yes."

"Cool," he said again, but this time he sounded happier, not false at all. "Cool."

"Who, the guy with the hair?" Layla said that night, when Verna told her about the date. Then she shrugged, sketched a cross in the air with her thumb, and said, "Whatever, my child. Go forth and fornicate. Our parents are going to hit the roof, though."

They were in Layla's room, Layla at her desk in front of her open calculus book and Verna sitting on the floor. Layla had gone to Justinian's house after school and Verna was almost starting to wonder if the two of them had argued, because Layla had been in a foul mood ever since. Her expression was cross, her color off; after she'd come home she'd gone straight to her room, changed out of the Black Sabbath shirt she'd worn again that day, and put on an old sweatshirt, the kind of thing she never even took out of her closet anymore.

Verna shifted uncomfortably. "We're just going to buy comic books."

"Doesn't matter. You're a girl and he's a boy." Her voice dropped, became as earnest as their father's. "'Oh, no, dear. You might hold hands and get pregnant and catch AIDS and go to hell. Wait ten or twenty years like a good girl and we'll find you a nice Christian boy who won't ever, ever give you an orgasm.'" Her voice went back to normal and she said, "And then Mother will call you a slut and Dad will say, 'Michelle, please,' and they'll both spend the rest of the night searching your room for condoms and automatic weapons."

Layla had the details wrong but the essence absolutely correct. There was no way they would let her go. On some level, Verna had known that, but she'd been trying not to think about it. Deflated, she said, "Mother hasn't ever called you a slut."

"You're right. She hasn't. In that one way, she's a fabulous fucking parent." Layla glared down at her notebook. "You know, I would care a lot more about solving for x if there was actual ecstasy involved. Do you like him?"

Verna nodded.

"Do you think he's cute?"

Cute? After a moment's hesitation, she nodded again.

"Does he seem like the kind of guy who's going to beat you to death and rape your corpse?"

Verna gave her sister an exasperated look. "Come on, Layla."

Something almost like a smile touched Layla's bitten lips. "Well, then, go. You have to live your life on your terms, not theirs. Otherwise, you're going to end up married at twenty to some dipshit like Toby and spend the rest of your life as a choir-singing, pew-scrubbing brood sow. So go to the movies. Have fun. Deal with them later."

Verna stared down at her booted ankles. Layla's carpet needed to be vacuumed. "What did you and Justinian do on your first date?"

"We didn't have one. I went over to his house and then we just— were."

Verna hesitated, and then blushed. If there was anybody she could ask about this—and she wasn't exactly overwhelmed with options—it was Layla. "When did you know you were going to—um—"

"Fuck?" Layla half-laughed. "I'll let you in on a little secret, Vee. Sex isn't nearly the big deal that Dad makes it out to be. Sex is a guy sticking his penis in you. Big deal. I stick a Q-tip in my ear every morning. The package says, oh, god, whatever you do, for the love of all things good and holy do not insert in ear canal, and yet for seventeen years I've somehow managed to avoid puncturing my eardrum. Sex is just sex. It's everything wrapped around it that's the problem."

"I'm serious. When did you know?"

Shrugging, Layla said, "I don't know. There just came a point when not doing it would have seemed like—splitting hairs. Like being a coke addict who won't use meth because it's bad for you." Layla was quiet for a moment. "We were obviously going down that road. I mean, I took off my clothes for him on the second day I knew him."

Verna, shocked, said, "Why?"

"Because I wanted him to know everything about me. No secrets. No hiding." Layla was looking down at her calculus homework, but Verna didn't think she was seeing it. She didn't look good. It was more than her poor color: the hairs at her temples were damp with sweat, and the hand holding her pencil was shaking. "Sometimes I feel like he's with me all the time, even when he's not. Like we could be a million miles apart, and he'd still be with me, inside."

"Layla," Verna said, "are you okay?"

The glance Layla gave Verna held something startled and furtive, but she nodded and smiled. "Ignore me, Vee. I'm just feeling morbid. Go to the movies with Wolf-boy. Have a good time. I've never actually been on a real date, you know. You'll have to tell me what it's like."

To have someone with you all the time. To never be lonely. "I'd rather have what you have than go on a date."

"Make him buy you popcorn," Layla said. "The guy is supposed to buy you popcorn."

In Bio, they scraped the insides of their cheeks with toothpicks, dyed the cells with methylene blue, and examined them under microscopes. The experiment gave the boys behind her lots of free time.

"Come on, Venereal," Kyle said, looking particularly handsome in his maroon and white letter jacket. A year ago, had Verna been shown photographs of Jared, Justinian, and Kyle, and asked who she would most like as a friend, she would have chosen Kyle. "Just show us. Just one little look and we'll leave you alone."

They wanted to know if she'd dyed her pubic hair. It had been going on all week and by now, she didn't even want to cry. She just wanted them to shut up so she could concentrate on her slide, and finish her lab, and get to Art. That day, sitting on the loading dock, Justinian had reached out and lifted her cross pendant with one finger. "Look at you," he said. "Spending all your time with us heretics, and you still believe." He dropped the cross, which felt warm from his touch, but maybe she was imagining it. "You're tough, Verna. You're titanium."

Maybe Verna swelled a bit when Justinian said that, allowed herself to think, why, yes, I am quite tough, aren't I? Never mind that sometimes she tucked her cross into her collar when nobody was looking; never mind that she felt ashamed every time she did it, and sent a silent apology to God. And never mind that she had avoided telling Justinian—any of them—about her date with Jared. I am tough, she thought.

"Pull out a few hairs," Brad said. She could practically hear him turning to Kyle for approval. "We'll look at them under the microscope. Maybe they'll tell us why you're such a slut."

Mr. Guarda was in the back of the room. Verna pressed her eye against the eyepiece of her microscope so hard that her eye socket hurt. She was going to have to fix her makeup after this. *I am titanium.*

"By the way," Kyle said. "Jesus told me he wanted me to come on your tits."

Anger surged inside her, hot as fresh blood, and she wheeled around, glaring at him. He smiled sweetly.

"Would you like that?" he said. "Would you like some nice, warm come on your tits?" and then the bell rang and Verna stood up. Out of the corner of her eye she saw the open bottle of methylene blue sitting on Kyle's lab table and before she even knew she meant to do it her hand darted out, grabbed it, and threw it right at his smug, beautiful face. Her aim was bad. It landed on the breast of his letter jacket, right under the curling letters of his name. Blue dye flew everywhere: on Kyle's lab report, on his face, on his open textbook, even on Brad Anastero, who clapped his hand to his eye and yelped. Kyle's hands flew up, as if he could somehow knock the dye away. He looked, in face and body, like he'd just been shot, only he was bleeding blue instead of red. As Verna watched, the blue dye beaded on the smooth leather of his sleeves and soaked into the white embroidery.

The look on his face was stunned. Beyond stunned: furious. From the back of the room, Mr. Guarda said, "Uh-oh."

Sure, Verna thought. Now you notice me.

Kyle stared at her and, in a voice full of wonder, said, "You bitch."

Verna's fists clenched. The tendons in her wrist strained against the bracelet Justinian had given her. "It was an accident."

"Like hell," Brad Anastero said, still rubbing his eye, and Kyle's face grew even more dangerous.

"I'm going to get you." He spoke quietly, so Mr. Guarda couldn't hear. "You're going to be sorry you were ever born."

She didn't care. She was tough. She was titanium. On her way up to Art, she felt like her heart was going to bounce right out of her chest. At camp, they'd talked about feeling the Spirit inside you. Verna had wanted to feel it, she'd told herself that she did. Now she knew she'd been wrong. This was what it was like: this power that came from somewhere else, running through your body and your veins and your soul like fire. Her hands wanted to clap, her feet wanted to dance, she wanted to jump up and down and make joyful noise after joyful noise. Instead she walked, her spine straight, her heart filled with a savage gladness.

·   ·   ·

She told her parents that she was going to see a movie with the non-existent (but increasingly useful) Brittany, something called *First Kiss* that she chose out of the newspaper because it sounded innocuous. The movie that Jared and Verna actually went to see was called *Fireblaze*. Jared told her it had been based on a comic book. Verna thought it must have been an extremely violent one. Whenever anybody was decapitated or impaled or incinerated, Jared laughed.

"I do?" he said after the movie, looking surprised.

Verna nodded. "Almost every time."

"I didn't know I did that. Maybe it's a startle reflex. Or cheesy special effects, I laugh at bad special effects a lot." He stuck his hands into the kangaroo pocket of his sweatshirt. "I guess I should have asked if you liked violent stuff before I bought the tickets. You had your eyes covered for half the movie." He sounded so downhearted and self-incriminatory that Verna reached out and touched his arm.

"I liked it," she said. "Maybe not the really bloody parts. But I liked the story."

He grinned. "It was awesome, when they were in the truck and it was on fire," he said. When they left the theater, he was holding her hand.

He took her to the graphic novel section of the bookstore. As it turned out, he knew a lot about comic books. "If you liked the Sorceress," he'd say, handing her a glossy paperback, "you're going to love this." He said it over and over again until the stack of books in front of Verna was ankle-high. His face was lit up, engaged in a way she had rarely seen in school; once, he actually pushed his hair back from his face instead of pulling it forward. He had a pierced eyebrow that she'd never noticed and Verna wondered: why get a piercing that nobody ever saw? She asked him if he wanted to draw comic books, and he said, no, he wanted to do video game design. "Why make static worlds when you can make them come alive?" he said. His fingernails were clean and short, and the face of his wristwatch was cracked, and he wore green canvas sneakers and smelled a little like Scotch tape. It was a nice smell; it made Verna think of Christmas.

Then it was only nine o'clock and Verna didn't have to be home until ten, so they went back to his house. She met his mother and her boyfriend, whose insistence on first-name familiarity was so intense that within minutes Verna could think of them as nothing but Call-Me-Keith and Call-Me-Carmen. Call-Me-Carmen was blond and wore a lot of necklaces, including a peace sign and an ankh and— Verna was surprised to see—a cross. Call-Me-Keith's shirt said *Beam Me Up, There's No Intelligent Life Down Here,* and no sooner had Jared and Verna walked through the door than he began grilling Jared about the movie: did they leave the supervirus subplot in, was the gay villain still gay, and what about the woman who played Kai-One, could she act at all because he'd seen the trailer on the Internet and it didn't look like it. And since when was Kai-One a redhead, anyway.

"Boys will be geeks, huh?" Call-Me-Carmen said with a smile. Her teeth were coffee-stained. Mother and Dad kept theirs perfectly white, they paid a lot of money at the dentist's to do it.

"I guess so," Verna said.

"Jared tells me you're a Christian. It's such an interesting story, the life of Christ, and such an interesting thing to be in this day and age. Religion has become so politicized, don't you think?" Call-Me-Carmen shook her head. "All of the moral legislation. You just wonder how much is the politicians and how much is the actual will of the people, don't you?"

Jared interrupted. "Easy there, Mom. Verna just came over to play some video games. Come on," he said to Verna. "Let's go downstairs." He led her through the kitchen, which smelled like beans and garlic, to the basement, where there was a couch and a television and what looked like four different game systems. The walls were covered with framed movie posters; there was a pinball machine here, too, but it didn't look broken. The lights were blinking.

"Sorry about that. My mom likes to think of herself as a student of all religions. That's what's with the necklaces." A small refrigerator hummed in the corner; Jared took out two bottles of soda, both red, and handed one to her. "Hang on a second, there's a bottle opener around here somewhere."

As he rummaged in a cabinet Verna said, "What did she mean, 'moral legislation'?"

"You know. Here." He opened her bottle; the cap came off with a hiss and a crack. "Gay marriage, abortion rights, all that stuff. Do you mind that I told her you were Christian?"

"Only if it makes her hate me."

"I'd be more worried about it making her annoy you."

"Do you mind?"

"If she annoys you? Yeah, I mind."

"No," Verna said. "That I'm Christian."

Jared flopped down on the couch and picked up the remote. "Are you kidding? Keith is all into animism and shamanism and that kind of stuff, and my mom's religious tastes change with the day of the week. If I weren't a reasonably tolerant person I'd lose my freaking mind." He took a sip of his soda and so Verna did, too. It was organic, with lots of quirky text on the label. *Be a free-drinker!* it read, in part. "Do you mind that I'm not Christian?"

She sat down next to him. "Well, the Bible says that you shouldn't yoke yourself to an unbeliever."

"So we won't pull any carts together," he said.

He taught her how to play a video game; not a violent one, a racing one, with a squirrel and a beaver in cute little cars. Verna was terrible at it. She was better at pinball. Upstairs, she could hear Call-Me-Carmen and Call-Me-Keith moving around, talking in the kitchen, flushing the toilet. According to the Price Above Rubies reading materials, rule number three for maintaining your virginity was *Avoid Temptation.* Do not be alone with a member of the opposite sex. Do not watch movies together in low light, or cuddle, or listen to soft music. These things were the worldly equivalent of Eve sitting beneath the Tree of Knowledge. Socialize in groups, in public, in well-lit, well-chaperoned places.

When Jared kissed Verna by the pinball machine, he tasted like her soda had: sweet and wet, with crisp little bubbles that tickled her teeth and her tongue. When he pulled her down to the couch, all she could think about was how many rules she was breaking. He put his arms around her. She could feel his breath on her skin, she could smell the soap he used. His tongue pushed tentatively into her mouth. *You're tough, you're titanium.* Only God was infallible but Justinian was usually right, even Layla said so. Jared slipped a hand up under her kitty-skull shirt and did she want this? Did she like it? She didn't know. She couldn't think. It was like there was a hole in the center of her and around the hole spun her father and Justinian and her mother and Toby and Layla and all of the faces from all of the prayer groups and church camps and lock-ins and revivals, and Kyle Dobrowski, too, all swirling like water around a bathtub drain. Jared shifted his body next to hers and she felt an awkward knob pressing against her thigh. He smelled like Christmas. She wanted to tell him to stop but she didn't know how. She wasn't supposed to have to tell him to stop. She wasn't supposed to be here.

He shifted again, pressed against her more insistently. Because he liked her. He had chosen her. Her, of all the girls in school. He was talented, he didn't treat her as if she were crazy for drawing pictures of angels. She didn't want him to think he'd chosen wrong. So she said nothing and did nothing except kiss him when he kissed her, and after a while he pulled back and looked at her. His lips were wet with their shared saliva and his temples were damp, too.

"Did you know that you're very cool, in a totally weird way?" he said, and Verna could practically feel her heart growing misshapen inside her chest.

He took her home. Layla was gone, Dad was in bed. Mother sat at the kitchen table, doing a jigsaw puzzle. The picture on the front showed an image that Verna knew represented the Sermon on the Mount. She'd memorized the entire sermon one summer, Matthew five, six, and seven. Dad said they were the three most important chapters in the Bible.

> *You are the salt of the earth; but if the salt has lost its taste, how can its saltiness be restored? It is no longer good for anything, except to be thrown out and trampled underfoot.*

"Thank goodness," Mother said. "A fresh pair of eyes. Come look at this thing with me, Verna, I can't make any sense of it at all." She scanned the pieces on the table in front of her. "Do you see three-quarters of a lamb's head? I need three-quarters of a lamb's head."

"Here," Verna said, and handed it to her.

FIVE

Caro found the note on Tuesday morning, scrawled onto a piece of notebook paper in watery ballpoint ink and fixed to the door with a hairy piece of Scotch tape. The hair caught in the adhesive was coarse, three inches long, black on one end and gray on the other. Dog hair. Caro heard that dog barking all the time. Its owners lived next door. They worked shifts and she thought they must crate the poor thing, the way it barked. Sometimes it woke her up. On hot days, the sweet nauseating smell of dog shit drifted over the high wooden fence separating the two yards. Last summer she'd tried to sunbathe out there a few times and the real or imagined buzzing of flies had made her itch.

> Please do not park your car in front of
> our house (149 Div), that space is our legal
> property and we will call the cops if we
> have to.

Caro didn't like neighbors. Neighbors made trouble. Standing on the porch in the sun, she squinted at the house next door. A wooden duck wearing a weather-stained bow tie hung crookedly from a nail on their front door, probably meant to be cheerful and welcoming but actually just cheap-looking and sad. Then she looked at the offending car, which Patrick said was barely drivable. It was, indeed, parked in front of 149 Division Street. The Cusimanos lived at 151. *Division* was a lousy name for a street. Residential streets were supposed to have bucolic, optimistic names, like Morning Dew Drive or Hibiscus Avenue. In Pitlorsville, Caro and her mother, Margot, had lived for a few months on Jenny Lane, which sounded like the sort of place where people walked around carrying baskets of flowers and bursting into spontaneous song. Not that anybody had done that, but at least it sounded that way. Division Street, on the other hand, sounded like the product of a late-night city planners' meeting where everyone had stopped trying. Which was appropriate since that was how Division Street itself felt: bedraggled and worn-out, both giving and given up. Dead leaves and garbage choked the storm drains and the neighbors could have bathed their stupid neglected dog in some of the potholes. But, hey. Why spend your time trying to make the world a better place when you could harass your neighbors for parking in a spot you didn't even need?

Inside, Mike was washing the breakfast dishes and Patrick sat at the kitchen table, staring morosely at a can of cherry Coke. At least she thought that was what he was doing. These days, they got along better when she didn't look directly at him. "Guess what we won," she said to Mike, and showed him the note.

His hands, scrubbing at fried-on egg, stopped. His lips moved slightly as he read. Then he scowled. "Assholes."

"What," Patrick said, and Caro held the note out to him wordlessly. There were heavy circles under his eyes. He'd been out late the night before. She could guess who with. He scanned the note quickly and shrugged. "Let 'em tow it. I don't want the damn thing anymore."

"We could put it in the garage," Caro said.

Mike's brow furrowed. "The garage is kind of full."

So it was; Caro had helped him fill it, the day she'd moved in, with boxes of the old man's belongings that the two of them packed, haphazardly, and stacked just inside the door. They hadn't taken much time or care over it. John Cusimano's room had smelled bad and Caro had been desperate to have at it with some good strong carpet deodorizer. When she was done the Summer Berry smell was strong enough to make your eyes water but she preferred that to vomit and old beer.

She'd said, why don't we just clean out *your* room, but Mike had been weirdly determined that they move into the big one. His room was just as he'd left it, with a blanket tacked over the window and the closet door falling off its hinges. They put stuff they didn't want in there now.

"Well, let me know what you two decide," she said. "If I can help or anything." Then she went upstairs to get ready for work. She'd never liked involving herself in any situation having to do with their father, not even before the Great Apocalyptic Mistake had napalmed her friendship with Patrick. You couldn't talk about the way things should be in somebody else's family. Families were like oceans. You never knew what was under the surface, in the parts you hadn't seen.

Caro's car had a bad battery. She kept meaning to get a new one but there were always other places to put that hundred bucks. That morning, when she turned the key—nothing. As Mike drove her to work, he said, "Maybe we should only have one car, anyway. Save money."

"Great idea. Except when you work swing and I get off in the middle of your shift."

"Darcy could drive you. Or Patrick."

Right, because what Caro wanted more than anything else in the world was to be alone in a car with Patrick, to watch him pull up at a stoplight and turn toward her the way Mike was doing right now.

They had good eyelashes, both of them, but Mike's eyes were brown and Patrick's a warm hazel. "I don't know if you've noticed, but Patrick's not driving much these days."

"His car's broke."

"So he claims." Her voice held an edge she didn't expect—that happened too often, these days—and she looked quickly out the window, down at the car waiting in the next lane. Mike's truck was jacked up high and she couldn't see anything of the driver except one arm, a floral rayon lap, and a manicured finger tapping the steering wheel.

"You think he's lying?"

She turned back. "He hasn't asked to borrow my car. Has he asked to borrow yours?"

Of course he hadn't. Mike took off the Steelers cap he wore and ran his hands through his hair, which was thick and copper-colored. (Patrick's was the color of coffee, black coffee.) It stood straight up as a result and he jammed the hat back down. "He's so fucking weird these days. Ever since he quit the warehouse, it's been Earth to planet Patrick." The light turned green and Mike sighed. "So what do you think, want to give up your car payment?"

"My car's paid off. If we're going to give up a car, it ought to be this big gas-guzzling penis monster of yours."

"I love it when you talk dirty." They pulled up in front of the restaurant. Leaning over, he kissed her, and she heard him inhale deeply. "I love the way you smell, too."

"Enjoy it now. The next time you see me I'm going to smell like high tide in a butter factory."

He smiled. "Tease," he said, and then kissed her again, and she got out.

Inside, Darcy said, "For crying out loud. The guy drives you to work and kisses you good-bye and even waits to make sure you get in okay. Tell me he's got a brother."

Caro grabbed her apron from behind the bar. "He's got a brother."

Darcy's face burned with sudden interest. "Seriously? Is he single? Is he cute?"

There was a bin of silverware and another of napkins on a table by the window. Caro sat down and began to roll: knife, fork, roll, flip, tuck. "Yeah, he's single."

"But not cute."

This flip and tuck, she'd learned it at a burger bar in Columbus. First restaurant she'd ever worked with cloth napkins. She'd dated the bartender, which was how she'd found the job, but after a while he'd dumped her for one of the hostesses. Caro had left Columbus not long afterward. It was not unlike what had happened in Athens, or Zanesville, or Wheeling, West Virginia. So many towns, so many boys. And now Ratchetsburg, Pennsylvania, which she'd never even heard of before getting off the turnpike here. "I guess he's cute. But he's a mess."

Darcy laughed. "Who isn't? Bring him in sometime. I'll buy him a drink."

"Maybe." Caro liked Darcy, who was a little worn-down but smart enough, all things considered. On average, Caro would rather Patrick sleep with her than some angst-ridden piece of jailbait. The pile of setups grew steadily on the table in front of her, her hands moving as if they belonged to someone else. Knife, fork, roll, flip, tuck.

That night was only medium bad. Some old guy, a big spender wearing too much cologne and a big onyx ring on one finger, put an arm around her hips as he placed his order and patted her ass when he was done, like she was a horse he was sending out to pasture. Caro clenched her teeth and put up with it. The bitch at table seven, whose shoes probably cost more than Caro made in a week, wanted "halibut, and I know halibut when I taste it so don't try pawning off some lousy piece of turbot on me. Lightly seared with real butter and sea salt, not table. Just a few grains." Where did the woman think she was, the Upper East Side? But Caro took the order anyway, and told Gary in back that they had yet another order for Ridiculously Specific Special Request Fish.

He made a jerk-off motion. "We ought to put that on the menu. Sells like hotcakes."

"If you put it on the menu, nobody will want it," Caro said, and the truth was that the cow at table seven didn't want it, either. A perfectly good, perfectly expensive piece of halibut, picked at for an hour and then scraped into the garbage. Sorry, fishie. You died in vain.

Halfway through the night she met Darcy at the register. "So how old is Mike's brother?" Darcy asked.

"Twenty-six."

"Young and uncorrupted. Just how I like 'em."

Caro tried to remember the drink order for table four. Was it two diet Cokes and one rum and Coke, or two rum and Cokes and one diet? "He has a shitty job, a car that doesn't run, and a different Led Zeppelin shirt for every day of the week."

"He's into Zeppelin?" Darcy's eyes widened as if at a divine revelation. "I love Zeppelin!"

Wow, you guys should, like, totally get married, Caro almost said, but didn't. Diet-diet-rum, rum-rum-diet?

"What's his name?"

Two diets and a rum. Because rum and Coke was the sort of thing you drank at a field party, not a medium-nice fish place. "Patrick," she said. "I've got an order up."

In the front, by the bar, there were two aquariums: the decorative one, where fish like gaily colored party favors swam in clear, cool-looking water, and the lobster tank. In the latter, brown lobsters piled on top of one another like old, discarded shoes. Caro didn't know anything about lobsters. Would they pile up like that in nature? Was it a stress response? Had the lobsters just given up? Because that was how they seemed to her. Like they'd lost all hope, like they knew that this murky holding cell was the last stop; barely even able to muster the energy to wave their claws, moving like dying soldiers pulling themselves across the battlefield. In theory, restaurant patrons could choose the lobsters that they wanted to eat for dinner. Caro would rather eat dog shit from the backyard of 149 Div than one of those sad, lifeless things. But people ordered the choose-your-own-lobster; they watched as she fished the poor thing out with a rake and grabbed it by its clammy exoskeleton, they cringed and laughed as she carried it into the kitchen for Gary to kill, they stuffed themselves on bread and clams casino while in the back of the restaurant, their dinner was dying. The people to whom this method of dining appealed were inevitably the same sort of people who felt the need to make macabre jokes about it. Naming their lobsters. Saying, "It won't hurt much." Like they knew.

Tonight that group was a bachelorette party, who giggled and squealed as Caro chased the bachelorette's chosen victim around the tank, then squealed some more as she carried it past them, holding it high and away from her body, its legs wiggling and twitching in futile struggle. The silly twit who'd ordered it didn't even know how to eat it. They were campers, taking up the table for almost three hours; no big deal, since it was only a Tuesday, but who scheduled their bachelorette party for a Tuesday, anyway? When they finally left, most of the lobster remained in its carapace. The bachelorette, proclaiming herself both bored and icked out by the lobster-eating process, had ordered two desserts instead. Caro was almost used to scraping nearly full plates of food into the garbage—like table seven, the halibut nibbler—but it was worse when you'd seen the thing die, when it had been alive and then killed and then thrown away.

Staring down at the semibroken lobster in the garbage, Caro was hit by a wave of sadness that stabbed the core of her, a place where she would have thought she couldn't be hurt. For a moment, she was overwhelmed. For a moment, she almost cried. But then she didn't. The choose-your-own-lobster dinner was expensive. The drunk bachelorettes had been good tippers. You did what you had to do to survive. That was all.

· · ·

Mike picked her up just after eleven. When they walked through the door, Patrick had already left for work and the television was off. The unnatural quiet reminded her of the first morning she'd woken up there, standing in the kitchen making breakfast before anyone else was awake, her feet bare, mist lingering in the overgrown backyard; the smell of French toast and bacon, a cup of coffee warming her hand. She had just met Mike the night before and hadn't met Patrick yet at all, although she'd noticed his coat thrown over the back of a kitchen chair and wondered about him, this brother. At the time, the house had felt peaceful, like a sanctuary—not to mention a hell of a lot more comfortable than the backseat of her car, which was where she'd woken up for the fourteen previous mornings, ever since arriving in Ratchetsburg—but now she knew that feeling had been a fluke. The house was almost never that quiet. Almost never *this* quiet.

And even as she thought that, Mike was in the kitchen, wasn't he, filling up the red cooler that lived next to the armchair in the living room with beer. She could hear the clatter of ice, the muted clink of beer cans. Caro hated that cooler. The uncleanable (she'd tried) pebbled surface of the thing, the old man's name written in huge Magic Marker letters on the side; the way that Mike sometimes came home with a bag of ice and a case of beer and she would instantly know that once again they were going nowhere, once again they were staying exactly where they were. Mike wrote letters to his father—one, anyway, after she'd moved in, *Her name is Carolyn but she is called Caro not Carrie, you'd like her since she is real nice and makes good chili*—but Patrick didn't, and Caro thought she understood why. The too-smooth repaired spots on the drywall, the smell of that bedroom before she'd cleaned it, the fact that Mike and Patrick had never moved out or found their own lives but instead lay piled on each other like dying lobsters. She didn't have to meet John Cusimano to know she didn't like him, and they'd never be free of him as long as that cooler sat next to the armchair, leaching a steady, constant trickle of despair.

She'd asked Mike once, early on, if they could get rid of it, trying as gently as she could to explain that his father's habits had not necessarily been good ones, but Mike had just looked blank. "Get rid of the cooler?" he'd said. "We'd have to go all the way to the kitchen every time we wanted a beer."

And Caro, whose mother was a paranoid-type schizophrenic and who had grown up as steeped in that woman's fear and despair as Mike had his father's, who still flinched every time a hinge squeaked and had to resist pulling her sleeve down over her hand every time she used a can opener or turned a doorknob ("Why do you do that?" Patrick had asked one night, back in the days before the Great Apocalyptic Mistake, when they were still friends; "Do what," she'd said, and, sharp enough, he'd said, "Nothing"), did not bother trying to tell Mike that there were worse things than walking ten feet for a beer. Like stewing in an ancient soup of somebody else's poison, for instance. Mike was strong and good-looking and he made her feel safe, but that wasn't the kind of thing he thought about. Patrick might have understood, but Caro thought Patrick had grown acclimated to misery, and even as he knew the cooler was poison he wouldn't have been able to get rid of it.

She took a shower, scrubbed the day off her body. When she came out of the bathroom, the television was back on; she could hear cheering and rock music, which meant sports highlights. She put on a T-shirt and sweats and went downstairs.

"Hey, gorgeous. Just waiting for the score on the Pirates game," Mike said. He didn't even watch baseball, he just didn't want Pittsburgh to lose. Next to him, ice and silver beer cans sparkled in the open cooler. "You want a beer?"

She shook her head. "Darcy wants me to fix her up with Patrick."

"What about the girl with the car?" Mike's eyes were fixed on the screen, watching the crawl at the bottom.

"She's in high school. She's a kid. He shouldn't be dating a kid."

"Dating?" Mike laughed. "What, you think he's taking her to the movies? The Eat'n Park buffet?"

"I don't care what they're doing. A twenty-six-year-old guy has no business with a seventeen-year-old girl." She heard the heat in her own voice and made herself speak more calmly. "At least Darcy is an adult."

He put an arm around her and pulled her down into his lap. "Don't worry about Patrick. If that girl gets him thrown in jail, he'll have nobody to blame but himself. Who knows? Maybe she'll even be good for him. Like you were for me." His nose rubbed against her jaw, the oil on his face making his skin slick against hers. The tickle of his stubble was friendly. "You saved me, you know."

"The only thing I saved you from was your laundry," Caro said, mollified.

It was a nice thing for him to say, the sort of thing that always got to her. Caro needed to be important. It was boring and typical and transparent as hell, even to her, but she couldn't turn it off any more than she could quit having arms. That night, she and Mike ended up doing it right there in the living room. She wished he'd shaved first. That friendly stubble felt like sharkskin against her face before too long, and she couldn't help worrying that Patrick might somehow come through the door at any minute, even though she knew he worked until dawn. As Mike's breathing reached a ragged pitch in her ear, she closed her eyes. For a second—just a second—she let herself remember a room with silver light, that night, the Great Apocalyptic Mistake. Patrick's hair was softer and there was less of it on his body. His mouth tasted different. His hands—

Caro pushed the thoughts away. The first time you had sex with somebody was always the best, anyway.

The next morning, Mike jumped Caro's car and drove it to work so Patrick could use his truck to cart away trash from the garage. Caro caught a ride with Darcy for the lunch shift, which turned out to be a wasteland. Nobody came in except a woman filling out a job application. Caro was wiping the dust off the liquor bottles when Mike came back at two, his dirty jeans and old T-shirt out of place among the restaurant's white tablecloths and fresh flowers. The warehouse hadn't been any busier than the restaurant and he'd been sent home. Gary happened to be up front right then checking the reservation book, and he told Caro that she might as well leave, too. "I kind of need the money," she said, and Gary said, "And I'd kind of love to give it to you, but it doesn't grow on trees. See you tomorrow."

"That guy's an asshole," Mike said, when they were in the car.

"No, he's okay." Back when she'd just started working for Gary, one night they'd found themselves alone after close. The sky was full of pretty summer stars and they'd had a few glasses of wine. She hadn't met Mike yet then and there'd been a moment—hardly even a moment, really—when she'd maybe looked a little too long at Gary, thinking only that he was nice and she was lonely. He was twice her age but that didn't matter, that had never mattered. He caught her look, smiled sort of sadly, and said, "Caro, you're a pretty girl but I'd no sooner fuck a good waitress than I'd key my own car." For the briefest of instants the rejection had stung, but then the sting had swelled into something like pride. She was a good waitress. She *was*.

Mike called Patrick from the bar to see if he wanted them to pick him up a cheeseburger on the way home. Mike had a mobile phone, like everyone else in the universe, but minutes cost money. Cheeseburgers cost money, too, along with gasoline, cable television, water service, sewage service, garbage pickup, electricity, and beer. Sometimes she thought, guiltily, that she should press the boys to cancel the cable, but the truth was that she didn't want to give it up. Sometimes, after a long shift, all she wanted to do was sit in one place and listen to somebody tell her about humpback whales or black holes or the interior life of the hippopotamus. It made her feel like there was a world out there beyond stupid people and their stupid problems. So she let Mike have his cheeseburgers and beer, and kept her cable. Fast food was cheaper than cooking, anyway.

When they got to the house, Patrick was standing in the garage, waiting for them. He'd actually made some progress; several full black garbage bags sat in the back of the truck, glistening in the sun like the giant eggs of some slimy alien monster from one of his movies. Caro could smell them even from where she stood. "Nice," Mike said, sounding impressed, as they sat down on the retaining wall to eat their cheeseburgers.

"Yeah, well." Patrick's face was flushed and the long hair at the back of his neck was damp and sticky-looking. He seemed agitated, like a tweaker trying to act straight: he stretched, he ran his hands through his hair, he cracked his knuckles. He wouldn't look at her.

"Hey, Patrick," she said, mildly. "You got lipstick on your neck, champ." He did: two perfect pink crescents, like a kiss on a cheesy greeting card. "And here we thought you'd just bagged the garbage."

She was pleased by how playful she sounded. Mike laughed. Patrick's hand went straight to the kiss—he knew exactly where it was—and rubbed at the spot, his cheeks flushing even deeper. "I didn't invite her," he mumbled. "She just came."

"I bet she did," Mike said.

"Yeah, that's funny. That's hilarious." Patrick rubbed at the mark again. By now it was nothing but a vague pinkish smudge. "By all means, bust my ass. I've got an eight-hour shift tonight and instead of sleeping I've been spending all day digging through the old man's crap."

Still managing to sound playful, Caro said, "Not quite all day."

Why did she say these things? Why? Patrick glared at her, his eyes full of something. Mercifully, he kept it to himself. "You know what?" he said, instead. "Fuck both of you. I'm going to go get some sleep." Then he turned and went back into the house, letting the door slam shut behind him.

"What's with him?" Mike said.

Caro shrugged. "I guess that girl is just really good for him. Should we go through some of this stuff?"

Mike said sure. It quickly became clear, though, that he had no interest in getting rid of his dad's stuff. He wanted to look at it, and touch it, and talk about it, but he didn't actually want to make any of it go away. He'd pick up an ancient, half-empty pack of gum, shake his head, and say, "The old man always chewed Doublemint." Or, about a T-shirt from the 1989 Teamsters picnic: "My dad wore this shirt all the time." By the time they found the old man's porn stash, tattered copies of *Hustler* and *Playboy* from the eighties that were full of soft-focus girls with fluffy hair and blue eye shadow, Caro had had enough. When Mike laughed and said, "Oh, we used to sneak into his closet to look at these, these are awesome," she threw down the stack of utility bills she was flipping through and said, "No. No, they're not. They're twenty years old and at least three different men have jerked off on them. Throw the damn things away."

"Oh, relax." Mike flipped to the letters section and started to read: "Dear Advice Lady, My new boyfriend makes me come like crazy."

Meanwhile, a car pulled into the driveway of 149 Div; the engine turned off and a heavy-hipped woman got out, carrying two plastic Wal-Mart bags and a big bag of dog food. Open space hadn't been a priority when Division Street was laid out, and the two sunken driveways were separated only by a scant patch of grass, browned and crisp from the summer heat. The woman was close enough for Caro to see the cartoon dogs printed on her scrubs, right down to the colorful flotilla of balloons each one held in its paw. She was definitely close enough to hear Mike reading.

Mike didn't notice her, or if he did notice, he didn't care. He kept going. The woman paused as if listening, and then turned purple. "Mike," Caro said. "Lower the volume, babe."

"I'm just getting to the good part," Mike said, but Caro couldn't stand it. First Patrick and that simpering Valentine kiss, now this unpleasant bitch in her balloon-puppy scrubs— *Leave me alone,* she wanted to scream, *quit looking at me, go away.* She reached out, grabbed the magazine from Mike's hands, and stuffed it into the trash bag.

He stared at her. "What the hell?"

"Turn around, asshole."

Mike did; just in time to see the woman's balloon-puppied back-side disappear through her front door. "Oh." He reached into the trash bag and pulled the magazine back out. "Whatever. Those people are the assholes."

She was trying to be patient and cool but the air felt like mustard gas in her lungs. "Yeah, sure, but maybe we could not openly antago-nize the neighbors who already hate us, huh?"

"Who cares?" Mike said. Not angry or confrontational, just gen-uinely puzzled. But Caro cared, that's who cared, because she'd lived with Margot and Mike hadn't. Margot, who occasionally woke her daughter up in the middle of the night to help her tie inflated plastic bags to the branches of the trees. All of the trees. Theirs. Everyone else's. Having the neighbors wake up to a nightgown-clad woman chanting and tying plastic bags to their sugar maples was not a great way to fly under the radar, and not flying under the radar was a great way to get official-looking people knocking on your door asking if they could please see the kitchen and how old is your daughter and where does she sleep.

The door of 149 Div slammed open and a man came out. He wore a work shirt from the local gas company and a pissed-off expres-sion. According to the shirt, his name was Herb.

"Hey," Herb called, taking the browned strip of lawn in two huge strides, not bothering with the front walk. "You talking dirty to my wife? You think that's funny, talking dirty to a woman who's just bringing in the groceries?"

Mike stood up, the magazine dangling limp from his hand. "We're having a private conversation on our private property. You got a problem with that?"

"Yeah. I got a big problem with that. I got a big problem with all you lowlifes."

"Mike," Caro touched his arm. "Let's go inside."

"Up all hours, drinking and yelling, with the TV blasting, playing god knows what. And you two pigs, never closing your goddamned shades—now you're talking dirty to my wife?" He pointed a finger at Mike. "I know about you. You and your scumbag brother. You ought to be in jail just like your old man."

Mike's jaw went hard and his fists clenched and Caro had to stop herself from taking a step back. "Don't talk about my dad," he said. "You didn't know my dad."

"I know he was a lowlife drunk, just like you." The sneering contempt in the man's face and voice was almost cartoonish. "And I know those poor people whose kid he killed are going to sue that house right out from under you, and I know the day you get evicted I'm going to be standing on my front porch singing 'God Bless America.'"

When you got kicked or punched, there was always a moment before the pain signals made it up to your brain when all you felt was the impact. And in the numbness of this particular impact, a numbness she knew as well as she knew her own face in the mirror, Caro thought: of course. Of course the house was in John Cusimano's name, and of course nobody had ever thought, the first or second or even third time he'd been arrested for drunk driving, that it might be a good idea to transfer it to somebody else. Because that wasn't the way the Cusimanos operated. If they'd lived in a floodplain they just would have let the house flood and flood, moved the TV upstairs, tacked plastic sheeting over the parts of the wall that rotted away.

Then the pain: she'd just painted the bedroom. Put new curtains up in the kitchen. In the distance she could hear the roar of the highway, somebody's music somewhere, a dog barking—maybe even 149 Div's own dog, locked away next door. She should have known. Nothing would ever be hers. Nowhere would ever be safe.

Mike dropped the magazine and it fluttered to the cracked concrete with a soft whispering sound. "Why don't you come on over?" His voice was calm and somehow that was scarier than rage would have been. "Come over here and we'll talk about it."

149 Div curled his lip, spat in the grass. But Caro saw a flicker in the man's eyes and knew he was afraid. "I got better things to do with my time than teach you a lesson," he said. "I'm a grown-assed man." Then he turned around, stomped back into his house, and slammed the door, leaving Mike and Caro standing together in the suddenly airless afternoon, surrounded by the litter of old clothes and magazines. After a long time—or maybe it just seemed like a long time—he turned to her. But he didn't have to say anything, because Caro knew.

Mike had gotten the letter the week before. He didn't have it anymore. He'd thrown it away as soon as he read it. "Look, drop it, there's nothing we can do," he said, then loaded up the ice chest and turned on the television.

While he worked his way through the cooler and flipped restlessly from channel to channel, Caro sat on the couch, chewing her nails, the smell of onions and ketchup from the burger she'd eaten drifting up from her fingers. The numbness had come and gone, the pain had come and gone, and now the race was on. When she'd lived with her mother the starting flag had always been pink eviction notices instead of lawyer letters but after that it was the same: be faster than the landlord, faster than the sheriff, faster than the nosy neighbor who tried to see past you when you opened the door. Panic and defeat nipping at her heels, worry riding high on her shoulders, grind, grind, grind and don't stop moving, because a half a step ahead, a quarter, a fraction of a sliver of a hair—whatever lead they'd had, she and Margot, it was never enough, they were always about to lose it.

But they'd never stopped. They'd never just sat and drank beer and let doom overtake them. Caro had run this race a thousand times, she'd been running it all her life. What was needed now was a plan. She was an adult and Mike was an adult and that was an advantage she hadn't always had; both of them were employed, however unsatisfactorily, and that was another. Mike's credit was a disaster (that truck, that goddamned truck, if she'd known him when he bought it she would have dragged him out of that dealership by his hair if she'd had to) but hers wasn't too bad, she had no assets but she didn't have much debt, either. They could get a new place, maybe. An apartment, a little house. Somewhere nicer than Division Street. No beer cooler in the living room, no dead woman's thirty-year-old pots and pans in the kitchen. No worn dish towels covered in decades of stains. When she was a kid—during one of the last good phases, when Margot could still drive a car to pick her up and keep track of reality long enough to remember that she had to do it—Caro had once been invited for dinner at a friend's house. The friend's face was hazy, but the kitchen where they'd eaten was crystal clear. White counters and white cupboards with red knobs that looked like candy, the dish towels printed with bright red cherries, the floor a clean black and white check. They'd eaten real macaroni and cheese from white ceramic plates with red edges. At Caro's house mac and cheese came from a box, and they rarely had milk or butter, even in the good phases, so they mixed the powder with water. She remembered the rubbery, cooling pasta swimming in runny orange water, the way the sauce soaked through the paper plates that were all they ever used, and resisted a shudder.

How many places, she thought, since she'd left Margot's house? How many new starts? Five, ten? She didn't count. It would just depress her. And always, always, trying to wedge herself into somebody else's life, occasionally a roommate, but usually a boyfriend. Time after time: finding room in the closet for her clothes, room in the bathroom for her makeup. She thought of clean, empty cupboards, shelves waiting to be papered. Thick, creamy sauce, golden brown bread crumbs. White ceramic with cheerful red trim.

Caro wanted that desperately. A *real* clean start this time, a place as much hers as anyone else's. Maybe more than one unsolvable problem could be dealt with here; surely Patrick would want to get out, too, to get his own place, and then they could all start over. The Great Apocalyptic Mistake could fade peacefully into the distance and they would never have to think about it again. Just her and Mike—stable, sane Mike, who maybe drank too much and wanted too little but who got up and went to work every day regardless, who asked nothing of her but clean laundry and love. No Patrick, with his horror movies and outdated metal, his sulks and silences, the wounded-puppy set of his shoulders; with his legs that always seemed to be in his own way, his eyebrows that laughed before the rest of his face, and those too-clever hazel eyes that saw things, always *saw* things—

All at once the panic was back, coming up behind her closer than it had in years. She jumped to her feet. "Get up, get up." She grabbed at Mike's hands. "If we're going to get drunk, let's go do it in a crowd like respectable people."

Mike's face was surly and already stupid with alcohol. "I'm happy here."

"Oh, come on." She smiled with mischief she didn't feel and pulled harder, his body a dead weight on the ends of her arms. "There's no food in the house anyway, and we've got to eat, right? We could go to Jack's."

"They deliver."

But Caro cajoled and flirted and eventually, grudgingly, he stood up and put on a clean shirt and they left. They drove to Jack's Bar and Sandwiches—or rather, she drove; he'd kept drinking as he dressed and was already too blurry to drive. The Bar part of Jack's was dreadful, with a boring jukebox and chronically broken toilets and the same half dozen drunks roosted on the same half dozen bar stools; the Sandwiches, though, weren't bad. Fat hoagies on warm soft bread served with fluorescent pepperoncini on the side. Mike and Caro had met there, and now every time they went in, Lecia, behind the bar, winked and smiled smugly at the two of them, as if any happiness they shared belonged partly to her, too. When in reality, all she'd done was say, *I don't care what people say, Mike's a good guy.* Later, in the parking lot, he'd told Caro that his dad was in jail. She hadn't cared. Lots of people were in jail. She hadn't even cared that the old man had killed someone. Lots of people were dead. Later that night they'd done it in the back of his truck, and after that he'd taken her home and they'd done it again. God, she'd been so drunk. She remembered feeling surprised at how good it was. She remembered how happy she'd been. The first time was always the best, with anyone.

That night, Mike had taught her the two-step, made her laugh. Tonight his anger was diffuse and formless and landed anywhere that would hold it. He munched it the same way he munched his chicken parm sandwich, grim and relentless. Fucking mozzarella on his sandwich, fucking bosses at work. Fucking jukebox playing fucking Warrant, fucking Great White (all those people in Rhode Island died at that show and somebody got rich and how many people paid for it, fucking corruption, it was everywhere).

"You're not mad about Great White. You're mad about the house," Caro finally said. She leaned across the table, put a hand on his. "Maybe it won't be so bad, though. Moving."

His shoulders slumped, and he picked at the cheese on his sandwich with one chewed, callused finger. He'd asked for provolone and hadn't gotten it. "Me and Patrick were born in that house. I mean, at the hospital, but whatever. We've lived there all our lives. I remember Patrick sitting in his high chair at the kitchen table. My mom died there, practically. You know?"

Gently, she said, "People are supposed to leave home. They're supposed to grow up and move out and have their own lives. We could do that. We could have our own place, that we chose together. Our own stuff that we bought together. Not me living with you in your dad's house. The two of us living in *our* house."

She could see him thinking about it, turning it over in his mind. "What about Patrick?"

"Patrick can get his own place."

Mike snorted. "Right."

"What? He's not an idiot."

"No, but he's got no damn common sense. You know what Dad used to say about him? All brains and no balls. Look what happened at work."

All brains and no balls. "What happened at work?"

"He quit, that's what happened. One of the other guys made some crack about our dad and five minutes later Patrick left his jack in the middle of the dog food aisle and walked out. Later he tried to spin some bullshit about being afraid the ceiling was going to collapse, but that was a crock and we both knew it. He didn't have the balls to work there anymore. Everybody looking at him, knowing what he did." Mike shook his head. "He can't live with himself, Caro. He can talk all he wants about logic and rational decisions, but the truth is that it's his fault Dad is in jail and he feels so guilty he can't stand it. He destroyed our family. He knows it, and everybody else knows it. I mean, look at him. Screwing around with a high school girl. I wouldn't be surprised if he's trying to get himself arrested, you know? Like, subconsciously."

Caro felt her brow furrow. The stuff about Patrick trying to get himself arrested, or the ceiling falling in, none of that was beyond belief, but she'd always gotten the impression that the Cusimano family had come predestroyed. That if it hadn't, Patrick would not have been faced with such a horrible choice, and John Cusimano would never have forced him to make it. Did Mike actually believe that what had happened to the old man was his brother's fault? Because if he did—if that blame was what dragged Patrick down—then why would Patrick even want to stay? Why wouldn't he want to escape, to save himself before it drowned him?

There was a heat behind her eyes that she associated with crying, but she wasn't crying. Focus, she told herself sternly. Patrick is not your problem.

"If we leave him alone, he'll kill himself or something. I'm the only reason he's still alive, anyway. Anyone else would have kicked his ass to the curb by now." But it wasn't exactly worry she heard in Mike's words, was it; he sounded calm and sure of himself and, so help her god, even a little smug. He looked at her. "You're cool with him staying, right? You and Patrick get along okay. He's not a bad guy, really. You can't count on him for shit, obviously, but once you know that, he's not a bad guy."

"Of course he's not," Caro said.

"You know, the more I think about this, the more I like it. We could get a dog. A real dog, not like that barky little shit next door. I used to kind of want a dog, when I was a kid." Mike squeezed her hand.

You could smile when you didn't feel like it. Caro was a waitress. She did it all the time. "Sure. I like dogs."

He grinned, hugely and electrically. "See, this is what I mean. Here I am, all pissed-off and mad at the world because shit is just about as bad as it can get, and then you come along and say something that makes it all right. You save me. All the time. You just save me." And at that, Caro's own smile settled in a little bit, and she pushed the hot-eyed feeling away. Maybe Patrick would want to escape, after all. Maybe he'd see this for what it was, an opportunity to clean up the mess, to walk away. She hoped he would. She hoped it would be okay. She hoped John Cusimano had never said that thing about all brains and no balls when his younger son could hear, because that wasn't the sort of thing you should hear your dad say about you. Margot had used to tell Caro sometimes that her life force was draining and disruptive. She would make her sit facing an outside wall for hours, to angle the forces out of the house, and of course when Caro got older she realized that the life force thing was bullshit but when you were young, you didn't know.

Back at the house (the house that would be nothing but a memory someday, all she had to do was wait) Caro went upstairs to take a shower. There was a knotted muscle in her back and she hoped the hot water would ease it. The finish was wearing off the bathtub and as she stood under the spray, looking down at the grayish-brown smear, she wondered how many women had stood there: Mike's girlfriends, Patrick's girlfriends, the old man's girlfriends—did he have girlfriends? And before all of them, Alice, Mike's mother. Alice Cusimano had been sharp-featured like Patrick, with the same guarded intelligence in her eyes. Caro herself looked like her father, or at least that's what Margot had told her. Margot had also told her there was a kingdom of gnomes that lived in the walls of their house, logging the location and weight and body temperature of the two women every time they touched a moving metal object (like a hinge or a can opener or a doorknob; thus Caro's habit, which Patrick had noticed, of pulling her sleeve down to cover her hand before she opened a cabinet or closed a door). Sometimes Margot would stand at the mirror, staring at her own reflection, and Caro would stand with her. *Is that me, Carrie?* she'd say. *Is that you? Are you sure? They could have switched us. It could be a trick.* The two of them would stand there for as long as it took. Sometimes it took hours.

Don't lie to me. You're not you. It's a trick. They're very tricky. You're not you.

In the shower, Caro pushed her face under the spray, closing her eyes tight against the heat and the water. Stop it, she told herself sternly. You're fine. You're you. You'll get a new place and Patrick will move out and everything will be okay, everything.

That muscle was torture.

"You okay?" Mike said, when she came into the bedroom with a towel wrapped around her. He was lying in bed, drinking a beer and watching the little television that sat on their dresser.

She put on a T-shirt and lay down next to him. "Just my back."

"Roll over, I'll rub it," he said, and lifted the shirt.

But Mike always rubbed too hard, so she just said, "No, it's okay." Her shirt stayed bunched above her waist. Mike picked up his beer from the nightstand, propped his head on his elbow, and balanced the can on her bare stomach. The metal aluminum ring was so cold it burned but she knew he wouldn't keep it there long.

"Let's get married," he said. Caro laughed. Mike didn't. "I'm totally serious. We should get married and have, like, ten kids."

"Ten?" The muscle throbbed. She didn't want even one kid, kids were small and vulnerable and you could hurt them without even meaning to. You could hurt them just by being who you were. You could hurt them with your *genes*, your very DNA.

Mike drained the beer, crumpled the can, and set it down on the nightstand. He rubbed the place on her tummy where it had just been. "At least ten. You'd look so awesome pregnant, with your big belly sticking out."

"No," she said.

"Okay," he said, misunderstanding. Probably not deliberately. He wasn't the type to deliberately misunderstand things. "One kid. To start with. Unless you have twins."

"I don't want kids."

"Everyone wants kids." Excitement danced in his eyes. He got like this sometimes: a shiny idea lodged in him like a fishhook, pulling him along. "Come on, it'll be like what you were talking about. Like how you were saying we should get our own place? We'll start our own family. And we can do— What's that thing that people do when they get married, when they tell people what presents they want?"

"Registering." That knot in her back, it was almost making her weak.

"Yeah. We can register. Patrick can be best man. Maybe your mom would come."

"No," she said again. Meaning not just *no, my mom can't come*—Mike knew almost nothing about her mother, and how could he since Caro had never told him—but also *no* to all of it.

But Mike was off through the water. "Sure she'd come. What mom wants to miss her daughter's wedding?" He laughed with delight. "You know what? Don't say anything else. I want to get a ring. I want to do this right."

"I don't want a ring."

"Now that, I definitely don't believe. Girls always say they don't want engagement rings when they totally do." He pinched her leg lightly. "This is the best idea I've ever had. We're getting engaged!"

Later, when he was asleep, she thought again of Alice Cusimano, lying in that same room and staring up at that same ceiling; while inside her womb, the seed that would become Mike or Patrick or cancer wriggled and grew and settled in. Had she felt her life hanging above her, seen the glint of its edge; when she looked at the cracked plaster, had her chest squeezed as tight as Caro's, had she ever opened her mouth to take a breath and found nothing there to breathe?

Sometimes Caro watched sitcoms on television where the entire twenty-three-minute plot began with some simple but potentially madcap misunderstanding. They drove her crazy. She wanted to grab the characters, shake them, yell at them to just stop moving for ten seconds and explain themselves, and everything would be fine. And yet, the next morning, when she lay in bed half-awake listening to Mike move around the room—he was scheduled for the early shift—she couldn't make herself wake the rest of the way up, sit him down, and explain that she didn't want to get married and have kids, maybe not ever and certainly not now. There was no question in her mind that she should do it. It just didn't seem possible.

And so, while he was in the shower, she thought: maybe he was so drunk last night that he won't remember. When he came back in, she pretended to be asleep. The bed dipped and rocked as he sat down on its edge to put his boots on. She could feel every tug, every push, every tightened knot. Her eyes squeezed tight. When she won the lottery she was going to buy one of those mattresses you could put a glass of wine on, and then jump up and down and the wine wouldn't spill.

Dressed, boots on, he lay back down next to her and kissed her neck. "I'm taking your car so Patrick can finish the garage. You work dinner tonight?"

I don't want to get married because the idea of not being able to leave scares me. Because schizophrenia might be genetic and I don't want to do to any other kid what was done to me. "Mm-hmm."

"Can you get a ride with Darcy? I might be too late to take you."

Also, I slept with your brother, and I don't know why, and I can't stop thinking about it. "Mm-hmm."

"I have to go to the mall," he said, and kissed her again. "To the jewelry store. Have a good day."

Right, hey. No fucking problem.

After she was sure he was gone, she got up, put on some shorts and a T-shirt, and made coffee. Patrick's bedroom was silent and that was good because Caro loathed herself. She couldn't even think about Mike's trip to the jewelry store without starting to feel anxious, so instead of thinking and feeling she went into the garage. Patrick hadn't finished sorting the old man's stuff and she and Mike hadn't done much to advance proceedings, but alone, she thought she could probably get the job done before she had to go to work. It was way easier to deal with somebody else's garbage than her own.

Most of what was in the boxes was junk like worn-out clothes and old magazines. No more porn, for which she was grateful. She worked quickly and steadily, making one box of things she thought the brothers might want to keep—like pictures or important-looking documents or the old pocket watch she found—and putting the rest into piles: clothes, papers, other. So they could just take a quick look, and make a decision. She tried not to think about the man whose

possessions she was sorting, about the stench and the girlie magazines and the cooler in the living room. About his son, who saw nothing wrong with any of it, and who drank too much, and who wanted
to marry her.

She was reading an article about Baja California in an ancient
fishing magazine when she heard a noise behind her and Patrick said,
"You shouldn't do that. It's not your mess."

Give it ten years, it might be. "I don't mind," she said.

There were a few moments of awkward silence during which
Caro found herself inexplicably wanting to cry. She went back to her
article but it was hard to read with him standing there. She didn't
care that much about Baja California to begin with.

"I'm going for a run," he finally said, and she said, "Yeah, sure."

She finished the last of the boxes, filled three of the empties with
the piles that she'd made, and put everything else into the back of
the truck. The woman from 149 Div came home again while she was
working; today her scrubs had rainbows on them. Caro lifted a hand
but the woman just marched into her house, eyes straight ahead. The
door slammed. The dog barked. The curtain flicked.

Caro looked at Patrick's car, parked in front of their house. The
windshield was covered with some kind of grime—dust, pollen, who
knew—and the tires were sinking into nests of dead leaves. Mike
and Patrick could scoff all they wanted, but Caro knew the kind of
trouble neighbors could cause when they took exception to the way
you lived. She found Patrick's keys on the table next to the front door,
buried under several layers of sedimentary junk. Unlocking his car
felt weird, like she was looking through his drawers. But he'd said the
cops could tow the car, he'd said he didn't care. And he'd managed
to drive it home, bad alignment or no. She could drive it twenty feet
into the garage.

The inside of the car was almost unbreathably hot. She rolled
down the window and it got a little better, but not much. Patrick

was not a tidy-car person. One cup holder held an ancient Zoney's fountain cup with a mangled, chewed-up straw—she could see the imprints of his teeth on the soft plastic—and an overdue phone bill sat on the passenger seat. Sliding the key into the ignition felt oddly intimate. The engine turned over without even a hiccup and instantly the car shook with pounding music. Caro smiled despite herself; Patrick's taste in music was hideous. She had nothing against metal but there was a time and a place for Megadeth, and the time was 1987 and the place was tenth-grade study hall.

Then again, revisiting high school seemed to be Patrick's thing these days. She shifted the car into gear and pulled forward, turned and backed up a few feet, then turned again and pulled into the garage.

There was nothing wrong with the alignment. The alignment was fine.

She closed the garage door from the outside and went back into the house through the front door. In the kitchen, the back door stood open, and when she looked out she saw Patrick lying on his back in the grass with his knees bent and one arm over his eyes. His face was an alarming shade of red and his chest was moving fast. His MP3 player lay in the grass next to him. One earbud was draped across his chest, the other had disappeared into the tall grass.

She opened the screen door, took a step outside. He looked even worse close-up, drenched in sweat with gray patches under his eyes. "Are you okay?"

He nodded. His eyes stayed closed and his throat moved convulsively. "Ran too hard."

The way he forced the words out, he didn't sound good. "You want water?" she asked, and he nodded again, so she went back into the house and got him a glass of water and a dishcloth she'd held under the faucet. She put the water down in the grass next to him and lay the dishcloth on his forehead. She was careful not to touch him.

He already looked better, but she sat down anyway. "I finished the garage," she said.

He nodded, but didn't speak. The grass beneath her was cool, the soil damp. Next door, the dog was barking. A soft breeze blew, tugging gently at her hair and her clothes and carrying away the smell of the neighbor's dog shit. Patrick had pulled his T-shirt up to cool himself off. He was too thin, she thought. Almost bony, compared to Mike. All that walking and running. Mike was a big guy, anyway, his high school muscle softened after ten years of too little exercise and too much beer, but still. Mike's bigness had always made her feel safe. Patrick was rangy. His stomach was flat, almost concave. His skin was so smooth that in the dark it seemed unreal, as your fingers ran over it searching for a mole or a scar or anything, like—

His eyes were open. Watching her. The manic color in his cheeks had faded, the heaving in his chest eased; the hazel eyes behind his long lashes were the color of deep water.

"Come upstairs with me," he said.

She wanted to. Her palms pressed against the grass behind her, to push herself up. She dug her fingers into the dirt. "Mike wants me to marry him."

Patrick stared at her for a moment and then looked up at the sky. He didn't say anything.

"Your car's fine, isn't it?" She didn't know she was going to say it until she did. "You're not driving anymore because you hit that deer."

His shoulders moved, a faint rolling motion she took to be a shrug. "Doesn't matter."

Her fingers curled in frustration. She felt the dirt jammed under her fingernails. "Yes," she said. "It matters. It matters that you can't keep enough of your shit together to drive a car and hold down a job and pay your goddamned phone bill. And then you ask me—you want—"

She stopped. She didn't know how to say it, how to tell him that he couldn't just hit a deer and give up driving. That he couldn't just give up. She could say the words but the words were no good, the words weren't enough and now she knew why she hadn't been able to talk to Mike the night before, because those words weren't enough, either. Next door, the dog barked. Those people, they complained about a parking space they didn't even use, and their damn dog barked around the clock. Not that you could keep a dog from barking if it wanted to bark but you could keep from leaving it in a crate all day, you could avoid getting a dog if you had the kind of life that would make a dog miserable. If anyone had a right to complain it was them, it was her, it was the dog. Patrick stared up at the clouds. Looking into his face she saw nothing. She wanted him to say something, anything; she wanted him to come alive, to ignite the way he had in her arms on the night of the Great Apocalyptic Mistake. She wanted him to ask her upstairs again. If he asked her again, she would go.

But he didn't ask. His face was cool and inert as a block of iron. He stood up and went inside and left her sitting alone in the grass under the clear blue sky, and the dog barked.

When Patrick rolled open the garage door for the first time since the police had taken the old man's car, it was another beautiful day, clear and mild with just a hint of breeze. The last time he'd seen the interior of the garage had been from inside, and what he'd seen that time was the bloody-fendered Buick. This time, all he saw was the garage. Dingy walls smeared with grease, a fluid stain on the concrete floor. His old bike. Three garbage bags full of empty beer cans. Those had belonged to the old man, who'd insisted that the city recycling program was some kind of racket, specifically designed to steal his four cents a pound or whatever he got paid at the recycling plant. On the far side of the garage were one two three four five six seven eight cardboard boxes, scattered around the basement door where Mike and Caro had dropped them. Not even Mike had been willing to step any farther into the space than absolutely necessary. For a moment, Patrick seriously considered just loading the boxes into Mike's truck and driving them to the dump, except that he'd have to actually drive the truck to get it there. Also, they'd talked about that last night, and Mike didn't want to do it.

"He's not dead," Mike had said. Caro wasn't there, which made it easier to have this conversation. After the fight they'd had on the porch her mere presence made Patrick feel like a surly teenager. "He might want some of that stuff someday."

Patrick had thought about the old man's collection of truck stop T-shirts *(Mustache rides five cents!)* but said nothing. If Mike wanted to believe the prison sentence was just a temporary setback, Patrick wasn't going to disabuse him of the notion. Now, standing in the garage, he pulled a box cutter out of his pocket, walked over to the first box—ignoring the shrill mental voice that cried, *Right here! This was where the fender was!*—and slashed it open. A fog of smell wafted up: mildew, beer, sweat, cigarette smoke. It smelled like the old man, like sitting next to him on the couch listening to him cry, *Holy god, I really did it now.* It smelled like court dates and neckties and endless messages left with the public defender's office, with only the occasional call back. Then there'd been the sentencing, and after that a long stretch of nothingness, a dead silence like the middle of a blizzard. Patrick remembered that being at work had started to feel— frightening. He remembered standing by the time clock, unable to catch his breath; he remembered looking down the long aisles in the warehouse and feeling like they would collapse if he tried to drive his jack down them. He remembered Frank DiCriscio joking that nobody was safe with a Cusimano behind the wheel and he remembered quitting, knowing that it was stupid and also knowing that he had no choice, that if he tried to spend another minute in that building it would kill him.

He'd actually thought the building wanted to kill him.

Fucking crazy.

He steeled himself, and reached into the box. Flannel shirt. He tossed it on the floor and reached again. Dirty athletic sock, worn at the cuff and dirty brown at the sole. He reached again. Underwear.

The first box, all clothes, went quickly, but the second box took longer. He spent almost an hour sorting through a stack of papers that contained, among other things, the old man's birth certificate and Patrick's own vaccination records. The long column of his mother's faded signatures brought a brief and intense flash of longing for her. The third box was mostly clothes, again, but at the bottom he found a battered shoe box full of photographs, discolored and sticking together. He didn't know who any of the people in the pictures were. If these people were important to the old man, where had they been during the trial? If they were important to Patrick's mom, where had they been while she was dying?

No point thinking about it now. He put the box in the keep pile and kept working, vaguely aware of the ebb and flow of engine noise as cars drove down Division Street. He was arm-deep in the fourth box (from the closet: ancient neckties, baseball caps, jackets with pockets holding half-empty packs of powdery cigarettes and lottery tickets and—Jesus—condoms) when one of the engines grew loud and close and didn't fade. He could hear bass pounding deep in his eardrums.

His heart was pounding, too. The noise cut off. He grabbed something out of the box, hardly aware of what it was but listening keenly for the sound of her boots on the concrete. When it came he glanced up, nonchalant, as if he wasn't rattled at all. "Doing another drive-by?" he said.

"I was in the neighborhood." Layla's black jeans looked like they'd been painted on and a crimson bra strap peeked out of the wide collar of her shirt, which was also not exactly what you'd call loose. He hadn't seen her since she'd dropped him off on Monday night. They hadn't had sex in reality but he'd had uncomfortable dreams that night where they'd done it in dozens of (usually public) places, like the high school bio lab and the food court in the mall. On Tuesday morning he'd woken up feeling like a creep. He'd been trying not to think of her ever since. Now that she was here, in the disturbingly apparent flesh, the creepy feeling was back and stronger than ever, and it brought along a nervousness that felt suspiciously like excitement.

"You should be in school," he said.

"My demoralization and indoctrination quotas have been met for the day, thanks." Her nose wrinkled. "What's that smell?"

"My life. What time is it?"

"Around one." She sat down next to him. "Updating your wardrobe?"

He looked at the thing he held, an ugly teal sport jacket. When the hell had his father ever needed a sport jacket? Into the Goodwill pile it went. "Clearing some space. The neighbors are complaining about us having cars, and parking them places."

"So you thought you'd try the garage. Thinking out of the box, huh?"

"Yeah, well. We haven't used it much lately."

There was a beat. "Right." Her eyes were moving in great, interested sweeps, taking in every detail of the windowless concrete room.

He hated the way he felt. He hated that he wasn't telling her to go away. "Welcome to the death garage. You want the tour?"

She didn't even blush. "Thanks, I think I've seen what there is to see." Reaching into the box, she pulled out a black leather belt with an elaborate chrome buckle. "Can I have this?" He shrugged. "Whose truck is that?"

"My brother's."

She strapped the belt around her waist, letting it dangle loose. It looked cool like that and he found himself remembering a moment in the car when she'd been on his lap and he'd slid his hands under her ass, lifting her, pulling her closer. "So your brother's a huge shiny truck guy," she said.

Mike's truck was, indeed, huge and shiny, with oversized tires and the largest risers legally allowed by the state of Pennsylvania. Patrick had hated driving it even before he hated driving. "I guess so."

"Is he compensating for a small penis?"

"His car payment is certainly enormous."

"Foolish, foolish humans."

"Look who's talking." He pointed toward her car, parked at the curb. "If that thing cost your parents less than thirty grand, I'm a flying monkey."

"If God didn't want me to drive a nice car, he wouldn't have made all those teenaged virgins buy my dad's purity rings," she said primly. "Sometimes they even have ceremonies where the dads put them on the girls' fingers. It's like a wedding, except ickier."

He looked at her hand. "I notice you're not wearing one."

"Not my scene," she said, with no small amount of smug satisfaction. "Whose stuff is all this, anyway?"

"Guess," he said, and she said, "That's what I thought. Won't he eventually need it?"

"That's why I'm going through it instead of just throwing it away."

"Does it make you sad?"

"It makes me wish I'd busted his ass more about cleaning up."

"Personally, I would have focused on the drunk driving," she said.

He stared at her, stunned. "You and your refreshing candor can fuck right off."

She didn't even flinch. "If you weren't already thinking it, you should have been. Hey, does the inside of your house smell as bad as the garage?"

She stood up and walked through the basement door. He scrambled to his feet, but he was too late, and she had a head start. He felt angry and nervous and like he wanted to grab her and—he didn't even know what he wanted to do. He'd never hit a girl and couldn't imagine himself doing it but a pressure was building inside him, a dull, base something that strained and pushed and wanted out. He made it through the basement door just in time to see her combat boots disappearing up the stairs. By the time he caught up to her, she was in the kitchen, opening and closing cupboards.

"You have five packages of ramen noodles and no spices," she reported.

"I didn't say you could come in."

"I didn't ask your permission." She closed the cupboard and opened the refrigerator. "Beer, apricot jam, ketchup. Why are you not dead of malnutrition?"

He reached across her to close the refrigerator—uncomfortably aware of the proximity of her breasts to his arm—but she was already gone, into the living room. "Oh, this is rich. All you eat is ramen, but you have digital cable? And why is there an ice chest in here?"

"For beer," Patrick said, and she laughed.

"In case you can't walk the ten feet to the fridge?" Layla opened the chest, peered inside, and then closed it again. "You're right. This is about as far from a wonderland as you can get. What's the upstairs like?"

He tried to grab her arm, but those combat boots of hers were nimble. He caught up to her in the doorway to Mike's old room, which had become the room where they threw shit, and then he did grab her arm. Harder than he meant to, probably. "That's enough," he said. "You're leaving."

"No, I'm not." Her arm moved, pushing against his gripping thumb, and suddenly he wasn't holding her anymore. "I'm helping you see things with new eyes." She scanned the room disinterestedly—the CDs and cheesecake posters left over from Mike's high school days, the fake tree Caro had made them buy last Christmas, the blanket tacked up over the window to block the light—then moved down the hall to Mike's current room, where she picked up one of the sequined throw pillows and made a puking noise. "Pretty. Whose room is this? Not yours."

"Mike and Caro's." The thing inside him was growing.

She turned to look at him. "That would be your brother, and the girl who cheated on him with you?"

"My brother," he said, taking the pillow away from her, "and his girlfriend."

She smiled. "Whatever you say." She started to walk around the room, picking things up and putting them down again. "Do you think they have anything interesting in here? Sex toys or porn or something?"

If Mike and Caro had any sex toys, he didn't want to see them. She opened the closet and examined Caro's clothes. Standing by and letting her do it felt like showing her a love letter. He knew he should stop her but he didn't seem to be able to. Layla pulled out a flowered sundress that Patrick had seen Caro wear a few times; it had a way of floating around her knees that he remembered. Layla held the dress up to her own body and made a face. "Yikes. I'm guessing no on the sex toys. What is she, a grade school teacher?"

"No," Patrick said. "She's a waitress."

Layla looked at the tag in the back of the dress and then tossed it on the bed. "Size eight. At least she's not anorexic." She moved on to the nightstand, opening the drawer and looking inside. "Birth control pills, lip balm, boring, boring, boring. Not even a bottle of lube." She pointed to a picture on top of the nightstand. Mike and Caro at the restaurant Christmas party, Caro wearing a Santa hat. "That's her?"

"You know it is."

She made a noncommittal noise and then drifted over to the dresser, where Caro's makeup was stuffed into a wicker basket. "Wicker." She shuddered, but started to dig through the jumble of bottles and tubes and plastic cases anyway. "Wicker is the anti-goth. If you line it with pink gingham, it's like goth kryptonite. This room looks like somebody bought the bed-in-a-bag sales display at Wal-Mart."

Patrick was pretty sure that was exactly what Caro had done. "Not everybody can afford thirty-thousand-dollar cars."

"I don't think you get to play the poor card with digital cable downstairs and that monstrosity parked in the driveway." Layla fished out a tube of lipstick, inspected the end, and uncapped it.

"Goddamn it," he said, and tried to take the tube from her, but she squirmed away from him onto the bed and kneeled in the middle of it. He could have grabbed for her but it would have been too easy to overbalance and end up with both of them on the bed. She smeared Caro's lipstick over her lips, a deep, strawberry pink that looked odd with her heavy eyeliner and black clothes.

"Get off there," he said, and she said, "Make me." He saw from her parted lips and the arch of her back and the way her hands lay against her thighs that she'd had exactly the same thought he'd had about what might happen if he grabbed for her. Her eyes dared him.

He could, he thought. He could grab for her.

Then she tossed him the lipstick, and slipped easily off the other side of the bed, next to the dresser. She picked up a bottle of Caro's perfume, sniffed the cap, and then nodded approvingly and sprayed her neck. "Not bad. Hey, close your eyes."

"If I do, will you get the hell out of here?" he said.

"Just do it."

He closed his eyes. He heard a rustle as she moved closer to him. Then he smelled lipstick and Caro's perfume, woodsy and sweet and totally unlike Layla's rich spiciness; felt breath on his neck, and before he could react a pair of warm, sticky lips pressed themselves under his ear. He could feel her body down the length of his—soft places and hard places—and his hands went to her hips, where they'd been wanting to go since the moment she'd put on the belt. Right at the top, where they started to swell out. She bit his earlobe. Layla's sharp teeth, Layla's quick tongue. But the smell in his nose was all Caro, not just her perfume but the smell of the room itself, laundry detergent and that carpet crap she used in here and sex.

"You want me to put on the sundress?" Layla whispered in his ear.

He kind of did. "Very funny." His voice sounded a little thick. The thing inside him broke the surface and he kissed her. Caro's lipstick felt smooth and satiny between their lips; Layla's mouth opened and her hands went to the back of his head. He felt like he wasn't behind the wheel anymore, somebody else was driving and he was just along for the ride. He opened his eyes enough to see Caro's sundress, lying where Layla had thrown it, and was filled with a perverse desire to throw Layla herself down on top of it. For a moment he was afraid he was going to.

Then she pulled back. "Show me your room," she said, and laced her fingers through his.

So he led her down the hall, blood rushing in his ears. When they got there, she said, "Now this feels like you."

"How's that," he said. Trying as hard as he could to take control again, to put on the brakes.

"Chaotic. It's good, though. I like chaos." She lay down on his bed and propped her boots up on the windowsill. Her shirt had pulled up slightly when she lay down; her fingers drummed impatiently against the exposed flesh, as if to call attention to it. She looked as though she had no intention of getting up, soon or ever, and her expression was so blatantly come-hither that part of him wanted to laugh.

But that baser place in his brain said, *Hey, why not.* There were thousands of reasons why not—he didn't have time, he didn't like her, she wasn't who he wanted, it could get him arrested—but in the end, Patrick went to her. Right there, on his rumpled, unmade bed. Right where he had been with Caro, right where she had left him. *I will not fuck this girl,* he told himself, over and over again. As he pulled her shirt the rest of the way off, as she reached behind her back and unhooked the red bra, he kept his eyes closed. He didn't want to know what she looked like naked, didn't want to be able to call up her image later, when he was alone. The feel of her nipples under his palms, the way she shivered as his fingers moved over her ribs—that was bad enough. But she didn't feel bad, her hands, her mouth. *I will not fuck this girl.* As she unzipped his jeans, as he let her. He didn't tell her to do that. She did it on her own. *I will not.* She lowered herself down and took him into her mouth and his thoughts turned to noise, a rushing torrent of pleasure and disgust. There was no telling where one feeling broke off and the other began. The monster that had been growing inside him since the moment he'd seen her—since before that, since the car, since the long night of dreams, since Caro—raged, but Layla herself was warm and smooth and disturbingly practiced. He could have said *stop* but he didn't, he said nothing at all, her hands ran over his hip bones and the only thing he said was in his mind, where she couldn't hear it.

I will not fuck this girl.

Sensation shot through him, cold like steel but good. Blankness behind his eyes, abstract shapes of no-color on the insides of his eyelids.

When the burst had subsided he felt her tongue trace the length of his torso, her warm body moving to nestle in the crook of his arm. Without opening his eyes he reached for the sheet and pulled it over the two of them. He'd just come in her mouth but he still didn't want to see her naked. That base part of his brain had gone quiet, the monster had vanished. Where the raging torrent had been was nothing but silence. It was like jerking off—the burst of pleasure, and then the quiet loneliness—but a thousand times worse. The arm around her was his arm and the hand at the end of it stroked her shoulder as if of its own accord. Miserably, he wondered how soon he could get her to leave.

"There," she said, and the self-satisfied tone in her voice reassured him. This girl was no innocent, no shy little thing. "How was that?"

"Good." The word was hard to get out. Nothing in him seemed to work the way it should.

"I thought you'd like it." Now that she was covered, he opened his eyes. All he could see of her was her scalp and her blond roots. He'd dated girls who spent their whole paychecks to get their hair that color, and Layla dyed hers black. Who was this girl, why was she in his life, why was he allowing her to be? "I guess I'm not too young after all, am I?"

The last of the anger faded and all that was left was guilt and the sudden awareness that when he'd been eighteen, Layla had been nine. "No," he said, "you're definitely too young."

She rolled over, folded her arms on his chest, and rested her chin on her hands, her black camera-lens eyes fixed on him. "Maybe you're too old. Have you ever considered that?"

"I consider that all the time."

"Chronology is irrelevant."

"I think the legal system feels differently."

"The legal system can eat me. As if the moment I turn eighteen, I'll magically become capable of reason, but in the meantime my poor little underage brain is nothing but pudding." She ran a hand over his chest. "I know what I want. As you may have noticed."

He sighed. "You have some very strange ideas about pillow talk, you know that?"

"And you have some very strange ideas about when it's appropriate to be miserable. You're acting like you just got a root canal instead of a blow job."

"Sorry," he said.

She traced his collarbone with one finger and even as the motion sent a shiver rippling up his spine, he noticed that her whole postcoital thing had come straight from Hollywood: the folded arms, the finger on the collarbone. Except it couldn't be postcoital because there'd been no coitus. Technically.

I did not fuck this girl, he told himself.

"Do you love her?" she asked.

"She's cool," he said, carefully.

"What about me?"

And under Layla's own cool, he thought he detected a hint of urgency, some deep neediness—the kind of neediness, maybe, that led screwed-up girls to give blow jobs to scumbags that were way too old for them. His arm tightened around her in reaction. He stroked her back, the bumps of her vertebrae under his fingers like stones at the bottom of a river. The caress made him feel like a liar but at least it didn't make him feel like a scumbag. "You're cool, too."

She made a face, crawled on top of him. "I'm cool? I just swallowed your goddamned sperm, and all you can say is that I'm cool?" Her eyebrows were up, amused but expectant. He could feel the softness of her chest against his even if he couldn't see it.

"Very cool," he said.

She leaned down so that their noses were almost touching, so that her hair fell in a curtain around their two faces, and kissed him. "And am I pretty?"

"Very pretty," he said, but the words rang hollow inside him. This was the sort of stupid game you played with a girlfriend, silliness born out of familiarity and satisfaction. Here it felt wrong, like sitting down to a fabulous meal and realizing all the food was plastic.

She kissed him again, lingering a little longer this time, pulling back just far enough at the end to let her tongue dart out like a snake's and lick his lower lip. When she spoke again her voice was barely a whisper. "Prettier than your brother's slut girlfriend?"

All of the play, false though it had been, vanished. "Be nice."

"You'd like that, wouldn't you?" she said. "You'd like me to be nice to you." Under the blankets she was moving against him in a way that would have been tantalizing if he hadn't suddenly wanted her and her Hollywood sex kitten act as far away from him as possible, and fortunately just then his phone rang.

He pushed her away—not looking—grabbed a T-shirt from the toppled pile of folded laundry on the floor, and threw it at her. "Put some clothes on," he said, as he stood up and zipped his jeans. "And be quiet, okay?"

The look she gave him could have started a forest fire three counties over. He ignored her and picked up his phone, which was on the floor next to the bed. "Hey, how's the garage coming?" Mike said, on the other end of it.

"It's coming," Patrick said. Leaving Layla behind, he carried the phone down to Mike and Caro's room, where the flowered dress still lay across the bed. The sight of it made him feel slimy and he hung it back in the closet, glad it wasn't something Caro wore often.

"Well, I'm at the restaurant. Caro and I both got sent home. We're going to stop by Mickey D's, you want anything?"

Patrick returned the lipstick to the basket, fixed the throw pillow, and looked around for anything else Layla had left out of place. "I just ate." He hadn't eaten since that morning, but he sure as hell wasn't hungry now. They wouldn't be long—ten minutes, maybe fifteen if he was lucky. He went back down the hall to his room.

Layla still lay on his bed. She was wearing the shirt he'd thrown at her. Black Sabbath. It was big on her, made her look young, which she was. He wanted her out.

"Get up," he said. "You've got to go."

She stared at him. Her lips pressed together. "First shut up, then get out? Thanks for the blow job, summarily dismissed?"

"It's not like that." Though it was, kind of. "That was my brother. They're on their way home." He held out a hand to help her up.

She didn't take it. "So what?"

"So, you've got to go." He found her shirt on the floor and handed it to her. She stared at it as if she'd never seen it before. Then she threw it at him.

"Hey," he said, startled.

She grabbed her boots from the floor. "You're lucky it wasn't one of these, asshole," she said, starting to pull them on. The sex kitten was gone. She looked furious. "Sit down, shut up, and suck your dick. Very enlightened. I do have feelings, you know. I'm not just some toy for you to play with."

Stung, Patrick stared at her. "Wait a minute. You're the one who—"

"What's next in the script?" Her face was so ferocious that Patrick took a step back, but her eyes were glassy with tears. "Am I supposed to cry and plead and beg? Please don't kick me out, please let me stay so you can fuck me? Is that the way this goes?"

"Whoa. Who said anything about—"

"Oh, never mind." She finished with her boots, pushed past him, and stormed downstairs. He went after her. Partially because he wanted to make sure she actually left, but mostly because he felt like a slimeball. Most of what she'd said had flown wild but a few of those arrows had hit home. And, Jesus, what if she went to the police? She was just crazy enough to do it, too—concoct some insane story, land him in jail. She was almost at her car before he caught her.

"Layla." He grabbed her arm.

She pulled away again, wheeled on him. "Go to hell," she spat.

He put up his hands, as if she had a gun. "Just wait a second."

Her cheeks were wet. Some of her hair was sticking to them. Her eyebrows were low and her lip was curled in anger. But she waited.

"I was a jerk," he said. "I'm sorry."

It was the best he could come up with. Her lips worked for a moment and she swallowed hard. "You are a jerk," she said, finally, and blew a contemptuous huff of air out of her nose. "At least kiss me good-bye, jerk."

So he did. Because he felt guilty he put more into it than he might have otherwise, and she responded in kind. When her hand drifted down to the front of his jeans and stroked him, he didn't stop her even though he knew he should have. She was a lunatic, and Mike and Caro were coming, and he didn't even really like her—

She pushed him back and gave him a look full of disdain. "Enjoy that hard-on, loser. Take it to your brother's girlfriend," she said, and he winced and felt like the loser she'd very correctly pegged him as, and then she was gone.

Not fifteen seconds later, Caro's tiny Civic rounded the corner at the other end of Division Street. By the time they pulled in he was kneeling on the garage floor, elbow-deep in a box as if he'd been hard at work this whole time, as if he had nothing to be ashamed of.

When he left the house for work that night, Mike and Caro were out. The beautiful day had turned into a chilly night and he was wearing a jacket for the first time in months. In the sky a cartoon moon drifted between clouds and he was glad he was walking. The dirty little secret of his postautomotive life was that he rarely minded walking, particularly at the time of night when he was likely to do it. It would be worse at four in the afternoon, when the grassless Ratchetsburg streets were packed with cars and fumes and noise. At midnight, though, it was a kind of bliss, even if every cop on the road did slow down as they passed him.

Work was Layla-free, for which he was grateful. Caro had told him once that the definition of insanity was expecting a different outcome from the same actions, and if that was the case, he was out of his ever-loving mind. Because part of him wanted Layla to come in. Part of him wanted to drive off somewhere in her big black car, to find some empty cornfield where the fat cartoon moon could reach through the windows and make her pale skin glow. He counted his drawer, restocked drink cups, made new coffee; and all the while that loathsome part of him was back in his bedroom reliving that blow job, standing on the street feeling her hand on his cock. That part of him wished he'd pulled the sheets away from her instead of covering her. The rest of him would have liked to hit that part of him with a brick until it stopped moving, and then dump the corpse in the nearest and deepest body of water.

It bothered him that Caro knew he'd been with her. He didn't feel like it should, but it did.

When he got home, the sun was rising sweetly and pinkly in the east, but for Patrick it was still the day before. He took a shower and lay down, but he was restless and his pillow was thick with Layla's smell and with Caro's, from the perfume Layla had put on. The combination was erotic and upsetting. After a while he got back up and put on his running clothes. On his way out of the house he heard noises coming from the garage and went down to see.

It wasn't Mike, it was Caro, sitting on a milk crate in her bare feet with her hair pulled back, reading a magazine. Surrounding her

were other piles, clothes and papers and all sorts of random things—
Patrick's dad's things. She was very beautiful: her ankles crossed in
front of her, the delicate sweep of her neck. The smell was strong in
the garage and she shouldn't have to do this, he thought, she shouldn't
have to be the one to clean up the old man's mess. He said something
to that effect and she blew him off, so he left her to it, and went for
his run.

It was only nine thirty but the streets of Ratchetsburg were loud
and hot and that sweet pink sun from the morning bounced hard
scalpels of light off the cars. He ran until he reached the railroad cut,
and then he turned left and ran along the tracks, feet sinking in the
gravel, dodging beer cans and empty packs of cigarettes and round
plastic chew containers. Patrick ran and he thought about Layla and
he ran and he thought about Caro and then Layla and Caro and
Mike and the old man and Layla and Caro and he started to feel like
something was chasing him, he started to feel like he had that day in
the warehouse when Frank DiCriscio had made that dumb joke, the
aisles had started to close in, and all the air had vanished. His lungs
and his calves burned. The bones in his feet felt like glass. But he ran
harder and harder, pushing himself past the point when he knew he
should stop, out of the railroad cut and through the park and back
down Main Street. He could not run fast enough, he could not run
far enough. By the time he pounded his way through the alley to collapse in the cool grass of the backyard, the world was gray around the
edges and his heart was beating so fast that he felt sure it would stop,
that whatever was so loathsome inside him had wrapped itself around
the muscle and was squeezing. Killing him at last.

Dimly he heard a rustle. Caro said, "Are you okay?"

No. No, he was not. But all he could say was "Ran too hard."

She brought him a glass of water. A cold wet rag appeared magically on his forehead, where it felt like heaven, and then she told him
that she'd finished the garage and that was almost better. To not have
to go back in there. To not have to smell that smell again. She sat

down in the grass next to him and that was best of all. That simple act, that she hadn't gone back into the house and left him to whatever happened. Gradually the thing around his heart loosened and the air came back into the world. When he opened his eyes the infinite sky made him dizzy and he closed them again.

His pulse slowed, his sweat dried. She stayed. The silence between them was not uncomfortable.

Finally he opened his eyes. He had pulled up his T-shirt and she was looking at his stomach. Which didn't matter, in and of itself. She might not even have been seeing him, her thoughts could have been a million miles away. What mattered was that he'd lost her, the night they'd slept together, what mattered was that ever since then her face had been a dead end and now it wasn't. Now her face was soft and her eyes were sad, the way her cola-colored hair fell on her shoulders was sad, her everything was sad. She looked up, straight into his eyes, and then he saw a way through and the way was her, the way was them. The afternoon opened like church doors, letting in an airy brightness in which everything seemed possible, even her. Even the two of them in his room together, even that safe place he'd found with her that he'd never had before or since. Why had they made everything so complicated when all that was necessary was this?

"Come upstairs with me." He did not know the words were there until he heard them come out of his mouth. For half a heartbeat he thought she was going to say yes but she didn't, she said something else entirely. And he saw in her face that she felt it, too, the awkwardness and the wrongness and the despair, and maybe seeing it there should have made him feel better but it didn't. Mike was a good guy. He wasn't smart but he was loyal. He would never cheat on Caro, he would never fantasize about being with somebody else in her bed, he would never let another girl put on her lipstick and suck him off. She deserved nothing less and Patrick could give her nothing more. The sky above him that had seemed so infinite just moments ago felt too hard and too close, as if it was sinking in on him, and Patrick found that he had nothing to say. Sitting there with her under the closed-in sky hurt him. Like sitting with his mother had hurt him, once he knew she was dying. When he'd wished that if she was going to die, she'd hurry up and get it over with. That it was fair to none of them, this waiting, this long, excruciating falling away.

He'd wanted that to be done then and he wanted this to be done now. He forced his aching body to its feet and turned away from her, and went into the house. He gave up.

SEVEN

The sun was shining when Verna woke up on Saturday but by night-fall the rain sounded like a thousand tiny boots dancing on the roof. The noise was as persistent as her anxious thoughts. Because she, Verna Elshere, had kissed a boy; had let a boy put his tongue in her mouth and his hands on her chest, had let him press against her with parts of his body that she couldn't quite bring herself to think about. The skies opened and wept and Verna could not keep her mind away from what had happened in Jared's basement. She was accustomed to feeling uncertain about many things but her own status as a good girl was not one of them. *I'm bad,* she would think. And then giggle, and then want to cry. Part of her thrilled at the thought, both of what they had done and that they had done it at all, but part of her wanted to throw herself at her father's feet, confess everything, and beg him to send her away to a nice single-sex Christian school.

She tried to talk to Layla on Sunday but Layla only said, "Christ, Verna, fuck the whole football team if you want to. Leave me alone. I'm sleeping."

Layla had been sleeping, or out, all weekend. She insisted that she was fine and on Monday she woke up and dressed without complaint. As they drove to school, water ran in thick, gooey rivulets down the windshield and lay in sheets on the roads. Even after a mad dash into the building—no early-morning cigarettes on the loading dock that day—Verna's feet still squelched in her boots. The halls and class-rooms smelled like wet hair and the floors were slick with tracked-in water. In the grim light, the building seemed unfamiliar, the way it did at night for school board meetings or open houses.

Verna never saw Jared before Art. She looked for him, but she never saw him.

By second period, the low-hanging clouds were the velvet gray of woodsmoke. As Verna sat in Algebra, the wind came up and the drizzle turned into a storm, water lashing violently at the windows. Verna watched the trees outside bending and trembling and won-dered idly if rain obeyed the laws of geometry, if the vector of each individual drop could be predicted and chained down by numbers. When she was a little girl and it rained like this, Mother had told her that God was driving the world through a car wash. When it thundered, that was God bowling. Little Verna wondered: did God also mow the lawn and fix the mailbox and stand at the washing machine turning His socks right side out? Who made God's wash-ing machine? Why didn't He just create socks that turned themselves right side out? Did God even wear socks? Did God get cold feet, or blisters, or step on pointy things if He went barefoot? Who made the pointy things that stuck in God's feet?

She remembered how much it had bothered her, this business of the feet.

On a trip to the bathroom she ran into Justinian. "Come for a walk with me," he said. She was bad now. Why not? The gray light, the empty halls, the squish of her feet in her boots; the day felt unreal and lawless anyway. Justinian pushed open the exit doors at the end of the second-floor hallway and they ducked through. He propped the door open with a paperback book. Outside, a ledge and two walls made a brick cave, smaller than the inside of Layla's car. Mostly the storm stayed outside but occasionally a gust of wind swept in and brought a spitting spray of rain with it.

Justinian lit a cigarette. Being caught outside the school building during class would be bad enough. Being caught smoking would be worse. Verna's heart rattled in her chest but she kept cool, watching the wind whip the trees into a froth. Part of her could not stop listening for footsteps on the other side of the door. The other part thought, I'm bad now.

Justinian offered her a cigarette, which she declined, and then—as if he could read her thoughts—asked how her date with Wolf-boy had gone.

"Layla told you?" she said, although she wasn't really surprised.

"Are you ashamed of it?"

No. Yes. "We saw *Fireblaze*," Verna said instead. "It was kind of gory."

He blew a smoke ring. "What about Wolf-boy?"

I should be in class, Verna thought. "Jared? He's nice."

"Are you going to have sex with him?"

"What?" Her face was suddenly hot.

"Sex." Justinian was flipping his Zippo open, striking it, flipping it closed. Verna could smell the butane.

She shook her head. "Layla might—she can—but—we're different."

"You're both human. You both have bodies and emotions and nervous systems."

"That's not what I meant."

He smiled. "I know it's not. But you and I both know you're capable of more than most people give you credit for. So maybe you should think about whether or not he's worthy. That's all I'm saying."

Verna could feel herself blushing. "Layla said sex wasn't important."

Justinian flicked ash off the edge of the loading dock. "Sex isn't

important. Who you have sex with is. It's a distinction Layla occasionally misses." Verna heard something in his voice that, while not
exactly an edge, was definitely well-chilled. She remembered the way
Layla had been that weekend, distant and surly. She'd stuffed envelopes for an hour and barely talked, much less complained.

"Are you two arguing?" she asked, feeling sort of presumptu-
ous. Because since when did Justinian talk to her about his problems?
Since when did Justinian even have problems?

"Is that what she said?"

"She didn't say anything. She just seemed—unhappy."

"A person can learn a lot from misery," Justinian said.

What a weird day. On her way back to class, Verna heard people
in the halls barking. She wondered if it was some sports thing, some
rallying cry she didn't know. Outside the storm surged and intensified. In gym class they played badminton indoors, and Calleigh, as
usual, aimed most of her volleys near, if not directly at, Verna. At one
point, when a birdie whizzed past Verna's nose, she thought she heard
the redhead call out, "Fetch, Fido!" but Verna was thoroughly oc-
cupied with keeping her expression neutral, and couldn't really listen.

By lunchtime, water poured down the courtyard steps. They ate
in the gym lobby. When the bell rang, Layla hung back while the
others went on. "You don't look so good," she said, as if Verna's eyes
were the ones ringed with purple-gray circles. "Are you feeling sick?"

"I'm fine."

The bell rang and people milled around them. Layla was looking
everywhere but at Verna. "Maybe you should call Mother. Ask her to
come get you."

Genuinely puzzled, Verna said, "But I'm fine."

Layla nodded. "Well, think about it. I'm on the third floor most
of the afternoon if you need me."

Somebody passing by barked, and then laughed. "Why would I
need you?"

"I don't know." Layla sounded oddly grim. "Just if you do."

.   .   .

When Verna walked into Biology, there was a dog collar sitting on her lab table. Pink leather studded with rhinestones. At first, Verna thought it was a mistake, that somebody had left it there accidentally. She picked it up. In her hand, it felt not unlike the bracelet that Justinian had given her.

The room was weirdly quiet. She looked up. Every expectant face and every glittering eye was trained on her. They were her classmates, her peers, her fellow students. The way they looked at her was cruel and faintly hungry.

She began to tremble.

Kyle Dobrowski wore the cruelest smile of all. He didn't look hungry; he looked full. Sated. Rocking back on his chair, his arms crossed across his chest. "Try it on, Venereal," he said. "Let's see if it fits."

Laughter hit her like a wave. She almost stumbled with the force of it but managed to keep her feet. Giving him her most scornful, most Layla look, she said, "What are you talking about?"

More laughter. Kyle's grin broadened. "Oh, you know what I'm talking about, Venereal. You know exactly what I'm talking about."

Just then, Mr. Guarda walked in. "Okay, people, take a look at page eighty," he said, and Verna sat down. Feeling them behind her, watching.

All through class, the collar lay on her desk. There seemed to be a virus going around because not a minute passed when Verna didn't hear a cough coming from somewhere in the room behind her, and all the coughs sounded like barks. She held back when the bell rang so everyone else could leave first. Dad always said it was better to have a drunk driver in front of you than behind you, where you couldn't see them coming. As Kyle passed her he picked the collar up, threw it onto her pile of books, and said, "Don't forget this, Venereal. You might need it later."

Laughter.

Of all the indignities Verna had suffered, this was the most baffling.

She picked up her books and the collar came with them. Later she would wonder why she hadn't thrown it away, but at the time she was sunk in mystification and it didn't occur to her. She carried it with her to Art.

Where Jared waited at their table. When she saw him, everything that had happened Friday night came back in a flood—his taste, his smell, the chime of the pinball machine—and she wanted to cry.

She put her books down, the collar lying on top of them like a dead snake. Jared gazed at it, and then at her. He shook his head, his expression disgusted. "For the record," he said. "Nobody really likes assholes like Kyle Dobrowski. They just don't stand up to him because they're afraid they'll be next."

She stared at him, a bottomless feeling in her stomach. "What are you talking about?" she said. She'd said the same thing to Kyle but this was different. This time she genuinely wanted to know.

Jared's face fell. "I thought you knew." He picked up a pencil and studied the drawing in front of him, as if he'd just noticed a line he wanted to change. "There's this website. HighSchoolAnonymous. It's sort of like if Facebook met 4chan, or eBaum, or something like that."

None of those words meant anything to Verna. She knew about Facebook, but she'd never seen it. Jared must have seen her blank look, because he said, "You're not missing anything. It's a message board, yeah? Except on 4chan or eBaum, the forum topics are, like, anime or television or hentai manga. On HSA, they're schools. There's one for Ratchetsburg. It's all gossip and crap and nobody ever uses their real name when they post. Remember last year, that cheerleader who said she'd been in a car wreck, but everybody said she was just covering up her nose job? That was on HSA."

"But what does that have to do with me?"

Jared looked pained. "There's a thread about you." He turned back to his drawing, his hair falling in front of his eyes. "It's—pretty bad. I mean, everything on HSA is horrible. The Internet brings out the worst in people. But they're saying—" He stopped, and then started again. "They're saying there's stuff going on with you and Justin Kemper." He pointed at the dog collar. "Somebody made some dumb joke about— Well, it doesn't matter. Everybody knows it's bullshit." He looked at her. "It is bullshit, isn't it?"

His voice sounded too casual and the sinkhole inside Verna deepened. "What?"

"You and Kemper."

"You just said it was. You said everybody knew that."

He had the grace to look ashamed, at least. "I was just asking. Sometimes things are a little bit true."

Verna was angry. "No. Nothing is a little bit true. Things are either true, or they're not."

Jared flinched. Doggedly, he said, "But there's nothing. You know. Physical."

She stared at him. "You think there is? Just because some stupid website said so?"

"No, of course not. But people say a lot of stuff about Kemper, your sister—sorry—that whole group. Weird stuff. Sort of culty stuff."

"What kind of stuff?"

Jared smiled a thin smile. "Vampire blood orgies."

"That's ridiculous. You know that's ridiculous."

"I'm just telling you what people say." Jared's lips were tight and his neck was pink. He was angry, too. Verna didn't understand what he had to be angry about. She was the one on the website. She was the one who had to sit and listen to him say these things. "Because they're saying it about you, too."

"So, what," Verna said, "we're not friends if people say things about me that aren't true?"

"That's not what I meant," Jared said. But then Mr. Chionchio started teaching, and whatever Jared was going to say, he couldn't. When class was over Verna got up and walked out without a word, without looking back. She threw the dog collar in the first trash can she passed.

At Eric's, they read the thread aloud from Justinian's laptop. "Tales from the Slut Side," Eric said, as deep and sonorous as the announcer on *Masterpiece Theatre*. "Little Whore on the Prairie, aka Venereal Elshere."

Layla, bubbly, curved her syllables upward to make everything sound like a question. "Venereal Elshere acts all holy but she's the sluttiest ho around? Justin Kemper does her doggy style? Her and her slut sister? He makes them wear dog collars? And they love it?" She looked at Justinian and batted her eyelashes. "Woof woof."

Everybody laughed. Verna, too. The words were horrible but the way Layla was reading it, it was funny. It reminded her of the time she'd had a tooth pulled and the dentist gave her nitrous oxide. She was laughing, but nothing was funny, and it hurt.

"Lahl," Justinian said, with great gravitas. The screen said *LOL*. Verna thought she was going to break in half, she was laughing so hard. Tears pricked at the backs of her eyes. "Let's buy her some Milk-Bones. I hear she loves sucking cock."

"Layla is a stuck-up whore?" Layla said. "And her sister is, too? I hope they and that lesbo? Criss Elkin? All catch AIDS? And die?"

"See, this shit right here, this is why I dropped out," Eric said.

"As long as it keeps that freak from shooting up the school," Justinian said, in his newscaster voice, "I don't care who he sticks his dick in. Bet those sluts like it though."

Everyone shouted: *"Lahl!"*

Eric's filthy room was full of laughter. Their warm bodies sur-

rounded her like a cocoon, and Layla held her hand. The voices and
the gestures made the website funny but the words on the screen
remained black and white and ugly.

> **little elshere looks like she'd be into a good solid assfuck**
> **ive got gym with her she smells like old tampons**
> **i fucked her and her sister last week**
> **so did my dog lol**

"Should we post something back?" Criss wondered, and Justinian
said, "Why bother. Let the sheep get it out of their system."

> **she's fucking jared woodburn 2. he told me all about it.**

Even Jared.

When she could, Verna snuck away. To the living room, which
was just as dismal as the rest of the apartment, but deserted. The
grimy coffee table was littered with gun magazines and there was a
pyramid of beer cans next to the couch. On the wall hung a painting
of an eagle in front of an American flag, a single tear running down
its feathered cheek. The knotted wood frame was coming apart at
one corner.

Verna could still hear the others. Her face and her gut both ached
from laughing and her throat burned from holding back tears. Verna
tried to listen for the voice of God in the room but there was nothing.
Just the hum of the refrigerator in the kitchen.

After a while, the bedroom door opened and Justinian emerged, a
cigarette in one hand and a lighter in the other. The noise from inside
surged and fell away as the door closed behind him. He saw Verna
sitting on the edge of the threadbare couch. "Hey," he said. "I was
going to go outside and smoke. You want to come?"

Verna looked at the nearly full coffee can of butts on the floor.
"You can't smoke in here?"

"I could, but then you'd smell like smoke and Layla would smell like smoke and your fascist parents would shit their collective pants. Come outside with me. You can sit upwind."

Verna nodded and they went through the sliding glass doors to the backyard, where three plastic lawn chairs sat water-spotted in the grass. All of the chairs were broken, so they sat on the edge of the small patch of concrete outside the door. It was a communal yard, shared by the entire complex. The different sections were divided by short lengths of plastic fence, just a few feet long, jutting into a broad field of grass. The people who lived in the apartments had tried to fit everything people normally kept in their yards into their tiny little squares of protected space: barbecue grills, potted plants, children's toys gone gray with exposure. As if, despite the wide lawn, only the spaces between the plastic fences were sacred. Verna felt sad, thinking about the cramped space people called their own here, about how important it was to them. Or maybe she just felt sad.

"You know it's only noise," Justinian said. "Everything they say. They're just ducks, quacking themselves to death. You're the lucky one."

Verna didn't feel particularly lucky.

"Think about it. They play football together, they go drinking afterward—but they don't care about each other. They're alone. You're not. You have us."

He put an arm around her. Surprised, grateful, she let him. He wasn't Jared; he was Layla's boyfriend. He felt safe. Somehow this afterthought of a place, this measly scrap of land divided up sixteen ways, felt safe, too. Kyle Dobrowski and Brad Anastero surely lived in one of the subdivisions across town, maybe Sunset Lake or Paradise Village. They had never been here. They would never come.

"You saw the message about Wolf-boy, I guess," Justinian said. She nodded.

He flicked his cigarette. "We knew about the website this morning. I told everyone to wait, to give him a chance to defend himself. What did he say?"

"He wanted to know if it was true about you and me." She looked at him. "He was mad."

"Well, sure. He spends all weekend telling everybody he had sex with you, then come Monday it turns out that the whole school thinks he's just one of many. Sort of takes away his bragging rights."

The more she thought about it, the more sense it made. Jared should have been angry for her, he should have been concerned. But he wasn't either of those things. He was just mad because the entire world knew he'd taken a slut to the movies. She'd let him touch her chest through her shirt, she'd let him press up against her. His—she could barely think the word—his erection.

Verna closed her eyes, leaned her head on Justinian's shoulder, and wished for all the world to go away. Except for him. Except for them. Except for right now.

They wrote *I love it Doggy Style* on her locker. Big, white, sloppy block-print letters. When she opened the louvered metal door, dozens of slips of paper cascaded out: penises and vulvas and other unidentifiable body parts doing other unidentifiable things. Printed on somebody's dad's color printer, cut so they'd fit through the vents. How long had the project taken? she wondered. How early had they woken up this morning to torture her this way?

She went to the principal's office, a few of the pictures tucked into her math book as evidence. Mr. Serhienko didn't want to see them. He told her to throw them away. He was a big man with florid cheeks and a vast wardrobe of gray suits and gray ties. His hair was gray, his eyebrows were gray, the light outside his office window was gray. "Go down to Facilities. You know where that is?" Verna didn't. He told her, and then said, "Mr. Paul should be down there. Ask him for some solvent, tell him you've got some graffiti on your locker. I'll write you a pass out of first period."

"Why?"

Mr. Serhienko stared at her. "To clean it off. You don't want to leave it there, do you?"

"But why should I have to clean it off? Shouldn't whoever wrote it have to clean it off?"

"Do you know who wrote it?"

Verna's fists clenched in frustration. "It has to be either Kyle Dobrowski or Brad Anastero. Calleigh Brinker, maybe."

"Maybe. So you don't know for sure." He looked exasperated. "Okay, fine. I'll have a word with them. But meanwhile, Mr. Paul has his own job to do. If you want your locker clean, I'm afraid you're going to have to do it yourself."

Fuming, Verna went down to Facilities and got the solvent, which smelled sickeningly of lemon. It took the paint off, but slowly. She had lots of time to think. Lots of time to wonder what kind of weird world she'd found herself in, where someone else wrote obscenities on her locker and she missed class to clean it off. Solvent parching her hands, making her skin feel burned. As if it were a punishment. As if she'd brought this on herself.

At lunch, she told the others what Mr. Serhienko had said, and they merely shook their heads. Yes, this was what they'd expected. "He won't help you. He's one of them," Justinian said. "Let us take care of it."

"And don't let those psychos catch you alone," Layla said, and Verna remembered what they'd done to her hair. She began to regret going to Mr. Serhienko. She began to hope he wouldn't say anything to Kyle or Calleigh, after all.

On her way up to Bio, she dawdled as long as she could, and that was probably why she ran into Jared. Or maybe he was waiting for her. "I'm sorry about yesterday," he said, before she could say anything. "Are we friends again?"

"Not if you're telling people lies about me," she said.

He stared. "What?"

"Lies." Had he been planning this all along, all the way back to the angel wings? "I never did those things you're saying. And anything I did do, I only did because—because—"

She couldn't finish because she didn't know why she'd done those things. He wasn't who she'd thought he was. She wasn't who she'd thought she was. Jared said, "Verna, hang on," but she couldn't hang on, she couldn't look at him. She fled up the second-floor staircase and ducked into the first bathroom she saw.

The floors were teal, the stalls bubble gum pink. She ducked into one, latched it behind her, and waited until the urge to cry had mostly passed. Then she came out and splashed water on her face.

"Oh, look," a voice cooed behind her. "It's Venereal Elshere."

The back of Verna's neck prickled. She turned around.

Calleigh. Three others. One from gym class; the remaining two were strangers.

"I have to go to class," Verna said.

Calleigh smiled. Like Kyle, she had a beautiful smile. "No, snitch. You don't have to go anywhere."

At first, Verna thought it was just Bio, except in the second-floor girls' bathroom. She thought that if she just kept repeating *No, no, no,* that they'd eventually get bored and go away or a hall monitor would come. Something.

Nobody came. No students. No hall monitors. The four older girls drew in, closer and closer. The door was miles away.

It made Verna's ears hurt, the things they said. Did Kemper do Verna and Layla at the same time; did he make them do each other; did they take it from his dog, they'd heard he had a big old Great Dane, how did that feel. What about Criss, the fat little carpet muncher. Had she taken a bite out of that tuna fish sandwich. How many cocks could she fit in her mouth at once. They heard she was an expert on blow jobs. Maybe she could give them a lesson.

By the time Calleigh brought out the banana, Verna was crying, from fear and humiliation. Not hard, not sobbing, but the tears were there. And Calleigh gave her that sweet, sweet smile, and held the banana out.

"Here, honey," she said. "Show us how you do it and you can go."

"We want lessons."

"We're not cheap sluts like you who give it up to everyone who asks."

"Show us, Venereal."

Verna looked at the banana. "I can't," she whispered.

Calleigh began to wave the fruit in the air. Back and forth, as if she were teasing a dog with a bone. "Suck it. Now. Or we'll beat the shit out of you."

No, Verna thought, dimly; they wouldn't. These were popular girls, respectable girls. Volleyball-team-starter girls. Honor Society, Homecoming Court girls. Not the kind who tore at each other's hair in the stairwells. This was all a joke, an impossibly cruel joke. "No," she said.

Something heavy—a book—hit the back of Verna's skull, and she felt her knees hit the tile floor.

More books. On her legs, her back, her arms. Everywhere but her face. When Verna cried out, they told her to shut up. On and on and on it went. Verna had never been hit in her life. Reduced to a writhing thing on a bathroom floor, flailing and reaching and finding only cruelty—had she thought the door was miles away? It was light-years away. Galaxies. She could barely see it through her stinging eyes.

She had always wondered how the martyrs bore their flaying and breaking and stoning and now she knew. They bore it because they had no choice. Verna bore hers as long as she could. After an eternity of pain, she let them pull her to her knees. They held up their phones as Verna, sobbing and shuddering, took the banana from somebody's outstretched hand and, shakily, put the stubby end of it into her mouth like a Popsicle. It tasted bitter and unclean.

"Not like that," Calleigh said. "Like you mean it."

Verna didn't know what they wanted. Calleigh grabbed her wrist and forced the banana in and out of her mouth. "Like that."

Verna tried. She wanted them to go away. She wanted this to be over.

"Jesus Christ, don't you know anything?" Calleigh grabbed Verna's hair, pulled her head back.

"Careful," one of the girls with phones said. "Don't get in the shot."

But Verna's face, yes, that they wanted. All she could see were the unblinking black eyes of the camera lenses on her.

"Like this, slut," Calleigh said, and her strong hands forced the banana deep into Verna's mouth. Farther. Into her throat. The rough end scraped the back of her throat but Calleigh kept pushing. Verna started to gag and still she pushed. Deep, deep, the horrid bitter taste of banana peel in her mouth and nose, the fibrous peel under her teeth as she bit down, she couldn't help it, she was choking. The girls laughed.

"All right," Calleigh said, "that's enough."

In the terrible soft silence of her bedroom and the terrible soft silence of her mind, time bled. The quiet was pressure in her ears like water, like the bottom of the lake at church camp, weeds brushing her legs and soft muck sucking her toes. The murky water, the brown light. The taste of lake water. Sometimes another kid dared you, said, *let's see who can hold their breath longest*, and so down you went to the bottom and your lungs cramped with the need to breathe and finally you pushed up toward the sun and the surface of the water broke into glinting shards of summer daylight and you laughed, laughed with the relief of the air and the light.

All Verna could taste was banana. When she inhaled she smelled banana. There was no *up*, no relief to be had.

For a while, Layla was there, lying next to her on the bed and stroking her hair. Whispering that everything would be okay, that it was over, that she was safe. Verna could not believe her and could not respond.

At dinnertime, without her, Verna's family talked. Down the hall, the dining room light stopping short of where she crouched at her cracked-open door, she listened.

"Poor thing," Mother said, "when I went to pick her up in the nurse's office, she was just green," and Dad said, "Must be a bug. Is it going around, Layla?"

"Oh, yeah. It's going around, all right. The whole girls' volleyball team is sick."

"That's awful."

"They deserve it."

The faint clink of silverware on china, like a wind chime three houses away. "You know, Layla, high school—your whole life, really—will be exactly as difficult as you make it. I was pregnant in high school. How easy do you think that was?"

"Less easy than getting an abortion would have been, I bet."

"God wanted us to have you, Layla."

"In His infinite wisdom, huh?"

Mother said, "His works are perfect, and all His ways are just. My point is, if you put sweetness out, you'll get sweetness back."

"Exactly what kind of fantasy land do you live in?"

"The same one you used to live in," Dad said. "The one where God helps us see the good in the world instead of only the ugliness."

"There's a fuckload more ugliness."

"Layla, language!" But Mother's protests were halfhearted, without conviction.

"You see what you look for, Layla," Dad said. "When Toby first started coming to Worship Group, he used to tell me how jealous he was of you girls. Because you grew up in a world full of the brightness of God and he was only just now starting to experience it. Now listen to the way you talk, the contempt you have for everything. The cynicism. Toby fights so hard to find just a little bit of that brightness, and you seem determined to drown every last bit of it."

"So adopt Toby." There was the screech of a chair being pushed back.

"Go ahead," Dad said. "Leave. I'm getting tired of trying with you, Layla."

Alone in her bedroom, Verna was Bathsheba. She was the Whore of Babylon. She was all four of the Horsemen of the Apocalypse, she was Salome, she was the Beast, she was the apple. She was one of the nameless children who died in Sodom when fire and brimstone rained down from the sky.

EIGHT

Caro worked that night and for once she was glad. To put up her hair and wear earrings and stand in Gary's nice clean white-tablecloth restaurant as if she belonged there, as if her life was as tidy and careful as the space around her. She had a table that night, two couples eating together: one ordinary and the other beautiful, unrumpled, effortless, and expensive. The man, particularly, or maybe their kind of good grooming just stood out more on a man. His hair was cut as well as his jeans, and when Caro took their drink order she smelled interesting cologne that he clearly hadn't bought on special at the drugstore. He and his wife—she had a big fat diamond on her ring finger— were both in their thirties, with about ten years on Caro, and Caro could not help thinking that she did not expect the next ten years to treat her as kindly as the last ten had clearly treated them. When the man ordered his cranberry and soda he looked straight into her eyes, friendly and warm with just a hint of a smile. The part of her brain that kept track of such things found him extremely attractive but the rest of her merely made a note and moved on. Because the beautiful man had a beautiful wife and no doubt their life together was beautiful, too. A magically silent dishwasher and someone to fill it, real art on the walls, vacations to islands where all the signs were in French. She imagined them lounging about in thick white bathrobes, like people in hotel advertisements, drinking Italian coffee and reading smart books. Classics and current events and biographies of major political figures throughout history. Somewhere, they probably had beautiful well-behaved children whose noses never ran.

He ordered the roasted beet salad and the grilled mahimahi. Fancy but earthy. The others ordered the usual stuff, crab cakes and stuffed sole and lobster ravioli. When she brought their apps the beautiful man was saying, "You don't have to use the money on a car or a vacation. You could start a foundation in his memory, or a scholarship. I can put you in touch with my accountant, if you want."

"But if a car or a vacation would relax you, don't feel bad about that," his wife said. Unlike her husband, she did not look at Caro at all.

"Won't be much money, after the lawyers take their cut," the plain man said.

Later, when she brought their entrees, the beautiful man gave her the same warm look again, the eye contact, the half smile. It felt like a touch on the back of her hand. A waitstaff basic: make people feel important, make them feel noticed. At one of Caro's many schools she'd been sent to see a counselor. (She'd been getting into fights; utterly unlike her, looking back, but Margot was in a bad state then and Caro hadn't been sleeping much.) The counselor, a fat man who smelled like cigarettes, had given her that same look. So sincere, so earnest.

So, Carolyn. What would you like to talk about today?

Nothing. She would like to talk about nothing. That's what she'd said, over and over. The counselor had seemed about to give up when Margot decided that they needed to live near running water, and with the crumbling house by the creek came a new school district and she'd never seen the counselor again. Maybe the beautiful guy was a shrink. Would she go to him to get her head shrunk? Would she lie on a couch in his office and tell him everything? She brought him another cranberry and soda, and again, his look felt like a caress.

She got a text message from Mike—*are u alurgic to nickle?*—and wrote back, *no idea why?* even though she knew exactly why.

No reason ☺ *luv u.*

Caro hesitated, and then wrote, *<3 you too.* It looked like an algebra equation.

She filled water glasses. The beautiful man's wife never checked her hair or the collar of her blouse. Her husband would not leave his phone number on the bill. Nothing that touched this woman would dare to be less than perfect. Holding a napkin to the base of the pitcher to keep condensation from dripping onto his clothes, Caro imagined herself taking the perfect woman's place, sipping fair-trade coffee in her well-appointed kitchen and admiring the landscaping outside. Later, applying expensive makeup at a lovingly lit vanity table, one of those sticks-in-a-jar air fresheners nearby, exuding some woodsy, sophisticated odor—sandalwood, cypress. She could feel the carpet under her feet. She could feel the plush of the robe against her skin. She could hear it. The silence, the peace.

The vividness of the fantasy scared her. What was wrong with her? Was she just killing time, or was this the first sign of her own brain chemistry turning against her? Daydreamed rich-lady life today, warring gnomes in the wall tomorrow? What if she married Mike and then two years from now, three, five, she woke him up in the middle of the night to beg him over and over for reassurance that they were each their very own selves, to show him the eyes she'd carved into the palms of her hands? Would he say, *Hey, babe, no big deal,* and offer her a beer?

Caro thought of the day she had come home from work to find that Margot had removed every doorknob in the house. It had been winter; the Christmas decorations were still up in town, but they had that sad January nothing-to-celebrate feeling, and the cold wind howled through the holes in the doors.

Terminal, Margot had said. *Terminal collateral. Cat herd. Capture cat herd.*

Caro had stood in the living room, listening to the howl of the snow and the word salad coming out of her mother's mouth, and she'd realized that if she stayed in that house even one more night, it would kill her. Her heart might be beating but she'd be dead inside; a life-support system, one of those hospital machines that went *blip-blip-blip,* marking off the moments not of her own life but of Margot's. She had turned around, right then, and walked out the door. She had called the police from a rest area two hours away and told them that there was a woman in a house who could not take care of herself, and then she had hung up.

If she married Mike. If, god forbid, they had a kid. If she went crazy. There would be hard decisions to be made. Would Mike be able to make them? Would he make them well? Would he leave her the way she had left her mother?

As Caro cleared their dessert, the two couples were deep in conversation and she tried to remain invisible, to not interrupt. The beautiful woman was saying, "She's just incredibly frustrating right now, you have no idea."

"You're doing the best you can," the normal-looking wife said.

"I just tell myself, God has a plan for her," the beautiful man said, touching his wife's hand. "There's a reason we're all going through this."

Caro ran the crumb sweeper over the tablecloth, careful to keep her face pleasant.

"It's Verna that really has me worried," his wife said. "She's a sweet girl, but she's not exactly what you'd call strong-willed."

"Yes." The beautiful man sighed. "That's a problem."

It should not have made her feel better to know that the beautiful couple had unbeautiful problems with their children, but it did. Caro's mood lifted and she could see the crow's-feet at the corners of the woman's eyes, the man's knobby Adam's apple. After she brought the check, Caro watched from across the room as he pulled out an expensive-looking mobile phone and bent over it, pulling up the calculator to figure the exact tip. When she picked up the check, she saw that he'd rounded down a few dollars.

Caro wondered if God had a plan for cheap tippers. She hoped this cheap tipper's daughters were blowing speed freaks in the park. She hoped God's plan for them included growing up to be tip-starved waitresses, that he would pay back every cent he'd stiffed her in bail money and STD treatments.

After close, her car wouldn't start. The only person left was Gary, who rolled his eyes and said, "Again?" but still pulled his SUV nose to nose with her Civic in the parking lot and gave her a jump. Mike had told her that it took five minutes or so with both cars running for a jump to take. Standing there in the crisp fall air, surrounded by car exhaust, Caro said, "Hey, Gary, you ever been married?"

"Once."

"You like it?"

He laughed. "You make it sound like a restaurant. Marriage isn't a place you go or a thing you do. It's a thing you are. There's some people it works for and some people it doesn't."

"Which are you?"

"I'm a damn good chef, is what I am." They laughed again, together this time. Caro liked Gary. She was glad he hadn't wanted to sleep with her.

Picking at the edge of a burn on his finger, he said, "This about Mike?"

His tone was neutral, noninvasive. She shrugged.

"You want to hear something funny? Small town. I knew his mom."

"You did?" Caro's interest was piqued.

"Allie Gensler. We waited tables together at Eat'n Park back in high school. Sharp girl. I always liked Allie." He smiled a wry smile. "Damn, I'm old."

"Did you know his dad?"

He shook his head. "Just from him coming in to see her. They went to Ratchetsburg, I went to St. Joe's. He seemed okay. People aren't their parents, Caro."

"Believe me, I'm aware." She waited for him to say something else. When he didn't, she smiled and said, "Any other sage advice?"

"Get a new battery."

"Give me a raise."

He grinned. "Put it on your wedding registry."

Carefully, she said, "Not so sure about that." The words were hard to push past her tongue.

"You're a sharp girl, too. You'll figure it out," he said, and then he told her he'd see her tomorrow, and she thanked him for the jump.

There were hard decisions to be made. There would be more in the future. She did not think Mike Cusimano was capable of making them. She wasn't sure either brother was. The one Patrick had made had nearly broken him; or maybe it had, maybe he would fall apart with a touch.

Caro drove to the all-night discount grocery store. She had no list in mind; she just wanted to go somewhere public, with music playing. Somewhere other than the house. But once she got there, she realized that she needed to keep her car running for another twenty minutes, or the battery would die again. Two weeks earlier she might have gone to Zoney's but that was out of the question now, she didn't trust herself.

So she sat in her running car, under the dingy lights of the parking lot, and thought about the beautiful man and his beautiful wife. She wondered if they and their two messed-up daughters were tucked safely into bed. She hoped the daughters weren't blowing speed freaks in the park after all. Through the open window she heard the whistle and rush of a freight train heading west through the cut. If there was a lonelier sound than that, she didn't know what it was. A tired-looking woman pushed a full shopping cart through the parking lot, her steps heavy, her body swaying with each one. Caro sat in her car and let it run. Mike was at home, with the ring. She had nowhere to go.

NINE

Mike dropped by Zoney's around dawn on his way to work, smiling like a jackass. He showed Patrick a tiny velvet box containing a ring with a minuscule diamond, a heart worked into the yellow metal. The ring was a godawful cheap-looking thing. It wasn't Caro's style but Patrick thought she'd probably take it anyway. She had no reason not to, if you didn't consider having slept with him a reason not to. And as reasons went, sleeping with him didn't seem to rank. Mike and Caro would get married. She would get pregnant and shrewish. A year from now, he'd be bouncing their shit-smelling baby on his avuncular knee, looking at Caro's double chin and wondering what he'd ever seen in her. Mike would drag him out to Jack's and bitch about his screechy wife and bit by bit, Patrick would lose her: the smell of her hair, the broken glass of her laugh, the quick, stunning creature she'd actually been.

Or he could move to Oklahoma, join the rodeo circuit, and get stomped by a bull.

He went home. Fell asleep. Woke up just after six to a terrifying clatter from the floor next to his bed and thought, I have got to change that damn ringtone. It was Layla. He'd given her his number that night in Pittsburgh but she'd never called him before. Which was weird, because he'd gotten the distinct impression that people her age were born with their mobile phones permanently implanted in their skulls.

And sure enough, the first thing she said was "Why doesn't your phone accept texts?"

"Because texts cost money."

"So get unlimited."

"Yeah, my mom and dad can pay for it."

"Oh, please don't be a jerk." She had the nerve to sound aggrieved. "So I got a little psycho last time. I'm sorry, okay? I'm a teenaged girl. I'm supposed to be mercurial and fucked-up. You're fucked-up, too, you know."

True enough. "What's your point?"

"My point is, let's be fucked-up together."

He sighed. "Enough bullshit, Layla."

"No bullshit," she said quickly. "Just a date. We'll see a movie. Eat some popcorn."

He didn't say anything.

"Please," she said, and then added with a not-so-convincing hint of sass, "If you're nice, I might let you get to second base afterward."

Patrick looked at the clock. Mike would be home by ten. Mike and his little velvet box. "Second, huh?"

"If you're nice."

"Pick me up at nine," he said.

He took a shower and got dressed, shaved and used some of Mike's cologne just like the date was real. He didn't stop to think about what he was doing. When he'd left for work the night before he'd heard Mike and Caro together upstairs, just like he always did. They didn't care that he could hear them. She didn't care, not about that or the way she'd looked at him in the backyard or the things they'd done together that night in his room. He didn't want to care, either.

Layla was a few minutes early. The light was nearly gone. In the mall parking lot, outside the movie theater, they sat for a minute. A few aisles over, a crowd of young people—around her age—tumbled out of a car like puppies. Patrick watched them laugh and lurch their way toward the theater and hated those kids, all the kids. The kids who luxuriated in their futures, who wanted for nothing, who had the time and energy to play games with people. Kids like Layla.

But next to him, she stared at the disappearing gang as if she felt the same way he did. Her physical presence intruded further and further into his awareness. He felt as much as saw the silhouette of her lips, the way she reached inside the wide neck of her sweater to scratch the back of her shoulder. The way her skirt rode up on her fishnet-covered thighs. When they got out of the car, the first thing she did was tug the skirt's hem down, which only made him want to pull it up again.

"So, this movie—" she said.

"Fuck the movie," Patrick said, and kissed her. He was taller than she was and he was faintly aware that the pressure of his mouth on hers was forcing her head back, that she had to clutch him to keep from stumbling when he pushed his tongue between her lips. He didn't care about that, either.

"Careful," she said, sounding a little stunned, when he let her go. "I might almost start to think you like me."

The kids were inside now. Nobody else was around. A sturdy breeze blew across the mall parking lot; the arc lights were on and each lamp had attracted a halo of nearly invisible insects, swirling like raindrops that had forgotten which way was down. Not a problem Patrick had. He knew which way was down. "Let's get out of here," he said.

She looked toward the mall and chewed her lip. "There's a place in the woods. My friend's grandfather owns it, but he's in a nursing home. Nobody ever goes there but us."

"Good," he said. "Let's go."

Layla drove them east, out of town. Eventually she turned onto an unmarked road barely wide enough for the car. Branches scratched at the windows and roof. When she finally stopped the car and they got out, he half-expected to see a bloody hook hanging from the bumper, like the urban legend. She'd been right; the place was deserted. He'd been picturing a hunting cabin, but he didn't see anything like that. Layla retrieved a six-pack from the trunk—bottles, not cans—and took a few steps into the undergrowth, where there was a kind of trail.

"Come on," she said. "There's a clearing."

He boosted himself up onto her hood. "I'm fine here. Give me one of those."

"But—" She stopped. "What the hell, you're right." She came back, forest detritus crunching beneath her boots, put the sixer down on the hood, and leaned on the car next to him. "We just always go to the clearing, that's all."

"We?" He cracked two bottles open with the opener on his key chain. The engine was ticking and the beer was warm and bitter. It was some fancy kind he'd never had before. He would have preferred a Coors, but beer was beer.

"My friends and I."

"Yeah, I bet," he said, and laughed. It sounded genuine enough but inside he felt as dry and crackly as the forest floor. "I bet you all drive out here in your expensive clothes and your expensive cars and then sit around and recite poetry about how much your lives all suck, right?"

"Maybe our lives do suck," she said. "You don't know."

"I know mine does."

She blew air out her nostrils. It might have been a laugh. "Well, then, Patrick. Tell us how you really feel."

Which was an expression that he hated, because when people said that—*tell us how you really feel*—what they meant was *don't*. Patrick looked at the sky, at the leaves he could hear but not see, beyond a vague suggestion of motion. "I feel like I'm dead but I haven't stopped moving yet, and it's only a matter of time before I get my brains blown out by somebody who survives the movie." He laughed. Really laughed. "Zombie extra number six. Zombie with Gas Pump Keys."

He lifted his beer to his lips but it was already empty. He felt numb but clearheaded, as if he'd lost his ability to feel pain and no longer had anything to fear. For once, Layla was quiet. He smelled her, patchouli and clove; saw her hair fall over her face as she looked at her hands. Fiddling with the coffin ring. He slid down to stand next to her, put a hand on either side of her waist, picked her up, and lifted her onto the hood of the car. She draped her arms over his shoulders, hooked her heels behind him so her skirt pulled tight across her thighs.

"I feel," he said, "like I want to fuck you."

In the gloom, she hesitated. "Just like that?"

"Just like that," he said.

Of course sex didn't work that way, so actually it was a few minutes later. But when you knew where you were going there was no need to wander around and Patrick knew where he was going: he was headed off a cliff. The last girl he'd been with was Caro and that had been in the dark, too. The memory of her was in his hands as he groped aggressively for this girl's neck, her hair, her back, her legs, her tits, as he pushed his hands inside her sweater, over her ribs. She shuddered and her fingers dug into his shoulders. She said his name and he said something back and immediately forgot what it was. For all he knew it was *shut up*. When he felt himself starting to come it occurred to him that he should probably pull out, but he didn't. Right then, in that moment, it didn't seem to matter.

Afterward she tugged her clothes back into place, took his hand

and led him to the backseat of her car, took his arm and wrapped it around her. He let her. He felt drained. No; vacated. He'd thought that she would erase Caro from his mind and body at the same time, that sex would ease the killing numbness he felt, but sex was nothing if there was nothing behind it and now that they'd done it, nothing had changed, except that this one part of his life—Layla—had reached inevitability, and he could stop resisting. He could give in. They could never do it again or they could do it every night for a week.

Although, now that it was over, he did wish one of them had brought a condom. Which wasn't the sort of thing you said to a girl you'd just had sex with.

"Look," she said, and pointed out the window.

He looked. Outside, he could see a small vague patch of lightness in the bushes. Her underwear, he realized. It hung from a branch like a decoration.

"I always wondered how underwear ended up in places like this. Now I know. Next time I come here with my friends, I'll see that and I'll remember this." She stretched languidly against him, made a small *mmmm* noise of satisfaction. "Because that was amazing."

Which seemed unlikely, since he hadn't given thought one to whether or not she felt good. Part of him wished that had been different—she wasn't anything like a virgin but she was young, how many guys could she actually have been with, he should have made a little more of an effort to be nice—but mostly he just felt restless and annoyed because she sounded like she was reciting movie dialogue again. Nothing about what had just happened had been amazing.

She pulled herself up to straddle his lap. "Mind you, it wasn't exactly the way I'd imagined this date going. I was thinking Denny's for ice cream and a kiss on my front stoop. My parents would shit an absolute brick if they saw you kissing me." She wriggled closer to him and ran her fingers down his chest. "You like me, don't you?"

"Of course I like you," he said, automatically. And he did, sometimes. Just not particularly right now. After they'd just had sex. His dim guilt flared.

"Do you like me more than her?"

"Who?"

"You know who. Your brother's girlfriend." Her voice was carefully neutral. He didn't answer. But Layla persisted. "Do you like me more than her?" she said again, and this time, the words sent knives through him. He forced the pain back down into whatever sticky, sore place it had come from and put his hand under Layla's skirt. Because Layla was here and Caro wasn't, because Layla had chased him and chased him and Caro had given up before they'd even started. Because he'd seen Caro naked, felt her back arch under him, and that time he had cared. He had cared and she had taken that from him and right now she was probably squealing and crying over the ugly goddamned ring and saying, *Oh, yes, Mike, oh, yes, I'll marry you.*

"Right now, I do," he said.

Layla smiled; not that sleepy bullshit smile, but a real smile that touched the corners of her eyes, and he realized that he'd never seen her smile like that before. She shifted on his lap. "Do you have to listen to them having sex?"

"Yeah." He pushed three fingers inside her.

She inhaled. "Maybe bring me over sometime. They could listen to *us* having sex."

He felt a flattened pang at the way her mind worked. Like a kid. Did she think they were dating now, would she expect him to take her to the prom?

He pulled his hand back. She put her own hands to his face and said, "Say something nice," and the desperation, the plea, was obvious. He didn't know how to respond. She wasn't beautiful, she was cute, and that wasn't what she wanted to hear. The sex had been decent, the blow job earlier that week had been decent, but neither had been spectacular. There wasn't anything nice to say.

"Come here," he said instead, which seemed to satisfy her. She leaned down and kissed him, and he kissed her back. He thought, I'll make it better this time, hooked his fingers under the hem of her sweater, and pulled it upward to take it off.

As his fingers brushed her rib cage he felt something strange on her skin. Like something hot was stuck to it. Her shoulders twitched and she made a tiny noise that didn't sound like sex to him. He pushed her back.

"Are you okay?" Then he looked down at her. Black bra against her white body, that much he'd expected—but below the bra, he saw faint marks on her rib cage. They were too straight and too geometric to be natural.

"Better than okay." She bent back down to kiss him again.

"Wait a minute." The marks almost looked like tattoos, but tattoos didn't feel like that, tattoos weren't sticky.

"No," she said.

He pushed her back again, less gently this time. Reaching up, he hit the switch on the map light. Layla went stiff and motionless, like a child caught disobeying.

The marks weren't tattoos. They were cuts, crosshatched slashes carved into her sides like the world's cruelest game of tic-tac-toe. Each cut was easily two inches long, clean and straight but not shallow. They were fresh. The tissue around them was a furious pink, swollen like a cushion, and the cuts themselves were crusted over with maroon. Behind the fresh wounds he could see scars from other, older cuts: some still pink, some faded to white.

His numbness snapped away like a window shade. "Jesus, what is that? Did you do that to yourself?"

"No." Layla's voice was very calm and she was making no attempt to cover either her bare skin or the wounds on it.

Feeling ill, he said, "Who did?"

Her chin went up. "A friend."

"You let somebody do this to you."

Her skirt was pushed up above her thighs, her arms draped over his shoulders. Tucking a lock of Patrick's hair behind his ear with a ghostly hand—the tenderness of the gesture made him recoil—she said, "It's a ritual. He drinks my blood and I drink his. It's not that different from sex, really. Just—more."

Patrick stared at her. "Jesus," he said again.

"Jesus is a fairy story." Misunderstanding him—perhaps deliberately. Her lips curled, faintly. "My parents used to say that if I loved Jesus I could keep Him in my heart. Well, Justinian is in my heart. And my veins, and my capillaries. I don't think that's quite what they meant, do you?"

Her voice was warm, even a little playful, but her face was as blank and molded as a plastic doll's. The sick feeling in Patrick's stomach was spreading.

"At first he just made little cuts, like on my arm. But he didn't want people seeing the scars. So he started on other places." Her fingers reached down, touched the gashes lightly. Caressing them, almost. "It used to be okay. But now it's never enough. There's always a new experience I need to have or a new emotion I need to feel. I need to be tied up so I understand freedom, I need to fuck his friend who hates me so I understand love, I need to let him hurt me so I understand pleasure. And it's always, *You're strong enough to take this, don't let your weakness control you, be brave, be powerful.* When I'm with him it makes this weird kind of sense. Like, of course he has to hurt me. How else could it be?"

There was soft upholstery behind Patrick and hard steel doors on either side. The spicy plastic smell of her car was choking him and her body on his lap was too heavy.

"One of the things he always tells me is that I won't be able to be with anybody else, ever, because I have too much of his blood and he has too much of mine. But he's wrong. Look at you and me. We understand each other. We're the same. Being with you feels good." She picked up one of his hands and pressed it against the cuts. They were hot, the raised ridges of them like seams. Patrick's brain was spinning. This was not okay. This was too far. Inside he was frantic but his body was paralyzed. Her eyes closed and she made a small, harsh noise that reminded him of the noises she'd made on the hood of the car; her body stiffened. "Just like that. It feels good."

His fingers were sticky, and he smelled blood. He looked down and saw that one of the scabs had reopened as she touched it, and blood smeared them both. The hot-copper smell. The car exhaust. Outside there was only forest but inside there was a concrete floor, cinder-block walls, the crash of the world falling around him; the stickiness on his fingers, the certainty of death. He pushed her. Hard.

She fell backward, and hit her head on the door. For the briefest and longest of moments she stared at him. Her hand moved slowly to the back of her head and he didn't know what his face looked like but her eyes, staring at him, widened with shock, and then she started to cry.

"Don't look at me like that," she said. He could barely look at her at all. His fingers fumbled for the door handle and then he was outside. Hunched over on the ground, certain he was going to throw up.

But he didn't. In the car he could hear her screaming, rhythmic thuds that were probably her fists pounding against the seat, sharper thuds that might have been her boots kicking the inside of the door. He walked with shaky legs to sit on the front bumper. Above him, the leaves rustled in the wind. Somewhere in the distance he heard cars. The air felt clammy and damp.

After a while, the noises in the car quieted and eventually she joined him. She'd put her sweater back on. Sitting down next to but not touching him, she stretched her legs out in front of her and played with her coffin ring, flipping it open and closed and open and closed. He didn't look at her. He did not understand her. They were not the same. The garage, the trial, the old man with his head in his hands—

his mother, struggling to breathe—those things were horrors. The mess under Layla's clothes was a game and he hated her for making him a part of it, for ever coming near him.

"I thought you were special," she said. Her voice was filled with a dead, preternatural calm. "But you're just another Ratchetsburg primate with sludge for brains. I thought we could save each other, but there's nothing in you worth saving. Justinian says we're better than you and he's right." She looked at him. There was nothing there. "It's bizarre to think that fifteen minutes ago I was fucking you."

"You and your friend don't know anything about me," he said.

"I know the Czerpaks are taking your house. Ryan's dad told us all about it in Worship Group, how Jesus wants them to take all your money and teach you a lesson. So looks like you're homeless, asshole. Serves you right. I used to babysit Ryan. He was a sweet little kid who liked balloons and hot dogs and SpongeBob SquarePants—"

And then he knew he really was going to throw up. He stood up and lurched over to the bushes, where he retched and choked on the warm beer he'd drunk and then on the noncontents of his empty stomach. Distantly, he smelled cigarette smoke. He wished this was the kind of nightmare where you woke up and loved your life, the sweaty sheets and the feel of the carpet under your toes.

"You're pathetic," he heard her say. "Find your own way home."

A door closed. An engine turned over.

He was alone.

Patrick wiped his mouth on the back of his hand and his hand on the thigh of his jeans. He stayed where he was, crouched down with his head hanging between his knees; staring at the black ground in front of him, listening to the wind in the trees. The sky had been cement-colored and pregnant with rain all day and if he looked up, he knew he would see nothing. No stars, no moon. There was nothing to see.

He shouldn't have had sex with her. He shouldn't have had anything to do with her. She was as broken as a doll with the string pulled out of its back. He'd known it all along and he'd been stupid to ignore it.

But after a long time—or maybe it wasn't so long—his legs began to cramp and he became aware that he was crouched over a pool of his own vomit. He could smell it, the bile and the beer, and bent over like this he could smell the sex he'd had with Layla, too, the peppery smell of the last time he'd touched her. His fingers had a sticky-powdery feeling from the dried residue of her blood. His hair was too long, it fell in his face, it tickled. Whoever he was, whatever he'd done, he was still here. The world wasn't going to fade to black and his legs hurt and there was nothing to do but stand up. So he stood up.

It took him forty minutes to walk to a place he recognized. Halfway there, the sky started to spit hard needles of rain down at him. Soon he was shivering, his toes numb inside his soaked sneakers, and it occurred to him that this was the first time it had rained since he'd stopped driving. Eventually he came to a closed Citgo station, where the twenty-four-hour pumps blazed under white lights and drops of water jeweled the plate-glass windows. Taking refuge under the narrow concrete overhang outside the garage bays, he pulled out his phone.

To his credit, he did try both Bill and Mike before he called Caro.

Her Civic pulled into the parking lot a half an hour later. When she leaned over to unlock the door for him he saw through the rain-spotted window that she was wearing her pajama pants, black flannel with red skulls on them. Once he'd thought they were hilarious. Now they made him think of Layla and he wished she'd worn other clothes.

"Get in before my car dies." She sounded annoyed. "You are making me miss the most amazing show about sharks."

"Sorry. Can you turn the heat on?"

She turned it all the way up. "Are you drunk?"

"I don't think so." He unlaced his shoes and took off his sodden socks. "I slammed a beer earlier, but I threw it up."

"That explains the smell," she said, aiming the vents toward the floor.

"Yeah. Sorry about that, too."

Then there was silence. Road-silence, the steady hum of tire on road. Caro's stereo was broken, it had been broken as long as he'd known her. He felt like he had to talk, to empty his brain the way he'd emptied his stomach back in the woods. "Tonight—"

"Did you know that a great white shark can smell a dead great white shark from miles and miles away? They did this experiment, where they distilled dead shark into, like, dead shark extract, and one tiny little drop—"

"Caro."

"One tiny little drop, and all the great whites for miles just vanish. It's the world's best shark repellent."

"Caro."

"Can you imagine that being your job, dead shark distiller? Can you imagine what you'd say at your high school reunion?"

He lost patience. "Caro, will you listen to me?"

"No." Her voice was higher than usual. "I will not listen to you because you're going to tell me that you had sex with that girl, that *child*, and I don't want to know that. I don't want to think that about you, that you'd do something like that."

"I had sex with you, didn't I?"

"Oh, god, please shut up." She sounded desperate, almost moaning.

He ignored her. "You're my brother's girlfriend and I slept with you without even thinking twice about it. Would it be a worse thing to do than that? I called the cops on my own goddamned father. We didn't even call a lawyer first. Would it be a worse thing to do than that?" He discovered that he was angry. "She kept coming at me and coming at me and coming at me and maybe there's a guy out there who'd keep saying no, but what the hell makes you think that guy is going to be me?"

"Because you're good!" She pounded the heels of her hands against the steering wheel in frustration. "Because you're the only person I know who thinks about things before he does them! Because you're too smart and too decent to have sex with that child and then come to me with this bullshit about how much she wanted it when you and I both know that she doesn't even know what she wants, that what she wants is a date to the goddamned prom and somebody to be nice to her—and you—*asshole*!"

She punched him, driving her closed fist deep into his thigh. Her other hand stayed on the wheel. The car never even swerved. His leg seized and cramped and he grabbed it but didn't say anything, couldn't say anything. It hadn't been playful. She'd meant it to hurt, and it had. The pain was brutal and he couldn't argue that he hadn't deserved it.

For a few minutes there was no sound but the road-silence.

Finally she let out a long sigh. "Oh, Patrick." She shook her head. "Why couldn't you just leave her alone?"

"I know you don't believe me, but it really was the other way around." He rubbed his leg. "To be perfectly honest, I've been way too miserable about you to chase anybody."

Sounding fairly miserable herself, she said, "This is my fault. If I hadn't—"

Patrick's anger rose again. "How is it your fault? Were you there tonight? Did you crawl inside me and make me have sex with her?" After the accident, he'd never told Mike about the garage, about the baby tooth. He'd never told anyone, because the words were too horrible to say. Now he wanted to tell Caro about Layla, about the cuts on her ribs and the way she'd made him touch them but he couldn't do that, either, couldn't tell her how the ridged flesh had been swollen and hot under his fingers.

"If I hadn't come into your room that night," she said, "you wouldn't be so pissed off about everything and you never would have got involved with her. I messed everything up. Things were good before that."

"Things were not good before that. Things have not been good for a long goddamned time." As if a key had turned, everything unlocked, his tongue and his brain and everything, and he found himself saying, "She lets her boyfriend cut her. Drink her blood, and—other stuff—Jesus, I knew she was crazy but I didn't know, I swear I didn't—"

The words tumbled out of his mouth like broken teeth. Caro pulled the car over and pressed the heels of her hands against her eyes. "This is bad, Patrick. You could go to jail. I don't know what the age of consent is in this state."

"You think I'm a scumbag?" Patrick said, quietly.

Caro dropped her hands. She stared out the front window. "Yes. No. I think—" She paused. "I think you're like me."

"I love you," he said.

"You can't possibly."

"Why not?"

"Because there's nothing to love," she said, and pulled back onto the highway.

They didn't talk again the rest of the way home. When they got there, Patrick took a long, scalding shower, and scrubbed his entire body twice. Then, leaving the water running, he got out and crossed dripping to the cabinet under the sink, where he found the stuff that Mike used to clean his hands when he'd been working on the truck. He used the whole bottle. It smelled like turpentine and cologne and as he scrubbed he could feel it stripping the moisture from his skin.

Back in the living room, Caro was sitting on the couch, one leg drawn up to her chest and the other tucked beneath her. The television was on and he heard splashing and shouts and ominous music; the light cast on her face by the screen was flickering and beautiful, but her expression was distant and sad. He didn't know what to say to her but he wanted to say something.

"We're losing the house," he finally said, and then felt like a jerk, because that was a lousy thing to drop on her, on top of everything else.

But she surprised him. "I know. Mike got a letter. Your brother has a profound talent for ignoring things he doesn't want to deal with." Caro turned the television off and placed the remote control carefully on the cushion next to her. Then she looked up at Patrick. "What you asked me the other day. In the backyard." Her voice was steady. "Ask me again."

A wave rippled its way up his back and across his arms. A long moment passed before he said, "I'm not sure I should."

The corner of her mouth twitched. "I'm not sure you should either."

Mike worked in the morning, Patrick knew that. He could hear his brother snoring from here, the sound faint enough in the living room but surely deafening upstairs. Mike only snored like that when he was drunk. Caro waited on the couch in her flannel pajamas, watching him. He wanted her. Not just somebody, not just a cessation of loneliness, but her, specifically. Caro: funny, fucked-up Caro, who hid her hands in her sleeves, who knew things about sharks. Who had come into his room that night, so brave and stupid, and torn what was left of his life right down the middle.

"No," he said. And then, trying to explain—"I can't keep screwing up, Caro. I have to be—better."

She put her hands to her face. He remembered standing in this exact spot, telling his brother and his father that he'd just called the police. Mike had said, *Why, Pat? Why would you do that?* in a voice turned querulous with disbelief and injury, but the old man had only put his head in his hands, just like Caro was doing right now. And he'd felt like the worst person in the world but he hadn't felt like this. He hadn't felt—

Wrong.

He was crouched in front of her in two steps, pulling her hands away and sinking his own into her hair and kissing her. She was like water pouring over him, like ocean water, deep and teeming. He had to quit screwing up. He had to be better than he was. For the dampness on her cheeks and the clutch of her hands on his chest and the fierceness that he felt catch fire inside him, for all the long days that stretched before them.

Eventually, he did ask her to come upstairs with him, but by then, he already knew the answer.

She had to sleep in her own bed because she had to be there when Mike woke up, but after he was gone she came back to Patrick. And he didn't care at all that she'd just come from his brother, that she smelled a little like him and the sweat on her body was part his. In fact, he cared so little that he sort of marveled at it—but not for long, because Caro was with him, and he had other things to think about, other things to do. There was this scene that happened in your lousier horror movie, when in the middle of closing the gate to hell or fleeing from the demon parakeet or whatever, the two protagonists stopped to have sex. Whenever he saw a scene like that Patrick always groaned and thought, Who stops to screw at a time like that? But that morning, when Mike could get sent home at any time and Layla could be sitting at the police station right that minute filing a report with her parents and somewhere in some legal office their house was undeniably, inexorably being taken away from them—somehow, all of that seemed to stop existing entirely. The sun streamed through his window, glorious and warm; the eggs he fried for their breakfast flipped over perfectly, and although his eyes were sandy from lack of sleep he wasn't tired at all.

Later, he stood shirtless at the refrigerator, staring at the empty shelves and seeing only a lone piece of leftover mushroom pizza he hadn't liked the first time around. The refrigerated air was cool on his bare chest. Caro came up behind him and leaned against him with the whole length of her body; her head on his shoulder, the smell of her sweet and hot, outdoorsy, because she'd been sitting outside in the sun and she'd carried the air and light and warmth in with her. He turned, wrapped his arms around her, and told her she was very, very beautiful—which she was—and she pushed him away and asked him if he had any idea how many times she'd heard that, how much she hated it. He laughed but she said, "I'm serious, I don't want to hear that shit, not from you," and he saw her face and the way her chest was rising and falling too fast and the pink cast to the skin on her nose. He stopped laughing immediately but it was too late, the spell was broken. She apologized but it was too late for that, too, and anyway, it wasn't her fault. In life there were problems and in humans there were scars and the world was what it was, and you couldn't lie around screwing your brother's girlfriend in a warm patch of sunshine all day, even if it felt good, even if you were in love.

You could, however—Patrick discovered—spend an entire night shift at a convenience store reliving that patch of sunshine. Over and over again, even as the rain drummed on the asphalt outside.

By Sunday morning, Patrick's exhaustion finally caught up with him. He walked home from work in the rain and went straight to sleep. When he woke up, the air downstairs felt moist and cool. The rain was still coming down and Mike had the back door open. He was sitting on the threshold with a beer can in his hand. The dog next door was barking, the sound sharp as hammer blows.

He gave Patrick a forced, wry smile. "You want to go out to the mall with me today? Return an engagement ring?" He shook his head. "If that isn't the saddest thing I've ever heard."

"Sorry." Patrick was a little surprised to find that he felt no joy when he spoke the word, that some part of him was, in fact, sorry. Caro hadn't mentioned the proposal at all. "When did you ask her?"

"Friday night, while she was at work. Got down on one knee and everything. Wore a tie. You should have seen me. I looked like a god-damned idiot."

"What did she say?"

"She said no, you stupid shit."

"Besides that."

For a moment Mike said nothing, just sucked on his beer and stared at his feet. Then he said, "Just that she wasn't ready to get married, she didn't think she was the marrying type, bullshit, bullshit, bullshit." Mike scratched his face. "Me, I think she's screwing some-body else."

Patrick's insides turned to liquid. Mike knew. They'd messed up, Mike had figured it out. Then he realized that if Mike knew, they would not be sitting here calmly discussing it. "What makes you think that?"

"This morning. We left it okay, you know? I mean, I was bummed, but whatever. If she doesn't want to get married yet, we won't get married. But she still didn't want to—you know. Do it. Said she didn't feel like it."

Patrick felt an unpleasant sting of gladness. "Maybe she didn't."

Mike nodded. "Yeah, but Caro almost always feels like it. I don't mean to sound like a dick, but it's true. You remember she had that flu right after New Year's?" Patrick nodded. "The night before she got sick, that was one time she didn't want to. And then a couple weeks ago, I think she was mad because I wouldn't take her to that stupid cemetery. It's not like we have sex constantly. I mean, half the time we're both too damn tired to even think about it. But most of the time, she's pretty up for it. Until this morning."

"You proposed and she turned you down," Patrick said. "Maybe she felt like it was weird."

"No. Something's up. She's hiding something. I love her so much it makes me sick to my stomach, you know? The thought of her with some other guy—I don't even like thinking about her ex-boyfriends. Guys say the whole if-I-can't-have-you-no-one-will thing and they sound like psychos. But you find yourself in that position, you start to understand." He dropped his beer can onto the concrete step and brought the heel of his sneaker down on it hard. Patrick thought that he'd probably heard the crack of beer cans being crushed in the womb. It was a primal noise, heavy with all twenty-six years of his life.

"You going to do something stupid?" Patrick said, careful to make his voice light.

Mike laughed. "Yeah, I'm going to do something stupid, all right. I'm going to play it cool, let her get it out of her system." He leaned down and disengaged one of the remaining beers from the plastic rings. "No point asking her about it. She'd just lie."

"Caro's not a liar."

"Try asking her about her mother sometime. She's a psych nurse. No, wait—she's a social worker. No, wait—she's sick, she's got lupus or arthritis or that chronic fatigue thing. I think the night we met she told me she was dead. Not that I care, I really don't. She could tell me the sky was made of Silly Putty and French fries and I'd believe her. I love her, that's all. I really love her."

Patrick looked at his brother. Mike's cheeks were unshaven. His shirt was spotted with oil and paint and god knew what else. The way his shoulders slumped and his hands hung slack between his knees made Patrick think of the old man, and with that came a sliding-on of weight, like he was betraying everyone, everywhere, in the whole world, just by being himself.

"I know you do," he said.

"When you love somebody, you don't just give up on them when they do bad things. You fight for them." He didn't look at Patrick but there was a faintly self-righteous note in his voice that made Patrick wonder if he was still talking about Caro. He didn't ask.

She came to see him at work, that night and the next: on her way home from the restaurant, in the weird nowhere-time of the night shift, Mike at home sleeping before an early morning punch-in. Wearing her restaurant clothes, white blouse and black skirt, she leaned across the counter toward Patrick in his candy-striped Zoney's shirt, their four hands laced together on the scarred Plexiglas surface. They talked. When they were done talking, on Sunday, he took her into the storeroom and they made out for a long time before she had to go. On Monday they didn't bother with the storeroom; she just came behind the counter. If anybody had ever bothered to review the security footage, Patrick would have been fired, but he didn't worry about that. It was the night shift. There was nobody in the world but the two of them.

T E N

"Get up," Layla said.

It was—when? All Verna knew was that the sky had been light and now it wasn't; she'd heard noises in the house and now it was quiet. Layla stood next to her bed, holding Verna's boots. She was dressed to go out.

Her voice was grim but not unkind. "You can't just lay here. You have to get up."

Verna turned her face to the wall but Layla wouldn't leave. Finally, creakily, Verna managed to pull herself out of bed. Hard fists of pain throbbed everywhere the girls had hit her, and drawing air into her lungs was pulling against an incredible pressure. The world was full of glue.

But every time she faltered, Layla's hands were there: pushing her into the bathroom, brushing the tangles out of her hair—after Mother picked her up from school she'd taken a shower but hadn't been concerned with things like combs—and getting her dressed and into her boots.

"What day is it?" Verna said, dully, as Layla pulled out of the driveway.

"Wednesday. Don't worry, you didn't miss anything." Layla turned the car toward town.

Verna wondered where they were going. The lost time bothered her. "Nothing at all?"

Stopped at a red light, Layla tapped her fingers against the steering wheel. "What do you want to hear? Neither Kyle Dobrowski nor Calleigh Brinker was struck by lightning. Jared Woodburn failed to tell me to ask you to the prom. The cafeteria served tacos."

Verna said nothing.

The light changed and Layla gunned it, sending the car jerking too fast through the intersection. "Yeah, Vee. Everybody's seen it. The world is full of liars and assholes and the only people worth anything are us."

What was left of Verna's spirit crumpled inside her.

"Reactions from theatergoers were mixed." Layla bit savagely at the words as they left her mouth. "But the girls who clucked their tongues and said 'oh, poor thing,' watched it just as many times as the guys who asked me where my little sister learned to suck a dick like that." She paused. "A couple of people told me you ought to go to the police. Your would-be boyfriend was one of them."

The police. The mental image of Calleigh Brinker and the others being led handcuffed into the police station with their RHS volleyball sweatshirts pulled up to hide their faces brought Verna a dim burst of satisfaction. Like when the guy who killed Ryan Czerpak had been arrested and they'd all cheered. But Verna also remembered how hollow Rachel Czerpak's face had grown by the time that guy was sentenced. How Danny quit talking in Worship Group, how their two surviving kids became as watchful and nervous as squirrels. And the drunk had pled guilty. Calleigh would never plead guilty to anything. There would be a trial, there would be testimony. The video would be evidence. They'd bring a television into the courtroom, or one of those computer projectors, like Mr. Guarda used. Her father would be there. He'd see it, he'd watch it—she could imagine his face—the disappointment—

"Should I?" Verna said.

Layla sighed. "Dad will make it a *thing*, Vee. He'll send that goddamned video to every news site and talk show he can find. Save the children, and all that shit. Never mind how you feel about it."

Verna imagined her father: *This particular issue is bigger than whether or not Calleigh Brinker made you suck off a banana, Verna. It's about all of the girls and all of the bananas in America. You have to stand up for them, to bear witness. It comes down to everyday battles like this and everyday people like you.*

Verna did not want to stand up and bear witness for all of the girls in America. Verna wanted to die.

"I can't," she said.

"Wise decision. Sadistic fucks like Calleigh Brinker have been working their special kind of magic since we came down from the trees, or left the Garden, or whatever. They're not new and they're not going anywhere. The only way to protect yourself is to separate from them. Make yourself strong so they can't hurt you."

"Where are we going?" Verna said.

There was a pause. And then, "Justinian's."

Justinian lived downtown, in a dingy brick house squeezed between a tae kwon do academy and a bar. "His mother works nights," Layla said, letting herself in through the unlocked front door. The inside of the house was plain, nearly undecorated except for the scented candles on every surface—the place smelled like a mortuary—and a few ceramic figurines, mostly birds. The beige carpet was studded with cigarette burns. The walls were deep shades of red and brown, and the curtain rods looked like wrought-iron spears.

Verna could barely imagine Justinian having a mother, let alone living here with her and her collection of scented candles and bird figurines. "What's she like?"

"His mother?" Layla shrugged. "Nice enough. She does whatever he wants. I think she's a little in love with him, actually. Not that he minds. He says every overlord needs a minion. This way."

From behind a door off of a winding, unlit hallway, Verna heard music playing. As they grew closer she smelled cigarette smoke and incense. Then the door opened and Justinian stood there: tall and gangly, black-clad as always. When he saw them he didn't smile. "Good," he said. "Come in."

They did. It was like moving from a cave into a smaller, darker cave. The walls of Justinian's bedroom were painted black and the room itself was immaculate, almost ascetic. The bed was neatly made, the black comforter taut and lint-free. All of the spines of the books were pulled forward to form a perfect line at the edge of the bookshelf. Philosophy, mostly. Lots of Nietzsche. Arranged like relics on the top of the bookshelf were two stubby red candles, a rosary, and a small wooden box. A chrome chain was wrapped around one of the bedposts. When Verna realized what it was, she cringed.

Justinian followed her gaze. "The dog collar is a joke. Layla bought it for me last year. That didn't start with you, you know. Look." He unwrapped it and put it in Verna's hands, where it felt unpleasantly greasy. She wanted to drop it but it seemed to cling to her. He put his hands over hers. They were warm.

"Just a thing." He took the chain and wrapped it around her wrist, fastening the clasp. "It can't hurt you. See?"

Verna nodded, although the heavy feel of it made her shudder. He dropped her arm and the chain clinked as it slid to rest against her hand. Layla, meanwhile, had taken off her coat and hung it carefully in the closet, removed her boots and placed them next to the door. Now she was sitting, motionless, on the very edge of the bed, as if she was afraid she'd muss the comforter. Her hands were smoothing the cloth beside her, almost nervously, and Verna could see her toes curling and uncurling inside her tights. She clearly knew this room, what to do with her coat and her boots, but the way she held herself didn't seem entirely comfortable.

"Come on, Vee," she said, and patted the bed next to her. "Sit down."

Verna did. Justinian crouched on the floor in front of her and put his palms on her knees. "I saw the video," he said.

She stiffened.

"All of it. What they did, what you did." His Siamese eyes bored into her. She couldn't look away. "The world is destroying you, Verna. Your way—your dad's way, being nice and meek and compliant—it isn't working. It's making you powerless and weak. Other people take advantage of that weakness and the result is pain. The result will always be pain." He looked at Layla. "Right?"

Layla nodded. He nodded, too. "Your dad's way got your face splashed across the Internet with a banana down your throat. The Internet is forever, you know. That video will find you wherever you go. Every guy you meet, every job you have. Some sicko in Arkansas is probably jerking off to it as we speak."

He was right. She knew he was. She could imagine the sicko in Arkansas. She could see him, as clearly as Justinian had seen what happened in the second-floor bathroom. Someday, years from now, Verna would walk into a party or a restaurant or a college classroom and someone she'd never seen before would gasp and say, *Oh my god, you're Banana Girl!* It didn't matter if she went to the police or not. The police couldn't help her. For the rest of her life, Banana Girl was all she would be, ever. And that life would be a ruin, a wasteland.

All at once, Verna blazed with a deep, all-consuming anger, unlike anything she'd felt before. There was no soothing this fire, no talking it gently into subsidence. She wanted to be back in the bathroom. She wanted to fight. She would have to fight for the rest of her life and she hated herself for not having fought then, when it counted. She pictured Calleigh Brinker's face and wanted to claw it like a cat. Mar that pure, milky surface. Make the blood flow.

"Time to try something else," Justinian said, softly.

It was hard to bring herself back to the present, to look at him. "Like what?"

"Does anybody mess with me, Verna? Does anybody try to hurt me?" She shook her head. "That's right. You know why? Because they're scared. Because I have power and they know it. My way works. Their way"—and somehow, he managed to include the entire rest of the world with a simple jerk of his head—"doesn't. When you do things their way, you get hurt and humiliated and used. Layla knows. Layla has tried." He turned to Layla, who was still sitting on the bed with her hands in her lap. "Haven't you?"

Layla nodded slowly. "Justinian is right," she said. "His way works."

Verna thought of the effortless glide in Layla's walk, the impermeable barrier of strength that seemed to surround her. Layla had always been confident but something had taken that raw confidence and molded it into armor. Dad talked a lot about God's armor, shielding you from the world; about being protected by your faith, and the conviction that the things of this world were unimportant. But Verna's body, her life—they were not unimportant. No matter what happened after she was dead, this was the place she was now; these experiences were the ones she had to endure. Whatever she had to do, whatever Justinian's way turned out to be, it couldn't be worse than being beaten to your knees in a high school bathroom and having a banana shoved down your throat.

In Layla's face she saw love and sympathy and worry and grief. In Justinian's she saw only love.

"How?" she asked.

He had a knife: a small, silver knife with an elaborately worked handle that looked as if it had been looted from a pagan tomb. His hands, as they rolled up her sleeve, were gentle but determined, like a doctor's. With the knife, he made a small, shallow cut on the meaty part of Verna's arm, well away from the veins. The pain surprised her but faded quickly. A thin line of blood welled up from the cut and for a moment, the three of them sat and watched the line grow fat and shiny. Verna felt an alien satisfaction.

Justinian bent down over her arm. His hair fell around his face. She felt the hot slick of his tongue, a sting, as he licked the blood away, again and again. Each lick was another thin sting, shooting up her arm and behind her ribs. The pain was negligible but her breath caught. This was the most intimate thing Verna had ever done. His hands, holding her arm like he was holding all of her. His breath, his mouth, on her skin like a kiss.

The cut was a minor one and it stopped bleeding quickly. When Justinian raised his head, Verna was almost sorry. Her arm felt too bare. Layla pressed a gauze pad over the wound, and her hand felt warm and good.

Then Justinian showed her his own arm, etched with countless scars, and cut himself. He didn't even wince. His blood looked darker than hers. Was that possible?

From somewhere over her shoulder, she heard Layla's voice, barely even a whisper. "Verna," she said, but she didn't say anything else. Verna didn't turn, didn't look at her. She put her mouth to the cut on his arm, and she licked. His blood tasted like salty metal.

"That's good," he said. "That's exactly right. Just like that."

He said he wanted a lock of her hair, so she made a thin braid and let him cut it off. Layla brought the wooden box from his bookcase. He opened it and said, "There's something from each of you in here. Something that represents your potential transformation." The box held a crumpled tissue, a cheap-looking pin shaped like a rainbow, and a braid of golden hair. He picked the last up and looked at Layla. "Remember this?"

Layla nodded. "The day Calleigh tried to burn it off."

"Your first time," he said, and she said, "For a lot of things."

He smiled and twined Verna's purplish braid around the golden one. "There. Now you're together."

Layla called Criss and Eric. They had seen the video like everybody else in the universe, but they treated Verna normally. She was grateful, but not surprised. Here, with Justinian and his people, was the only place she would ever feel safe again. The cut on her arm stung a little, like a cat scratch. It was a song, singing: *you are more than this, you are more than that moment.*

"Welcome to the family," Eric said. The can of beer in his hand, the handcuffs on his wrist, and the oily skin on his face all gleamed in the dim, twitching light. The way he looked at her had changed, become more appraising. This pleased her. When he was around she'd always felt shrunken. Now she didn't.

"Thanks," she said.

Criss handed Verna a beer and she took it. She had swallowed Justinian's blood; what was a little alcohol? "Doesn't it feel good?" the blue-haired girl said, sounding dreamy. Judging by the slackness of her expression, the beer in Criss's own hand was not her first. "When the knife cuts into you, the way it pulls?"

"Makes me want to get laid," Eric said, and Criss grinned.

"Me, too," she said. "Oh, me, too."

Verna didn't say anything. The bloodletting had not made her want to get laid, but in this room, with these people, she felt like a puzzle piece that had finally been put in the right place. Justinian had shown her on his arm the places where he'd first cut himself for the others, first Criss and then Eric and finally Layla, naming each scar. *This one is Layla's,* he'd said, as if that little piece of his body belonged to her, always. *This one is yours. It will always be yours. And this*—touching the cut on her own arm—*this one will always be mine.*

Verna had wanted to see Layla's scars, but Justinian had laughed and said later, maybe. The expression on Layla's face had almost been relief, and Verna realized that, given the nature of Layla's relationship with Justinian, some of Layla's scars were probably on more interesting places than her arm.

Justinian, like everyone in the world except for the Elsheres, had a video game system, and when he and Layla came back from the kitchen, they turned it on. This game was about killing zombies. Because they didn't look human, it felt less horrible than the war games Eric sometimes played where agonized faces disintegrated on-screen and detached limbs spurted scarlet blood. Verna tried her beer. It was bitter and the bubbles nipped at her throat. She didn't like it, and thought she wouldn't drink any more, but the game continued and after a while she took another sip, and then another. When she stood to go to the bathroom she discovered that she was tipsy. Her joints seemed too loose, and she had to put a hand to the wall for balance as she walked down the hall. In the bathroom—more candles—she put her fingers under the tap and pressed them to her temples. Staring into the mirror, she thought, This is what I look like when I'm drunk. The reflected image seemed to gaze back at her from a great remove. Maybe this was what other people saw all the time: tangled hair, grease-smudged eyeliner, eyes watery and red.

From the living room came the sound of an electronic explosion, and laughter.

Verna looked under the sink for a comb and found a pornographic magazine tucked against the inner wall of the cabinet like a book on a shelf. Opening it, she looked almost clinically at the stretched, distended places where flesh met flesh. All of the models' bodies were hairless; their faces looked angry, or pained. On one page she found a woman with her mouth stretched wide around an immense veined penis. The man's face wasn't in the photo but one of his hands held the back of the woman's head—caressing her or gripping her, it wasn't clear which. Verna studied the woman's face for a long time. When I get married, she thought, I am never going to do that.

She put the thought away. No boy, ever, would be able to look at her and see anything other than Banana Girl. She had Layla and Justinian and Criss and Eric. Nobody else would ever want her. She put the magazine back under the cabinet, found a comb in the medicine chest, fixed her hair, and went back out into the living room.

Criss was very drunk. "So are we going to get some serious revenge on these assholes, or what?" she asked, as Verna sat down.

Justinian paused the game and it froze on an image of a hand reaching for a door. "Yes. We are going to get serious revenge on all of the assholes."

Criss clapped her hands. "Excellent. What's the plan?"

"The plan is that Justinian and I are working on the plan," Eric said, "and they're all going to pay."

"I wish we could just leave," Layla said.

Justinian nodded. "I was thinking Montreal. It's not too far, and it's out of the country."

Leaving. In her head Verna saw her bedroom at home, her closet, her slippers. "Why do we have to leave the country?" she asked.

Eric laughed. "Because your psycho father doesn't have an international calling plan."

"And because you and Criss and Layla are all minors," Justinian said. "Until you turn eighteen, you're property. They think they can do whatever they want to you. But they can't. Not without going through me."

He sent Criss into the kitchen for more bottles of beer, and one of them was for Verna. She drank it. Later there was another and eventually Verna found herself in the bathroom, throwing up into the toilet. Somebody else had discovered the magazine and left it splayed open on the floor. The angry, copulating figures stared up at Verna as she kneeled on the cold tile. When she was done she squirted some toothpaste on her finger and rubbed it around the inside of her mouth, then stumbled and lurched out into the hall. The ground would not stay level and the walls would not stay straight and halfway down the hall she decided that she'd better sit down.

Outside Justinian's room. The door was closed. Light shone underneath it. She squinted even though it was her hearing she was trying to focus, and heard her sister, talking too low to be heard.

"Be quiet," Justinian's voice said, clearly. "I told you not to talk." Verna held her breath. Nothing. A faint rustle, maybe a whimper. "Stop moving. Do you want to fix this or not?" He sounded stern, commanding. Verna had never heard Justinian sound that way before and she felt like she was going to be sick again, so she crawled back down the hall to the bathroom.

A few hours afterward, when they left, everything seemed fine between Justinian and Layla; he put his arms around her, they kissed. It felt the same. In the morning—the dragging, nauseous morning—it was easy for Verna to look back on that moment in the hallway, and decide that she'd imagined it.

The sisters went to school the next day. Despite the fact that Layla's eyes were bleary and Verna's, in the mirror, were the same; despite the fact that Layla's movements were stiff and awkward, and since Verna's entire body hurt she figured that hers were, too. Somebody had scrawled the word *slut* on Verna's locker and she barely even felt a pang. The world seemed to flicker just as Justinian's living room had flickered, and her ears felt dense, as if they were filled with water. While they ate lunch on the loading dock Justinian talked about Montreal. The vision he painted of the five of them living in a house together, being responsible only for and to themselves, was compelling beyond words, the kind of dream you were sorry to wake up from, but it felt like a fairy tale. She no more believed that she would be in Montreal on Monday than she believed that the faithful would be pulled into heaven Tuesday afternoon, that surgery patients would disappear from operating tables and planes would crash.

In Bio, she found a banana on her desk.

She picked it up. It was cool and smooth and repulsive. She could feel the expectant faces behind her, waiting to see how she would react, what she would do. Would she cry? Flee the room? Throw it in Kyle Dobrowski's face? He wasn't wearing his letter jacket. She hoped she'd ruined it. She hoped the stain never came out and his parents couldn't afford to buy him a new one. She hoped that when he found it forty years from now, reliving his high school football glory in some dusty old attic, he saw the blue stains on his embroidered name and hated her. The very idea brought a nasty, unexpected pleasure.

But right now, Verna did nothing, because there was nothing she could do. There was no comeback withering enough, no put-down clever enough. The Kyles and the Calleighs of the world would always win and the world would always love them. Justinian had sworn that he would never let anything like the second-floor bathroom happen to her again. *I swear it on the blood we share*, he'd said. The tape holding the gauze over her cut itched and the pain was a low comforting throb. She tried to pull strength from it the way he'd told her, to feel the throb and know that she was special and strong and capable of things other people weren't, but the other pain was greater. There would always be more bananas. There would always be more second-floor bathrooms.

Right then, standing in the bio lab. That was the moment. That was when she started to believe. There was no other option; she could no longer endure. Even as flickering and muted as the world had become, she, Verna, could not exist in this place and this time. There was no room for her here.

In art, Mr. Chionchio talked about shading. Imagine the light source. Fill in the shadows where they'd fall naturally. He told them to draw an object from memory, something simple that they could easily imagine in multiple situations. Verna chose the paper coffee cup she'd seen on the floor of Layla's car that morning. She could think of nothing else except knives and bananas.

Jared pulled his hair down in front of his eyes. "So Justin Kemper says I'm not allowed to talk to you anymore."

A coffee cup was a cylinder, tapered toward the bottom. No. Too much. Erase. Erase erase erase.

"Although his exact words were 'Stay away from Verna or I'll cut your fucking throat.'"

Stay away from Verna. Jared had seen the video, he would not need to be told to stay away from Verna. The plastic lid had the same degree of taper as the cup, but inverted.

"At the time, it was actually your sister that I wanted to talk to. I was trying to get your phone number."

The hole in the lid: a rectangle with rounded edges. "Why?"

"Because I was worried about you. Because I wanted to make sure you were okay after—" Verna heard a snap and a tiny conical piece of graphite shot across the table. "Jesus," Jared said, and then, "Sorry."

"Say whatever you want," Verna said. "I don't care."

"Whoever wrote that post about me saying things about you was lying," he said.

Because of course, if it was true, he'd just admit it.

"Verna—" There was a pleading note in his voice. "Don't be one of them. Don't get all creepy and obedient."

Verna didn't say anything.

"I know the rest of humanity hasn't exactly treated you supergreat lately, but that guy's a psychopath. He talked about you like you were his property, Verna. Like he was Count Dracula and you were one of his vamp-whores."

"Are you calling me names now, too?" Verna said, softly.

"No." Jared sounded exasperated. "I learned that word, *vamp-whore,* from a comic book. The only person I've ever heard use it in real life is your sister. Somebody asked if she was Kemper's girlfriend and she said, 'I prefer vamp-whore.'"

"A joke."

"She called herself his whore, Verna."

"You don't know anything about it. You don't know him. You don't know anything."

"I guess I don't," Jared said.

Around them people were talking and laughing but there was a heavy silence.

Finally he said, "If you're not going to listen to me about Kemper you're probably not going to listen to this, either, but your parents should take that video to the police."

The video. She wondered if he'd liked it. She wondered if, when he watched it, he'd imagined that the banana in her mouth was his penis, if he'd imagined his hand gripping her head.

Lick it. Suck it. You like that, slut?

Jared was saying, "My mom said, if your parents wouldn't do it, she would."

Call-Me-Carmen, with her pantheon of religious jewelry, who didn't even have enough sense to suggest that Jared and Verna drink their sodas upstairs, in the family room. Who'd done nothing but dishes as in the basement, her son had pushed Verna's legs apart with his own and groped inside her clothes. "Tell your mother it's none of her business."

"She's trying to help you. I'm trying to help you."

The way Dad would try to help her, her and all the girls like her, the way he would take the video on television and play it over and over again. "It's none of your business, either."

"Verna," he said. "Don't let them do this to you."

Let who do what? The bell rang and the hallways filled with noise and chaos and jostling and laughter and all of the noisy chaotic laughing jostlers had seen the video, all of them. Jared waited a minute but she didn't say anything else. She could feel the empty space she was supposed to be filling with words but she had no words, words were pointless.

After school she went with Dad to pick up a new batch of brochures. While Dad paid, the printer's old basset hound, who Verna had known since he was a puppy, came out from the back and pushed his wet nose into Verna's hand. His eyes were rheumy and he moved as if his hips hurt. When she bent down to pet him his coat felt rough and dirty.

Her hands still smelled of sick-sweet dog when Dad dropped her at home with the brochures and headed for the copy shop across town. Mother was out, and the house was silent. If Layla's bag hadn't been on the entryway floor and her car next to Toby's in the driveway, Verna would have thought nobody was home. Her arm stung as she carried the heavy box of brochures down the hall to the office door, which stood half-open. She nudged it with her knee and then stopped.

Layla was inside. Layla and Toby. Toby sat on one of the old swivel chairs and Layla kneeled on the floor in front of him. Verna could only see her from the back, her head moving, her hands on his knees; Toby's eyes were closed, his lips moist and parted. She could see his tongue moving behind his teeth.

"Oh, God. Layla." Verna could barely hear him. "Oh, God. Oh, please."

Like that, slut.

His hands were in Layla's hair, not gripping but stroking, petting; the sweet dog smell was not unlike banana and Toby's face turned red and screwed up. He let out a noise that was halfway between a grunt and a cry. His eyes opened.

And then, seeing Verna, widened. "Oh, God," he said, again. "Oh, shit."

He shoved Layla back and fell off the chair, hands fumbling at his pants as he tried to hide himself. She saw anyway: that part of him, still half-tumescent, slick and wet-looking. Not distended and massive, like the ones wielded by the men in Justinian's magazines. Then he was standing and, white-faced with horror, shoved his way past her out the door and into the hall. His belt, which he hadn't bothered to fasten, flapped at his waist, and Verna could hear the jingle of the buckle end all the way down the hallway.

Layla spat calmly into the wastebasket and wiped her mouth. Most of her lipstick was gone. She looked at Verna, her face expressionless. "What?"

What. How could she, was what. Here. With Toby. At all. Verna put the box down. Her hands and her face felt hot and her legs felt unsteady.

"He loves you," she said.

"Who, Toby?"

Verna shook her head. An inscrutable emotion passed over Layla's face, something that pulled at her mouth and furrowed her brow. Her eyes grew shiny with tears and then she, too, pushed past Verna. A moment later, through the poorly insulated garage walls, Verna heard her car start.

When Layla missed dinner, Verna didn't bother to lie. Dad asked where her sister was and she said she didn't know. As they ate he grew more and more agitated. Afterward, table cleared and dishes washed, Verna was in her room, staring pointlessly at her history book, when she heard a knock at the front door, and then Toby's voice, and Dad's, moving into the kitchen.

Quietly, she crept down the hall to the living room and out the front door. The night smelled like wet concrete. Up and down the street, drapes were closed and porch lights were on. The few visible stars shone feebly, as if they might flutter and die at any moment.

She walked around the side of the house, the lawn soft under her feet, to the kitchen window. Mother always left it open to let out the cooking smells and the heat. Staying back so the warm light didn't reach her face, she could see Mother and Dad and Toby sitting at the table, a plate of cookies between them. Verna could sense the tension from here, she could see it in the way Toby held his back. Mother's eyes were fixed on her lap and Dad's were staring out the sliding glass door. He looked like he wanted to stop the world as much as Verna did.

"It was a m-m-mistake," Toby said.

There was a brief, suffocating pause.

Dad's voice was tight. "I think you should leave."

Toby stood up. Verna pressed her back against the rough wall under the window.

"This is the closest thing I have to a family." Toby sounded as if he were crying. "The four of you."

Something shattered. Verna pushed closer to the wall, trying to disappear. "Go!" Mother cried. "Get out!" And then Verna heard the heavy falls of Toby's combat boots retreating through the house. Distantly, a door slammed and an engine revved.

In the kitchen, a chair scraped against the floor. A cupboard opened. Verna heard the swish of the hand broom and fragile tinkling sounds: cleaning up whatever had broken.

"I'm sorry," Mother said, and Dad said, "It was my mother's. I never liked it."

Footsteps. More tinkling. The chair scraped again.

"Oh," Mother said. The syllable stretched into something guttural and enraged. "That girl. Why would she do such a filthy, shameful thing? Why Toby?"

"Because she could. Because she knew how it would make us feel." Dad sighed. "She's out of control, Michelle. It was one thing when she was only hurting us. But now——"

There was a long pause. Then Mother said, "You're thinking about Renewal."

"It's a good place. A Christian place."

"You hear things about those camps. Kids dying of heatstroke and——"

"It's hiking. That's all it is. They go hiking, and there are counselors. They pray."

Mother half-laughed but Verna felt as if her insides had turned to concrete. "I'd like to see the counselor that can get Layla to pray."

"They're professionals, Michelle. It's what they do."

There was a long pause and when Mother spoke again her voice sounded helpless. "Sending her away, though."

"Getting her back," Dad said. "Think about Verna."

The chair scraped; a cupboard opened. Water filled a glass and somebody drank.

Then Mother said, "Soon, okay? Before I lose my nerve."

Underneath the quiet, waiting night, the world was surging, rising, out of control. Verna's fists clenched. All she wanted to do was sit down exactly where she was, put her hands over her ears, and let the stillness fill her. Instead, silently, she went back inside. Into her parents' bedroom, where she took the extension receiver into the bathroom and sat down on the edge of the bathtub because she was shaking so hard that she could barely press the buttons. As Layla's phone rang, Verna stared at the perfume bottles on the counter: each a different shape, each a different color. All elegant, all beautiful. A crystal sea of golden fluids and sweet smells. Layla would be in wilderness camp, dehydrated and hot with a heavy pack on her back. Layla would be dying, and the perfume bottles would still be here, still be shining.

"What," Layla said. Sounding annoyed. She thought it was their parents.

"It's me," Verna answered. "Don't come home."

ELEVEN

Wednesday night, before Patrick's shift started, Mike wanted to grab a beer at Jack's Bar and Sandwiches, so they did. Just the two brothers. It had been a long time. Before the accident, they'd gone out together three, maybe four times a week; sometimes they'd bring the old man with them, and sometimes they'd meet him while they were out. Not that they ever planned it that way, it just happened. Patrick would be shooting pool or watching a game or something, and he'd look across the room and there the old man would be, sitting on a stool. As he and Mike walked into Jack's that night, Lecia called out, "Double trouble!" just like she always had. Out of habit, Patrick almost asked her if she'd seen the old man, and then remembered exactly why he didn't like going to Jack's anymore.

There weren't a lot of people he knew out on a Wednesday, but there were a few: guys he'd worked with, people he knew from school. They looked at him curiously, maybe said *hey what's up* if they happened to find themselves standing close enough to make silence awkward. "They're not being weird, dude," Mike said at one point. "It's you. You look at everybody like you think they're about to stab you in the brain. Why don't you relax, for crying out loud?"

And maybe Mike had a point. Mike liked people, and people liked him. The old man had been the same way, back before he'd completely pickled himself. When Patrick had started high school, the things Mike was good at—sports, girls, the kind of friendly disobedience that made teachers roll their eyes without making them mad—seemed important and for a while, Patrick had tried to cultivate those skills himself. It hadn't taken too long for him to realize that those weren't exactly skills that could be cultivated, and he was better off concentrating on areas where he was actually talented, like running or drawing gross cartoons.

Now he found himself marveling anew at the way Mike could sit on a bar stool and shoot the shit with Lecia like nothing had ever happened. Even when she put one hand on her hip, shook a schoolmarmish finger at them, and said, "Now, which of you boys is driving tonight, because that's the one I'm cutting off early," and Patrick heard the layers in her words, the way she pretended to be stern because she didn't want them to notice that she really was being stern, Mike just laughed. She'd never cut either of them off before. To the best of Patrick's memory, nobody had, which was probably part of the problem. But here she was, doing it anyway. And Mike thought it was funny.

Except that five minutes later he was morose again, telling Patrick about some new way that Caro had found to spurn his devotion. And then it was himself Patrick marveled at, that he could simultaneously sit here and nod sympathetically and say things like *oh, man, who knows,* while another part of his brain hoped that Mike would be passed out when Caro got off work tonight so that she could come see him at Zoney's. So maybe Mike wasn't the only one in the family who could ignore the obvious.

"Did I tell you that asshole with the dog practically called her a slut?" Mike said.

"Yeah," Patrick said, feeling sapped. Mike was on a loop, saying the same things over and over. There were no clocks in Jack's but Patrick guessed the loop was maybe twenty minutes long. Twenty-five, tops.

"Right there in front of me, like I wasn't going to do anything about it." Although to the best of Patrick's knowledge, Mike hadn't done anything about it. "And like it was his goddamned right to tell her about the house. I was going to tell her. I was going to tell both of you. I just hadn't yet." Mike paused. "Do you think that's why she doesn't want to get married? Because we're getting sued?"

"No." Which was true. "I think she doesn't want to get married because she doesn't want to get married." Also true, albeit with a potentially damning lie of omission. "Besides, we're not the ones getting sued. The old man is the one getting sued. We're just the ones getting evicted." The Czerpaks' lawyer had given Patrick the details over the phone that afternoon, after keeping him on hold for fifteen minutes.

"Same difference." Mike was on his fourth beer. Patrick was nursing his first. "Probably the thrill of their fucking lives, taking away our house."

"I'm pretty sure they'd trade our piece-of-shit house for their kid any day of the week," Patrick said. He certainly would.

"Our house isn't a piece of shit."

"Come on, Mike."

"I'm serious. How can you say that? You grew up there, man. Mom died there, for Christ's sake."

"Mom died in the hospital."

"Same difference." God, Patrick was starting to hate that phrase. "She was sick there, wasn't she? She lived there, didn't she? We had some good times in that house." Mike hammered back the rest of his beer and signaled Lecia behind the bar for another.

"Yeah? Name one."

"The barbecues."

The barbecues. When the aunts drank wine coolers in the kitchen and bitched about their husbands and the uncles drank beer in the backyard and bitched about their jobs; when the kids filled water balloons at the outdoor tap and hurled them at whoever was closest. The later it got, the less careful the adults were about keeping track of their drinks, which the older kids finished off in the alley. And their mom, having spent days beforehand making potato salad and pasta salad and barking at anybody who came too close that they better not touch a damn thing in the refrigerator or so help her god she'd start cutting off hands, would be worn-out and snappish by the time everyone went home. But he also remembered seeing the old man grab his mother around the waist in the kitchen and, only slurring a little, say something like *Al, baby, you throw one hell of a party,* and she'd answer, with a smile in her voice, *Go pick up the backyard, you lazy drunk. I'll deal with you later.*

That moment existed only in Patrick's head. It wasn't at 151 Division Street and it never would be again. "It's just a house, Mike."

Lecia came over with Mike's beer. "You sure you're not driving, big guy?" she said, and Mike answered, "He is," with a nod at Patrick, although Patrick hadn't driven in weeks and Mike knew it. When she was gone, Mike leaned over and pointed an accusatory finger. "It's not just a house. It's our home. Don't you even care about that? Doesn't that bother you, even the tiniest goddamned bit?" He sat back. "But I guess if it did, we wouldn't be here right now, would we?"

Patrick stared at his brother. "What's that supposed to mean?" Even though he knew, they both knew. But if Patrick was going to have to hear it then Mike was going to have to say it. If they were going to have this discussion, they were going to have it.

"You did what you did, that's all I'm saying. Maybe if you hadn't—" Mike stopped, and then pushed on. "Maybe Dad wouldn't be in jail. Maybe you'd still have a real job and I wouldn't be so fucking broke from carrying your ass. Maybe me and Caro would be engaged. Maybe we'd be married, have our own place. People are supposed to do that, you know. Get married and move out and stuff."

There it was. "So none of that's happening because of me?"

Mike spread his hands, lifted his shoulders. "Like I said. You did what you did."

Jack's was crowded, the room was warm; the bottle in Patrick's hand, which he'd been holding for over an hour, felt warm, too, having taken on the heat of the air and his hand. A hole in his right sock bound uncomfortably around the tip of his second-smallest toe. Mike's coppery hair was starting to creep back at the temples, he noticed. Just like the old man's. He had the old man's long earlobes, too. Patrick felt calm. Not angry, not upset.

"So what if I hadn't done it?" he said.

"Then we keep living our lives, brother."

"What about the car?"

Mike blinked. "What do you mean?"

"I mean the Buick. We couldn't just leave it there, close the doors, and pretend it doesn't exist, like *Garage? What garage?* So, what?"

"Wash it." Mike's voice was uncertain. "Fix it up."

Patrick shook his head. "The minute we touch that car, the first dent we take out, we're accomplices, *brother*. And then it's our asses in jail, too." And everything the world had said about them, everything Mike had managed somehow to ignore—all of that would be true. If it wasn't already.

"Sure," Mike said, "if we get caught."

"You couldn't even look at that car. You closed your eyes when they towed it out of the garage. You expect me to believe you could have washed off the blood and scraped the hair off the bumper?"

The big muscles in Mike's jaw tightened and worked. "You think you're better than us. You always fucking have. But he's worth ten of you, you little shit, and because of you he's in a goddamned prison cell and I have to spend all day every day not punching you right in your fucking face. And don't think it wouldn't feel good, you selfish prick."

Mike had always been the one with the temper. The smooth places in the walls where the drywall had been repaired, a lot of those belonged to the old man but a handful of them were Mike's. Mike was bigger and stronger than Patrick, and he'd fought more and harder, but Patrick was unafraid. "So do it," he said.

There was a long pause and Patrick saw, with some incredulity, that there were tears in his brother's eyes. If Mike was turning into a weepy drunk, that was another way in which he was like the old man. "Everything's just so shitty right now," Mike said.

"I know it is," Patrick said, but then Mike said, "What the hell is wrong with her?" and to that, Patrick said nothing.

The next night, Mike wanted to do it all over again. The minute he walked in the door from work: pointing a finger at Patrick, dropping his thumb as if firing an imaginary rubber band. "Come on, man, Jack's ain't Jack's without at least one Cusimano in it, and I ain't drinking alone." Then he went to take a shower.

Caro, getting ready for the dinner shift, watched him go, her brow wrinkled with worry. "I've never seen him this way."

"I have," Patrick said. Thinking of those bleak months after the accident, when Mike had done almost nothing but drink and brood, and burst out into poisonous, abbreviated rants. The old man's rants just washed over you after a while, like the way you could be in a room thick with cigarette smoke and not realize how bad it was until you went out in the fresh air and smelled your clothes. Mike's anger was more like a brick through a window: loud, startling, and afterward the room was cold.

Fucking people. Who lets their fucking kid play in the fucking street? They deserve what they get. Fucking praying in the courtroom. Why didn't Jesus swoop down and save him, huh?

"I don't know what'll happen if he gets drunk and you're not there to take care of him," Caro said.

"Screw that, Caro. I'm dead on my goddamned feet." And, it was on the tip of his tongue to say, he was tired of taking care of angry drunks. He'd been taking care of angry drunks his whole life. "Last night he threatened to punch me in the face."

"He won't do it," Caro said. "Go. For me, okay?"

So he went. Thursday was payday almost everywhere, and Jack's was hopping: crowds of drinkers dancing, laughing, having a good time in that live-fast-die-young way that people had when one day was just like another and if you weren't living for the moment you weren't living for anything. Mike and Patrick found stools at the bar and ordered two beers from Lecia. They hadn't been there ten minutes when some drunk girl leaning over to order fell against Patrick.

"Hey, there," she said. A little horsey, a little pudgy, too much makeup but the whole package was cute, nonetheless. "Come dance with me, slugger."

Patrick smiled despite himself and pushed her back upright. "No thanks."

"Your loss," she said, merrily, taking her fluorescent-pink drink from Lecia, and then the crowd swirled and she was gone.

"You should have gone for it," Mike said.

"Not my type."

"You can't see her face when she's sucking your dick." Mike laughed. "Man, the girls at Jack's. Remember when we used to call this place Jack-offs, Blow Jobs, and Sandwiches?"

"Yeah, I remember." And then, on some malicious impulse, Patrick added, "Hey, isn't this where you met Caro?"

Mike stared down at his beer. "Yeah."

"Guess you got an okay look at her face," Patrick said, and even as he said the words he wondered what was wrong with him. Pushing Mike. It was almost like he wanted to fight and as soon as the thought rose in his brain he realized that it was true. He wanted

Mike to hit him. He wanted to hit him back. He was tired of living in this weird paralyzing stasis, tired of listening to Mike's sad line of shit, tired of seeing Caro worry. It was the jump-in-front-of-a-train thing, all over again.

Mike's face turned surly. "That was different. Don't talk about her like that, anyway."

"Sorry," Patrick said, and he was—but for Caro's sake, not Mike's.

The music was loud and for a few minutes they didn't have to talk. Mike finished the rest of his beer in one long pull and then leaned against the bar. His face blandly pleasant, he scanned the crowd. "You see that drunk girl around anywhere?"

"Why?"

"Why not? Caro's sleeping around on me and you've got your little high school girl, which makes me the only one of the three of us not getting laid. You want to come? Maybe she has a friend who won't land you in jail."

In Mike's expression, Patrick read both challenge and plea, and with a sad frustration he realized that as much as he might want to go straight home and tell Caro that Mike was cheating on her, he had no intention of doing it. "Actually, I think I'm done for the night. I think I'll head home."

Mike nodded. "I'm just so tired of losing," he said. "I'm so tired of being the one getting screwed."

Patrick went home, watched some television—he wanted the machine to distract him from his own thoughts but it failed—and then took a shower. When he turned the water off, he heard music playing somewhere in the house, music he hadn't left on. *Dark Side of the Moon.* Caro listened to sentimental indie rock and Mike liked country and angry over-produced Top 40 crap. This music was coming from down the hall. His room.

Layla. In the house. In his *room.* Hands not quite operating smoothly, he pulled on his clothes. He considered grabbing the can of Raid from under the bathroom sink but, ultimately, went unarmed.

She was sitting cross-legged on his bed, reading one of his horror movie magazines. The room had an intimate, bedtime vibe, which he realized after a moment was because the only lamp she'd turned on was the little one next to his bed. The dim bulb treated her kindly. When she looked up at him, he could almost see the girl she'd once been, under the makeup and hair dye.

"I've decided to forgive you," she said.

The fragile bubble of sympathy inside him popped. He turned on the overhead light, flooding the room with surgical illumination. "You got a funny way of showing it, breaking into my house."

"I didn't break in. I came in. The back door was unlocked." She held up the magazine. The page showed a young woman being decapitated. Arterial spurt, wild staring eyes, the whole nine yards. "I have to say, I'm surprised that someone with your taste in entertainment was thrown by a little blood."

"That's not blood. That's corn syrup."

"Whatever. I saw you with your brother's girlfriend, you know."

He waited, warily.

"On Monday. I was out driving around, thought I'd go by Zoney's and see what you were doing, make sure you made it back from the woods okay. And what to my wondering eye should appear?" She looked back down at the magazine. Flipped a few pages. "I have to say, you move pretty fast, making out with her on Monday night when you'd fucked me the Friday before. I assume you didn't tell her."

Her tone was casual, but he didn't trust it. "I told her."

Layla's camera-lens eyes fixed on him. "Let me guess. Your love was just too overwhelming to be stopped by such petty details. Don't worry, stud. I won't tell your brother you're porking his girlfriend."

Jesus. Patrick hadn't even realized that was on the table. He should have seen it coming long ago. "Why not?"

She tossed the magazine down. "Why do I need a why? Can't a girl just do a favor for a friend?"

"You broke into my house to tell me that you're not going to do anything?"

"I told you, I didn't break in." Staring down at her hands now, picking at her nail polish, she looked like a little kid in time-out. When she finally looked up, her face was carefully set—the practiced half smile that he found so infuriating, the lowered lashes—but the act seemed off tonight. Like a wig that was just crooked enough to feel wrong. "You know, you never gave me my new name. Remember, that night at the SuperSpeedy?"

Patrick stared at her. "Are you serious?"

"As a heart attack." She stood up. She was wearing a short skirt, her leather jacket, and a top that was a little too short. A strip of flesh showed above the band of her skirt, just below where he knew the hidden scars started. She came close to him, stopping an arm's length away. "Give me a name." Her words came too quickly now, as if she thought that she could convince him by not giving him a moment to think. "You give me one and I'll give you one and we'll run away together. I'll sell my car. We'll go to Mexico, live on the beach."

"No."

"You hate being who you are. I hate being who I am. Let's be other people." She took a step closer. "If it's the scars—they'll fade, they're not that deep—"

What a horrible mistake he'd made with her. "Layla—"

"I can't live here anymore. I want away. I want out. Justinian"—he saw the way her eyes skittered at the very sound of the guy's name, the way her tongue licked at her lips—"I told him about you. Look."

She lifted her shirt and Patrick didn't want to look but he felt like he had to. On Friday night there had been four cuts. Now her ribs looked like a scratching post. Gashes over gashes in various states of healing and nonhealing, red and inflamed. Her hand fluttered near the wounds, as if she couldn't quite bring herself to touch them.

Patrick felt sick. She dropped the shirt. "Every day. He says he has to get you out of my blood." Her voice was trembling and rough. "I can't make him stop. I can't tell him no."

He put his arms up toward her, but he didn't know what he planned to do with them. Downstairs he heard the faint sounds of somebody working the stuck front door—then the squeak of the hinges—then footsteps. For a moment the two of them stood frozen together, listening as the creaking floorboards sung of two people moving through the house: one into the kitchen, one into the living room. They didn't hear any voices.

Layla's face was pleading, almost desperate. "Do you know what I did tonight?"

He didn't know. He didn't want to know.

"I sucked my dad's assistant's dick. And he's lame, he's a pathetic little hypocrite, but—"

"Then why did you do it?"

Her eyes shone with tears. "I don't know. One minute we're talking and the next minute we're making out and he's telling me how hot I am and then— I don't know how it happened, I don't know." The despair in her face was like smoke, clogging the air, choking him. "My parents hate me. School's a disaster. Justinian hurts me but he's the only one who loves me besides my sister, and she— He has her now, too. I guess I thought if there was somebody else—"

"Layla," he said. "You need help."

She took one of his hands, like she had in the car, and he stiffened. But she only brought it to her face, closed her eyes, and then opened them again. "Then help me. Let's get out of here. I'll do anything you want. I'll *be* anything you want."

The toilet flushed. As gently as he could, he pushed her away. "No."

He may as well have slapped her, the way she looked at him. "No?"

"No," he said.

Her eyes narrowed. "What were you planning to do instead? Be homeless and fuck your brother's girlfriend?" She bit savagely at the words, close enough for him to see the smears of lipstick on her teeth and the purplish-gray patches under her eyes. "Are you two going to run off to Mexico together? Whose car are you going to sell?"

"I don't know," he said evenly.

"You two. Your brother. It's all going to blow wide open, you know." She bared her teeth. "Maybe I'll blow it open for you. I'm amazing at blowing things. Or maybe I'll just go to the cops. That's what you're really afraid of, isn't it?"

"If you do that—" he said, instead, keeping his voice calm, but then he stopped. He couldn't say what would happen if she did that. He could barely even conceive of it. "It would be bad."

"Stop me." The bravado in her voice was Hollywood-perfect but when he looked at her all he saw was desperation.

He knew he should be scared, and some distant part of him was, but mostly he just felt sad. "Layla. Honey." It was the first time he'd ever used such an endearment with her. He didn't mean to, it just fell off his lips. Even now, even as far gone as she was, her mouth and her eyebrows twitched and she took a hopeful step toward him.

He stepped back. Her face fell. "Wait here," he said. "Just wait."

Downstairs, the television was tuned to Comedy Central—some stand-up comedian in front of a brick wall—and the laughter from the studio audience made the room seem even grimmer than it already was. Caro sat on the couch in her work clothes, legs crossed, looking pissed. The cooler was closed and presumably empty; Mike sat in the armchair next to it. He seemed somehow incomplete. It took Patrick a moment to figure out: no beer. Mike wasn't drinking.

"Hey," he said. Layla upstairs, Mike and Caro down here, the horse-faced girl back at the bar—he didn't know what else to say.

"Do you smell hand lotion?" the comic said. It was a punch line. Only the TV people laughed.

"Hey," Mike said. "Do I seem drunk to you?"

Patrick glanced at Caro, who stared at the TV screen with nothing on her face. All her doors and windows were closed. "I don't know. I just got here."

"Caro thinks I was too drunk to drive." Mike's tone was contemptuous, but Patrick remembered the beers Mike had slammed at Jack's, and who knew what else while he was with the horse-faced girl. All in less than two hours. Yeah, Mike probably had been too drunk to drive. And he'd picked up Caro, driven her home. "Don't know, wasn't there," Patrick said, although the words stuck in his throat. He had to get Layla out of the house in a way that would not encourage her to destroy his life. He had been hoping, somehow, that Caro would be able to help him with that, since she clearly had more experience than he did with messed-up teenaged girls, but looking at her face he knew that wasn't going to happen.

"If I was too drunk to drive, Patrick would notice," Mike said. "Nobody's a bigger pussy about drunk driving than my little brother."

Booted feet tromped down the stairs and Patrick's heart fell through the floor. When Layla entered the room she was pulling at her shirt as if she'd just put it back on and all of his sympathy for her, every misplaced shred, vanished into a thick cloud of rage. "That was fun, *honey,* but I have to— Oh, hello!" she said, exactly like she hadn't known full well that Mike and Caro were there.

Mike stared at her. "Hey. You must be Patrick's girlfriend." Caro's coat lay on the end of the couch. He leaned over, grabbed it, and threw it on the floor. "Don't run off. Stay. Hang out."

"She has to go," Patrick said through clenched teeth.

"I have a few minutes." Entirely too pleased with herself, Layla sat down not two feet away from Caro. Whose face was a black hole, who wouldn't look at him.

Mike seemed oblivious. "Want a beer?"

"Absolutely," Layla said.

"Absolutely not," Caro said.

Layla gave her a quick, desultory glance. "Don't be a bitch, Caro," Mike said.

"Not being a bitch. Just trying to keep the number of felonies we commit tonight to a minimum."

"I'm sorry," Layla said. "I don't think we've met. I'm Layla. You must be Mike and—" She turned to Caro, her expression sweet. "Carrie, was it?"

"Charmed," Caro said. "You still can't have a beer."

"Jesus, since when are you such a prude?" Mike glanced at Patrick. "You going to sit down or stand there like an asshole?"

"I'm going to stand here like an asshole," Patrick said.

Layla laughed. "Why does your brother want so desperately for me to go, do you think?"

Mike grinned at her in his amiable Mike way. "I have no idea."

"Maybe he's afraid you'll get grounded if he keeps you out past curfew," Caro said.

"He's definitely afraid that *somebody* is going to get in trouble," Layla said, and that was it, Patrick was going to get her out of his house if he had to drag her by her intestines. She must have read his intentions, because she sighed and stood up. "But I suppose he and Carrie are right. We've probably had all the fun we can legally have in one night." Standing up, she blew Patrick a kiss, and left.

Patrick was so angry he couldn't move.

"No wonder you wanted to race right home," Mike said.

"I didn't know she was here," Patrick said. "She broke in while we were at Jack's."

Mike laughed. "Yeah. Sure she did, you goddamned liar. Not that I blame you. She's hot even if she is jailbait."

Outside, Patrick heard Layla's car rev up, the pounding heartbeat of her music, thought again of the bloody wreckage of her ribs and wanted to rip himself in half, set himself on fire. And then do the same to her.

Caro abruptly stood up and walked into the kitchen. Mike said,

"Ignore her, she's been a bitch all night," and Patrick made some vague noise that he hoped could be interpreted as supportive, or whatever it was that Mike wanted him to be. He could hear the clash of dishes in the kitchen, the slamming of cabinet doors. The neighbor's dog was barking and the comic on the television screen pranced around the stage, body contorted, arms bent and elbows pointed to the ceiling. Patrick waited for what he hoped was an appropriate period of time, staring at the screen but not really seeing it, and then said in what he hoped was an appropriately casual voice, "We got anything to eat?" and went into the kitchen.

She was standing at the stove, staring down into a frying pan where a cracked egg congealed in a slick of butter. Two slices of bread, an unwrapped slice of American cheese, and a jar of apricot jam sat on the counter next to her. Caro ate apricot jam on almost everything. The egg frying in the pan might as well have been cooking under the heat of her scowl.

Patrick heard nothing but commercial jingles from the living room. He came up behind her—choosing the side farthest away from the spatula she gripped in one hand like a weapon—and put a hand on her other shoulder, so his arm was almost around her.

"That girl is trouble, Patrick." She didn't look at him. Her voice was acrid.

He pressed his face into her hair—shampoo, hot butter, a vague oceany smell that was probably lobster—just in case she was about to tell him to go to hell and he never had the chance again. "I didn't ask her to come here."

"I hope not." She tried to flip the egg over with the spatula. It refused to flip, folding on top of itself like a greasy half-moon. "God-damn it. I suck at frying eggs. It repulses me that you slept with her."

"Nothing happened tonight, if that's why you're mad at me."

"I'm not mad at you."

"You're mad at something."

"I'm mad at everything."

"Caro," he said, "how much longer can we do this?"

She didn't answer. She didn't need to. Her chin sank and her shoulders crept up toward her ears. She picked up the pan and dropped it to another burner with a clatter. Yellow yolk promptly oozed out around the hardening white.

"I ruined my egg," she said.

Her voice was thick. Gently, Patrick took the spatula out of her hand. "Go sit down. I'll make you another one."

Tears spilled over Caro's eyelids. Patrick wanted nothing more than to wipe them away, but she dashed at them with her fists and took the spatula back. "Never mind. You'll be late for work. Just go."

So he went upstairs, put on his candy-striped shirt, came back down. Where Mike was moving the cushions off the couch. "I have a feeling I'm sleeping down here tonight. You want a ride?"

Patrick stared at him. "You're kidding, right?"

Mike tossed a pillow down with extra force. "I'm telling you, dude, I'm sober, no matter what she says. Come on. Get in the damn truck."

Patrick didn't have it in him to argue, not that night. Once they were in the truck, Mike bent over the steering wheel for a moment with his hands covering his eyes. When he sat up, Patrick realized, incredulously, that Mike was crying. "Why did you let me go after that girl tonight?" he said. "What the hell is wrong with me? I love her, man. I love her so much. Everything's such shit." Wiping his eyes, he ground the truck into gear, and turned around to back out of the driveway.

The next seven minutes were among the longest of Patrick's life. All too soon—by the time they'd reached the end of Division Street, in fact—it became abundantly, harrowingly clear that Mike was hammered. Patrick tried to remember, as he clutched the door, if he'd ever been in a car driven by somebody so drunk when he wasn't at least as drunk himself. He didn't think so. Mike drove too fast, missed corners, bounced over curbs. Stopped for stop signs halfway through intersections or not at all. When they reached the two-lane highway Patrick was transfixed by the way the center line drifted beneath the truck's tires. The thing was jacked up so high his perspective was skewed, he couldn't tell how bad it really was. And all the while, Mike talked—*I don't know, man, she's been through some messed-up shit, she won't talk about it, maybe that's why she doesn't want to get married, we can just live together for all I care but she's been so goddamned weird lately*—and Patrick tried to figure out how he'd gotten here, in this truck on this night. How he could have avoided it. How many things had gone wrong.

When they finally got to Zoney's, Mike let the truck roll to a stop, coming dangerously close to the gas pumps. Patrick opened the door and the air outside hit him like a song. Before he could get out, Mike said, "Dude, she trusts you. She talks to you, right? If there were somebody—if she were fucking around—you'd tell me, wouldn't you?"

"Sure." Patrick was half in and half out of the truck, his foot dangling uncomfortably in midair. "I got to get to work."

"Because I didn't think Caro was like that."

"No, of course not."

Mike rubbed his eyes. "Why'd you let me go after that slut at the bar, man? Why didn't you stop me?" His voice was sad, pleading, with a hint of whine. This was just like talking to the old man, and Patrick reacted the same way he always had.

"Sorry. I should have," he said, automatically; dismayed by how quickly he fell back into the old, placating patterns, and chilled by how comfortable and familiar those patterns felt.

"Without her, I got nothing." Then, as an afterthought, "And you. Just her and you and that's it. I love you, little brother."

Patrick managed a laugh. "You're drunk as shit. You want me to call somebody? I could get you a cab, call Caro to come get you."

But of course Mike didn't want a cab and Caro's car was dead, so Patrick watched him drive away, wondering who he'd kill on his way home and knowing that this time, without a doubt, it would be his fault. Mike was dangerous, and Patrick had let him go.

The no-time of Zoney's was a relief.

By the time his shift was done, he was wiped out. When Bill showed up to take over he asked Patrick if he wanted to go smoke a joint, but Patrick didn't need chemicals to feel out of his head. He stumbled home in the glaring faraway world to a silent house. The tangled blankets on the couch and the nearby litter of beer cans told Patrick that Mike had, indeed, slept there the night before. Patrick tapped on Caro's bedroom door but there was no answer. When he opened it a crack he saw the slash of her hair across her pillow and decided to let her sleep. He told himself he was being considerate, but actually, it was just easier.

Downstairs, he let himself fall into the beery mess of blankets on the couch so that he'd wake up when she left for work. They would talk. They would figure something out. But when he woke up, it was almost six. He'd slept for ten hours, and the bedroom was empty. Patrick showered and got dressed in silence. The house had changed. All of their stuff was there, but it already felt abandoned.

He wished Caro had woken him up before she left. He wished he'd woken her up that morning, that he hadn't been too cowardly and tired to deal with whatever fallout remained from Layla's little performance the night before, from Mike's adventures with the horse-faced girl, from the broken egg. The thought of her hair on the pillowcase stung him and if he could have kicked his own ass he would have.

He couldn't do this much longer. He couldn't do any of it.

Mike came in with a greasy bag that smelled like hot wings. "Dig in," he said, dropping it on the coffee table. "I had the worst god-damned hangover of my life this morning. I think I was still drunk when I got to work."

Patrick didn't feel like eating. "Hey, what ended up happening with that girl last night?" he asked, instead. It seemed important, somehow, to know if Mike had cheated on Caro.

"Nothing." Mike ripped open the bag. "The real question is, what happened with *your* girl last night? Did she really break into the house?"

"Yeah. And she's not my girl."

"That's hilarious."

"Actually, it's kind of creepy."

"You got no sense of adventure." Mike ripped a wing in two, stuck half of it into his mouth, and sucked at the meat. Then he took the bone out of his mouth and dropped it back in the bag. "Listen, man, when we get kicked out of here, how do you feel about finding your own place?"

Mike's tone was casual, but from the way he looked at Patrick out of the corner of his eye, Patrick could tell that this conversation was one Mike had been thinking about. "Sure."

"Cool. It's just, I think maybe Caro and I should get our own place. I think things might work a little better if it was just the two of us."

For a dreadful instant Patrick was afraid he would laugh.

They ate the wings and watched some television and it was just like a thousand other times when one or the other of them had been surly about some girl. Mike didn't mention Caro and Patrick didn't mention Layla. It lulled Patrick into a bleak, familiar stupor, and even as he hated it, the stupor was hard to shake off.

At eight, somebody knocked on the door. Patrick knew imme-diately that the man standing on the porch was Layla's father. The resemblance was strong: Layla's chin, the shape of her face, her round cheekbones. His clothes and the car parked at the curb both looked expensive, but his face was haggard. He was younger than it seemed like he should be. In one hand, he held a sheaf of papers.

"I'm Jeff Elshere," he said. "I'm looking for Layla."

They could sit and drink beer all they wanted; outside, the world continued to spin. Behind him, Patrick heard quick footsteps as Mike made himself scarce. "She's not here," Patrick said.

The man lifted the papers. "The GPS device in her car says she was here last night from ten forty-five to eleven thirty. So you might as well tell me the truth."

"I'm not lying." Judging by the guy's coffee-stained shirt and the grim worry in his face, the truth was the last thing he wanted to hear, anyway. "She was here. She isn't now. You want to come in, see for yourself?"

"I want to find my daughter," Elshere said doggedly, but when Patrick stepped back from the door he stepped through it. Patrick offered him a beer and he shook his head. "I don't drink."

"That's right. You're the minister."

Elshere sank down on the couch. Everything about him seemed crumpled, concave. "I'm not a minister. I'm a home church leader."

"Water?"

Elshere nodded.

When Patrick came back, the guy had picked the cable bill up from the table and was staring at it. "You're Michael Cusimano?" he said, in a tone of faint disbelief.

"Patrick." Patrick handed him the glass. "Mike's my brother."

Elshere studied him. "You're Patrick."

"I just said that."

"I should tell you," he said, "I know the Czerpak family pretty well."

Patrick sat down in the armchair. "Yeah?"

"You're the one who called the police."

Patrick didn't say anything to that.

"You're the one who did the right thing. Eventually." There was just the faintest hint of emphasis on the *eventually;* the resounding certainty in the way he spoke allowed no room for doubt, either in himself or in anybody else. Patrick saw how it could get old quickly, growing up with that voice in your ear.

"Eventually," he said.

"How exactly do you know my daughter? You're quite a bit older than she is."

"I know her from the night she walked up to me and told me she wanted to be friends because my old man killed the Czerpak kid," Patrick said. "She hasn't left me alone since."

Elshere looked stunned. "She did that?"

Patrick nodded.

"Why would she do that?"

"If I had to guess, I'd say because she knew you'd hate it."

Elshere's shoulders slumped. "Yeah." That note of certainty was gone. "That sounds right." He stared down at his sheaf of papers, flipping through them, but Patrick didn't think he was actually seeing them. "Tell me," he finally said. "When did you know you were going to have to do it?"

"What," Patrick said, "call the police?"

Elshere nodded. "It must have—" He stopped, and then started again. "It must have felt like such a horrible thing to do. When did you know?"

When had he known? When he saw the car? No. Before that. He'd gone into the garage knowing what he would find. When he saw the old man, crying on the couch, right where Jeff Elshere sat now? That felt wrong, too. When they'd come off shift, all three of them, and the old man had said, *Hey, boys, let's go hit the Strike;* when Mike and Patrick said, no, they were going to go sleep, they were hungover from the night before, and the old man had gone anyway?

When they'd come home from Patrick's mother's funeral?

You boys go find something to do with yourselves. Your old man's going to get drunk.

He had no intention of answering Elshere's question, but—he'd always known. It had to be him. There was nobody else. Mike cruised along. Mike coasted. Mike found the path of least resistance and took it. He had a lousy job, unsteady pay with no security, surrounded by people who looked at him and saw his father; but looking for a new one would be too hard. Like moving out on his own would have been hard, or drinking less, or sorting through the boxes in the garage. Mike didn't do things that were hard unless somebody forced him. In a way, Caro had been perfect for him: she was easy to look at, she could cook, and she washed a mean load of laundry. She had no family, no friends, no other loyalties. As far as Mike was concerned, she had sprung fully-formed from the tap at Jack's Bar and Sandwiches, filling the hole that the old man left when he went to prison. Mike could fit himself over her like a wheel on an axle and spin happily away without ever wondering where they were going, if they were moving at all.

"Have you had sex with my daughter?" Elshere asked. "The age of consent in this state is sixteen. Layla's seventeen. We probably wouldn't bother with a corruption charge. We—we have bigger problems right now. Layla is—" He stopped talking.

Patrick thought of Layla, of the cut-and-paste sexuality she'd taken straight from the movies. Layla, with whom he'd engaged in two separate acts of explicit sexual congress, and he couldn't imagine how either had brought her any pleasure and after both he'd wanted her out of his sight so badly he could barely look at her. Layla and her lacy purple bra and the mess she'd let her friend make of her body, the coffin ring and the skeleton earrings and the death fixation and the wild teary look in her eyes the night before. *I want away, I want out. Justinian hurts me but he's the only one who loves me.* "What?" Patrick was surprised at the challenge in his voice. "Layla is what?"

"I've made abstinence my life's work. You said it yourself. She does things just because I hate them. Even if those things ruin lives. Even if one of those lives is hers." He looked at Patrick and his eyes were tired. "I know I've failed her. All I want to know is how badly."

As if he couldn't see that just as easily by taking one look at Layla, by listening to a tenth of what came out of her mouth. "Pretty fucking badly, I'd say," Patrick told him, and was satisfied to see that the guy at least had the decency to wince. "You tried the clearing in the woods?"

Elshere nodded. "There, everywhere. All of her friends' houses. I even drove into Pittsburgh. I've been driving all night." He shook his head. "Layla is so *smart*," he said, and the mystification and hurt in his voice was so great that even Patrick felt a little sorry for him.

"I hope you find her," he said. "I really do."

The business card he gave Patrick before he left said, *Price Above Rubies. Treasure your teen for all she's worth.*

TWELVE

Caro's car died Wednesday night. This time, all the jumper cables in the world couldn't bring it back to life. Darcy tried, Gary tried, a drunk guy who'd been slamming back martinis at the bar all night tried. But no matter which battery they hooked the Civic up to, when Caro turned the key there was nothing.

Somebody said it was probably the starter coil, or the fuel pump, or the something else. Caro wasn't listening. She sat behind the unresponsive wheel of her corpse of a car, which had taken her away from Margot and Pitlorsville and Columbus and Athens and who knew how many other places, she didn't, not anymore. It had been her shelter and her refuge and her friend, it had waited for her in countless parking lots like other people's mothers waited for them at bus stops in grade school, but when it died she was surprised by how quickly it became nothing to her.

She left it in the parking lot and got a ride home with Darcy, who said, "That car's been giving you nothing but trouble as long as I've known you. Sayonara, garbagemobile. Right?"

"Right," Caro said, and climbed her exhausted way up the incredibly steep and dangerous front steps to the Cusimanos' house. Her feet and back and shoulders shrieked in three-part harmony. A tall, narrow window was set into the wall on either side of the front door; they were both dirt-spotted and shrouded with cobwebs, but through one of them she could see Mike asleep on the couch. Passed out, more likely. He and Patrick had gone to Jack's that night. By now Patrick would be at Zoney's but judging by the open cooler on the floor next to the coffee table Mike had come home and continued the night's good work. His boots were off, his feet propped on the arm of the couch. The bottoms of his socks were ashen. His jaw hung slack and through the walls she could hear his snoring, and the television laugh track.

Drive that boozy look from his face and slap the dust off his jeans, and he would be the Mike who had danced with her, joyful and laughing, under the disco ball at Jack's. Who had found out the next morning that she was sleeping in her car, looked outraged, and said, *Like hell you are.* One night she'd had a bad dream—not just an eek-I'm-falling dream but a Margot dream, a real scorcher—and he'd stroked her back until she stopped shaking and could get back to sleep. She remembered how gladly she had burrowed into his chest, how grateful she had been then for his safe solid bigness.

And—still standing on the porch—she also remembered the night of the Great Apocalyptic Mistake (although maybe she couldn't call it that anymore, since she'd made that mistake half a dozen times since), when she'd stood exactly here and looked through the dirty window exactly as she was now. To the couch where Patrick had been lying, almost exactly as Mike was now, but awake. She'd had a bad shift, not unlike the one she'd just finished, with her feet and her back and her shoulders and all of it. Patrick played his cards close. Most of the time his expression was cool and removed or cool and amused or just cool, but watching, always watching, with those dark-water hazel eyes of his, so impossible to read. But that night, from the darkness, she had looked into his face and seen keen, intelligent despair, and while she thought she appreciated Mike's optimism and cheerful determination, what she saw in Patrick reached into her and held her. Because Mike's optimism was the stubborn kind and it felt increasingly like a lie, a willful ignorance in the face of all the facts. It made her feel like she didn't know what she knew, like the world wasn't what it seemed to be, and it made her feel crazy. What she saw in Patrick was what she felt in herself. She had walked through the door and bitched about the lock and watched him eat pasta with his fingers, and all the while she had known what would happen. Mistake or no. Apocalypse or no.

Inside, Mike slept on.

Caro felt like she was driving on rims. She was afraid all the time. When she lay on Patrick's pillow she couldn't relax, because what if she left a hair, what if Mike came in and found it there, long and dark and obviously not his brother's? When she lay on her own pillow, she couldn't relax, either, because what if Mike wanted to have sex and what if sex with Mike was the right thing, what if the right thing was just to let this mess with Patrick go and fall back into her old life? Sex and takeout and Jack's Bar and Sandwiches. Could she even do that, if she wanted to, or had things gone too far? Making out in stolen moments the way she and Patrick did was for kids. The co-brushing of teeth, the payment of bills, poking Mike when he snored to make him roll over—that was grown-up life, that was stability, that was what she'd wanted as long as she could remember. A world that didn't change between going to sleep at night and waking up the next morning. How much was she willing to give up, she'd wonder, what was she willing to lose?

Then Patrick would just—be there—watchful, aware, his eyes growing murky with tension. And she would think: maybe, maybe . . . but wasn't that always the way, didn't she always think *maybe, maybe* when she met a guy? Wasn't it the potential of the relationship that caught her heart and the drudgery that dulled it? Would Patrick, in time, come to seem just as clumsy and predictable as Mike sometimes did; would he turn out to have a thing for car sex or baby talk or sexy nurse costumes that at first seemed harmless and easily indulged but that grew and grew and pressed and pressed until she wanted to scream?

Caro walked around to the back door. She took off her shoes, opening the screen door slowly and carefully so that it wouldn't sing or cry, and then she crept upstairs to their bedroom, lay down on the bed, and pulled her knees to her chest. Closed her eyes, tried to sleep, eventually succeeded. Sometime in the night she felt the bed move as Mike lay down. All the way on the other side of the mattress, as far away from her as he could get.

On Thursday night, Mike wanted Patrick to go drinking with him again. Patrick was clearly running on fumes but Caro begged him to go. She told him she was worried about what would happen when Mike got drunk, at Jack's or elsewhere, and Patrick wasn't there to run interference. Which was true, but even truer was that when Patrick and Mike were drinking together, neither of them was with her. She was tired of being confused and torn. As the night passed at the restaurant, she started to think: if she could get her car fixed, she could just leave the whole damn mess behind. Chalk Patrick up to Wrong-Place-Wrong-Time and add Mike to the long list of Boys. The Boys were the true division of Caro's life. Schools blurred together, because she'd start the year in one and finish somewhere else and a year later find herself back in the first, but the Boys came one after another in a steady march, occasionally overlapping but never repeating. Before Mike there was Scott and before Scott there was Andrew and before Andrew there was Dave, the burger-bar guy from Columbus; before Dave were Robbie, Matthew, Steve, Bryan, on back to Brent, who had been their landlord when Caro was in sixth grade. The things she hadn't known then, the things she hadn't known. Brent had bought her dinner sometimes—Boston Market in a flimsy plastic container—and given her a couch when Margot got too wild. After the first time they'd had sex, she'd thought he was her boyfriend. *Are we going to get married?* she'd asked him, once. Imagining a sort of dollhouse life, with turkey dinners and lawn sprinklers and lots of cute clothes. Not the shabby thin-walled duplex where they both lived, where sometimes he had to tell her to turn it down so her mother didn't hear how much fun they were having (although it hadn't been that much fun, she'd only made noise because she thought she was supposed to). He'd laughed at her, and then grown quiet, and not long after that they'd moved and he'd hung up on her when she called him.

Lately, she found herself thinking about Brent a lot, and for the first time, feeling angry. Because she had been twelve years old and all she'd wanted was a safe place, and now she was twenty-five and she wanted the same thing, and life shouldn't be so fucking hard, you shouldn't have to give so fucking much up.

That night, after close, Caro was surprised and unhappy to see Mike's truck pull up in front of the restaurant. She was standing at the window, looking out at the street; he saw her, tapped his horn twice, and she lifted a hand in greeting. Darcy, emerging from the back, said, "Guess you don't need a ride after all. Hey, are you ever going to give his brother my number?"

"Trust me," Caro said, "you don't want to get involved with his brother."

The cab of Mike's truck reeked of beer. "Hey," he said, as she climbed in.

She forced a smile. "Hey, yourself."

"You look pretty."

"I look like ass," she said. "Hey, don't take this the wrong way, but it kind of smells like a kegger in here. Are you cool driving?"

"Of course I am. Me and Patrick went to Jack's, that's all."

"Yeah, I know. That's kind of why I was asking."

"I'm not drunk. You think I can't have a beer or two without getting drunk?"

"I didn't say that."

"Because I can. I totally can."

Caro didn't want to fight. "How was Jack's?"

"Good." He hesitated for a moment. "Lots of people."

A quiet warning bell rang in Caro's head. "Yeah, well. Thursday night, huh?"

"We met on a Thursday. You remember?"

"Sure."

"You know what else I remember? I remember how pretty the stars were."

The warning bell got louder. Mike Cusimano, in his natural state, did not notice stars. Also, he was wrong. Her memories of having sex with him in the back of the truck were blissfully dim but she remembered the soft cotton of his shirt under her hands, the cool of the metal truck bed seeping up through the jacket he'd laid down for her—and the gray clouds hanging over them like a downy blanket. "There weren't any stars."

"Sure there were."

"No. It rained that whole week." She would know. She'd listened to the rain drumming on the roof of her car like impatient fingers as she tried to sleep, cramped and awkward in the backseat.

"No way. Because you and me, we were talking about them, you said—" He stopped. Probably remembering which girl that had actually been. When he spoke again, his tone was sheepish. "I guess maybe that was another time."

"I guess so."

Then his words came out all in a rush. "But that's how it is for me, you know. I barely remember any other girl I've ever dated, but you. Caro—"

"What?"

"You know things have been kind of rough lately, with us."

"I know," she said. Wary.

"Well, I wanted to tell you—there was this girl, tonight, at Jack's. And I was drunker than I am now." He glanced at her. "And I sort of fooled around with her a little bit."

Great! an illogical part of Caro wanted to cry. *Because I've been sleeping with your brother, and now we're even. Let's get a pizza!* She bit her lip hard to keep from laughing—although what she felt inside, she didn't know what it was but it wasn't laughter—and said, "What does that mean, fooled around with her a little bit?"

"I kissed her. You know. Fooled around." Another sidelong glance. Was he checking to see if she was upset? Was she upset? "I didn't have sex with her, if that's what you're worried about. Here's the thing, though—I wanted to. I mean, part of me wanted to. But mostly I think that was because things have been so weird with us, and— Look on the floor, there, under the seat, will you?"

She bent down, looked, and picked it up. An unused condom, although the package was torn across the top as if someone had opened it, and then changed their mind. She could feel the hard ring of it inside the package, slipping around in its envelope of lubricant. An empty, harmless sort of thing, like the empty mussel shells Gary threw away at the end of the night.

"I think I left it there on purpose so you'd find it, but now I'm just telling you," Mike said. "Because that's how close I came."

Sitting there with the condom in her hand—and feeling unaccountably angry, given the circumstances; screw the girl or don't, she thought, but don't make me play this stupid game—she said, "Exactly what reaction are you looking for, here?"

"No reaction. I just want you to listen to me. Because I could have done it, but I didn't, because I love you. And I don't care what's been happening, or going on, or what I don't know about, or what. Because I still love you and I always will."

His words were coming too fast again, and too sincere, as if he'd rehearsed them. Caro realized what this was: it was a declaration of love, the Mike Cusimano version. She couldn't help it. She laughed.

"Why are you laughing?" Mike sounded hurt. Justifiably so, maybe. "What are you laughing about?"

"You," she said. "You just gave me a half-open condom that you almost used to fuck another girl. What am I supposed to be, touched?"

"I'm being honest, aren't I? Most guys wouldn't be. Most guys would have just done it and then lied to you afterward. Especially since—"

He stopped. An ominous silence filled the car.

"Especially since what?" Caro said, no longer laughing.

"You know."

"No. I don't know."

"Don't make me say it."

"No," she said again. "If you've got something to say, say it." Feeling like a tide risen as high as it can, a wave about to break.

They were at the house now. He pulled into the driveway too fast—she lurched against the door—turned the key, and then sat in the sudden silence. She could see his jaw working, his fists clenching on the steering wheel.

"Caro," he finally said, in a voice gone tuneless with deliberate calm, "the point is, I still love you, despite all the shit you're putting me through. So don't be a bitch."

A broken shard of guilt pierced her. Right then, she knew, if she reached out and touched him—a shoulder, a knee—if she spoke to him gently and lovingly, even if only to say his name—that would be all it would take. He'd forgive her everything. Like he had forgiven Patrick everything, she thought; and then remembered what Patrick had told her earlier that night, that Mike had threatened to punch him in the face, and she knew that Mike had never forgiven Patrick for a single thing.

"Well," she said, "thank you for not fucking the drunk chick you met at a bar. I guess."

His fists on the wheel clenched again, and this time they didn't let go. "Yeah, well, you know why else I didn't fuck her? Because the last girl I fucked at a bar turned out to be a slut."

"You're an asshole," she said.

"I'm an asshole who's faithful to you. Which is more than you can say."

Then he got out of the car, slammed the door behind him, and went into the house. He slammed that door, too.

How much longer can we do this, Patrick asked her, later, after his stupid little goth twit with her silly boots and overwrought makeup finally left, and Caro didn't answer because they both knew the answer.

The answer was: not very long.

Mike slept on the couch that night. As she fell asleep Caro thought that if they hadn't passed the moment of no return before, they might well have passed it now, and with that thought came an odd feeling of calm, and stillness, and pause. Like the wind had died down but the current had yet to pick up. She wondered if other people felt like this, if every life change was an exercise in drift. Somehow she didn't think so.

When she woke up, Mike was there. Sitting next to her, holding a cup of coffee. The room smelled of it, bitter and burned.

"Peace offering," he said, "and I'm working really, really hard not to puke right now, so take it, okay?"

She sat up and took it. The sky outside the window was gray and early-looking. The coffee tasted as bad as it smelled.

Mike looked forlorn. "I wanted to take you out to breakfast. Do this right."

"It's okay," she said. "It's too early for food."

His neck drooped and his forehead came to rest on the mattress. When he spoke, his words were muffled. "I'm a bastard."

She felt a sudden, sad burst of kindness toward him. He had been right, after all. She was cheating on him. "You're just hungover."

"No. I mean last night. I'm sorry for last night." His head swiveled so he could look up at her. "If I heard some other guy saying those things to you, I'd kick his ass. I'd put him in the hospital."

"That's very sweet."

"Seriously," he said. "I'm sorry."

His eyelids were pink and puffy-looking, the lines at the sides of his mouth deep and unhappy. She shouldn't be snide, she thought. Mike wasn't a word person. He wasn't like Patrick, he didn't need seventeen ways to describe *miserable*. When Mike was sad or sorry or pissed off he said so; when he was attacked he fought back. He wasn't sophisticated or subtle but you mostly knew where you stood with Mike.

"I know," she said, softly. Her hand reached out to stroke his hair. The thumbnail was broken and jagged. She watched it move through his hair and wondered when she'd done that, and how.

Mike sat up. His face was hopeful. "Look, I'll tell you what. This weekend, let's go out. Anywhere you want. I'll even drive into Pittsburgh. We'll start over."

She didn't think so. She didn't think they would. But there was no way to say that to him, not now, not at five thirty in the morning. He turned greenish and groaned and his head dropped back down to the mattress.

"I think I'm dying," he said.

"Let's talk about it sometime when you're not," she said.

"Tonight? When you get home from work?"

He would forgive her. He would never forgive Patrick, but he would forgive her. "Sure."

He smiled, wanly. "It's a date."

Then he left, and she dumped out the horrible burned coffee and went back to sleep. She was surprised at how easily it happened, as if even the most animal parts of her brain knew she couldn't deal with this. Not right now. At some point during the long morning, she woke to the sound of the door opening gently, knew it was Patrick—who else could it be—and pretended she hadn't heard. She needed more sleep, more time; she needed to be able to figure out what she was going to do.

But when she woke up she had nothing. Patrick was asleep on the couch, wearing his candy-striped Zoney's shirt. He looked ragged, unwashed. If she was his girlfriend, she thought, she would make him get a haircut and shave, she would make him buy some T-shirts from bands that still recorded music once in a while, she would make him find a job that didn't require a stupid uniform. Or maybe she wouldn't, because Patrick would hate all of those things, and she would hate herself for doing it again, for taking her shitty life and tossing some ugly throw pillows across it and pretending it was more than it was. Pretending *she* was more than she was. But she had nothing else for him. She couldn't even break up with his goddamned brother for him. And so she dressed for work and did her hair quietly, and he was so deeply asleep that he didn't wake up at all, and she crept out of the house, and let him sleep.

Her last table that night was a bunch of jerks from some computer company, all wearing khaki pants with mobile phones clipped to their belts and celebrating somebody's last day at work. She knew it was a computer company because one of them spent half the meal standing by the kitchen door shouting into his phone about rollouts and debugging, and she knew it was somebody's last day at work because they wouldn't shut up about it. They wouldn't shut up at all, in fact. Was there chicken on the menu tonight because one of them was really hungry for a couple of breasts and a thigh, what kind of tomatoes were in the salad because another only liked his tomatoes cherry, and so forth. Caro, who was nervy in a way she hadn't been since leaving her mother, bore it patiently until the end, when one of them—she thought it was the guy who was leaving, and she hoped he was leaving the country—said, "You've been a good sport, Carolyn. How about a cocktail?"

She smiled her automatic waitress smile and started to say she couldn't drink on the job, but he cut her off. "I'll bring the cock, you bring the tail."

"Eat shit," she said. Pleasantly enough, she thought; but the guy turned purple, snatched the black leather check presenter out of her hand, and scribbled out her tip on the credit card receipt inside it.

"I want to speak to your goddamned manager," he said.

Gary bawled her out about it later. "A five-hundred-dollar tab, Caro. Five hundred dollars, and nobody from that company is ever going to come back here again."

"Well, that leaves me in tears."

"I'm serious, Caro. You get a customer who's treating you badly, you come tell me about it. You tell me about it and I'll kick them out on their ass, never let them back through the door." He pointed a callused, knife-scarred finger at her. "But you can*not* tell them to eat shit. You can't let other customers *hear* you telling them to eat shit." They were in the kitchen. Darcy was outside, wiping down tables. Gary slammed a cupboard door. "Come on, Caro. What's wrong with you? Why would you just take that garbage all night?"

Caro gritted her teeth. "Because it's a five-hundred-dollar tab." Knowing, even as she said it, that it was a lame reason, that she'd just put a price tag on her own pride.

For a long moment, Gary looked at Caro, his face grim. "Next time, just tell me about it, okay?" he finally said, and her face burned.

She was still fuming when she got home. The way she felt—impatient, angry—she didn't want to talk to Mike. She didn't want to talk to anyone. So she came in through the back again, hearing the television blaring the late late show in the living room. Which meant it was midnight, or close to it. She crept upstairs, closed the door behind her, took off her shoes and her hose, lay down and closed her eyes. She wished she had somewhere else to go. Anywhere.

Somebody was moving around downstairs. The fridge door opened, a cupboard slammed. Then she heard feet on the stairs. There was a light knock on the door. It opened.

She squeezed her eyes tighter.

"Babe?" Mike said. "You okay?"

"Yeah, sure." She was surprised at how normal her voice sounded. "Come in."

The door swung wide and she heard a damp glassy clank as he put the beer bottle he was carrying down on the nightstand. Beer in bottles: Mike was breaking out the good stuff. A vague sense of dread bloomed in Caro. She felt the bed shift as he curled his body around hers, slipped his arm around her waist. His breath smelled like alcohol. "I heard you come in. Why'd you use the back door?"

"I thought you might be asleep."

"No, I was waiting for you." His unshaven cheek felt scratchy and unwholesome on her neck. "You missed a hell of a night around here."

Caro's eyes flew open and she rolled backward, looking up at him. Her chest was fluttering, nervous. "Why? What happened?"

"That chick Patrick's seeing, that high school girl?" Mike pulled a piece of her hair out of her face and smoothed it back. "Her dad showed up looking for her. Had some GPS thing proving she'd been here, you believe that?" Mike's words were crisp enough, but the look on his face was almost merry. She couldn't tell how drunk he was. "He actually came right out and asked if Patrick had slept with her. Right there in the living room."

The fluttering intensified. "What did he say?"

Mike laughed. "Nothing. Patrick's too much of a pussy for jail and he knows it." Shrugging, he added, "The guy said he wouldn't press charges, but Patrick still kept his mouth shut. For once in his life."

Caro's chest felt tight because she hadn't been breathing and now she made herself inhale. "Well. That's good."

When she'd rolled toward him, Mike had thrown an arm over her. He'd been massaging her hip gently through her skirt as he talked and she'd barely noticed, because she'd been thinking about Patrick. Now he started playing with the lower buttons on her blouse. "So, where are we going this weekend?"

"I don't know. I might have to work."

"Ask for the night off. You never take off. That guy owes you." His fingers moved up her chest, toying with a button and then the one above it, until they were between her breasts. "Starting over, re-member? We'll go out, have fun. Next week we'll start looking for our own place, maybe, like you said that night at Jack's."

Jack's. She'd been so panicked about the house that day, the world had felt like it was falling away under her feet. There had only been one Great Apocalyptic Mistake, not a dozen of them. She remem-bered thinking about turkey dinners and lawn sprinklers, cherry sourball drawer pulls with matching dish towels.

Mike was still talking. "Patrick said he's cool with getting his own place."

I want to stay right here, he'd said to her, the morning after she picked him up at that Citgo. *I don't ever want to move.* He hadn't meant the house. "He did?"

"Well, I kind of told him he had to."

She stared at him. "I thought you said you didn't want to do that."

"I'd do it for you," he said. "I'd do anything for you. You're the most beautiful girl I've ever met and you just drive me crazy. Even right now." Mike's fingers pressed and the button beneath them popped open. When she looked down she could see the tiny bow at the center of her bra, the lace at the edges of the cups. He rolled on top of her. Caro was frozen, she didn't know what to do. His mouth was on hers, his tongue pushing its way behind her lips, his knees angling and nudging to part her legs. She tried to find that gentle place of resistance that would communicate *not now* instead of *stop*, but he was too drunk to pick up on it. The hem of her skirt rose to the tops of her thighs as her legs spread apart, and then his erection pressed against her through his jeans, hard enough to hurt. She felt not aroused but sick. Her bare legs felt exposed; the hot fog of his mouth on hers was suffocating. She tried to turn away. His mouth chased her.

All of this took seconds.

If she gave him her body, things would snap back into place between them like a dislocated shoulder going back into joint. Sore, but functional. It would take five minutes but the thought—the thought that she was having the thought—made her teeth and fists and toes clench. When she was twelve, she had let Brent take her clothes off not once but multiple times, because in her television-fueled vision of the way the world worked, you had sex, and you fell in love, and you got married, and somebody took care of you, and you were safe. Lies. Lies. She wasn't safe. She had never been safe.

Suddenly furious, she bucked and pushed and he fell off her with a surprised grunt. She yanked her skirt down and moved away. "No," she said, and discovered that her voice was shaking with rage.

Mike looked confused. "Why not? We're getting our own place. I thought things were okay." When she looked at his face, she saw the same Mike he'd always been. His face was a boy's face, a yearbook face, the kind of face that seemed made to pose with sporting equipment: kneeling with a football, baseball bat poised and ready, holding a big dead fish on a string or a limp-necked deer with foggy eyes. He loved sports. Sports were clear and defined. They had rules. You scored points. You won.

"Because I don't want to," she said.

He made an exasperated noise. "That's a bullshit reason."

Which wasn't what he meant, exactly, and she knew that, but all the same anger burst from her like vomit and her hand darted out and slapped his arm so hard her palm stung. He snatched at her wrist and twisted her arm over and now they were fighting, actually fighting. He was stronger than she was. He held her to the bed, steel grips on both arms as she twisted under him. Her head full of radio static, rage and frustration grown inarticulate with the passage of years; spitting words—not even words, half words, guttural animal noises—up at him. Her own hair was in her eyes and her mouth and nothing she did made any difference, he was just there, solid as a building above her. It was like attacking the ceiling, doing battle with a brick wall. Her anger turned to panic and she fought harder, she had never fought like this, not once: thrashing her legs at the mattress, making the headboard slam against the wall.

Mike pinned her arms against her body and lifted her off the bed. "You're—not—making—any—sense!" he shouted, right into her face, slamming her down against the bed with each word—it didn't hurt but the impacts made her dizzy, the world lashing sickeningly over his shoulder. One final slam and he was back on top of her, his legs between hers, and she gasped and the hair in her mouth went down her throat and she started to choke. Air. She couldn't get air.

Above her, she saw dim alarm dawn on his face. "Jesus." He pushed himself up on his arms so her own arms could move. His legs still held hers apart but her hands could claw the hair out of her throat and she could draw in deep gasping breaths. "Jesus." He was helping her, pulling strands of hair gently out of her face. "Are you okay? Caro? Honey?"

She couldn't talk.

"Are you okay? Jesus, did I hurt you? Can you breathe?"

She nodded and was in fact filling her lungs with air again and again while he hovered above her, his eyes watching her anxiously. He pushed her hair back again, running his hand over her skull. "Jesus," he said again, and then dropped his head to rest on her breastbone. As if he was the one who needed shelter.

"Get off me," she said, when she could talk.

His head lifted and he looked at her. "This has gone all wrong."

"Get off."

But he didn't move. "I didn't mean to hurt you. I'm sorry. I just— Say you're not mad. Say it's okay, okay?"

And still, that desperate part of her whispered that if she did it, if she told him it was okay—just this one time—but when she looked at him she saw the bartender from the burger bar, she saw Brent the landlord; she saw herself, eyes as dead as Margot's, every time she'd ever given it up out of desperation or hope. Not just sex. More than sex. Every backseat, every blanket, every meal she'd cooked, every toilet she'd cleaned. Every time her ass had been pinched and she'd said nothing, every lobster she'd heard dying in a pot of boiling water. *I'll bring the cock, you bring the tail.* All she had ever wanted was a world she could count on and every time she thought she had it somebody took it away from her, somebody kicked her out or traded her in or walked away without a word. She never learned. Nothing ever changed. That sad sick little part of her was urging her to stay, to try to fix it. Say, *oh, honey, it's okay,* and then he would get up and she could leave and she would never have to do it again.

But the rest of her knew that wasn't true. She would always have to do it again.

"Tell me who it is," he said. "Tell me who you've been with. I've been trying to figure it out but I can't. If it's not Gary—or someone from the bar—"

And then the hand she'd been allowing to drift toward the nightstand wrapped around his beer bottle and she brought it down on the side of his skull.

The beer inside sprayed over the bed in an arc. He yelped and fell to the other side. Grabbing at his head, rolling back and forth. She'd intended to hit him with all her might but at the last minute she'd held back. The bottle hadn't even broken.

"Jesus!" His voice was thick with pain. "Jesus, what did you do that for?"

"I told you to get off me and you didn't listen," she said. "You never listen. Nobody ever listens."

He stared at her, drops of beer sparkling in his hair. "Are you fucking crazy?"

But Caro was already up, already running. Her car was dead in the municipal lot downtown but Patrick's keys were on the end table where she'd left them, there was a pair of sandals by the door, her coat, her purse. Dimly she was aware of Mike behind her, stumbling a little—from booze or the blow from the bottle, she didn't know—and leaning against the wall. He kept saying her name, over and over. "Caro. Wait, please—baby—" but it was like she was hearing Margot talk to her imaginary wall-gnomes, like he was talking to somebody who wasn't there.

THIRTEEN

Dad was out late into the night looking for Layla. The house phone rang again and again; again and again Mother ran to the computer, double-checking the report they'd downloaded from Layla's GPS unit. Looking up addresses, finding phone numbers. They didn't know that Verna had warned Layla about the wilderness camp. They thought she wasn't coming home because she was afraid of being punished for what she'd done to Toby. After Dad found her car abandoned in the high school parking lot, her phone in the console, he came home. It was almost one o'clock in the morning but he came into Verna's room, woke her, and asked if she knew where Layla was. Verna answered, honestly, that she didn't.

"Verna." Gray hollows nestled under Dad's eyes and spilled coffee spotted the front of his shirt. He sat on the edge of Verna's bed; Mother stood in the doorway. "I know about Toby. I know everything. You can't help Layla by keeping her secrets anymore."

But it was not just Layla's secrets that Verna was keeping. She told him nothing. He asked her if she was sexually active and Verna shook her head mutely, feeling like a liar. Mother took a step into the room and said, "Jeff," but Dad stared at Verna as if he'd never seen her before. She felt like he was peeling away her clothes, her skin, her muscles, down past her skeleton to whatever made her who she was. With the feeling came a sick, bilious shame.

Then Dad said that he was having a lot of trouble believing anything she said right now, and they left her alone. Verna lay awake long into the night. Her twin bed seemed huge, her blankets flimsy, and her eyes kept moving toward her door. She could never remember a time like this, when she hadn't been comfortable in her own bed, when all of the wrongness in the world seemed so irrevocable. She tried to pray but the act felt just as cheap and worthless as everything else. A motion she went through, an echo in an empty room.

The next morning, he was gone again, with the latest printouts from the GPS website. "Dad didn't mean anything by last night, Verna," Mother said in the car, on the way to school. "He's just worried about your sister. And he's worried about you, too, because you've been spending so much time with her."

"I know," Verna said.

"You really don't know where she is?"

Verna shook her head.

"I believe you." But Mother sounded as if she was trying to convince herself more than Verna. She pulled into the parking lot, stopped at the curb, and told Verna she would pick her up at the end of the day. With a faded smile, she added, "Don't worry, honey. Everything is going to be okay."

But *okay* had become some distant land that Verna could hardly even imagine. Before the first bell, she went to the loading dock even though she knew nobody would be there and ate an apple even though she wasn't hungry. She didn't know what else to do. When she lay down, the hard concrete was rough against her back. In the distance she heard the thrum of industrial compressors, forcing air into the building; beyond that the swell of traffic on the highway down the hill. Verna felt anesthetized, insulated from the rest of the world. It wasn't entirely unpleasant. Like at the dentist's, how they wrapped you in that lead blanket, and it was heavy and awkward and smelled funny but felt almost good when they draped it over you, like a hug.

In Algebra, she stared down at the page of numbers and symbols in her book and they made no sense, no sense at all. She didn't even try. She didn't see the point. The school schedule was staggered; halfway through class the bell rang and the halls filled with voices. Suddenly a great thump shook the building, as if a book the size of a parking lot had fallen on the roof. The panes of glass in the windows trembled in their frames and a few of the girls squeaked. Verna's algebra teacher just had time to say, "Oh, my," before there came a second impact, and then a third and fourth. Outside the classroom a door slammed, and somebody cried out, and the fire alarm went off.

Mrs. Bergman looked confused. "All right, everyone. Fire drill. Let's go." As they crowded out into the hallways, there was a strange smell in the air, like burning paper and matches, and teachers and students alike looked nervously over their shoulders. One of the other math teachers put a hand on Mrs. Bergman's shoulder, whispering in her ear. Her face went white.

She clapped her hands. "Come on, people." Now her voice was shrill and frightened. "Move. Let's go."

Verna let herself be herded with all of the others, through the parking lot and across the street to stand in the front yards of the neighboring houses. Sirens wailed in the distance, growing ever closer. The motions of the teachers urging students forward were stiff with fear. Verna passed Mr. Chionchio and he grabbed her arm. His eyes were wild.

"Verna," he said, "where's Layla? Is she in school today?"

"No," Verna said.

The art teacher closed his eyes and some of the rigidity left his frame. "Thank God. I hadn't seen her. I was afraid she—"

Then he stopped. The sirens were earsplitting now, coming from all directions, and over Mr. Chionchio's shoulder the first of the screaming vehicles roared into view: four fire trucks, a huge black van, more police cars than she could count, and still they kept coming. Mr. Chionchio turned, too, and the two of them stood and watched as masses of firefighters and policemen flowed out of the cars and trucks into the parking lot. The black van was full of men in bulky black suits wearing helmets with clear plastic face shields. It looked like one of Eric's video games. It looked like a war.

"Mr. Chionchio," Verna said, "what's going on?"

He tried to look very teacherly and reassuring, but failed. The tie he was wearing today bore a repeating pattern of cartoon cats with mouse tails sticking out of their mouths and the words *carpe diem*. "There were a few bombs in lockers. But they were very small," he added, quickly. "The police are just here to make sure there aren't any more."

Another vehicle with flashing lights appeared at the top of the hill. An ambulance. Two ambulances. One of them stopped a few houses down, where a tighter cluster of adults had gathered, including Mr. Serhienko and most of the guidance counselors. The ambulance door opened and two blue-shirted medics pushed their way into the cluster. "Who got hurt?" she said.

Instead of answering, Mr. Chionchio said, "Verna, what class are you in right now?"

"Algebra. Mrs. Bergman." The other ambulance parked in the lower lot. There, the medics were stopped by the men in the padded suits, who didn't seem to want to let them inside.

"You should go stand with her. She'll want to make sure you're safe."

Verna doubted very much that Mrs. Bergman could have picked her photo out of the yearbook, even, but she nodded and went to stand with her classmates anyway. They were scattered in hushed groups, whispering and staring across the street at the school building.

Mrs. Bergman stood with the other math teachers. They whispered and stared, too. Everybody seemed afraid, Verna thought, even though they were theoretically safe. But nowhere was safe. Maybe that was why Verna wasn't scared. Maybe that was why, when a hand fell on her shoulder and somebody said her name, she wasn't even startled.

It was Criss, looking anxious and grim. "Come on."

"Where are we going?" Down the street, the cluster had broken, and she saw a medic helping someone into the back of the ambulance. It was Calleigh. Her face was red and tear-streaked and her hands were wrapped in thick bandages.

"Just turn around and walk," Criss said. "Quick, before anybody notices."

And so Verna did, because nobody *would* notice. The two girls slipped around the back of the nearest house, through a backyard and a stand of trees into another backyard, emerging into a nice residential neighborhood where all of the houses were well-kept and all of the window shades were pulled. Police radios crackled faintly over the hill but in a few moments, even that faded.

Criss had Justinian's car. She was breathing hard, her face purple and her blue hair indigo with sweat. Her driving was erratic, too fast one moment, too slow and careful the next. She zoomed around corners and then swore, as if it were the car's fault. At Eric's, the other three—Eric, Justinian, and Layla—were gathered around the television, which showed a helicopter shot of the school and the surrounding chaos. By now there was a second black van and even more cops in riot gear. "Verna," Layla said, sounding glad, and hugged Verna. She smelled like somebody else's soap.

"What's going on?" Verna said.

"The assholes had to pay," Justinian said.

"Although they're saying three injured, which means that one got away." Eric was frowning. "I don't see how. I built those things solid."

Verna felt a twitch of fear, and yet part of her almost wanted to laugh, because the situation seemed so impossibly absurd. It couldn't be true, but she had no doubt that it was. "I saw Calleigh," she said, hesitantly. "Her hands were bandaged."

Justinian shrugged. "I guess that's something."

"I wish there was more fire," Eric said.

Now a stiff-haired female reporter with perfect lipstick was talking about how much of the building remained to be searched, about how they had finally managed to get the third, most seriously injured student into an ambulance. None of the injuries were expected to be life-threatening. Verna found herself hoping, despite herself, that the third injured student was Kyle Dobrowski. The twitch of fear intensified.

She edged closer to her sister on the couch. "Layla?"

"Relax, Vee," Layla said. Her eyes were glued to the television screen but her voice sounded normal. "It's all going to be okay, I promise."

It wasn't. Verna knew that. But nothing had been okay before, either. "They made bombs?"

"Eric and Justinian," Layla said, "yeah. For you."

There was no accusation in her voice. None. For me, Verna thought numbly.

It was almost two o'clock. Justinian said it would take hours to finish combing the school, and more hours after that to connect them to Eric, because he'd been out of school so long. They were safe for now, and would be until after dark. He never said the word *police* but Verna felt it there anyway.

"What happens after dark?" Criss said.

"Phase two," he said. "The Elshere sisters. I think Verna needs a formal welcoming, don't you?"

Verna didn't know what he meant. She didn't know what else there could be after letting him cut her and drink her blood, but she didn't believe she could be hurt anymore, anyway.

"You said sisters, though." Criss sounded uncertain.

There was a moment of icy silence. Layla, next to him on the couch, seemed suddenly shrunken, folded into herself.

"Right. I guess we should talk about Layla." Justinian said her name slowly, as if he was tasting it. "Layla strayed from us. She lost faith. After all this time, you'd think she'd know how the world treats people like us, but I guess sometimes you have to learn a lesson over and over before you truly know it."

"Wait," Criss said, and Eric said, "What did she do?"

"She let one of them contaminate her," Justinian said.

There was another pause. Then, "Fuck her, you mean," Eric said, and looked at Layla. "Whore."

Layla sat up straighter and glared at Eric, some of her old nerve asserting itself. "Right. You hate when I fuck other guys, unless of course it's you."

"You were a whore when I fucked you, too."

Verna said nothing about Toby. She hated the words Eric used. She hated them.

"Layla, be quiet," Justinian said, calmly. Layla's mouth snapped shut and her body contracted back into itself. He turned to Eric. "You've got a right to be pissed. But for what it's worth, she came to me on her own, confessed everything. She's had to be very strong, this week. If she didn't want to be here right now, she wouldn't be. Don't get me wrong; she betrayed you. And me, and all of us. But now she's asking to be taken back."

"I don't hear her asking," Eric said. "I hear you."

Justinian's voice was cold. "It's the same thing."

"Who was it?" Criss said.

Layla shifted uncomfortably. "This loser who works at this gas station."

Gas station. The one they went to for coffee in the mornings? Verna had never seen Layla talk to anybody there.

"Such a loser that you couldn't stop yourself from having sex with him," Criss said. She sounded bitter and wounded.

"It wasn't like that." Now Layla seemed genuinely pained. "Crissy, I swear. He was— When I was with him—" She stopped. Her hands were twisting together almost convulsively. "When I was with him, I could pretend I was like him. Like I was normal." Her eyes scanned the room, landing briefly on each of them, even Eric. Searching for sympathy, or maybe refuge. "I'm not normal. I'm not like them. I'm like you. This is where I belong."

"You know that now," Justinian said.

She nodded. Quickly, as if she were afraid she would miss her chance.

"And you'll be faithful, from now on."

The same quick, desperate nod. Verna had never seen Layla like this, cowed and cringing. It frightened her.

Justinian smiled. "It's like I always say. You find pleasure through pain and power through submission and wisdom through doing stupid things. So now Layla is a little wiser. I think this was her last mistake. I think if we give her a chance, she'll be more than willing to prove how loyal she can be."

"Maybe I'm just a cynic," Eric said, "but I can't help wondering if you'd be forgiving her quite so easily if you weren't so into fucking her."

Justinian's eyes narrowed and his face went hard. But his voice, as always, was controlled. "Every time I look at her, I see his face. Every time I touch her, I feel his greasy skin. She tastes, and smells, exactly like sewage. Exactly how *easy* do you think that is for me?"

Eric didn't answer. Layla's cheeks were black-streaked with tears. "Every human being on earth who truly loves me is in this room," she said. "I know I screwed up. I know it's bad. I know none of you are ever going to come near me again without wondering if I caught something from him. But I don't have anywhere else to go. If you don't forgive me, I might as well be dead." She said it matter-of-factly, as if it were obvious, and then she fell silent.

Justinian nodded.

Verna didn't understand what was happening. "Layla," she said, but her sister only looked at her, and didn't answer.

Criss sighed, long and pained. "Of course we forgive you. We love you," she said. "We want you with us."

Eric rolled his eyes. "You just want her, period."

"Good, then," Justinian said. "It's settled," and whatever had been in the air was gone, just like that, and all that was left of it was the nervous feeling in Verna's stomach and the mascara on Layla's cheeks. Layla quickly wiped away the mascara, and after that there was nothing.

Justinian produced a bottle of wine and they drank it as they waited for dark. Verna drank as enthusiastically as any of them. It didn't seem to matter anymore if she got drunk. Justinian told them again about Montreal, the old Victorian they'd buy; they'd fix up the house together, and it would become a place of love and freedom. People would flock to them, they would be happy. Verna let the wine and the words wash over her and didn't believe that any of it was going to happen. What she believed was that night would roll around, and somebody— probably Criss—would decide to go home, instead. Or the police would find them; she wasn't sure it would take as long as Justinian thought for them to look at the absentee list and figure out who the bomber was most likely to be. If that happened, Verna thought, they would probably all find themselves in a great deal of trouble.

"It's going to be okay" was all Layla would say. "Everything is going to be okay."

If they made it to Montreal, Verna would never have to worry about her father seeing the video. She would never have to stuff another folder with Layla's face on it, never have to sit through another cookie-and-punch Worship Group reception, never see Amberleigh Costa again. Never set foot in school. Never hear Calleigh's voice.

Calleigh. She wondered if Calleigh was in a great deal of pain. It was awful, but she hoped so.

The numbers on the clock moved smoothly, almost magically. The time when her mother would have been waiting outside of the high school had long since passed. No cars pulled up outside, no bomb squads, no lights and sirens; maybe Justinian was right. Eight o'clock, nine o'clock, ten. Then he said it was time. He and Criss and Eric shut themselves away in Eric's room while Layla sat on the couch and smoked silently, one cigarette after another. When the others finally opened the door and let the Elshere sisters in, Layla stood and walked in, still silent, and Verna followed.

Eric's room—was clean. Cleaner. The floor had been cleared and a blanket spread out. The lights were off, and the room was filled with candles that looked and smelled like the ones from Justinian's house. The warm dancing flames were friendly, the smell of the wax otherworldly.

Justinian sat in the middle of the blanket with his eyes closed. The rest of them arranged themselves around him. Verna looked out the window—it was fully dark now, she could see stars—but found her eyes drawn to the white terrain of Justinian's throat, the ribbons of tendon under the skin.

Finally, he said, "The other day, I saw a dead deer by the side of the road. Stiff, with its legs sticking up in the air. Everybody else was just driving by, but I stopped. I looked. I saw the blood on its hide, the flies crawling in its mouth. I could smell it decaying, returning to the earth. It was like a poem that somehow contained the whole world, birth and death and rot and color and everything that ever was, the sum total of every possible experience. It was like being on the best drugs in the world. It made me want to live, to do everything that my body could possibly do: fight and fuck and eat and laugh and cry and sing. Everything."

He paused. There was no noise.

"All those cowards driving by, too scared to look because the truth might be ugly. We're not scared. We take the blood and the shit and the beauty and the agony and we use it to make ourselves stronger. We wanted power, and we took it. We wanted our freedom, and we took it. We want revenge on everybody who's wronged us, and we're taking that, too."

He turned to Layla. The set of his mouth was stern. "Layla, you lied to us, and that was wrong. But in a way, I'm proud of you. You saw something you wanted and you went for it. If you hadn't tried to do it alone, you could have had him. Instead, he has you. I can see him looking out of your eyes. We can take you back from him. We can make you free, if that's what you want."

Layla's voice sounded choked, as if she'd been crying. "Yes," she said, and then, when he still waited, "Please."

For a moment, his eyes held hers. The room felt as if the very walls were waiting. Then he turned to Verna.

"And then there's you. I can't even count the number of people who have a piece of you. Your parents, Calleigh Bitch Brinker, Wolf-boy—all inside you, chewing on you, carving you up. You'll never be whole while they're in there. You'll never be fully *you* and you'll never be safe." Passion rose in his voice. "We can make you free, too. And when you're free and Layla is free, then we'll all go together as a unified force and break the chains that hold us. When the sun rises tomorrow, we'll have ultimate power. Nobody will be able to stop us, ever."

Engulfed in the fog of his words, Verna nodded. He opened his hand, and Verna saw the ritual knife shining in his palm.

"Verna first," he said.

She held out her arm but he told her to lay down on her back, so she did: first staring up at the ceiling, then looking out the window to the night sky. Stars like silver fireflies, friendly and alive in the blackness. Criss held one of her hands and Layla held the other. Eric crouched above her head, out of sight. Some Christians drank strychnine, Verna thought, trying to reassure herself as panic began to blossom in her chest, or draped themselves with rattlesnakes. Some sat by while their children died of fevers because they believed in the will of God over all things. This was only pain, not danger. She was tough. She was titanium. Justinian let her watch as he rubbed the knife down with an alcohol swab. Then he lifted her shirt and bared her rib cage. Verna's stomach had never been exposed in front of other people. She'd never even worn a two-piece bathing suit. The air in the room felt clammy.

He stroked her ribs, pressing her flesh gently to feel their edges. She had never been so aware of her own skeleton. Then he leaned down over her, so close that she could feel the strands of his hair against her, and kissed the skin just above her bottom rib. She could feel his tongue and when he drew back she could feel the kiss, too, turning to ice as the air moved over the saliva he'd left. She shivered.

Then he cut her. She clutched fiercely at Layla's hand. The scratch on her arm had been nothing compared to this. The blade moved like a brand across her ribs and she heard herself cry out; her whole body was a high-tension wire and the gash he carved was the core of her. Criss was gripping Verna's arm and Eric's hands were on her shoulders, holding her down as Justinian pressed again to make the blood well faster. The experience did not make her feel powerful. It made her feel terrified and imprisoned. She could hear herself crying like a puppy; he pressed again and she felt a hot line of blood snake down her side.

"Be strong," he said. Then he bent over her ribs and Verna felt his tongue again, his lips, and this time they stayed. Moved.

Not a kiss. There was new pain and the pain was a river. It flowed. It endured. Never in her life had Verna felt pain that didn't flash and instantly began to ease, pain that persisted, pain that pushed into her very being until the rest began to fold around it. He was sucking on her, drawing out her blood. It went on and on. Distantly she became aware of other things: a hand stroking her cheek. The stars. The mortuary smell of the burning candles.

Herself. Her body. Her own heartbeat.

"Isn't that enough?" she heard Layla say, her voice strained and oddly distant, and Eric said, "Shut up, bitch."

Finally, she felt Justinian's tongue travel down her body, catching the first drop of blood that had spilled, and she thought it must be over. But his fingers were still on her ribs. "Eric," he said. "Your turn."

There was a pause. Verna felt Eric's hands grip and flex on her shoulders. She opened her eyes but she could only see Eric's nostrils and mouth, which hung open as if he was panting. But she could feel his eyes. She could see his tongue flick out, swipe at his upper lip, recede.

"Wait," Layla said. Her hand was tight on Verna's. "One at a time, we do one at a time—"

"Not tonight. Now, Eric." The command in Justinian's voice brought with it a dim memory of rough hallway carpet on Verna's face, the taste of beer in the back of her throat. *Be quiet. Stop moving.* He and Eric switched places. Eric's hands were hard and merciless against Verna's ribs and his mouth was rougher. The pain rose and swelled again and this time the world faded into a thick haze of gray. As he drank he scraped the cut with his teeth, biting at its edges. New agony broke through the gray and Verna heard herself shriek.

Eric laughed; he sounded manic, almost drunk. "Don't be afraid," Justinian said. "It's just pain."

The dim forms above Verna moved again. Now it was Criss at her side. Her tongue fluttered gently at the wound and her cool hand hardly pressed at all, but the pain surged anyway. All the words for pain were wrong. Pain was not bright, it was not electric, it was not hot, it was not a wave. It simply *was*. It was everywhere and it was everything. From the other side of it, Verna felt Justinian's hands on her shoulders, heard Layla whispering in her ear, telling her to hold on, it was almost over. They were almost done.

Justinian didn't make Layla drink. She and Verna already shared blood, he said. When Criss was done, they helped Verna sit up. From somewhere a gauze pad was produced and Layla held it in place while Verna whimpered and Justinian used the silver knife to make a cut on the fleshy part of his arm. Verna's side throbbed and her whole body ached. She was covered with icy sweat and sick with heat.

"Drink," he said, not unkindly, and put his arm to her mouth. "Drink, and it'll all be over."

There was nothing in the world but him, and blood, and pain. Verna drank.

They gave her more wine. A lot of it. She couldn't get the taste of his blood out of her mouth. Later she lay curled, fernlike, on Eric's bed. She shivered and a dirty-smelling blanket was tucked around her.

Layla's voice, soft in her ear. "Keep your eyes closed. Don't watch."

But she was aware, anyway, as Justinian took blood from Layla— aware enough to see that her sister bore more than one gash on her ribs, and also that Justinian was not as gentle with the elder Elshere as he had been with the younger. His hands did not stroke and press so much as they dug and pinioned. Layla did not cry but she writhed and moaned. When Justinian was done he spat into the garbage.

"Christ, I can still taste him in you," he said.

Then he held Layla down for Criss, and for Eric.

In the bathroom, Layla dressed Verna's cut. The wine was burning its way out of her system, leaving a remote, empty horror. She noticed how Layla kept her torso stiffly upright, how she didn't twist or bend, and she realized that she'd seen that stiffness before without knowing what it meant.

Layla rummaged through the cabinet, found a tube of Neosporin. "It's not that he likes hurting us," she said, squeezing a greasy worm of ointment onto her shaking finger. "But the world will hurt us worse, and we have to know we can take it." She smeared the ointment onto the cut in Verna's side. The split skin burned and Verna gasped.

"Sorry." Layla taped the piece of gauze over Verna's wound. Then she took off her own shirt, and Verna gasped. Her sister's ribs looked flayed. Behind the new gashes Verna could see older ones, some scabbed hard and some fresh enough that the blood crusted and crumbled. Looking at them made Verna feel sick.

Layla rubbed ointment into her own cut without even wincing, but there were tears in her eyes and the smile she gave Verna was twitchy, unreliable. The fluorescent bulbs in Eric's bathroom flickered and under their light Layla looked sickly and greenish. Verna was glad when she put her shirt back on.

"You let him do that to you," Verna said.

"It's like—therapy." Layla's voice was too high, too fast. "He used to tell me my blood tastes like chocolate. He says, every time we do it I feel a little closer to the way I used to. You know, that guy I was with? His dad was the one who killed Ryan Czerpak."

None of the words Layla said were foreign or unfamiliar, but somehow the things she was saying still didn't make any sense. Verna couldn't focus enough to figure them out. "Eric bit me," she said.

She nodded. "He always does. You don't have to share with him again if you don't want to. I only do it when Justinian tells me to."

Realization flashed in Verna. "Is that why you had sex with him? Because Justinian told you to?"

"I told you. It was profound."

But Layla would not meet her eyes. Verna felt sick; her side burned. "I want to go home." She didn't even know the words were true until she heard herself say them.

"You are home," Layla said.

They went into the living room. Justinian was outside, loading the car with Eric, and Verna was glad. He had been looking at her in a new way and she didn't think she liked it. It was still loving and wise and gentle—almost Christlike, in fact, as if he'd studied one of the famous paintings of Jesus and practiced His expression in the mirror—but underneath all of that was something akin to triumph. Like Verna was a prize he'd won. Criss, red-eyed, lay on the couch. She barely even looked at Verna as she said, "Oh, Layla-love, come here, come be with me," and even though not an hour before Criss had sucked at Layla's blood while the boys held her down, while Justinian urged her on—*Come on, Crissy, she's yours, take her*—Layla went, falling into Criss's arms and burying her face in her neck. Criss stroked her hair, looking tremulous and ecstatic.

Verna took refuge in Eric's dad's bedroom, huddling on the pilling, staticky bedspread. Her side hurt. The tape Layla had used to hold the gauze in place pulled and itched and her mouth tasted like blood. Everything felt wrong. She was in the wrong place, she was the wrong person. Verna closed her eyes and tried to be elsewhere.

She heard the door open. "Oh," Eric's voice said, sounding mildly surprised. "I didn't know you were in here."

"It's okay," Verna said, without opening her eyes.

The closet door squeaked open. Objects moved.

"You all right?" His voice was closer now. She opened her eyes to see him standing next to the bed. A skull grinned horribly at her from beneath his unbuttoned flannel shirt, and his handcuffs glinted from his wrist, but the expression on his acne-purpled face wasn't unsympathetic, and unlike Criss he actually looked at her, he actually seemed sort of concerned.

"It hurts," Verna said, in a small voice.

"It's supposed to hurt." He put down the thing he was holding—a long black case, which looked like the soft-sided guitar cases the counselors at camp had sometimes carried but was the wrong shape—pushed up the sleeve of his flannel shirt, and showed her the row of parallel scars marching up the inside of his arm, past the twin silver hasps of the handcuffs. His voice was, again, not unkind. "You can't take a little scratch on the ribs, how are you going to handle the rest of what the world dishes out?"

They kept saying that, all of them. As if pain canceled pain. Eric pushed his sleeve back down. "Hey, what was it like when the bombs went off? Was it loud? Did the building shake?"

Verna nodded.

"Was there a lot of smoke? Were people scared shitless? I bet they were scared shitless." Eric's expression was eager, his eyebrows lifted expectantly.

"People were scared. There was some smoke. I don't know. Not a lot." She wondered where Eric's father was. She wondered if he ever came home.

Wistfully, Eric said, "Man, I wish I could have been there. I wish I could have blown up the whole fucking school. That's what I wanted to do. But we got the bitch's hands. And that guy who told everyone he nailed you, we got him bad. So that's something."

Jared? Verna flinched, huddled more tightly into herself. Eric's lip curled.

"What, you think I'm creepy now? Your sister thinks I'm creepy, too." He leaned down close. Verna smelled alcohol and cigarettes. She turned her head, pressing her face into the pillow, but she couldn't get away. "But when I fucked her, she came so hard she cried."

Verna started to shake. Eric laughed. "Your poor little virgin ears. Wait until—"

"Eric." Justinian was standing just inside the door, his face stern. "What are you doing?"

Eric stood up, too quickly. "Nothing."

"Leave her alone. Go put that in the trunk with the other one." Eric picked up the black case that wasn't a guitar, gave Verna an unpleasant grin, and left. As soon as he was gone, the sternness on Justinian's face melted away. As he crouched down next to the bed, his expression was almost rueful. "Did he scare you?"

Verna was still shaking. "Did Jared get hurt today?"

"Did Eric tell you that?" Verna nodded. Justinian shrugged. "Wolf-boy has a lot more people taking care of him right now than ever took care of you, I promise." He reached out, stroked her hair. Verna wished he wouldn't. She never wanted to be touched again, by him or anybody else. "Why would you care, after what he did to you?"

Verna suddenly remembered Jared, sitting at the art studio table, looking angry and unhappy. "Maybe he didn't do anything to me," she said. "Maybe whoever wrote that post was lying."

"Maybe. So what? Even if he didn't do anything to hurt you, he would have eventually. Whoever wrote that did you a favor." Again, she heard that self-satisfied note in his voice. Justinian had called her attention to the message. He'd told her what it meant. The website was anonymous. He could have posted it himself. He could have posted any of the messages, or all of them. Had he? Knowing Kyle and Calleigh would read them, knowing it would egg them on?

She didn't know. She would never know. But the post *felt* like Justinian, and nothing like Jared. Poor Jared, who was—where, now? In the hospital? Intensive care? Because of her? No. She hadn't made the bombs. She hadn't planted them. She hadn't even known. Because of Justinian.

"I want to go home," she said.

"That's just aftershocks. You've had an intense night." The smile he gave her was the same wise, kindly Justinian smile, but all at once Verna found it galling. It was almost midnight and her head throbbed with wine and her side throbbed, too, where she'd let herself be cut open and bled like a plague victim in a medieval woodcut; her parents couldn't be trusted and Toby couldn't be trusted and, for the first time in Verna's life, home didn't feel like the safe place where she belonged more than anywhere else in the world, but it felt safer than here. Her universe was as inside out and backward as an Escher drawing; the stairs led nowhere and the doors opened onto walls and nothing could be relied upon, but this, right now, the look in Justinian's eyes, the quality of his voice: this was familiar. Once again, she was being told what she thought, how she felt, what she wanted.

Suddenly—and *suddenly* was the right word, it was like putting
on a pair of 3-D glasses and watching a distorted image resolve into
clarity—the kindness and wisdom thinned, became transparent.
Behind them, Verna saw calculation and pleasure. As if he were an
overindulged child and they—all four of them—were toys, his to play
with and break in any way he liked. Nobody had ever hurt Verna like
this. Nobody had ever crawled inside her and cut her to pieces and
hurt her. And Layla—what he'd done to Layla—

She had never hated anybody as much as she hated him. Not
Kyle, not Calleigh, not anybody.

"Come out," Justinian said. "There's some pizza left."

Pizza. Verna sat up. "I don't want pizza. I want to go home."

He looked at her for a long moment. Verna felt those Siamese
eyes boring into her, trying to pull her apart. Finally, he sighed and
said, "Come with me." Calmly, sorrowfully. She knew she was supposed to feel embarrassed and forlorn, that her heart was supposed to
break at the idea of disappointing him. Instead, she felt a hot flare of
anger. He held out a hand. She didn't take it. Her side felt like somebody had stuck a sword through it, but she stood up on her own and
followed him stiffly into the living room, where the others waited.
Criss and Layla perched on the edge of the couch, Eric stood, impatient, by the sliding door. Layla watched Verna anxiously and Verna
noticed her sister's bitten lips, the hollows under her eyes. That was
what you looked like when Justinian loved you.

She felt a new burst of fury. Layla had let this happen. She had let
it happen to herself and then she had let it happen to Verna, and now
she was still letting it happen.

"Are we leaving?" Criss said. "I thought we were leaving."

"Soon." Justinian put an arm over Verna's shoulders. She didn't
want him touching her but she bore it, anyway, so she could get out,
so somebody would take her home. "There are a few more things we
have to take care of first. It's like being sick. If you stop the antibiotics
too soon, the infection comes back. You can't just drive it away. You

have to kill it." The arm around Verna tightened. "Running from the world won't do any good. It'll just come after us."

"So what's the plan?" Layla's voice was nervous and her skin was the color of clay.

"First, we're going to kill the subhuman that polluted your blood and tried to ruin you," he said. "And then we're going to kill your parents."

Verna screamed. Every part of her mind screamed along with her. She tried to twist away from him but Justinian's grip on her was too strong. He glanced mildly at Eric. "Eric, help me out?"

Then Eric had her by the upper arms, fingers buried in her flesh, and she couldn't get free. Layla's eyes, black pools in her ghostly face, darted between Eric and Justinian and Verna. Her hands twitched as if they wanted to move and she was stopping them.

"Wait," she said. "No."

"That corruption is always going to be inside you, Layla. The only way to eliminate his power over you is to kill him. Same with your parents." Justinian's voice was calm, reasonable. "Besides, you've told me a thousand times that you wanted them dead. I'm just giving you what you want. I'll make it easy for you, even. The only one you actually have to kill is the corrupter. Eric and I will take care of your parents."

Layla's voice shook. "When I said that, I didn't mean it."

Justinian smiled. "Yes, you did. They don't love you, Layla. You're a mistake, you know that. A plan that didn't work out. They want to send you to that wilderness camp so you'll come home dead or broken—I doubt they care which. As long as you're not out there embarrassing them, because that's all they care about. If we run, they'll only hunt you down. You'll never be free while they're alive and you know it." He turned his beatific smile on Verna, too. "Besides, you don't need them. Neither of you do. We're your family now."

Verna writhed in Eric's arms, willing herself desperately toward the back door and the black expanse of freedom beyond. But foul-smelling Eric held her by the arms. And he was *strong*. Even as she struggled he picked her up bodily and pinned her against the wall. She screamed and then his hand was over her mouth, pressing her against the unyielding drywall.

"Leave her alone!" she heard Layla cry, but Verna could see Criss holding her sister, lips close to Layla's ear, murmuring.

Justinian sighed. "Eric," he said, "where's the key to those handcuffs?"

Eric handcuffed Verna to the cold radiator in his bedroom. She fought and kicked the whole way. Right before he snapped the hasp home she got him good in the middle of the thigh, her boot heel driving hard enough into the muscle to make him cry out, but his grip on her didn't slacken. When the handcuffs were locked, he drew back a hand to hit her.

Justinian stopped him. "No. She's confused, but she's one of us."

"Bitch kicked me," Eric said.

"She's scared. Go check on our supplies. Let me talk to her."

Eric scowled, but left. When he was gone, Justinian crouched down next to Verna. "I'm sorry. I know this is freaking you out. But it's for your own good. You just have to trust me."

He put a hand on her shoulder and she pulled back, as far as she could. The radiator was covered in dust and grit. "Come on, Verna," Justinian said, sounding exasperated. "I'm not going to hurt you. I'm not going to *rape* you. That's for Calleigh Brinker and Kyle Dobrowski and your father." He saw her face. "Oh, please. Don't tell me it's never occurred to you that there might be a reason why your father is so afraid of you two becoming sexual beings. He's been fucking your mind for years, anyway. It's really only a matter of time."

"My father never handcuffed me to a radiator," Verna said.

"But he did. That's totally the problem here. He did handcuff you to a radiator, psychologically, and you don't even know it." He shook his head. "Look, just be patient and try to relax, okay? This will all be over in a few hours. Then we'll go to Montreal and a week from now you'll be thanking me." He leaned down toward her; she tried to pull back even farther but there was nowhere to go. He kissed her cheek. "I love you so much, Verna. You just have to trust me."

Verna was crying. "Where's Layla? Where's my sister?"

He reached out, found the cut he'd made on her ribs, and pressed down. Pain surged through Verna and her mouth opened and she wailed, a high, wavering sound like an animal would make.

"Feel that," he whispered. "It's real. It's life. Open yourself up to it. If you let it in, it'll illuminate all the darkness."

She squirmed, arms uncomfortably twisted behind her, feet scrabbling at the filthy carpet. The expression on his face was probably meant to be kind but she saw it for what it was, now, she saw the pleasure, the cruelty.

"My blood is inside you," he said. "This is where we join."

And he pressed harder, and Verna screamed.

FOURTEEN

Patrick wanted Caro to come by that night. He didn't know what would happen between them, he didn't know how they would end up, but he needed to see her. The encounter with Layla's father had left him rattled and angry and he needed to tell Caro about it, about how lost and broken they all were: Layla, her father, Patrick himself. He needed her to tell him it wasn't true. She'd said he was good, that night in the car. He needed to hear it again.

But when she did come—only minutes after the cop left, the one who stopped in every night for a scratch-off and a Snickers—when the door jingled and it was her, the burst of relief he felt withered and died as soon as it was born. She didn't look right. Her hair was falling out of the careful twist she always wore at work and the legs under her black skirt were bare. It wasn't October yet, but it wasn't warm enough for bare legs. Her eyes were too wide, her cheeks too pale.

He came around the counter. "Are you okay?"

"I have your car. It's outside." Her voice sounded high-pitched and strange. "Also, I hit your brother in the head with a beer bottle. He's okay, though. I don't think I really hurt him."

When the old man had cowered on the couch, moaning, the words running through Patrick's consciousness had been *what did you do this time, what mess are we in now and how am I going to fix it,* but in the private spaces of his mind, that mental territory he could barely admit existed, he'd been thinking, *I am so tired of you, so tired of this.* But this time, in that instant when it had seemed like Caro had done something dire to his brother—his oldest friend, the only family he had left—he'd wondered frantically where they would run, how he would hide her. The difference terrified him. He knew he had done the right thing when he called the police to come and get his father. He didn't want to think that he'd only done it because he was tired of cleaning up after a sad old drunk.

"I think we broke up," Caro said.

Would he have hidden her? Would he have sold his car and fled to Mexico with her? Patrick took a deep breath. "Tell me what happened."

"We had a fight. He told me I was crazy." She looked at him. Her eyes were bombed-out, desperate. "That's not why I hit him, though."

"So why did you?"

"Because if I didn't, I was going to stay with him. And I didn't want to stay with him. Maybe he's right. Maybe I am crazy," she said. "I do the same shit over and over again and it always turns out bad and I keep doing it anyway."

"You're not crazy," Patrick said.

"I meant to hit him as hard as I could, but I pulled it at the last second. I pulled it because I was scared that if I hit him too hard he might not take me back. I don't even want to be with him."

He put his hands on her tense, trembling shoulders. "Caro, it's okay."

"It's not okay. It's a long fucking way from okay."

"You said he was fine."

She laughed. It sounded brittle and pained. "He is. I'm not."

"It's okay," he said again, and put his arms around her; but even as he felt her start to shake against him, he knew he stood at a crossroads. In one direction lay Mike, Division Street, the old man, his mother, all of the bricks and pebbles that had piled up through the years to make him the person he was. In the other: Caro. Caro, and an empty stretch of uncertainty. He could still go back. Let Mike think she stole his car and vanished. Try to pick himself up, somehow. The way Caro clutched at him, the way her nervous fingers couldn't keep still, he wondered if she was thinking along similar lines. Nothing held her here. She could leave. Be free. Start again.

She smelled like the restaurant. Brine, sweat, perfume. He kissed the corner of her eyebrow, the space between her temple and cheekbone.

The bell over the door rang. Patrick and Caro didn't step away from each other, but their heads turned at the same time and they both saw Mike standing in the doorway, holding an aluminum baseball bat that Patrick dimly remembered from their childhood, his wide eyes taking in the two of them.

"You?" Mike said, staring at Patrick. "It's you?"

"This isn't real," Layla whispered to Verna, as the three girls pressed together in the back of Justinian's car. "They won't really do it." But Verna's wrists were still handcuffed in front of her and she thought the conviction in Layla's voice was more wishful thinking than true belief.

"Shut up," Eric said from the front seat. "You don't get to talk."

Justinian, behind the wheel, said, "Eric."

They were driving across town. Verna was in the middle, between Criss and Layla. There were other cars on the road and if Verna had been sitting at the window she would have pounded on it for all she was worth, written *Help* in scarlet lipstick letters across the glass. But it was like Layla had been drugged, or knocked semiconscious. She just sat staring at her hands in her lap, as limp as a broken doll.

And maybe that was what she was. Broken. Verna understood, sort of, how a person could get that way. Remembering the look in Justinian's eyes as he had watched her try to squirm away from him, the fierce spear of pain in her side as he'd squeezed and pinched her cut flesh in Eric's room. Criss had heard her crying afterward, had come in and hugged her and suggested that they share blood. She'd looked insulted when Verna recoiled. *This is all for your own good,* she'd said, trying to sound like Justinian, but even through her pain Verna saw the fearful dart of Criss's eyes, and if Criss was scared— loyal, devoted Criss—then when Layla said this wasn't real, Verna didn't believe her. Not one bit.

In this world, in this car, the rules were different. For Verna, the change had been instantaneous, but Layla was like a lobster in a pot, not noticing how hot the water had become, not understanding the danger she was in. Or understanding it too well, maybe. Either way, Layla did nothing.

The car pulled into the gas station. Justinian stopped on the far side of the lot, away from the flood of light through the store windows. The last time Verna had been here was the day they'd dyed her hair, when she had wanted nothing more than to absorb even a little of Layla and Justinian's cool, a little of their nerve. Two other cars sat in the lot—a battered blue compact and a showy, jacked-up truck— and she let herself imagine for a moment that their drivers would be able to help her. But Justinian had two shotguns in the trunk and she thought Eric had a gun, too, and most of Verna knew that no rescue was coming.

Justinian turned around in the front seat and looked at Layla. "You should use the shotgun. The derringer would be easier for you to handle, but the shotgun is a surer thing. All you have to do is stand in front of him and pull the trigger. Then you'll be free."

"Justinian." Layla's voice was pleading. "Please. This is ridiculous. I don't need to kill him to be done with him. He's not inside me. He's barely even inside himself."

His voice didn't change. "He had enough power to make you lie to us. He had enough power to make you fuck him."

Verna felt Layla shrink back. The older girl said nothing.

Justinian sighed. "Here are the options, Layla. We get out of the car, you and me. We go to the trunk and we get the shotgun and then we go in there and you kill him. I'll be with you the whole time. You'll never be alone. And then it'll be over. Convenience stores get robbed all the time. Nobody will think twice about it."

"There's somebody else in there," Eric said.

"That's unfortunate," Justinian said.

Mike hefted the baseball bat in one hand. "I brought this," he said, "because I knew she'd go straight to whoever she'd been with and I wanted to bust their head in." He stared at Patrick, looking bewildered. "Tell me I'm wrong, dude. Tell me this isn't happening."

Caro pushed Patrick away. "You're a prick," she said to Mike. That high-pitched strangeness was gone. She sounded sharp and alive. "I just came here to ask him if I could buy his car, that's all. And he saw that I was upset, and he gave me a hug. So sue the guy, he's got a tiny little shred of empathy."

Mike looked at him. "Is that true?"

She was trying to give him a chance. Patrick could hear the strain behind her words, could see it in the hunch of her shoulders. When she'd pushed him back he'd felt her fingers linger on his arm for barely a split second. He could still feel them there. They had been smooth and soft.

But there were no half-truths. There was truth, and there was what you chose to do about it. Living with yourself afterward; that was where the *half* came in. Because you could half-live pretty much indefinitely. You could half-live until you died.

He sighed. "No. It's not. Sorry."

Next to him, Caro let out a long, shaky breath. Like she was deflating.

"What's the other option?" Layla said.

Justinian glanced at Verna. "Verna can do it."

"No," Verna said, at the same time that Layla said, "She can't. She wouldn't."

"If killing him could guarantee the lives of other people she loved, I think she might." He looked at Verna. "Wouldn't you, Verna?"

Verna was horrified. "I could never kill anyone."

"What other people?" Layla said.

"Your parents, to start with. Because if Verna can kill your friend inside, then maybe their brainwashing doesn't go as deep as I'd thought. Particularly since killing a complete stranger who's never done anything to you—like she'd be doing—would be a lot harder than killing somebody who made you feel as dirty and violated as you've been saying all week."

"Let me do it," Criss said. "I'll kill him. I will."

"No. It won't be the same." The expression on Justinian's face was a reasonable facsimile of heartbreak. "Don't think I want to do this, Layla. I don't. I love you more than anything in the world, you know that. But this life that we've chosen—it's not easy. If you don't have the strength for it, then love won't be enough. We can't risk having you with us. So you can kill him, and show us that I'm right about you, that you're strong enough to do what needs to be done. Or you can stand by while Verna does it, which would take a different kind of strength from both of you—strength for her to kill him, of course, but also strength for you to risk letting her be the powerful one for once, now and in the future. I think killing a stranger might change Verna in some very interesting ways, don't you?" He looked at Verna. "You might even find that you want your parents dead, after this. Once you see how easy it is."

"No," Verna said.

He said nothing.

"Not much of a choice," Layla said, her voice almost a whisper.

Justinian and Eric exchanged a look. Justinian sighed. "There's a third option, if you want to take it. It came to me in a dream last night. We were in the clearing, all of us, drinking from you. Like tonight, except at the same time." He paused. The sorrow in his voice was convincing and, numbly, Verna wondered if, on some level, Justinian was truly sad.

"In the dream," he said, "I was making love to you as your heart stopped. It was beautiful. I woke up crying."

"You weren't surprised," Mike said slowly. "When I told you she didn't want to marry me. You weren't surprised at all." He gripped the bat so hard that Patrick could see the bloodless moons of his knuckles. "Did you sleep with her?" His eyes, fixed on Patrick, were desperate. *Say no,* his face begged.

"Yes," Patrick said.

Caro made a faint, exasperated noise, almost a moan. In front of Mike's body, the bat drifted as if in a breeze. "Why?"

Patrick marveled at how the opportunities to walk away kept coming, like easy pitches right over the plate. Even now he could say, *Because she threw herself at me, dude, she came into my room at night. She's a liar. She's no good.*

But he and Mike had lived this moment before. And that time, when Mike had said, *Why, little brother?* Patrick had answered, *Because it had to be done.*

"Because I wanted to," he said now. "Because I love her."

Caro flinched. As Patrick watched, Mike's eyes filled with tears.

When Mike spoke again, his voice was thick. "I spent my whole life taking care of you, you ungrateful little shit. Ever since Mom died. Even after what you did to Dad. And the moment I get something for myself—the moment I'm happy—"

"I didn't do anything to Dad," Patrick said.

"Bullshit."

No. Patrick had betrayed Mike. He would take that guilt; it was his and he would accept it (because he did love her, even now as she stood between them with her wild eyes going from brother to brother; because loving her was the best thing he'd ever done). Not the other, though. Not Ryan Czerpak. Not the old man. "He killed that kid. He knew it and he didn't even stop."

"It doesn't matter." But Mike's jaw was tight and the bat was shaking.

Patrick took a step toward him. "You never looked at the car. It sat in our garage all night and you never even looked."

"It doesn't matter!" Mike screamed. The sound ripped through the stale air. Thick cords stood out on his neck.

Patrick spoke softly. "There was a baby tooth stuck in the grille, Mike. A little, tiny, broken-off tooth. Looked like a pearl."

Justinian said, "It wouldn't be like dying, Layla. You'd be inside all of us, forever."

Layla's face was desperate. Verna thought of the eternal life she'd always believed in, and imagined spending eternity inside the sinister red canyons of Justinian's veins. If hell was the absence of God then life in Justinian's world, that was hell—but as Layla stared at Justinian, her lips parted, and scared as she seemed Verna thought she saw something helpless and yielding there. Layla was trapped. She couldn't see her way out, couldn't see a life beyond him. If he told her that bleeding to death in the clearing was the right thing to do—

"I'll do it," Verna said. "I'll kill him."

Criss gasped. "Right on," Eric said, sounding impressed.

Layla grabbed at her hand. "Vee—"

"But not my parents." Verna's own voice surprised her, how strong it was, how certain. "You leave my parents alone. That's the trade."

Justinian smiled. "Like I said, you might feel differently later."

"No," Layla said. Her nails dug into Verna's hand and words tumbled out of her. "No. I'll kill him. I never loved him anyway. I always loved you. Let me do it. I want to do it."

"It's too late." Justinian pulled the trunk release lever. "You made your choice. Verna made hers."

"She's not like me," Layla said. "She's too good. It will destroy her."

"Let Verna out, Crissy," he said.

Verna slid out, awkward because of the handcuffs and not sure that when her feet touched the ground she wasn't going to crumple to meet it. Justinian helped her, lifting her by the elbow like a child, and she walked with him to the back of the car, where he removed the handcuffs from her wrists and pulled out the case Verna had seen earlier, the one that had reminded her of a guitar case.

"He works here, so he'll be wearing some sort of uniform. The spray pattern on this thing is huge. Just point it at him and fire. It'll be quick." He unzipped the case and took out the shotgun. The lights over the gas pumps gave the long, dark barrel a reptilian sheen. Verna half-expected it to wrap around his arm and slither up to his shoulders. He showed her how to hold it, where to put her hands. The endless world stretched around them but Verna didn't run.

She searched his face for the Justinian who had loaned her books and played music for her on the loading dock. "Don't make me do this," she said.

He reached out and touched her wrist where it was still sore from the handcuff. She flinched away from him but he didn't seem to notice or care. "I'm sorry about the handcuffs. That's not how I planned this. But they're off now, right? We don't need them. We trust each other, don't we?"

Verna said nothing.

He glanced at the store, at the road, and then looked back at her. "Look, I'll make you a promise. Do this well and when it's done, we'll get in the car and leave town."

"You'll leave my parents alone," she said, uncertainly.

"If that's what you want."

"Of course that's what I want."

"Then you want the wrong thing. They don't care about you."

"What about the other people inside?"

"They don't care about you, either," he said, and she said, again, "Don't make me do this."

"I'm not making you do anything. You understand the situation, and you're making a choice. A strong choice." He put his arms around her. The long, brutal line of the gun between them was hard against her body. This hug smelled like every other hug he'd given her; it felt the same, with his rangy body pressed against hers and his wiry arms strong around her. The Justinian she thought she'd known had been a lie. Verna wanted to die. She hoped she would die.

He told her he was proud of her, then put the gun into her hands. He said that she had to carry it in.

Mike raised the bat up over his shoulder, like he was waiting on a low inside pitch. Not that he would know that. Mike had never given a shit about baseball. Baseball had been Patrick's thing, Patrick's and the old man's. Like horror movies and metal music and why was he thinking about this right now? "You and me, Pat," Mike said. "We'll go out back and I'll do what I should have done a long time ago, and kick your ass." The tears had dried on his cheeks. His eyes never left Patrick's face.

"Not exactly a fair fight," Patrick said, "me against you and that bat." But his fists were clenched, his arms aching to swing. For all of it. For his whole life. It wasn't Mike's fault but Mike was here, and Mike was ready. Patrick was ready, too.

"This isn't a fair fight." Mike's voice was even. "This is you getting what you deserve."

Caro yanked the baseball bat from Mike's hands and threw it to the floor, where it hit the linoleum with a hollow aluminum ring. It was a sound Patrick associated with sunny weather and endless bitter scrambles in the dust. "Yeah?" she said. "And then what?"

Mike stared at her. His hands hung in the air, as if the message that they were empty had yet to get through. "What do you mean?"

"You take him out back, you beat the shit out of him. Then what? Go back home, watch a little tube, drink some beer? No harm, no foul, and he got what he deserved?" Patrick had never seen her like this. She was so angry she was practically spitting. "What about what I deserve? If Patrick deserves to get his head knocked in with a baseball bat, what about me? I cheated on you, Mike. I've slept with more guys than I can even count. What do I deserve?"

Hands still hovering, Mike said, "I never hurt you. Not once, in all the time we were together."

Going home, watching TV, drinking a little beer. Wistfully, Patrick thought how easy those things would be. But when Caro said, "Not being hurt isn't enough," her voice overflowing with weariness and frustration and sadness, he knew that going home might be easier but it would also be death. Parts of him had already died. In his own way his earth was just as scorched as Layla's and Caro's and even Mike's, although Mike would never realize it. The dead parts grew heavier and harder to carry each year, each day. And some of what was left was callused and corrupt, some of it had led him to Layla and allowed him to sit in the living room drinking beer with his father while the dead kid's blood dried on the Buick; but some was still good. It had to be, or Caro would not have given everything up for him, or he would not have given everything up for her.

Patrick realized: he was giving everything up for her.

"I'm sorry," she said. He wasn't sure who she was speaking to.

"There's no settling this, Mike," Patrick said. He was surprised to find that what he felt wasn't anger but resignation, and maybe a dying ember of sorrow. "You want to beat me up, fine. But it won't change anything. It won't do a damn thing except screw up your knuckles and my face."

"It'll teach you a lesson," Mike said, and Patrick said, "Not this time."

Caro closed her eyes.

Mike's eyes were flinty and hardened. "Fine. Fuck both of you."

The door jingled. All three of them turned.

Standing at the door, just next to the height strip, were two teenagers, a boy and a girl. The boy was tall. His sallow cheeks were speckled with the stubble of a patchy adolescent beard, and his dyed black hair hung lank in his face like crow feathers. With him was a girl whose hair was an unnatural burgundy and whose face was an unhealthy white.

The boy's weird blue eyes cruised over Mike and Caro and then fixed on Patrick.

"There," Justinian said. "You see him?"

One of the men in front of them wore a candy-striped shirt: the uniform Justinian had told her about. His dark hair needed badly to be cut and his face was narrow and ferretlike. Verna was only vaguely aware of the other man in the store, or the woman. Her eyes were too full of the man she had to kill. She had never seen him before. In the car, killing him had seemed terrible because killing was wrong but he had just been an idea, a concept that had thrust them all into this nightmare by having sex with her sister. Now, in front of her, he was human. *His dad was the one who killed Ryan Czerpak,* Layla had said, and Verna hadn't absorbed the meaning of the words then, but she did now. Nothing changed.

She did not want this to happen. It was happening anyway.
There was nobody to stop it, nobody to save her.
Verna lifted up the gun.

"Oh, what the fuck," Mike said, contemptuously, and Patrick understood why. This wan mouse of a girl, dwarfed by the shotgun in her arms, seemed too comical to be threatening. But the more he stared at her the more familiar she looked. Something about her, the creep standing next to her. Then the dots connected and Patrick understood. This boy was the monster. Which made the fearful girl standing next to him, the girl at the end of the gun—

Layla's sister. He saw the way the shotgun trembled and the panic in her eyes, and knew that she was not the danger here. What had he done, Patrick thought miserably; what had he gotten them into? He wanted the others to be somewhere else. He wanted Caro to be somewhere else, somewhere safe; away from Layla's terrified little sister, away from the psycho, away from him.

"Shut up, Mike," he said.

"Verna," the psycho said. In his voice Patrick heard warning, encouragement, and command, and understood that it didn't really matter what he wanted. The girl had the gun but the psycho had the girl. If he made her pull the trigger, Patrick would die. The long hellish night after Ryan Czerpak died would become a moment's mention on the local news and the moonlit night with Caro, the morning patch of sun—those things would become nothing, they would vanish as if they had never been. The girl had the gun and the psycho had the girl and there were no more decisions to make, no more choices, no more betrayals. His life was no longer under his control, and Patrick had felt that way for years but now that it was true—absolutely, irrevocably true—he understood how wrong he had been, and how much time he had wasted.

"Verna," the psycho said again.

. . .

Verna thought desperately of her parents. Home right now, probably. Waiting by the phone. Drinking herbal tea. Maybe some of the people from Worship Group would be there, supporting them in their time of need, waiting for news of their wayward daughters. If Justinian was telling the truth, unlikely as that seemed—if she could do this and get in the car and leave, they would continue to drink tea and pray through the night and into the next morning, when somebody would say, *Oh, Michelle, you look exhausted. You have to sleep.*

If Justinian was not telling the truth, everyone in the house would be dead by the time the sun came up.

What had she done, she thought, miserably. How had she come to this place?

Even if Justinian was telling the truth. Even if killing this man meant that her parents could live, did that make it okay? She knew what was happening at her house because she had seen it happen at the Czerpaks' after Ryan died, when her father had spent all night with Danny and Rachel while this man had—what? Watched television? Drank beer? He was not a good person. Her parents were. Her parents tried to help people. They tried to make the world better.

But the man in the candy-striped shirt didn't look like a bad person. He looked like a scared person, like an unhappy person. He was sweating and his eyes darted back and forth between Justinian and the woman next to him (who looked awful, too, now that Verna noticed) and finally to Verna herself.

There was something intelligent in the set of his face. He would have been good-looking had he not been so thin.

"I know who you are," he said to her. "I know your sister. Don't do this."

When Patrick spoke the psycho looked at him with utter contempt, and Patrick realized that in the psycho's world, he, Mike, and Caro weren't even real. They were less than nothing. The bad skin, the stupid hair, the cold eyes: how empty you would have to be, how desperate, to take this guy's act seriously, to let him do the things he'd done.

"You don't understand," the girl said, in a voice Patrick could barely hear. But the gun barrel wavered.

The psycho moved closer to her. "Verna. Consider our discussion."

Her mouth was quivering, her eyes full of tears. She hesitated a moment more.

Then she raised the gun again.

If Patrick was going to die like this—wearing his Zoney's shirt, listening to the Eagles, all of his life and his mother's life and the old man's life and every crushed beer can and every slam of the screen door and every smell of smoky coconut and hair conditioner and butter and brine reduced down to a nameless convenience store death immortalized in grainy black-and-white security footage—if this was how he was going to go, he'd be damned if this trembling overwhelmed girl was the last thing he saw. If he was going to die, he was going to die looking at Caro. Burning every detail of her into his brain: her eyes, her chin, the slump of her shoulders; her glorious hair, her messed-up heart.

Her eyes met his.

The door jingled again.

"No," Layla said. Her face was pink and blotched and streaked with black and she would not look at Patrick. She lifted her hands to the psycho's face, turned his head toward her. "Don't make her do this. She can't do it. Let me do it. I'm the one. I have to."

Her tone was unlike Patrick had ever heard it. The closest was the last time he'd seen her, in his bedroom, when she'd pled for help, but this went beyond pleading. This was begging. Her hands stroked the psycho's sallow cheeks, his hair, his chest, and Patrick saw that, incredibly, she still loved this asshole.

She'd never had a chance. He wished he'd been nicer to her.

He turned back to Caro.

. . .

Hope flared like a candle in Verna—if anyone could sway Justinian, it was Layla—but the flame died as soon as it was born. Because Justinian's face as he gazed down at her sister was sad and disappointed, and that was all. "You had your chance." He sounded genuinely aggrieved. "Layla, Layla. You should have stayed in the car."

"I couldn't stay in the car," Layla said. "She's my sister."

"And now she has to kill all three of them," he said, sadly.

Verna's heart seemed to stop beating, and the world blurred at the edges. Justinian's face remained clear. Dumbfounded as she was, somehow she managed to speak. "But you said—"

She'd turned, almost without realizing it, and now the gun was pointed at him. He put his hands up, as if to try to placate her, but Verna saw his eyes flick upward, toward the security camera.

Again, sudden clarity.

Justinian knew where the security cameras were. He knew how it would look, Verna turning the gun on him, him raising his hands—the gentle rebuke in his expression wouldn't show on film, probably, and he knew that, too. Until Layla came through the door he had said nothing but her name, and *consider our discussion,* which could have meant anything at all. This was a show. Verna killing somebody on camera, sure. Witnesses to Verna killing somebody, sure. Witnesses to the fact that he was making her kill somebody, no. Justinian was telling the world a story, and the story was that Verna had killed everyone on her own. And once she did, his control over her would be complete and permanent. He would always be able to say that she was the one who'd killed those people, not him; that she was a murderer, and her only hope was to let him protect her. She could even hear him saying *You wanted to do it. If you hadn't wanted to do it, you wouldn't have done it.*

He would say it over and over, and there would be nobody to tell her differently. And after a while, she would begin to believe it.

. . . .

Mike bolted. He grabbed Caro's arm and pulled her down the household goods aisle, toward the emergency exit. Patrick heard the bang of the panic bar and the creak of the hinges, and then they were gone and it was about damn time. If their places had been reversed, if it had been Mike staring down the barrel of the shotgun, he would have—he would have—he didn't know. He wouldn't have known he'd call the cops on the old man, either, or sleep with his brother's girlfriend. You didn't know how you were going to act until you had to act, not really, and Mike had done the right thing.

For an instant, Patrick thought he would go after them. But—Layla.

He would not have been able to predict that, either.

If Verna killed the man, Justinian said he'd let her parents live, but she doubted it. Just like he could make them drink each other's blood, just like he could make them handcuff her to a radiator, he could make them kill people, even people they loved. He could make them do anything. She knew that it would never be enough, that they could never give enough or suffer enough to satisfy him. There would always be more he could do to them, and he would. Over and over, he would.

Layla looked at her and Verna saw the same realization reflected in her sister's sandblasted eyes. The gun in her arms was heavy, her muscles burned. She remembered being in the car, her hands cuffed in front of her, thinking that if she were only at the window, she would do anything to escape from this, she would do anything to be free.

"Do it, Verna," Justinian said. "There's no going back. Kill him and this will all be over."

The other two people were gone, she didn't know where. Why didn't the man run, too, she thought; why didn't he go after them? Justinian's eyes were fixed on her, not the man she was supposed to kill, not the people who had escaped. They didn't really matter. It was her that he wanted.

She thought of Ryan Czerpak. She thought of her parents, her teachers, Kyle Dobrowski, Calleigh Brinker; Mr. Guarda, Mr. Chionchio, Mrs. Bergman and Ms. Kiser and Mr. Serhienko. Everyone she had ever known, everyone her eyes had ever seen. She thought of Jared. She thought of her sister.

To kill was to be doomed. To kill was to die, yourself.

She lifted the gun. She had never fired one before but Justinian had implied that it would hit whatever unfortunate thing lay in front of it, so she pointed it at his face. Right between those Siamese eyes.

Behind him, Layla's face contorted in despair. "Vee, no."

His eyes widened, but his expression was more curious than afraid. "Do you really think you can, Verna?" he said, softly.

"I can try," she said.

But before she could, Layla dropped to her knees, scrabbled on the floor behind him, and came up holding a baseball bat. A baseball bat? Verna thought, dimly perplexed, and then Layla screamed—a wild, almost inhuman sound—and brought the bat down on the back of Justinian's head.

He collapsed forward, into Verna. The gun fell to the floor with a clang but the dead weight of his body knocked her to the floor, trapping her beneath him. The smell of him, of blood, was thick in her nostrils, his rangy heron's body against hers, his coat entangling her like a web. Her boots slid on the floor and something warm fell on her face as she fought and clawed and scrambled. Away, out from under him.

Layla was still screaming. Now, she was screaming his name.

The psycho was still. Clear fluid leaked from his ears. There was blood on the bat that Layla had dropped and more spreading in a puddle on the floor. Inexplicably Layla had thrown herself across his motionless body, wailing. Her sister's eyes were blank in her blood-splattered face, her feet and hands slipping in the growing slick as she tried to crawl toward the candy aisle.

Patrick ran to Layla, put his hands on her shoulders, meaning at least to pull her away from the thing on the floor—but then the door opened again with the same surreal jingle and now it was two more people he'd never seen, a bald-headed boy and a chunky girl with blue hair. The bald-headed boy's face blasted insane fury at Layla, still crouched sobbing over the psycho's body. "You fucking *bitch*! What did you do? What did you *do*?"

He, too, had a shotgun. Patrick just had time to feel weary, to wonder why these teenagers were so well-armed, and then the boy pointed the gun at Layla. A bubble of saliva swelled and popped between his lips.

The blue-haired girl jumped on his arm. "Eric! Stop!"

The bald boy pushed her away hard, so that she fell back out of the door. He was howling like Rambo, like this was a movie. He aimed the gun at Layla and this time he fired.

Patrick felt a scattering of searing pains on his arm and Layla fell against him. He tried to catch her. Her sister screamed but Patrick didn't see what happened to her because just then the gun fired again.

Somebody doused the left side of his body in boiling water. He was looking at the kickplate of the coffee bar, dirty and scuffed. Something cold and hard was against his cheek. A pink stirrer lay on the floor a few inches from his nose. The cold hard thing was the floor. Somebody shouted his name, it sounded like Caro but he knew it couldn't be because Caro was gone, and he just had time to wish that it was her, anyway, before his vision went white and silence—

FIFTEEN

He was working again, finally. Landscaping. Who knew what he'd do come winter, but for the time being at least he was earning money. He could drive a ride-on mower or use a weed whacker even with a sluggish arm that didn't always do what he told it to do, and the other stuff—hedge trimming, and so on—was getting a little easier, when his bosses let him do it. Which he asked for, sometimes; he couldn't afford the kind of physical therapy he was supposed to be getting, and he figured working a pair of hedge clippers was as good as anything. The supervisors felt sorry for him and usually let him try, but they never liked it. Exposed them to all sorts of liability. He'd noticed that the other workers tended to clear out when he picked up a pair of clippers, find things to do in other parts of the site. He didn't blame them.

His left shoulder, collarbone, and upper arm were mostly held together by metal. In the heat of midday it felt like he was burning from inside and out. In the cool of the evening, like now, the external burn was gone but the internal remained, and the rest of his body ached from compensating for muscles that didn't work the way they should.

When he climbed out of the truck that had driven the crew back to the office, he winced as his feet hit the ground. Bit it back. Ordinary shit hurt now. Always would. No point whining about it.

He still drove the same car. That was where he found her, waiting for him, just like he'd found her sister behind Zoney's almost a year ago. Unlike her sister, she wasn't leaning against the car like she belonged there. She simply stood next to it, a bit uncomfortably, as if she were afraid to take up too much space.

He knew her instantly. When he was a few feet away from her, he stopped. There was a thick pause, during which they both looked at each other, and waited to see who would speak first. The two of them had never had a conversation. For most of the time they'd spent together, she'd held a gun on him. He didn't know what to say to her and he didn't want to know what she had come here to say to him. The familiar parts of her face were hard to see because they reminded him of her sister, but he was relieved to find that he was glad to see her, anyway; or at least, to know that she was—okay. The bald boy had shot at her, too, but missed. Patrick had known that, but he'd wondered more than once about what had happened after.

Her hair was much shorter than it had been, and appeared to have been dyed an unremarkable medium brown. There was no sign of the silver-streaked burgundy that he remembered. She wore jeans and a plain T-shirt. She looked older. It was as if the terrified goth teenager in his memory had been wiped off the face of the earth, replaced by this new girl whose demeanor spoke not so much of any desire to stand out or blend in as it did a complete refusal to take part. As if the only statement she wanted to make was *You expect clothes; here are clothes. Now leave me alone.*

It made him sad. She'd given up. He didn't even think she could legally drive yet. Then he saw a tattoo on her wrist, a thin bracelet of vines or something, and felt a little better.

"My dad's assistant drove me. He's waiting." She gestured, and

Patrick saw a truck idling across the lot, a figure inside it. "When I asked him to help me find you he promised not to tell my dad about it, but I think he will. If he does, you can probably expect a call."

"Your dad probably has good reasons for not wanting you here," Patrick said.

"My dad has good reasons for everything he does." Her voice was oddly affectless. "He sent me away, you know. I just got back."

Patrick wanted to speak, but something was blocking his throat.

"It wasn't so bad. There were horses. It turns out that I like horses. I didn't know that before. My dad can barely look at me. My mom is better. They moved to a new house."

"Layla," he said. The word came out choked and strangled. It was the thing that had been blocking his speech, and it hung in the air between them for a long moment, during which neither of them said anything. Layla was dead. The psycho was dead. The bald kid and the blue-haired girl were dead, too, shot by state police outside of Harrisburg. Of the five kids who had set off that night to kill Patrick, only one had lived. One kid, and him.

"Did you care about her?" she said.

He hesitated, and then told the truth. "Not the way she wanted me to."

"Then why did you have sex with her?"

"Because people don't always do the right thing." It was a cop-out, and she knew it, and he knew she knew it. Her eyes closed briefly, and then opened again, full of dispirited hopelessness. Suddenly he wanted very much to do better by this girl, to be better than all of the well-intentioned people who had left her like this. One of whom, when you thought about it, was probably him. "Because I was angry," he said. "I was angry and sad, I thought it might make me feel better, and I knew she would go along with it. I knew it was the wrong thing to do and I decided I didn't care. I decided the world didn't care about me, so why should I care about it?" Now that he'd started the words flooded out of him, a deluge that he couldn't stop. "She came to me for help. I didn't help her. I was ashamed of what I'd done and I wanted her gone. If I could change it—"

"Why did you and your brother wait so long to call the police?" she said.

He stared at her, surprised. "He was our father. He was all we had. We did the best we could."

She nodded. "I had the gun. I had the gun and I'm the only one who didn't get hit. My dad says—everyone says—that was God's hand at work. But I think that if God were merciful, He would have let me die."

She said it calmly, emotionlessly. For the first time, she reminded him of Layla. It was hard to see her that way. "He didn't. You're alive."

"I know," she said. There was another pause, and then she asked him if his arm hurt him much, and he said that it did but that he was dealing with it. She nodded and told him she had to go. He wished her well.

That night, when Caro came back to the apartment and saw how upset he was, she made him tell her about it. Then she said, "You know, Patrick, you're alive, too."

Because it had been her, that night in the store. That night, and all the nights since. He said, "Well, I'm trying," and put his arm around her.

ACKNOWLEDGMENTS

This book, like all books, would not exist in its current form without the help, influence, and support of more people than I can possibly count. Here's my attempt to count them anyway.

Julie Barer, as always, proved herself stalwart, patient, and wise throughout the five years it took me to write this book, and Zack Wagman's insight and enthusiasm carried it the rest of the way. The support of everyone at Crown was truly enheartening, and I owe great thanks to each and every last one of you, even those of you I haven't met yet.

Elisa Albert and Amanda Eyre Ward both read this book in its nascent form, Lauren Grodstein read it twice, and Owen King read it about seventy times. All were smart, loving, and totally badass readers, and their assistance was invaluable. Robert Johnston of Belden Law in Greensburg, Pennsylvania, spent several hours with me explaining the subtleties of DUI law in Pennsylvania, and Rosemary Fretz, Brian White, Heather Mock, and Nate Hensley (among others) helped with the guns. Any errors are mine, not theirs.

More intangible thanks go to Brittany Statlend, Elizabeth Horwitz, and Steve and Tabby King, all of whom gave me the help I most needed at the times when I most needed it, sometimes with very little notice. But the most intangible and all-encompassing thanks of all go to Owen King, who already got a nod but who deserves about sixty million more. He is possibly the most patient and goodhearted and generous person in the entire universe. Without him, nothing would be possible—particularly not that most infinitely sweet thing, that thing that is by far the best thing we've ever done.

SAVE YOURSELF

EXTRA
LIBRIS

ESSAYS,
READER'S GUIDES,
AND MORE

Introduction to "Hung Up"

Somewhere around a thousand years ago, I wrote a short story called "Hung Up." The title was a rodeo reference; it's what the announcers call it when a rider has already been bodily thrown from the back of the bucking animal, but stays bound to it by a strap or a stirrup or whatever. When I wrote the story, I had finished promoting my second novel but didn't have a fully formed idea for my third, and was feeling a bit hung up myself. That's reflected in the story, which I can now see is, in large part, about inertia, and loss, and letting things happen instead of making them happen.

That story turned into *Save Yourself,* the book you've (hopefully?) just read, which is about many of the same things. Novels and short stories have more in common than, say, wedding cakes and haiku, but they're still entirely different forms of storytelling. Turning one into the other is a little like taking a boat apart so you can use the wood to build a house: some of your raw material is still useful, but you're rarely going to use it in the same way, and those few things you keep are rendered nearly unrecognizable by all the new material around them.

Some of the differences are obvious. The novel is told in third person, the short story in first; the *Save Yourself* Patrick works at Zoney's, but the "Hung Up" Patrick is unemployed. In the short story, Mike is nobler, somehow, and Patrick and Caro are a little too glib, too comfortable with each other. Reading it feels to me like looking at their baby pictures, their features familiar but not quite cohesive yet. But there are also moments here I love, like Patrick's memory of going to the unemployment office with his father. Even though that moment didn't make it into the novel, it's a part of the life he lives in my head. And this story, flawed as it is, is where that life began.

An Excerpt from "Hung Up"

I remember going to the unemployment office with my dad when I was a kid. We waited in a long line. I don't know how old I was, but the counter at the front of the line was high above my head. My dad lifted me up so I could see the woman behind the window—or, more likely, so that she could see me—and said, *Say hello, little man*. I said hello. There was green linoleum, the smell of cigarette smoke, fluorescent lights; we stood between cold chrome rails that made me think of the ones outside the roller coaster in Kennywood Park. I remember all of this because it's one of the few memories I have of being alone with my dad and that kind of shit feels special when you're little.

Unemployment's not like that now. Every week, all I have to do is pick up the phone and press one for yes or two for no: am I still unemployed? Am I actively seeking employment? Have I been offered employment in the last seven days? The answer to the first question is always one for yes; the answer to the last is always two for no. The answer to the middle one is blurrier—I get a bit stuck on that word, *actively*—but what the fuck, I usually just lie. They send me a check, I sign it over to Mike to help pay the mortgage or the cable bill or whatever, he says something along the lines of, "I can get you back on at the warehouse anytime you want, dude," and I tell him thanks but no thanks.

The next day, the day when Mike is supposed to take Caro to Homewood Cemetery, is check day. I sleep until two in the afternoon. Then I turn on the television. Sometime around four o'clock I find a rodeo in one of the upper channels, and I pass an entirely enjoyable hour listening to all of the cowboys' accents and thinking about how if I were from Oklahoma or Texas or Montana instead of Pennsylvania, that's how I'd sound. Instead of saying *younz* I'd say *y'all,* and instead of being *unlucky* I'd be *snakebit.*

Maybe I'd have a cool cowboy name, like Cord or Cimarron or Camo. When the bull riders come on, I watch in horrified fascination as one of them is dragged around the arena by his left arm, clearly dislocating the fuck out of it, while a couple of guys wearing desultory clown makeup try to get him free or at least make the bull stop running. After it's all over, the poor guy walks out of the arena, but just barely. His arm hangs strange and useless at his side and the cornpone announcers say things like *Good golly, he shore did get hung up there dint he* and *I tell you what that is one tough Okie.*

Later, I take a nap.

It's almost eleven when Caro comes home, smelling like lobster again. Every day, when she leaves for work, she looks like a movie star, but now, at the end of her shift, she looks like hell. Her makeup is smudged and caked under her eyes and the way she walks in the door makes me think of that poor hung-up cowboy making his way out of the arena.

"Hey there, little cowgirl," I say to her in my best Oklahoma accent—although, sixty minutes of televised rodeo notwithstanding, I wouldn't know an Oklahoma accent if I was snakebit by one—and she says, "Patrick, you freak."

I explain that I've been watching rodeo.

"Another productive day, then?" She shakes her head. "Patrick, Patrick, Patrick."

I hate that goddamn thing she does with my name, but I let it slide. Her eyes are red, and I know it's just the exhaustion, but she looks like she's been crying. Kicking off her shoes, Caro flops down next to me on the couch and swings her feet into my lap. She wiggles her toes. "Rub my feet and I'll do your laundry."

"I'm not sure that's a fair trade." I take her left foot in my hands and start to rub anyway. Her feet are small and moist and warm.

She yawns. "I've seen your laundry, cowboy. Believe me, it's fair."

I'm digging into the arch of her foot in a way I know she likes. There's a hole in the bottom of her sock, and when my fingers move across it I can feel the rough callus on the ball of her foot. I'm fairly sure that the skin there is too thick for her to feel my touch. I stroke the spot lightly. She doesn't react.

"You got a hole in your sock," I tell her.

AN EXCERPT
FROM
"HUNG UP"
317

"Who cares? I spent all day watching sea creatures being boiled alive. One after another, into the pot. Scrabble scrabble." She shudders. Her toes curl in my hands. "I'll never eat another crustacean as long as I live."

"*Crustacean* is kind of a tasty-sounding word, though. Crispy and fried on the outside, but hot and gooey on the inside."

She makes a disgusted face. "How about *lobster*? That sounds so—globby and stupid, like a snail with a digestive problem."

I feel myself starting to grin. "How about crabs?"

"You'd know more about that than I would," she says.

I push my finger into the hole, against the soft damp skin of her arch. She makes a strange noise, kind of like the sound I imagine a boiling lobster would make if it had the physiology to create sounds, and yanks her foot away.

"You sure know how to ruin a perfectly good foot massage," she tells me, but she's smiling for real now and some of the color is back in her cheeks.

"I told you that you had a hole in your sock."

"I didn't think that meant you were going to molest my goddamn feet. Now I have to take a shower, because you made me feel dirty." Standing up, she pulls absentmindedly at the elastic around her ponytail, and her hair, which is the color of sun shining through a bottle of cola, falls around her shoulders. She is already unbuttoning her work shirt as she walks into the bathroom.

Five minutes later, the phone rings. Mike has a

chance at a second shift, good money at time and a half, and he's going to take it. "Tell Caro we'll go see the cemetery some other time," he says to me.

Behind the bathroom door, I can hear the rush of the water. "She's not going to like it."

"I don't like working double shifts. Everybody's going to do shit they don't like." He laughs. "Except you, apparently."

He sounds friendly enough, and it's what I'm thinking, but I still wish he hadn't said it. I keep my voice light when I answer, "Don't think it doesn't take work to be this much of a bum."

"Tell her she'll like the extra money," he says, and hangs up.

The shower cuts off and I hear Caro's footsteps pad softly down the hall to my parents' room. I don't like to go in there; the history of that room is charted in smells for me, and its current smell (shampoo, aftershave, leather, the subtle tang of sex) is too like that of my earliest memories. Makes me think of my mother, who died of cancer when I was eleven. For most of my life, that room has smelled like cigarettes and beer and vomit and sour sheets. Like my dad.

In a few minutes Caro emerges, wearing jeans and a necklace that Mike gave her for Christmas. Her cola-colored hair is clean and pulled back in one of those plastic clips. She's washed off the caked, smeary makeup, maybe put a little new stuff on in its place, and instead of exhausted and sad her eyes are young and sweet-looking. When I tell her Homewood is off, they fill with disappointment. It's like somebody pulling the shades on a sunny day and making the room go dark. I flip through the channels on television until I find a rebroadcast of the rodeo I saw earlier. "Watch this," I say to Caro, trying to distract her. "I'm telling you. It's hard-core."

"This is how I wanted to spend my Friday night, all right," she says, but she sits down anyway. She reaches her arms up and over her head until she can drum her fingers on the back of the armchair. We watch together in near silence until some guy in chaps lowers himself onto the bull in the chute, tying his hand into the rigging. The bull thrashes in the chute; the guy stands up on the rails again, starts all over, and I realize when I see his face that he's the same one I saw get hurt this afternoon. It's like one of those dreams that feels like you've had it before, where you know all of the nasty surprises but can't do anything to get away from them.

Meanwhile, Caro's unrest is palpable, even from the other side of the room, her arms still twisted over her head and her fingers still drumming. She doesn't know what's going to happen, but I do. The chute opens. The bull bursts out into the arena, and is it wrong that I want the outcome to be different this time? The cowboy's free hand is held high above him like it should be, his head up, his eyes never leaving the bull's head as it leaps and twists under him.

Suddenly Caro's fingernails scratch fiercely at the upholstery and for the second time that night I find myself comparing her to a lobster in a pot. "Fuck it," she says. "Let's go anyway."

On television, the announcers are saying *Good golly, he shore isn't lettin' that bull get ahead of him* and

I tell you what that is one beautiful ride, but milliseconds from now they're going to be saying something very different and all at once I can't watch. "Come on, Patrick, leave the house, see what it's like," Caro is saying, and I say, "Yeah, okay."

To enjoy the full story, please visit *www.kellybraffet.com.*

AN EXCERPT
FROM
"HUNG UP"

Recommended Reading

Trying to come up with reading recommendations for a specific book is like archaeology: everything you read leaves a layer, and after a while you have rock, and with luck that rock can be carved into something like a story. So, with that in mind, here are some of the books that leap to mind when I think about *Save Yourself*. Some are terribly obvious—I don't really have to tell you to read Donna Tartt, right?—and some are quite basic, and I'm not saying that any of them are the best of their kind. But all of them contributed, in some way, to the gritty, convoluted hunk of rock that is *Save Yourself,* and maybe they'll contribute something to your life, too.

DARK FICTION ABOUT DARK PEOPLE DOING DARK THINGS:

The Cement Garden—Ian McEwan
The Secret History—Donna Tartt

WHERE I'M COMING FROM, IN A LITERARY SENSE:

The *Mammoth Book of Pulp Fiction*—edited by Maxim Jakubowski

They Shoot Horses, Don't They?—Horace McCoy

The Talented Mr. Ripley—Patricia Highsmith

NONFICTION ABOUT BEING POOR, RELIGIOUS, OR TEENAGED:

Nickel and Dimed: On (Not) Getting By in America—Barbara Ehrenreich

Columbine—Dave Cullen

The Case for God—Karen Armstrong

The Unlikely Disciple: A Sinner's Semester at America's Holiest University—Kevin Roose

For additional Extra Libris content from your other favorite authors and to enter great book giveaways, visit ReadItForward.com/Extra-Libris.

ESSAYS, READER'S GUIDES, AND MORE